THE
BLONDE

THE

BLONDE

A NOVEL

ANNA GODBERSEN

Printed in the United States of America.

Cataloging-in-Publication data for this book is available from the Library of Congress.

ISBN: 978-1-60286-222-7 (print)
ISBN: 978-1-60286-223-4 (e-book)

Published by Weinstein Books
A member of the Perseus Books Group
www.weinsteinbooks.com

Weinstein Books are available at special discounts for bulk purchases in the U.S. by corporations, institutions and other organizations. For more information, please contact the Special Markets Department at the Perseus Books Group, 2300 Chestnut Street, Suite 200, Philadelphia, PA 19103, call (800) 810-4145, ext. 5000, or e-mail special.markets@perseusbooks.com.

Handgun photo © Coprid used under license from Shutterstock.com

Book design by Natalie C. Sousa

First edition

10 9 8 7 6 5 4 3 2 1

FOR ERIN

PROLOGUE

SHE was a beautiful child.

There was no one else left to remember, and yet her memory of the little girl she used to be wasn't sentimental. A woman like that puts about ten thousand miles between herself and the little girl she used to be if she has any chance of getting up in the morning. "Detached," her shrink had said on occasion, except that they never did so much of that kind of talk. (Mostly they both liked the sound of her voice, and of course he wasn't shy about prescriptions.) She wasn't beautiful the way the world wants children to be beautiful—pink cheeks, blonde curls. Her hair wasn't blonde yet, and she had learned to control a blush before she learned to talk. She was beautiful the way grown women are beautiful, all slim limbs and knowing eyes, which is perhaps why men were inspired to treat her like a woman early.

Those unflinching eyes went a long way to explaining everything that happened later. Not the fame—the secret part. The strange clicks on the line late at night, the trench coats in the crowd, the paranoia of being trailed. How she'd fallen in with dangerous people, and why she had pursued Jack in the first place. How she came to betray her country, and all of that.

When she was born, in June of '26, there had been no daddy to point to—her mother was wild and pretty, and she got low the way her daughter later would. She was her mother's third to come to term, and her mother wasn't any more prepared than she had been for the first two, although those babies at least had a father. The third baby was a child nobody wanted; that was the lattice upon which she grew. She was sent away to live with folks called Bolender, who boarded babies for people who couldn't care for their own, out on the fringes of Los Angeles County. Eventually her mother did manage to buy a house for them to live in together, on Arbol Drive. Doesn't that sound lovely, Arbol Drive? Her mother thought so, too. She bought a lot of furniture she couldn't afford, all in white. That was when the little girl first saw that white is sometimes just a story we tell, innocence a feint.

The Bolenders taught her songs about Jesus, but on Arbol Drive they listened to big band on the phonograph and the grown-ups played cards and drank gin until their laughter got loud and they danced around the living room. Her mother and her mother's best friend, Grace, worked at one of the studios, and they'd stare at the little girl sometimes and say how pretty she was, how she could be a movie star when she grew up, and they wouldn't have to worry about money anymore. There was never enough money—this was the Depression—and they were forced to take in boarders, a Mr. Kennel and his wife, but this seemed fine. The Kennels were actors, and they talked in a plummy, movie aristocrat way, and they'd invite friends over who worked in the pictures and always came with gossip about the business.

He was one of these. His name was Perry and he had been a bit player, too, but he'd shown up drunk at work too many times, and the studio terminated his contract. He wasn't a bad drunk, though. He got very happy and made everybody laugh. He was handsome, and when his eyes were red from drink they glittered in a way that made her feel special.

So it was on an evening when everyone was feeling loose and some tall, dark fellow was dancing her mother close. Perry came to the corner where she sat, observing the grown-ups from a safe distance. He must have noticed how Mr. Kennel stared at the little girl, touched her, asked her to sit on his lap, tried to get her alone whenever he had the chance. "A girl as pretty as you needs to know how to defend herself," Perry told her, with a grave and comical lowering of the eyes. "All men aren't so kindly as me."

She was so shy she could barely speak, but she smiled to reward him for looking out for her, and he gave her a dime and told her to go see the new Jean Harlow picture. Someday, he said, she'd be even bigger than Harlow.

Not long after that her mother stopped paying the bills or talking sense. Her eyes went dead and she was shouting up the stairwell for days before Aunt Grace called the ambulance and had them take her away. Grace said she'd look after little Norma, but she wasn't a real aunt, and she was busy trying to keep the attention of a younger man. For a while Norma Jeane went to the pictures every day. She watched Jean Harlow over and over and learned how her gaze changed after settling on a man. It was during that period that Perry made good on his promise—she was walking to Grauman's Egyptian, and he pulled up in his old Ford and told her to get in. "Today's the day I teach you how to defend yourself," he said.

As they drove, she was very impressed by how fast you can leave a place in a car, how smoothly this one rolled into the sun-dappled afternoon. It was a hot, dry day, the dirt rising off the road and the hills that scorched, California umber. The air smelled of eucalyptus and chaparral, and as they traveled away from the familiar streets, she was conscious of the earth spinning very slowly and how truly alone she was.

They pulled off the road into an open space with a lot of long, dry grass and a hazy view of snowcapped mountains. First he set the cans up on an old split-rail fence and then he showed her the gun, and it was just like the six-shooters that men in the movies wear in holsters under pinstriped suits.

"Do you want to load it?" he asked, gently putting six bullets in her palm. Then he showed her how to open the chamber and slip them in. She must have appeared frightened, because he told her that there was nothing to be afraid of and brushed the hair off her forehead. Then he warned her that when the gun went off it would make a loud noise and that its force might knock her backward. She'd have to stand firmly, legs apart, and hold it with both hands, and he bent to put her feet in place. Then he moved her fingers, showing her how to cock the gun so that it was ready to hammer a bullet.

The first shot was a thunderclap inside her ears, and she was sure she'd never hear again. But then she noticed him chuckling, and knew she hadn't hit a thing. Determination rose up inside her. That was how she'd always been—by that age she'd figured out nobody was going to stick around long enough to raise her right, and so she took her lessons where she found them, paid fierce attention when there was something to learn.

The canyon was quiet, and she gripped the gun and concentrated on the cans glinting in the sun. She imagined the bullet inside the chamber and how it would hurtle straight to that can and knock it from the fence. She gave the bullet a little talking-to, so it knew she was going to have her way, squeezed the trigger, cocked the gun, squeezed again. The sound was just as loud but it didn't bother her this time, because she'd hit her targets. Two cans had flown right off the fence, and the burning in her palms was a pleasure.

Perry clapped his hands. "Hot damn!"

He'd been crouching behind her, and now he lay down, folding his arms under his head. She turned around for approval, but saw right away that he wasn't smiling in the goofy way he did on Arbol Drive. Now he was smiling like a wolf.

"Did I do it right?" she whispered and for a long time he made no answer. The sun was very bright, and sweat pooled on her upper lip.

"Forgive me, Norma Jeane," he said when he reached up her skirt. With one hard pull he took her underpants to her knees. "But I just can't help myself."

Perhaps he forgot the gun in her hand, or maybe he believed she was as she appeared. Whatever went through his mind at that moment, it was the last thing he ever thought. She stared down at him, childlike and trusting. Her eyes got wide, and there was a moist dark sliver between her lips. He grinned and she twice rehearsed how to do the thing. Then she cocked the gun, lifted it with both hands, and blew his face away. One moment his grin was there, framing his slick, shining slug of a tongue, and the next it was gone. There must have been a great deal of blood, but she tried not to see that. She dropped the gun on his belly and walked back down the canyon while her heart kept marching time.

It was almost thirty years before she heard her heart beat like that again.

"This isn't how you imagined it'd feel to be alone with Marilyn Monroe, is it?" she asked the man who sat across from her. He wore a black suit, an ominously straight tie, kept his eyes cold and impassive, but she held his gaze. "You figured I'd be a hundred and twenty pounds of quivering delight, whispering cotton candy and blowing kisses. Well. All that burbling sweetness isn't a lie, not totally, but men can be so stupid when it comes to vulnerability. They forget that vulnerability can be itself, and it can also be a shield, and also a knife. Any old thing can be a weapon, so long as you know how to use it right."

The man showed no reaction, only prompted her by clearing his throat. But she had known he would come eventually, and was not about to be hurried.

"You want me to get on with it," she observed. "Stop talking about myself, tell you how I met Prez, why I wanted to reach him so badly. Get me a cigarette and a drink, and I'll tell you everything. I deserve it, you know. All appearances to the contrary, the story I am about to tell you is a love story."

I

1959

O N E
New York, March 1959

THE biggest spectacle in Manhattan, on the eve of Easter Sunday, was at the corner of Forty-fifth and Broadway, where Billy Wilder's new picture was having its premiere and the press swarmed the sidewalk to document the famous faces emerging from the chandelier-dappled lobby of the Loews State Theater. There were so many onlookers and full-time fans jockeying for position in the street that the police several times had to push them back. The last of the film's stars to appear was the blonde who'd played Sugar Kane. The temperature had just dropped into the thirties, and she wore a sleeveless, low-cut gown that appeared to have been made out of a thousand silver filaments clinging by some magnetism to every rise and fall of her sure body.

"Here." Her husband, a step behind her, tried to pull the white fur over her pale shoulders, but she moved away from him, toward the crowd, the red heart of her mouth trembling and swelling before it spread into a broad smile. The camera flashes and the desperate waving of hands became orgiastic, and for a few moments, for anybody lucky enough to look on her, at her naked shoulders and her half-naked breasts wagging against their triangular silver constraints, the whole world was made up of diamonds and palm trees and soft, suggestive kisses.

The crowd convulsed and called her by her first name. Microphones were thrust in her direction. She had been famous a long time by then, and the rabidity of crowds had ceased to frighten or thrill her as before. Their pitch continued to increase, and the likelihood of some kook who meant her harm being out there, amongst the sweet boys who kept her picture under their mattresses, was surely the same as it had ever been. But the idea of harm no longer troubled her. In fact, she went toward it. By now she knew perfectly well that empty rooms could swallow her whole, even after the bright frenzy of a night like this. Anyway, it was too late; she had promised to be this way and was too familiar with the pain of broken promises to betray her public by being anything less.

"Marilyn, did you enjoy the picture?"

Resting a hand on her hip, she moved to face the reporter, a young man with his fedora pushed back on the crown of his head. In the movie, you could make out the curve in her middle and guess that she had been pregnant, and watching it had reminded her that the months she'd spent on set had cost her another one.

"I thought it was Mr. Wilder's best yet," she almost whispered, her breath suspended in the cool air between them like a veil. "Did *you* enjoy the picture?"

Of course she knew he hadn't seen the picture, and before he could attempt an answer, ten more questions were hurled her way. "What'll you do now?"

"Well, we all worked very hard, so I expect we'll go to the party and celebrate and enjoy ourselves a little."

Another voice, this one more charging than reverent: "Is it true that the studio plans to put a weight clause in your future contracts?"

Marilyn gazed back at the question, and her lids sank slightly to protect her eyes from the cameras' light. Suddenly her false lashes were too heavy, and she felt her stomach turning over the white chalk she'd had in lieu of dinner. The smile sank and rose again, curling the edges of her lips. "My husband likes me a little plump." She issued a soft, careless laugh and looked up at Arthur in his bow tie and black-rimmed glasses, who returned her smile enigmatically. He was so tall; for a moment she remembered why she had thought he could give her shelter. The creases of the smile lingered in his healthy, olive skin—the marks of a person so distinguished he was beyond intimidation. "That's all that matters, really. Don't you think?"

Another question: "Did you read Mr. Wilder's comments in *Parade* this morning?"

"No, I didn't. Is that a newspaper or something?" She winked and tipped herself forward. "I live in New York now, so I read the *New York Times* in the morning."

The flashbulbs had become explosive, atomic. They had no center.

"What do you think of Mr. Lemmon and Mr. Curtis?"

"Oh, they're cutups, both of them, and Tony especially is such a darling, I could just eat him!"

"All right," Arthur said, his mouth at her ear. Then he was steering her, and she let him, even as she kept her gloved hand raised and her lashes batted back and her face gently radiating her own girlish femininity, which she had once practiced so assiduously but now had the purity and force of habit. The white moon of her face turned toward the crowd, as though what she really wanted was to shine on them. "Come," he urged, once he had spotted the limousine the studio had hired, his big, tapered fingers strong and goading. "Come, my dear."

She loved it when he talked that way. They were still calling her name, and her heart stretched out, and she wanted to show them once more how much she had given. But she loved it when he said *my dear*, and couldn't say no. He opened the door for her, and lifted up her glinting train so that it would not get caught. Delicately he arranged it around her satin high-heeled shoes, and he paused a moment so that she could wave again before closing the door and coming around the other side.

They rushed toward her window. Several sets of eyes—human, and the bug-eyed camera kind—stared at her through the glass, and she gazed back from beneath drooping lids and tilted herself forward in offering. They were still taking her picture and she was still gazing back at them when Arthur slammed the door. The limousine was halfway down the block and the sound of her name was beginning to fade before she looked at him.

He was lighting a cigarette and did not meet her eyes. "Sutton Place and Fifty-Seventh," he said, playing up the Brooklyn in his gravel voice.

It was not the first time the sound of their home address had disappointed her. "But what about the party?"

She'd spoken in the high, childish cadence that once would have made him do anything for her—saying *party* as though it signified a kind of candy that little girls cannot resist—but now he went on without meeting her eyes. "I'm going up to the country early tomorrow." He exhaled in the direction of the passing city. "I'm going to work."

In the silence that followed, the crowds and the noise began to seem abstract, like something she'd read about once long ago, or a story she told when she was on the couch, and she felt the supple self she had been present-ing for the last several hours begin to frost over.

"If you want to go, I won't stop you," he went on without turning his head. "But I don't have the patience tonight."

"The patience for what?"

The flat, judgmental faces of New York's buildings passed by, and Arthur said nothing.

"The patience for what?" Now she was almost shrieking, even though it would worsen his silence. They both thought how it wasn't the voice of the woman he'd meant to marry. How it was the voice of some other creature, bent on making the party, and everything else, a special hell. How she would send him off to mix just the right amount of scotch and soda in a champagne glass so everyone would think she was drinking bubbly. How her pulse would quicken in his absence and her whole body would seek the most admiring male gaze. How she would purr at Billy and Jack and Tony and say flattering things to their wives and then, later, rage about how they'd trashed her in the press, the nasty, unkind things they'd said to put her down, keep her in her place, justify paying her too little, and on and on. The fury she'd set loose, and the unquiet night to follow.

"Who needs the party?" Her voice was weightless again, a very fine imitation of unself-conscious delight.

Arthur said nothing.

"Maybe I'll come with you, to the country. The dogs would like it, wouldn't they? I'll bake you bread while you write, and maybe a berry pie. It will be just like when we were first married, the night it rained so hard? I made you a pie and we drank bourbon and played cards and you knew how much I loved you." She smiled at the back of his head. But he didn't turn around, so she swung in the other direction and gave it to the passing street. The pale mask of her face was reflected in the window, not quite as vivid as the red on her mouth. "I have so much reading to catch up on anyway," she went on, although now she was speaking more slowly, as one does when they have begun to employ the future impossible. "And it would be so nice to see the Diebolds' children."

The night was silent, and so was Arthur, as their limousine glided along Fifty-Seventh Street past the Art Students League, where the bearded young man she'd gone down on in the bathroom of the Subway Inn last week had said he was taking figure-drawing classes, and past the diner where she sometimes liked to have a BLT alone in her black wig and pretend she was just another rich housewife wasting away the afternoon. The headlights of the passing cars were big as squid's eyes, and just as seemingly innocuous. She told herself they were not squid's eyes. They were celestial orbs; they were bioluminescent eggs; they were jewels sent from another planet to honor her otherworldly beauty; they were symbols of fertility; everything was going to be all right.

Everything is going to be all right, she thought as they went through the lobby, and she actually believed it until they were in the elevator, and she saw him press the button for the floor with his long index finger—the one he pressed against his temple when he was thinking about things she couldn't understand, the one he pointed at her when he was angry. The button said 13, and she shuddered, remembering how they'd fought over that one. He'd said it was a silly superstition, and she hadn't wanted him to think her silly, and let him win. The apartment was affordable, he'd insisted, the bookshelves already built in. Of course he didn't know, and how could he, how vigilant she was, how carefully she read the signs, how assiduously she avoided bad omens of any kind. Now the elevator was lifting her, slowly, to the unlucky apartment where she should have known everything would go wrong.

Arthur said nothing as he crossed the white carpeted living room and put Billie Holiday on the record player. The fragile music filled the room, and Marilyn lingered at the large entryway mirror while the door drifted closed behind them. She had hung it there—why? For this, she supposed. To see her mystery faded, her face slack with disappointment, with the sheer effort of buoying herself up, while all the while her hair remained set, a helmet of floss. Perhaps the things they said about her were true. She was crazy and unreliable and couldn't remember lines. She would never make another picture, for who would want to work with her? But this was the kind of thinking she could not allow, and with a brightening of the eyes she let her fur slip off her shoulders and went swiveling and tiptoeing across the floor to the chair where Arthur sat, smoking his pipe by a lamp, one long leg crossed over the other, his focus on the book spread open in his lap.

"Poppy?" she said as she sank down beside him. A strap slid down her shoulder; the dress strove to contain her breasts.

Arthur said nothing.

"Poppy, take me with you to the country, why don't you? I'll be a good little wife."

Not looking up: "I'm going there to work."

"But I won't make a sound. I'll darn your socks and bring you tea. Just don't leave me here alone. Please?"

The passage of Arthur's gaze from the pages of his book took an era—whole species came and went in the time it took him to look at her—and by then she no longer wanted to go to the country with him. She wanted to tell him: *One phone call, Joe DiMaggio will be over to knock your teeth out,* but she had used that line before, and Arthur had only laughed and left the room. His eyes were weary, and they barely blinked as they stared into hers. His nostrils were hatefully wide, and the sigh that came through them was violent with unsaid things.

"If you come to the country you'll miss your appointments with Dr. Kurtz . . ." Each word issued from his thick lips was a pretense of patience. "No, I think you had better stay here and let me get a little work done. It will go quickly, you won't even miss me. You have so many friends."

As he stared at her she blinked and blinked. Like a fish, her lips parted and closed, parted and closed. Her shoulders were so heavy and her feet so pinched and red and her heart felt waterlogged and ill-used. She knew what he was thinking. He thought of her the way Wilder did, as a bitch and a child, a destroyer of other people's plans. This was not paranoia (as Dr. Kurtz might carefully have suggested); she had read his diary, those many lines of eloquent disappointment.

"Oh, never mind," she said hatefully. She tore off the dress and left it in a heap on the carpet as she proceeded to the far side of the apartment.

When she was single and suffering sleeplessness, she'd at least had the consolation of the telephone. She'd get a man on the line (any lover or friend would do), provoke him to say reassuring things. Using a soft, halting voice, asking simple and naïve questions, usually did the trick. How big was the universe, and where did it end? How had he made his first fortune, and what was the weather like where he was calling from, and did he think everything might still turn out all right? She was soothed by the sound of their confident pronouncements, which perhaps they really did believe, and after a while her eyes might close and her thoughts grow quiet.

But she wasn't single, and she knew she'd just be crazy and wide-awake as long as she stayed in the apartment with Arthur. She was careening through the rooms, her mind lit up with some heady combination of emotion and pills wearing off and a sweating need for a stiff drink. An old slip going over her naked body, and a navy fisherman's sweater over that, and then the London Fog jacket she'd bought when she first moved east after divorcing Joe. She took Arthur's hat from the hook by the door and put it over her hair. *Ha*, she thought when she glanced in the mirror, *I'm Sam Spade.*

"Fuck you," she shouted at the living room as she went through the front door and put all her energy into jamming her finger against the elevator button, hoping he'd come after her, and hoping he wouldn't. In her mind: *fuck you fuck you fuck you.*

The cool, quiet air did nothing for her anger, and she walked several blocks without thinking of direction or registering any faces. She thought about how ugly New York was, how California would be better. They had already discussed it—a trial separation—and Arthur had tried to pass the arrangement off as her idea. Maybe she really would go now, see how he liked it, how he did without having her body when he wanted it. Perhaps if she'd had a father, she thought, he would have warned her not to fall for creeps, and she wouldn't find herself so often alone, on some street late at night.

She turned off an avenue and saw, through a canyon of apartment buildings, the lights of a barge on the water. Then she heard the voice, and wondered if she were hallucinating.

"N.J." The voice was quiet, almost disembodied.

"What are you, CIA? FBI? Isn't it enough you tap my phones?" She took three swift steps backward from the building's shadows, not wanting to catch the stems of her heels in the gaps of the sidewalk. She couldn't remember now if it had originally been Arthur's paranoia or hers, that sense of someone always listening in, or if she had been born with the fear of a constant, hovering presence that intended no good.

"N.J., it's me," he said again, and this time she could not pretend with herself that that vaguely accented voice, with its touch of European courtliness, was not familiar.

"Fuck you." She went toward the river, trying to loosen the fearful grip that voice had on her throat. But she wouldn't run, she wouldn't sacrifice the dignity of walking on the way she always did—ankles practically knocking against each other—just to get away.

It took no special effort for him to match her speed, and soon he was walking alongside her at barely more than an amble.

"N.J.," he said as he laced his arm through hers. It was a gentle gesture, but firm, and she had no choice but to turn and look at him. Those sun-washed blue eyes, the nose like a downward pointing anchor carved of gypsum. He smiled with one side of his mouth, revealing a dimple, and as he gazed at her his exhalation relaxed his shoulders. "Remember me?"

"Of course I remember. Nobody ever called me that but you." Her smile shone brilliantly through the darkness; the words were true, the smile false.

"It's cold—you'll catch cold. Let's get you indoors." She had forgotten this about him, the solicitousness. Unusual for her—when she noticed the impulse to protect in a man, she rarely forgot. Even now, there was a map of safe harbors fixed in her memory, men like Joe who were always willing to play hero when she was in distress.

"The Subway Inn. I like it there. Nothing fancy, but they treat me just like any other drunk," she said with a wan, self-effacing smile.

"I know you do. You spend too much time there," he said, with faint disapproval, and his arm swooped around her shoulder. "But it will do for now."

T W O

New York, March 1959

SHE let him lead her past the neon storefront into the mostly empty bar. The air was dense with cigarette smoke, and the only bodies left belonged to true drunks, the kind who wouldn't slow their march to oblivion by seeking trouble.

"I'll have a double bourbon," she informed him and crossed the tiled floor to a booth upholstered in cracked oxblood leather. There were no eyes to meet—nobody looked up. She threw her coat across the seat, but left her hat on.

Beneath the brim she let her eyes close, and for a moment she was in Schwab's again, and everything was different. There was all that wonderful electric light, for starters, and the cigarette smoke was mixed with wholesome smells, like cheese sandwiches melting on the griddle, and she was hungry (she hadn't eaten for days, and the hunger cut pleasantly into her torso), and she was desperate to catch anybody's eye. All around her were people who worked in the movies, some of them big time. That was why she'd worn a skirt that was too tight and her fur stole, in the hope of being noticed. She was already Marilyn Monroe, but the name didn't mean anything yet.

The hours passed and the crumbs of her grilled cheese got stale on the plate and the ice from her Coke melted in its voluptuous glass, and then she finished even that thin brown liquid. The boy behind the counter started watching her, and she knew he was beginning to suspect that she couldn't pay for lunch. They liked her there—people usually did at first—but they could smell bad luck. Show business people are worse than baseball players when it comes to superstition. The boy left the check in front of her without comment, and walked to the other side of the bar and put his elbow against the counter and started up a conversation with Joe Gillis, the screenwriter.

Seventy-five cents. She read the check like an indictment of every breath she'd ever taken. After her first divorce, when she was just twenty and it seemed every day a stranger told her how pretty she was, how the country needed a beauty like her to lift its war-trodden spirits, she thought if she could just get in the pictures she'd always be all right. Well, now she had been in the pictures. She'd done everything they told her to. She'd changed her hair and her walk and her name. She'd gone down on her knees on hard pool tile, and she'd let studio big shots poke at her with their geriatric cocks. But she didn't have a job or a home. She didn't have seventy-five cents for lunch, and if the collection people caught her, they'd take her car. The last time she'd had an audition her mind had gone blank, and the best she could do was mumble a little something and get out fast.

When she put her head down on the counter it was to forget what she had come for. She couldn't be fearless again, the way she'd been at the beginning, because she had tried, and her trying had come to dust. She was twenty-two, and washed up. For a while she stayed still like that, imagining every variety of suicide, until her mind put together what she was seeing. A five-dollar bill had been placed on top of her check, and after a few minutes the boy made change. Now that change was glinting at her.

"Oh." She straightened on the stool and made her features soft but no less sad. "I'm awfully sorry. That can't be very nice, eating your lunch next to a mess of curls."

"On the contrary. You have lovely hair, and I wasn't in the least bit hungry." There he'd been, with that prominent nose and the pale blue eyes with their intelligent, observant light. He spoke beautifully, in the kind of charming, unplaceable accent that a certain kind of man uses in the pictures. At first she'd thought it was put-on. His clothes had been nondescript, but they'd fit him well—she had noticed that right away—the white dress shirt tucked into dark blue slacks. "I've seen you here before," he went on in an easy, conversational way as he sipped black coffee. "Are you an actress?"

"I—I—I guess so." Her posture went slack, and she put her weak chin against her fist. "I don't feel much like one today."

"I think you'd make a fine movie star."

"That's swell; could you tell Mr. Zanuck over at Twentieth Century-Fox? He keeps giving me these crummy little parts and then firing me." She knew he wasn't somebody—he wasn't wearing anything flashy or expensive, and anyway by 1948 she recognized most of the big fish. He wasn't the type she went after when she needed a job or to meet somebody important. He was the type she went to when she wanted to be held: fatherly, distinguished in a conservative way, hair graying, on the cusp of forty—old enough that he probably really was a father already. Anyway, he'd paid her bill, and that was what mattered.

"You seem like you haven't been getting enough to eat."

She shrugged. "I'm used to it. I grew up being packed off from one orphanage to another."

"It's a terrible country where a pretty girl like you could grow up so deprived."

"Oh, that's all right." She winked at him. "Helps me stay trim, so I won't complain."

"Here, you keep this." He took a quarter from the change on the counter, to leave as a tip, and pushed the rest to her. "Why don't you use some of it to play a few songs?"

She made the most of her walk to the jukebox, moving slowly and with her slight, affected limp. She redid her lipstick with her compact, and then she put the Peggy Lee record on the juke and went back to the soda counter. After that it all happened very simply, almost too simply, like the first act of a picture.

The music was loud, and it created a wall of privacy around them.

"This was a good choice of song," he said. "Mañana, do you know what it means?"

"Of course." She closed her eyes and shimmied her shoulders. "It means tomorrow."

"Do you believe in tomorrow?"

She giggled, but the giggle was faint with sorrow, and her eyebrows lifted when she replied: "Can't be worse than today."

"I think it's going to be a great deal better." He paused when the boy returned to fill his coffee cup. His back straightened and his face got serious, and he gestured for him to fill her soda glass, too. When the boy was gone, he went on: "What would you say if I told you that I could make you a star? The most famous movie star in the world—wealth, fame, glamorous friends, everything you've dreamed of. You'd like that, wouldn't you?"

Suddenly the music was too loud. It shook her insides. Her body retracted and her throat went tight and her features got hard. "I'd say you must think I'm pretty dumb. And that you must be pretty dumb yourself. You could've found out I was an easy lay by asking anybody. You could have laid me for a lousy sandwich and a few songs on the jukebox. But I don't like liars. I don't like big, trumped-up lies like that. A child wouldn't fall for that line."

"Shhhh . . ." His eyes glittered, darted, his hand caressed her wrist, and she realized she'd been shrieking. "I know you're not dumb."

The tightness in her throat relaxed, but she didn't respond to his touch. "Well, I still wouldn't—can't—" she mumbled and broke off.

"Norma Jeane—that's what they used to call you, isn't it?"

They still did in some places, but she didn't like hearing it said out loud at Schwab's. "How did you know that?"

"Norma Jeane, this isn't what you think it is. I won't ever touch you that way."

"Then what *do* you want?" she asked, trying not to sound insulted.

His eyes scanned the surrounding area and he bent forward, gesturing for her to do the same. "My name is Alexei Lazarev," he began, speaking low and fast. "I've learned to speak this way, to comport myself this way, but in fact I grew up in a very different kind of world. My country and your country used to be friends—at least, we pretended to get along, during the war. But that is eroding now, and there are those of us who are here to watch, and to listen."

"You're Russian, aren't you?"

He smiled as a professor smiles on a favorite pupil. "Yes. You're a good watcher and listener already, aren't you?"

She wished that the praise didn't heat the skin of her ears. "Thank you, Mr. Lazarev, but I think I'll keep trying my luck at acting. It's the only thing I've ever been good at, and I'm too old to change my mind."

"That," he replied, as though for him the world held no surprises, "is precisely what we want you to do. And we know of a perfect role for you."

The dangled role made her heart tick, but she didn't let it show. She leveled her chin slightly, the way Bette Davis might. "How do you know my real name again?"

"These things are never difficult to discover, my dear. There are public records, of course, and your modeling agency used to send you out with that name. But we've been watching you longer than that. Marilyn is a good name for an actress, but I can't quite seem to match you with it in my mind. N.J. is how I think of you."

The revelation that he already thought of her intimately enough to have bestowed a nickname made her face cold. "I had better—" She stood to leave, and would have gone immediately, but he grabbed her forearm. In his fingertips, there was a superb lightness that held her more effectively than roughness would have.

"Don't be afraid. We've been watching you only to protect you. As long as you are one of ours we will see that no harm comes to you."

How long had she waited for someone to say words like that? With a deft hand, he guided her back to her stool.

"Tomorrow you'll go to the William Morris Agency and ask for an agent named Johnny Hyde. He'll look after you for me, for the time being."

"But why?"

"Why?"

"I'm just a little orphan nobody. Why would you do this for me?"

"You're not an orphan," he replied quickly.

Those blue eyes stared into hers, and she swallowed hard, taking in how much he knew. About her mother—alive, if not exactly well, in the institution. That her father was not dead but had simply never claimed her. Her eyes flashed back at his. "No, I guess not. But I do know nothing's free in this world."

After that, he was easy again. "Someday, a long time from now, once we've seen to your success, when everyone knows your name, we will call on you, and you'll do something for us."

"Someday? I can hardly imagine tomorrow."

"That's all you should think about now. Just think about tomorrow. But someday I'm going to find you again. All right?"

"All right."

When she stepped back onto Sunset she had been surprised by the daylight, as though she had fallen asleep in the afternoon and woken up to darkness with a dry mouth and hazy head. He'd glanced at her car disapprovingly, and then he had given her more money, and told her to look her best tomorrow. By the following day their conversation seemed a dream, but dreams were all she had in those days, and she had gone to William Morris the next morning, and Johnny Hyde had treated her exactly as Alexei had said he would. He had believed in her, and he had gotten her the role in Mr. Huston's picture, *The Asphalt Jungle*, and all her other roles had come from that.

She was glad when Alexei came back with their drinks, if only because it put an end to remembering, returned her to the Subway Inn. She didn't like to think of that time, when she'd had so little and been so desperate and done so many ugly things to get by.

"Here." He handed her a drink and slid into the booth next to her. The decade that had passed since she last saw him hadn't done much damage. The eyes were just as crystalline, and the new lines etched into the surrounding skin gave him elegance. The way he carried himself—confident and attentive, but so carefully scrubbed of desire that one might almost miss his presence—was the same as that day at Schwab's. His lean frame was clothed in the same tasteful, understated style. She guessed he must be around fifty now, but he didn't look it.

"You introduced me to Johnny Hyde," she said, as though only just realizing where they'd met before. She could feel the cracks in the leather through her silk slip.

"Yes."

"To Johnny." She raised her glass to his. "It just about killed me when he died. He had such a big heart—sometimes I think it got overworked, the way he cared for me, and that's why it gave out."

"You know it wasn't his heart."

She took a sip of whiskey and laughed. "I knew he wanted to screw me, if that's what you mean. He was a man, you know."

Alexei ignored this. "I meant that it wasn't his heart giving out that killed him."

"Oh." She exhaled audibly through her nose, blowing away her previous levity, as well as his insinuation. Tonight she had no interest in other people's shadowy insinuations. "Well, that's all about a million years ago, isn't it?"

"Yes, a lot has happened." Alexei folded his forearms against the table and smiled. The light in his eyes was just for her. "Look at you! A real star, like I always knew you would be. You've even exceeded my expectations—you're an artist, my dear. Beloved by the whole world. I cried, you know, when I went to see you in *Bus Stop*."

"Honey, I have publicity men and lawyers and husbands to tell me how wonderful I am and how I deserve it all and yada yada. They get paid pretty good for that service, too. But I'm low on funds these days. Why don't you just tell me what it is you want?"

If he was taken aback by her directness, he didn't show it. "You remember, that day in Schwab's, when I told you Johnny would help you? I told you we'd call on you someday. Well, now we are."

"You want a favor." She winked decadently. She didn't owe him any-thing—so many shysters had promised to change her life in those days that Alexei barely stood out; in fact, she had only thought of him once or twice over the years—but she didn't mind doing for others when she was asked nicely. "What kind of favor?"

"There's a publicity tour, for *Some Like It Hot*. They go to Chicago tomor-row. I want you to go with them."

They had been speaking in hushed tones, but when she laughed at that—a mirthless, one-syllable laugh—it rose above the quiet barroom mumble. A few heads lifted off the tabletops. Alexei swiveled, watching the others until they looked away, and she knew he cared if they were overheard. That he cared, but she didn't. "I haven't been on a tour like that since I was a kid," she snapped, her voice devoid of its usual breathiness. "I don't do that kind of thing anymore. I don't have to. I'm Marilyn fucking Monroe, and you're just some funny foreign fellow I met at Schwab's a lifetime ago."

"But my dear," he replied easily. "We made you."

"Let's say you did have something to do with it." The anger was at a boil inside her now, and she leaned toward him so that he could see it in her face. "Just for a laugh, let's say you did. What are you going to do about it now? Take it back? Make me *not* famous all of a sudden? I'd like to see you try."

"Of course we could take it away," he replied, quietly amused. "Though we haven't the least intention of wasting a talent like yours."

She gazed back at him, one eyebrow aloft. Her anger was under control now—she had it in a corner where she needed it. Without flinching, she lifted her whiskey glass and drained it. "Go right ahead." She put her coat over her arm and slid around the booth away from him. She was almost to the door when he called out for her.

"N.J." It was that gentle intensity again, and this time he didn't seem to mind the curious glances from the strangers in the bar. Slowly, with exquisite indifference, she turned toward him. "Don't you want to know why we chose you?"

"I guess I seemed like the most desperate girl in Schwab's that afternoon." She rested a hand on one hip and put her weight on the other. "Is that it?"

With a shake of his head, he reached into the hidden chest pocket of his coat. He pulled out a photograph, too large for a wallet but not large enough to frame, and put it down on the table. Someone came in behind her on a gust of cold March air, and she stepped toward Alexei just to get out of the way.

By then her eyes were glazed with tears.

How many photos like that had she carried around, from one apartment to another? Black-and-white snapshots of men posing with automobiles or marlins or doing whatever they did when they became fathers. There was the one of the man named Stanley who people said had been her mother's lover in '25, and after that a picture of Abe Lincoln, an idealized stand-in, staring at her with all the fortitude and intelligence in the world. The pulsation of her heart was loud and rhythmic as she moved, trancelike, back to the booth and sat down. She picked up the photograph, and her lips parted.

"Who is he?" She knew what he was trying to tell her but she couldn't believe it.

"Your father."

Her hand flew to cover her mouth. The picture was black-and-white, the size of her palm, and it showed a young man wearing a white T-shirt smiling at the camera. He had a shotgun rested over his shoulder in an easy way, as though he had just been deer hunting, and he had a mop of light hair falling over his face. The way he gazed into the camera was the same way she gazed into a camera—searching, charged with life, and not to be looked away from. His face was so like her face she had to breathe deeply just to find a few words. It was like seeing your markings on another body and realizing you were part of a tribe. "But I've looked for him. I—I was sure he was dead. I've hired private dicks and spent I don't know how much money trying to find him. I've made myself so conspicuous. I mean, what kind of person doesn't seek out fame when they have the chance?"

"Yes," he replied carefully. "What kind of person?"

She returned his stare blankly, tried not to show how much she wanted it to be true.

"Don't you think if your father were some ordinary person at least one of those detectives you hired would have found something? He's one of ours."

"Oh, god. Is he in trouble?"

"He's all right. He wants to meet you."

"When? Wh-when can I meet him?"

"In good time."

She felt faint with the thing she'd so long wanted, and before she could help it she had rested her head against Alexei's shoulder. It was stronger, larger, than she had expected, and she let her eyelids drop and her muscles relax. She had gone through just about every emotion there was since waking up that morning, and already before that she had been exhausted for years. "But I've waited so long," she said.

He kissed her lightly on the forehead. "I know. But first I want you to go to Chicago. Don't fret, my dear—I think this is a trip you're going to enjoy."

THREE

Washington, D.C., March 1959

WALLS was alive. The bed was unfamiliar; the sheets fragrantly feminine; the face on the pillow next to him obscured by heaps of strawberry blonde hair. As he blinked, scenes from the night before filtered back: the cocktail party in Georgetown to which his cousin Lucy (Mrs. Robert Bennington) had invited him; how he'd had two drinks fast, told himself to slow down, and immediately forgot the directive; the girl in the full, teal-colored skirt; how bright her eyes got when she told him it was late and she really ought to be going; how quickly she had accepted his subsequent offer of a ride home. When he remembered that, he had to suppress his instinct to make a noise—some hybrid sigh/groan. He would have given a whole month's pay to get out of that bedroom without waking her.

Her? She had a name, she must, and he was even confident that it was vaguely French. Renée, or Roxanne, though neither of those quite fit. In any case, she was a junior at Vassar, taking a semester at G.W. for reasons that she must have explained but were now lost to him, and her father, whom she plainly adored, was the principal of a New York advertising firm where one of his fraternity brothers was now employed. Her face, when she mentioned him, had led Walls to think precisely that: *Her father, whom she plainly adored.* It was a sign—though not the first, last, or most salient—that if he took her home (or rather, allowed her to take him home) he would regret it.

Walls (Douglass Everett Walls on his passport; Dougie to his mother; D.W. to his father; Doug to the world; but always to himself simply and purely Walls) was not in general so unromantic as the part of him that wanted to flee this girl, this bed. At New Haven he had been known as a ladies' man, and in secret he thought of himself as the one true romantic of his acquaintance. Women were to him so delicate and lovely, and he held a strong belief that they should be treated right. He lived in fear of doing anything that might suggest he was falsely promising them the happy futures they so obviously desired—he doubted that he would ever be fully capable of promising any such thing—and this was the crux of the carnal paradox that kept him rather lonely most evenings since he'd joined the Bureau.

Except on the occasions when he couldn't help it anymore, and called up the elusive charm bequeathed by his father. Almost always it worked, a little too easily to be fully satisfying. Most of the girls these days would let you use your hand, and if you did that part right, they were almost certain to submit to the rest. Then he'd find himself heaving over some debutante with silken hair, grinning like an ape as he listened for her dishonest sighs to yield to the real, unpretty moans, before ejaculating on her rosy, flat belly. That was more or less last night's order of events; and so he couldn't really be surprised by his current state of remorse.

Expertly, stealthily, he removed himself from the bed. The mattress barely registered its lightened load. Luckily he'd put on his underwear before falling asleep, and his under and dress shirts were on his side of the bed. The sleeves of the latter were over his arms by the time he was across the floor, and his pants were waiting for him by the door—as though *they* had been awake with the first light, and had been urging him to get on with it since. In the living room he found shoes, socks, and tie on the zebra-skin rug, near the glass coffee table where their half-drunk glasses of bourbon remained from the night before. His jacket, helpfully, was hanging on the brass coat tree by the front door. He almost couldn't believe how nicely his escape was going.

Already he was in the hallway, stuffing his tie into his pocket, summoning the elevator. He leaned against the wall opposite, as though the casualness of his pose might exonerate him for fleeing. The elevator was mirrored, and as he waited he regarded himself—the fair hair bluntly cut, the arms still muscular from Quantico, if not quite so lean as in his tennis-playing days, the deep-set hazel eyes that (as one of the more self-consciously intellectual girls he'd known once said) were "difficult to read," the serious, handsome features which appeared suddenly goofy and boyish when he smiled. He wasn't smiling now. The odor of the girl was still on him, her Chanel perfume and the smell of her body it was meant to mask. On mornings like these, he saw how like his father he was, and disliked himself. To distract himself from this knowledge he quoted Chekhov in his mind—"And he judged of others by himself, not believing in what he saw, and always believing that every man had his real, most interesting life under the cover of secrecy and under the cover of night"—a favorite from his undergraduate days. But really he was still thinking of his father, and in the next moment, with a surge of dread, he realized the flaw in his getaway.

The hat. It was the same hat his father wore the year he came back from Spain with the limp, and went to work for Uncle Edward's firm doing something mysterious and financial. (One night around Christmastime a few years ago, his father had explained that he had been in Spain running guns for the anti-Franco guerillas, and Walls had wanted to believe this noble, dramatic version of his family history, though he wasn't sure if he should.) Those had seemed happy days to Walls, who must have been about seven years old—his father home at last, and not at risk of being sent off to Europe or the Pacific, on account of the limp, returning to Greenwich every night for dinner on the 6:15. Now he knew it hadn't been a happy time. His father had hated sitting at a desk, and had used it mainly as a surface upon which to fuck his secretary (this according to Walls's mother who, it must be said, possessed a vivid imagination). That went on for some months until Walls's father absconded with what remained of his wife's trust fund, squandered it magnificently on a month-long spree in Atlantic City, and returned mainly to demand a swift divorce. He no longer imbibed grain alcohol, which for better or worse made him a far superior gambler—he hadn't worked in years—but Walls still preferred the version of him in the hat.

There was no choice but to go back in.

With a wince he turned toward the apartment where the girl in the teal skirt lived. He took five grudging steps away from the elevator, braced himself, and raised his fist. But the door drew back before he had the chance to knock. Several panicked seconds passed before he realized that he was not facing Michelle (there was her name!), but a different girl. A roommate, perhaps. She wore a powder-blue nightgown, and her hair was in curlers; he saw she was less pretty than Michelle, and felt oddly grateful to her for it.

"I guess you're Doug." As she spoke she lifted the grayish olive homburg, which rested on her open palms, as though offering him a tray of canapés.

"How did you know that was my name?"

"Michelle kept saying it last night." The corners of her mouth flickered mischievously. "The walls are thin here."

"Oh." He took the hat and put it on his head.

"I'm Gloria," she told him.

They both sensed the stirring in the next room, and glanced in that direction. Then Gloria looked back at Walls—she was still smiling, but more faintly now. She nudged the space between them with her chin, indicating the stairwell at the end of the hall.

Thank you, Walls mouthed.

Gloria held his gaze a moment, gave a nod of understanding, and closed the door to him.

As he maneuvered his black Cadillac Eldorado—a low, lumbering shark of a car, previously owned by Uncle Edward—through the lettered streets he thought how he had always liked the name Gloria. He liked, too, the idea of living in the capital, its quaintness and intentional backwardness. The redbrick façades of Georgetown (which he imagined full of crackling fire-places and children who still believed their mothers were the most beautiful women in the world) seemed, to Walls, moral and reassuring, especially at this hour, when only the servants were awake.

He wondered, as he had before on such mornings, if driving through Washington at dawn wasn't a little like waking up dead: the big gray obelisks, the reflecting pools, the weak blue sky, all quiet and peaceful, and there you were, speeding along a parkway, whistling to yourself, occasionally passing a fellow traveler entombed in his own hulking metal box, as you moved in an ominously tranquil circle.

He stopped at the diner he liked on D Street, bought the *Post* from the box outside, ate two fried eggs and four pieces of bacon and drank as much coffee as the waitress could pour in the time it took to read the headlines. When he got back in the car, he removed his holster from the glove com-partment and slipped it over his shoulders. Then he put his jacket back in place, checked his face for sufficient seriousness in the rearview mirror (he knew how much it set him back with the other special agents every time he showed the boyish smile), and drove to headquarters. It had become his habit to begin every day with target practice in the basement firing range, even on weekends and mornings when he woke up in strange beds. Perhaps especially on those mornings. He enjoyed the ritual, which made him feel disciplined, prepared for any assignment, and was surprised that so few of his fellow agents did the same.

At that hour on a Sunday the range was mostly deserted, but he spotted Pete Amberson, his roommate from training, in a stall near the entrance. Pete's jacket and fedora were hanging from the wall behind him, and the vision of a confederate in uniform for a moment made Walls a believer in the world's logic and reason. The spareness further settled him—the peeling paint, much pockmarked with bullet holes—and he took a deep breath of the stale basement air, which had the odor of an old gym where fireworks have been set off. "Pete!" he said, raising his hand with an accidental enthusiasm he soon came to regret.

"Walls," Pete observed. The muscles of his face flexed as though he were happy to see Walls, in a not exactly friendly way. He opened the chamber to dump the spent cartridges, kicked them into the coppery pile that spread out from under his stall, and replaced his gun in its holster. They shook hands. "You're here early."

"Yes." Walls shrugged and hung his coat and hat on the hook next to Pete's. "You, too."

"Got to keep sharp." Pete winked, and changed the subject. "Hope you haven't bought any furniture." The meaning of that facial tautness became clear to Walls: Pete had something on him, fodder for the variety of joshing one-upmanship of which he had been the foremost practitioner at Quantico.

"Some." This was a lie. Walls lived in a furnished room, and he'd paid so little attention to its décor that he wasn't sure if he could truthfully say what the color scheme was, or even whether he liked it. "Why?"

"I hear you got a new assignment."

"Really?"

Hope bloomed briefly in Walls. He was currently the most junior agent on a surveillance operation, the object of which was a group of supposed communists whose rhetoric seemed, to him, undergraduate in the extreme. They printed pamphlets, spoke only in the most abstract terms of any kind of violence, and though his superiors apparently regarded them as a threat, he felt sure their convictions would dissolve long before they did anything that justified arrest. Privately, Walls believed Uncle Edward to be behind this assignment—Uncle Edward was the type of man who, depending on the political climate, alternated between high government posts and big business, and who never sat through a meal without being called away to the telephone. He knew everybody, and though he never expressed any special fondness for Walls, it was in his nature to be gratified by the notion that he'd kept his baby sister's only child out of the line of fire, far from anything interesting.

"That's what I hear."

"From who?"

"Saw Special Agent Hoffman this morning—he's looking for you. That, and the last man on the job is a friend of mine."

"What happened to him?"

The way Pete's lips curled, Walls knew that the transfer wasn't going to make him any more impressive than he currently was. "Got himself on an organized crime case up in New York. Big-time stuff."

"What's the job?"

"Word is you're the Director's new peeping tom on Marilyn."

"Monroe?" The fact that the one name followed the other so automatically did not make its utterance in this locale any less outrageous.

"And I must say I think you owe it to all of us to end up *on* Marilyn."

Ignoring the comment, Walls asked, "Why me?"

"Maybe he thought it takes a blond to get inside the head of another blonde." Pete snickered. "Maybe he thought you'd look good in a bathing suit, soaking up the California sun."

"California?"

Though he would have liked an answer to this question, Walls was relieved when Pete shrugged noncommittally and went for his coat and hat. Once he was fully dressed it was clear the ribbing was over, and his features assumed a professional blockiness. He was Amberson again; the two men shook hands and agreed they'd see each other soon, disregarding how unlikely that future seemed now.

"Lucky man," said Hoffman, Walls's immediate superior, when he arrived some minutes later.

Walls was loading his weapon—the handgun he had been issued at the end of training—and was glad of the excuse not to be facing his boss. "Why the hell are we following a movie star anyway?"

"You know how the Director likes his Hollywood gossip." Hoffman leaned against the beige wall, arms crossed over his chest, shaking his head so that the cheeks of his fallen, gin-ruined face quivered; Walls had never seen him so happy. "She *is* married to a Red."

"That's all intellectual posturing." Walls turned away and lifted his gun, stared down the barrel at the target—the silhouette of a man in a hat, a mobster, maybe, which was as it should be. He'd seen the original production of *Death of a Salesman* on Broadway with his mother, and even as a teenager he'd recognized it as the work of an inveterate blowhard. "Are they really sending me to California?"

"Yes."

"But doesn't she live in New York?" he asked, not sure exactly how he'd come by the information.

"Seems the man currently on Marilyn"—Hoffman's tone indicated that he found this pun just as amusing as Pete had—"thinks her marriage is about to implode, and his sources indicate she's going to California to get away from it all."

"Why me?" Walls asked again. He kept his voice even, let the gun speak his displeasure. A boom in the ears, heat in the hand, and he watched the bullet rip through the target's forehead as though it were more than paper, as though the shot really had splintered bone, splattered brain. Smashed the target's head open, like a pumpkin against a concrete wall.

Hoffman was kinder than Pete. "Can't have a married man listening to all that late-night pillow talk" was his obviously fallacious explanation.

"You're not married."

This was cruel of Walls, and he knew it—Hoffman's wife had left him for good the last time he fell off the wagon. Hoffman knew it, too. "Guess it's probably because your mother's Mosey Moses," he said, in a voice that meant the conversation was about to be over.

Of course the minute Amberson said California, Walls had known why he would be given such a silly, dead-end assignment. His mother: Maureen "Mosey" Douglass, a.k.a. Mo Walls, a.k.a. Mosey Moses, lean and fair, wild and elegant, a hothouse flower with razor-edged cheekbones, she of the Long Island Douglasses, whose family fortune had been more or less wiped out in the crash only to be resurrected by her older brother, Edward; who had run off during the Depression with a well-connected gambler named Wes Walls; who had been socially ostracized for her excesses, and all but abandoned upon her divorce, only to triumph as the third wife of a studio head named Lou Moses. Of course her old friends who had left her for dead relished this final point of ignominy—that she had married a Jew. But that was before she started throwing famous parties at her Holmby Hills mansion (in fact, it was three conjoined properties), to which actors and actresses and foreign royals were invited, but none of the people she'd gone to boarding school with or known socially during the years she'd tried to be a Greenwich house-wife. Walls did not care that his stepfather was a Jew; this was, for him, the least of his mother's transgressions.

"Good luck, kid," Hoffman said, dropping the file on the floor before walking out. The papers hitting the cement sounded to Walls like an indifferent farewell to his entire career.

There were five bullets left in the chamber, and he shot them off one after another as fast he could, tearing the target at both knees, groin, stomach, heart. But his accuracy only increased his sense of futility. His ears rang as he shook the cartridges on the ground, jerked his things from their hooks, and left.

FOUR

Chicago, March 1959

IT had taken three Seconal just to stitch together a few hours sleep last night, and she asked for a second Bloody Mary when she realized that the descent into Midway wasn't going to be smooth. The plane was small, and she could hear every thrum of the engine and the wind through its walls, and that was before they hit the weather over Lake Michigan. For the first time in some years her fear of flying rose beyond a hazily pleasant fatalism, and she put her palm against the little oval window and let her eyes scan the blue surface below to the place where it met land. She wanted to make it there. If she had a father, somewhere in the world, then there was a reason to land safely after all.

The airport was coming up now, and she wondered what was in Chicago. Alexei had only said that it would be better for her to know less, and to be free to arrive at her hotel as she would for any junket. Mostly she disliked being told what to do, but in times of trouble she could on occasion enjoy surrendering to a task, especially when the promised reward was great. And Alexei had made the biggest promise of all. That the thing she was to do here would finally reunite her with her father was the most recurrent thought in the circle of her mind, and she didn't really snap-to until the steps were down and she saw that the publicity people had done their groundwork. A crowd of well-wishers were gathered under a gray sky, and they shrieked when they saw her descending to the tarmac. She took a moment, on the last step, to turn herself up a notch. *I'm Marilyn Monroe*, she thought, and reviewed a few of the particulars: the clinging, camel-colored turtleneck sweater dress, a long fur, high white pumps, her hair curling flamboyantly toward and away from the line of her jaw. She was glad that she had fixed her lipstick before disembarking. Her shoulders drew back as she moved into the waiting crowd, and she met the eye of as many well-wishers as possible to let them know she appreciated the welcome.

By the time her car pulled away from the airport she was feeling quite alive. Why did she always bitch and balk at these trips? It was invigorating, really, to arrive in some town where you didn't know anybody and have a lot of good people cheer for you. She saw that she had been afraid to leave New York, where her days were structured around visits with her analyst and acting classes. Perhaps all she'd really needed was a change of scenery. Arthur would be halfway up the Saw Mill by now, and she didn't miss him.

A light rain was falling when they arrived at the Ambassador East, but she kept her sunglasses on as she followed her public relations man across the sidewalk. Without so much as raising her chin, she took her key from Daniel (or David?), her publicity minder, and left him at the desk to sort out the practicalities of luggage and a room for her to get dressed in. There would be a luncheon with the local press in a few hours, and she had been firm that she would need time alone before that.

When she turned away from the reception desk the same thing happened that always happened when she walked across a room. A subtle combination of conversations breaking off and chairs creaking as people turned to look and a low murmur (the meaning of which she might read as hostile, depending on her mood). But the sense of freedom her early morning departure from New York had given her was still strong, and she breathed in the rare, reverent atmosphere. That hit lasted until she passed the final column and saw the row of brass elevators, and experienced a presentiment of danger. The old tells—a tingling along the skin of her ears and a tightening of her throat—and she knew she was being watched. Not in the way she wanted to be watched, but with predacious, hungry eyes.

Even so, she kept her shoulders relaxed and smiled brilliantly at the young man who was manning the elevators. He looked at her shyly and then looked away. As she waited for the brass doors to open she focused all her good will on him, letting her fur slip off her shoulders and down to her elbows. She remembered that David (or Daniel) was there to take care of her; that Alexei, too, was alert to any threats to her safety; that she had traveled far from the sorrowful, helpless feeling that had sent her out walking late last night; and that she was on the verge of solving the great riddle of her life. But the sensation of being followed persisted until the bell dinged and the doors opened.

"Tenth floor," she said with a wink.

"Yes, ma'am," he said, only half raising his eyes to her as she glided past him into the elevator. She leaned against the mirrored wall, relieved to be alone, and closed her eyes. The mechanism of the doors groaned as they reached for each other, and a man came in after her quite suddenly like an unexpected gust of weather.

"Going up," he told the boy brashly.

The veins in her wrists constricted, but she kept her body in a smooth curve against the mirror. The floor underneath sank a little before it lifted. Without any hurry she let her eyes open, lazily and only halfway.

"I'm Jack." He spoke in a fast, confident way, like a talent agent might.

His sport coat was dark brown and he didn't wear a tie and he was leaning against the wall opposite her with one ankle crossed over the other, in a posture of total ease. The loafers he wore were expensive mahogany leather, and the neat trim of his hair did not obscure its virile thickness. She could see her own face reflected on the mirror just behind him, as though they were some kind of two-headed astrological beast. There was a striking contrast between their faces—the skin of hers was pale, and his was so tan—and the opposing mirrors repeated them over and over and over. Of course she recognized him—he was one of the Kennedy clan the press so loved to fawn over, one of

Joe's boys ("that old Nazi," Arthur used to call him)—but she wasn't about to pass up the satisfaction of acting like he was nobody to her.

"Jack." She half whispered the name, but the tentativeness was for him, not her. Her full lips trembled toward each other without meeting, and she went on, in a voice she might have used to tell some fellow he was her king: "You're awfully impressed with yourself, aren't you, Jack?" The sound was sweet, but she meant it mean.

"I'm awfully impressed with you," he answered, unfazed. "That's no crime, is it?"

"Oh, I wasn't really alleging any kind of crime. But I don't care much for pretty boys."

"Lucky me." His gaze shifted slightly, so that he was meeting his own eyes in the mirror behind her. The jauntiness of his grin and the intensity of his look remained the same, and she was briefly sorry they weren't focused on her anymore. "There's no way anybody would call me pretty when I'm standing next to you."

His eyes were focused on her again, almost blindingly, and she returned his gaze long enough to let him know she could take it. The thing he wanted to do was plain on his face: He wanted to shove her against the elevator's wall and lift her skirt. She turned, very slowly, and showed him her profile. "You're a real womanizer, aren't you, Jack?"

It wasn't a question, and before he had time to attempt an answer the bell dinged and the brass arrow overhead pointed to the number ten. Languorously she stepped away from the wall. Jack moved faster, already ahead of her, and for a moment she thought that he was going to block her way, but he didn't—he just straddled the entry, one foot in the elevator and one in the hallway, holding the doors for her. Slowly, exquisitely, she advanced onto the thick golden carpet of the hallway and rotated to face him. Perhaps two feet of air separated their bodies, all of it electric. Just the hint of a smile as she paused, daring him to come up with a line worthy of her.

His grin held steady. "Going to the Pump Room later?"

"I don't know," she answered, trying not to show her disappointment that he hadn't tried harder. "The studio always has something planned."

"Hope you disregard them, and show at the Pump Room." His tone was practical, staccato, with nothing of her feathery suggestion. He stepped back inside and didn't meet her eyes again until the doors were closing. Then he lifted his chin slightly, and put his gaze on her. "You're even better looking in the flesh," he said, and though he was still grinning, his voice had grown grave.

Before she could reply the doors closed, and she heard the shifting of metal gears lowering him down. What a good idea it had been—she reflected for the second time—to get out, away from the rut she'd dug herself, to be reminded that she still had it. And not in some grubby half-punitive way, with bearded, emaciated boys in dirty barrooms, but with beamingly wealthy men pretty much anywhere.

The room the studio had reserved for her was good—as sprawling and anonymous as she could've hoped. As soon as she entered she let her fur fall to the ground, pulled her dress over her head, unhooked her bra, kicked off her pumps, shimmied out of her half-slip, and slid against the sheets. She pressed her face into the silken pillow and her nipples against the mattress. In minutes she was asleep.

The sleep must have been deep because when she awoke it was very suddenly and without any sense of time passing.

The telephone was ringing, and her mouth was dry. It wasn't until she was across the floor, pouring ice into one of the cut-crystal glasses on the bar and over that scotch from one of the decanters, that she remembered that in her dream she had been lying on the sun-warmed deck of a boat next to Jack Kennedy, naked, his fingers nestled between the two halves of her bottom. The phone was still ringing.

"Hello?" She picked it up, took in the beige-and-ivory surroundings, remembered she was in Chicago.

"N.J."

"Oh, it's you." She sank into the stuffed chair next to the telephone and put her tumbler against her forehead.

"You made it."

"Yes."

"Is everything all right? You're comfortable there, I hope?"

"Yes, the room is lovely, just like I told them it had fucking better be."

"Good. I want you to be comfortable."

She drank, letting the ice rattle close to the receiver, and waited for him to get to the point.

"What's the schedule that the studio gave you?"

"I have a luncheon with the local press. Some local columnist, bunch of photographers. And after the premiere I suppose a dinner with notables and plenty of opportunity to have my picture taken."

"Good. And perhaps later a drink at the Pump Room? The hotel is famous for it, you know—all the greats have been there."

Her eyes took a luxurious roll. So much secrecy and allusion, and suddenly he was talking like an eager travel agent, and not even a particularly inventive one. "Yes. I went once, when I was married to Joe. Frankie was playing. Frank Sinatra? They were friends, maybe they still are. Anyway, why does everybody want me to go there so bad?"

"It's the local—how do you say?—hot spot. The man I want you to meet is the kind who likes pretty women, and I'm counting on the fact that it will be a story that Marilyn Monroe is in the hotel, that he will be looking out for you. That he'll be looking out for you to make a pass, and the Pump Room is where he might expect to find you."

"Oh, yeah?"

"Yes. He's a United States senator, from Massachusetts. He's going to go for the Democratic nomination next year. The establishment likes Johnson if he runs. But we think this man is going to be the next president of the

United States."

"Uh-huh . . ." She curled in around her drink, closing her eyes. So that was it—they wanted to bring down a politician with a little sex scandal. And what did she care? After the lies Wilder had spread about her, who knew whether she'd work again. This was Alexei's game, and he knew how to play—that Jack Kennedy was a womanizer, and she was perfect bait. Perhaps he had only underestimated Jack's appetites, didn't realize they would have met already. "How'll I ever know which one he is?" she asked, in false ingénue.

"He's handsome, and a good talker, and I don't think you'll have trouble spotting him. But my guess is he'll find you."

"Yeah, well." She shifted in the chair, eyed the decanter. "I've already met him. In the elevator. Saw me in the lobby, I guess, and followed me."

On the other end of the line, Alexei chuckled. "You see, my dear? That's precisely why we picked you."

"You didn't think I knew who John Kennedy was? His little brother was with McCarthy, you know. They invited Arthur over for their little committee—Arthur hates those boys. You must think I'm pretty slow."

"My dear, don't talk that way. Of course I don't think you're slow. I only wanted you to meet naturally, as I knew you would if you were staying in the same hotel at the same time. . . ."

"Anyway," she went on, standing up and moving across the floor with the telephone in one hand, scotch in the other, the receiver tucked between ear and shoulder. "This bit you did get right—he *is* going to be at the Pump Room. He told me he hoped to see me there."

"Good. Good. Go there tonight, get to know him a little. Don't fall in love with him, though—he's said to be quite charming."

"Don't worry about that. I can't fall in love." Was it true? She'd never said anything like that before, but it sounded right, and suddenly all the romantic disturbances with which she'd filled her years seemed like irrefutable proof.

"Anyway, what do you want me to do to him?"

"That, my dear, is entirely up to you. The important thing is I want you to get something out of him. A secret."

"Like what? You want to know whether or not your Senator Kennedy has a big dick?"

This time the amusement was fainter, just an exhalation. "That I know already. No, whatever it is, you're going to have to tell me."

The mirror opposite the bed was framed in gilt flourishes, and she regarded herself, listening to the faraway sound of Alexei breathing. Her full, uptilting breasts, the swelling of the abdomen like something from a Rembrandt painting, the whiteness of the flesh. *In the flesh*, Jack had said. Her mind was bright—she hadn't imagined they'd meet again, but now she was excited to see him, to put Alexei's scheme in motion, to see what she could learn. She only wished she wasn't quite so heavy at the moment, but that never mattered once she was playing a part; and anyway, there was lots of time to make herself up. She was practically a genius at that by now.

"N.J.?"

"I'm here."

"I'll find you again soon. Don't drink too much; I want you to remember as much as you can." He paused, and for a moment she thought the line had disengaged. But then he went on, softly: "And do take care of yourself, all right?"

FIVE

Chicago, March 1959

EVEN in the early days, when she was so intimidated by pretty much everybody including the catering people that she was mostly mute around them, her eyes had been her friends. They had always known how to return a gaze; words sometimes failed her, but she didn't shrink in that way. One prolonged look, and she could tell the story of all the carnal possibilities. She could make love with her eyes. Jack, it seemed, had the same talent. Besides her, he was the shiniest object in the room—he wore clothes the way she wore clothes; they hung lightly, temporarily, on a body well aware of its value—and even in a room packed with the fashionable and rich, he never lost sight of her.

When she arrived at the Pump Room, off the hotel lobby, he was sitting in a booth, surrounded by men wearing white dinner jackets and deep in conversation. That was two hours ago, and though they'd both flitted from table to table—saying hello to acquaintances (people she'd met at parties, or through her husbands; others who admired her and merely wanted to touch her hand), occasionally accepting invitations to dance—they had not yet spoken.

What the old studio bastards called procrastination, she called patience. This was the essence of performance. She would never shout for attention when she could wait and draw it to her. Occasionally Jack glanced in her direction. Then she looked at him, looked away, lowered her lashes, let her shrouded eyes roll lazily back in his direction. Other women might have worried that they were losing their mark. Not her. She could feel the tension building, and knew the moment he made his move. He rose from the booth—the steaks his party had ordered for dinner lay half eaten on platters, and the ashtrays overflowed—and began to maneuver through the crowd. She rested an elbow on her table, lifted her chin, relaxed her posture, held steady.

"Marilyn Monroe," he said, when he was standing before her. He said her name low, emphasizing all five syllables, as though it signified some gorgeous stretch of landscape that he was appreciating for the first time. Then he thrust his hand forward and flashed his grin. "I'm Jack Kennedy. I hope I'm not interrupting. I wanted to tell you I enjoy your pictures."

"Thank you, Senator." A silly, suggestive wink as she dangled her fingers in the vicinity of his. "Any picture in particular?"

"All of 'em." He caught her hand and pulled. "Will you dance?" Glancing in the direction of her publicity man, he added: "If that's all right."

She'd worn her publicity man down—he only waved his hand indifferently as she allowed Jack to draw her onto her feet. The evening dress she wore was black, spangled with jet, and though the neck was somewhat higher than usual, the back was open down below the narrow of her waist. As Jack led her to the dance floor, he put his hand on the naked skin of her lower spine. One of her straps slipped, and she left it resting there, halfway between elbow and shoulder.

"I've been thinking about you," he said, leaving one hand on her back and using the other to draw her into a gentle sway. The band was playing mild jazz from a slightly raised stage in the corner, and she smiled at him mistily, as though she might have been thinking about him, too, or might not have. "You're dangerous. They shouldn't let you out looking like that."

"They?"

"The government, I guess."

"But you are the government."

Neither had blinked since they began dancing. His face was lit with his gaze, and though he was not quite smiling anymore his mouth hung open. "I guess I'd be a hypocrite if I tried passing any laws against you."

"Please don't. I make people happy, you know."

"I only care whether you make me happy."

"How am I doing so far?"

"Grand." Others in the room had noticed them, but he didn't seem to mind. "I haven't felt this happy in months."

"Good." She let her heavy lashes kiss the skin of her cheeks. "I think I'd enjoy making you happy."

They were quiet for a while after that. Now she saw that he wasn't really so handsome—it was the combination of tanned skin and confident, intelligent eyes that made him seem so. In fact, his features were rather piggish. But he was more appealing for it, more original. He was a good dancer, too, and she enjoyed being led. Though he gripped her loosely, she could feel the energy of his body—its heat was concentrated on her.

Time passed before she spoke again, and the pitch of her voice changed, as when something meaningful has occurred. "Where did you come from?" she asked.

"Washington," he replied bluntly.

"Mmmmm . . ." she purred, as though he were just making sounds and she was in no state to absorb any information, instead of pressing him, on Alexei's behalf, for some secret detail. "So you're here on business?"

"Pleasure. Come to my room tonight." It was half command, half request. His voice had lowered, too.

She shook her head faintly, a drop of sadness. "I can't," she whispered, as though denying herself something she wanted badly. She did want him, a little. But if they went to bed too quickly, she knew he wouldn't talk at all. They couldn't both have what they wanted. "But don't leave me yet. Talk to me. I like the way you talk. Tell me anything—about your work. Did it bring you here?"

"In a way," he replied evasively, without meeting her eye. The tautness of his muscles changed—abruptly his interest had slipped.

She summoned a pink warmth, let it spread over her cheeks. She averted her gaze before raising it to meet his, the vulnerability quivering and dense. Her body got heavy with it, so he almost had to hold her up. "If I did," she went on, helpless and hopeful as a child. "If I came to your room, I mean, you'd forget about me as soon as you were done, wouldn't you?"

"A broad like you?" He shook his head in disbelief at the suggestion. The moment of his flagging attention had passed; she had him again, and stronger this time.

"Maybe we could meet in Los Angeles. I keep a bungalow at the Beverly Hills Hotel." Her voice was halting, as though she were afraid of the suggestion—afraid of what it might mean, afraid it might be rejected. "My husband prefers New York, so I'm more free on the Coast. Plus it's so nice in the sunshine, don't you think? When the sun makes your skin real hot." When she said *hot* she wrinkled up her nose, just like she had for Wilder's picture.

"I'm going there in a couple of weeks. Maybe I'll call you."

"Would you?" she whispered, as though she wanted to trust him but was afraid to. They looked at each other, and she knew he couldn't wait for it, for balmy California, to hammer her on the sand. She made her eyes big as buttons, like Betty Boop. "But tell me something now," she went on in the breathy voice she used when she performed. "Tell me a secret. Tell me something real, something you don't want anybody to know. That way I'll have a little dirt on you, and you'll have to come back and treat me nice." Many times she'd practiced saying *nice* like that—girlishly, but so that any man who wasn't queer couldn't help but think of the word *naughty*—but it had never come out of her mouth quite so perfect.

He gave her that swanky grin, and turned her so that she was facing the direction he had been facing a moment ago. Over his white tuxedoed shoulder she could see the booth where he had eaten dinner, a table full of men who had just been staring at her. They'd changed their postures quickly, but she could always tell, and suddenly she knew what Jack had been doing. He'd been holding her, on that spot, so that his friends would have the best view—the open back of her dress, that channel of white skin pointing down like an arrow to the fat black-sequined apple of her ass. The corners of her mouth curled, and she let her irises drift up till they were half obscured by her eyelids. Alexei had been right—she was going to enjoy stealing from Jack.

"See that man with the little glasses and the big sausage nose?"

"You mean at your table?" she asked innocently.

"Yes."

"The one in the middle? The one who's talking like everyone should pay attention?"

"Yes, that one. And everybody *is* paying attention. That's Sam Giancana—he runs Chicago."

"What do you mean, *runs?*" She gave him her widest eyes.

"I mean he's the capo, baby. La Cosa Nostra. He's in the mob. He *is* the mob."

"Oh." She let the fear shudder down her spine so that he'd feel it in his palm—which, now that she was turned around and only the band could see her backside, had drifted south. "You mean he's one of the bad guys?"

Jack just kept giving her that grin, that fence of strong, bright teeth.

"He doesn't hurt people, does he?"

The same teeth.

"But what are you doing sitting at a table with him? I mean, if you're a senator, isn't it your duty to bring him in or something?"

"That's not how it works, baby. Not in this world."

"What are you meeting with him for, then?"

He told it as matter-of-factly as though it were the story of how he was going to order his sandwich. "It's business. When I make my run for president, he's going to see that Cook County goes for Kennedy."

"I see," she said and closed her eyes. She rested her head against his shoulder and let her body relax against his. "I mean, aren't you big and important," she cooed drowsily. But she wasn't tired. Her mind fizzed with the information. It had been so easy—all she'd had to do was act a little dumb and frightened, and he'd told her something she already knew was even bigger than Alexei could have hoped for. She was almost sorry that this would be the end of her spying, because in fact she found it quite satisfying. She was a natural, which was probably why they chose her. Perhaps she'd always liked digging for secrets.

Then her mind really did drift from their conversation, and she let him sway her for a few more songs. She enjoyed that part, too—his appealing, assertive features, his ragged energy, the way the room spun around him like he was its center. After that she yawned—girlishly, theatrically, sweetly— and told him she had better get her beauty rest.

"But I'll see you on the Coast," he said when she stepped away.

"You better mean it. Remember, if you don't call me, I'm going to the papers with your secret." She winked and let him lead her over to her publicity man. Jack was back at the booth of cronies before she was out the door, talking about what a fine ass she had, probably, but she didn't care. After she got back to New York she was going to meet her father, and maybe fix things with Arthur, or if not start fresh in California—she'd buy a place in the desert, and make Father bacon and eggs for breakfast every morning.

The elevator sank fast through the hotel, the following morning, but she wasn't frightened. She hadn't slept much, and for once this caused her no agitation. She was alert, and her eyes in the mirrored walls that had contained her first meeting with Jack were shining and focused. She felt everything— her hair framing her face, a pulsing from the soles of her feet, the collar of her fur coat against her jaw as she hugged it close to her body. When she stepped onto the curb outside the Ambassador East, she saw Alexei right away. He was carrying a sign that said TWENTIETH CENTURY-FOX, and wearing a chauf-feur's hat and the suggestion of a smile that was for her alone.

Leaving her publicity man to deal with her luggage, she wordlessly allowed Alexei to hold the door for her. She situated herself in the backseat—crossed legs, compact held aloft so that she could check her lipstick. It wasn't until he'd pulled onto the freeway that she put away her makeup things and met his gaze in the rearview mirror. He had been watching her already, and she gave him the knowing, mischievous smile of a former lover who has never really gone away.

"How was last night, my dear?" he asked, returning her smile.

"Good." She beamed. "I think you're going to be kinda impressed with me."

"The senator liked you, then?"

"Yes, right away."

"Does he trust you?"

"Oh, I don't know about that. I don't think trust means very much with a man like that. He thinks I'm not too sharp, that's the important thing—he didn't worry much about telling me important things, because he believes I'm too dumb to understand."

The face Alexei gave her was better than any she'd ever gotten from a director. "You really got his number, didn't you?"

"Yes." She savored the *yes*—they both did—as he maneuvered the car across the vast lavender ribbon of expressway.

"And what did he tell you, my dear?"

"He told me . . ." She bit her lower lip and closed her eyes. "He told me the reason he was in Chicago."

"Which was?"

"He was in Chicago to see Sam Giancana, the man who runs the Chicago Outfit." The story, as she recounted it, sounded almost harmless and quaint, like the oft-recited words of a fairy tale on the lips of a child. She closed her eyes and listened to herself tell the ending: "He was there to make a deal with Giancana, so that when he runs for president, Illinois will go for Kennedy."

Beneath her white pumps, through the floor, she could feel the car's wheels slow slightly; Alexei was changing directions to bring her to her father. He was close by, and as a reward she would be taken there in time to make him coffee and read him the headlines. But when she finally opened her eyes she saw that the car was moving along in the same path—it was only that other cars were denser around them now, so he couldn't maintain the same speed—and his gaze was no longer focused on her.

"Isn't that what you wanted?" She hoped her voice wasn't really so pathetic.

"I knew that already," he replied quietly. He didn't need to express his disappointment, because it was obvious in his changed posture. "How do you think I knew he'd be in Chicago in the first place? We have a girl in Giancana's organization."

The skin of her face went cold and her stomach made a fist as she apprehended what Alexei was involved in—what she, by extension, was involved in. She thought of the little man at Kennedy's booth, his small glasses and thin lips, his shoulders creeping up around his neck like the shoulders of all corrupt people. About how he was a killer. The nameless girl who reported to both Alexei and Giancana was a killer, too. And so was Alexei, probably, if the situation demanded.

"You're not going to introduce me to my father, then?" She didn't sound like a child anymore, and her face was turned away.

He ignored her question. "How did you leave it with Kennedy?"

The fur coat was draped over her shoulders, and under its cover she fixed her arms across her chest. "He said he'd call me when he's in California next," she replied vaguely to the windowpane.

"Good. Then that's where you're heading. I'll take you to the airport and get you a ticket. It will appear natural enough—it's what Arthur's been asking for; he won't object. And if you stay longer than planned, you can tell him that you're seeing to his business, both your business, by trying to convince Mr. Gable to be in the picture. We understand Arthur hasn't been able to convince Mr. Gable to play Gay yet."

"That's because Arthur doesn't understand Mr. Gable," she snapped bitterly, before she thought to ask how Alexei knew about *The Misfits*, Arthur's latest obsession, or what she and Arthur fought about in private. "He doesn't understand anybody besides himself."

"But you do. It will be good cover for you, and if you're doing a little business it will be a perfect excuse to go to parties and see a lot of Kennedy."

Suddenly her head hurt, and the miles of expressway, the tangle of traffic, the great distance that lay between her and the airport lounge and a good, strong drink seemed impassable, impossible. "When do I get to meet him, Alexei?"

He glanced at her in the rearview, and must have seen how her eyes burned when she asked this. He knew she meant her father, and did not make her say so out loud. "Once you've done this one thing for us, then you can meet him." He was patient again, but some of the kindness was gone. "Go to California. Wait for Kennedy. Let him romance you. Get him to tell you something. Anything. I want to know something about Mr. John Kennedy that no one else knows."

SIX

Los Angeles, April 1959

THERE was always a moment, returning after a long time away, when she thought California could hold her. It was so quiet in that dry, clear atmosphere, and she would squint, and see nothing harmful in its fine light. But despair can creep up in the sunshine, too, an old lesson she was reminded of by two days spent waiting in her hotel for Jack to call. Alexei had assured her he was, in fact, in Los Angeles, but she had yet to hear from the senator, and so on Saturday she set off on the business that had officially brought her west. On the freeway she turned up the radio and let her consciousness drift, so that by the time she had descended into the orange groves of the San Fernando Valley she had almost forgotten her troubles.

The air, when she stepped out of the car, was fragrant with orange blossoms, and the quiet was so complete that the studios on the other side of the hills seemed like another country. Clark Gable was coming toward her from the house, his arm raised in greeting, rather bowlegged as though he were a real cowboy. His face was charred from the sun, and even at a distance she marked the silver glint of his eyes, the ruffled brow and half-cocked smile. She unknotted the scarf that she had worn to protect her hair during the drive, and tossed it through the open driver's side window.

"Hello, honey," he called out. "Don't you look like a dream!"

She smiled shyly in reply. In fact, they were dressed rather similarly, in white slacks and suede loafers, his collared shirt unbuttoned to the chest, hers designed to open wide. She stepped out of the driving loafers and into the red high-heeled pumps she kept under the seat. "And you look just like I knew you would."

When he reached her he put an arm around her shoulder and drew her in the direction of the house. "Pleasure to meet you, honey. Thanks for coming out to the boonies."

"Oh, well, you know, the pleasure is all mine. It's a relief, really, to get out of town."

He chuckled. "Where you staying, honey?"

"My usual bungalow at the Beverly Hills."

"Welcome to Encino, then. When you've been in this business as long as I have, you learn to get away."

"Oh, I've been away plenty, only for me it always seems to . . ." Her words grew faint and fell away, no match for the weight of all that running away failed to fix. "You know my mother used to have a framed picture of you on her nightstand? For the longest time, whenever I saw your face, I thought *you* were my father."

"Yes, I've heard that one," he replied genially. It was a story she liked to tell reporters. Grinning down on her, he asked, "Is it true?"

She grinned back, and answered in the same easy manner. "Who can remember anymore?"

His arm remained rested on her shoulder as they went into the shadow of the house, up the brick steps framed by eruptions of bougainvillea, and into the cool foyer. "Kay!" he yelled, loudly but in no direction in particular. "Kay! Miss Monroe is here."

A big blonde emerged from around a staircase, skirt swinging. As she wiped her hands on a towel, her lips—where red tint had been recently applied—stretched in welcome. Her hair rose off her forehead in brass curls that must have set the night before, and Marilyn saw right away what had happened to her: She was pretty enough to get into pictures, but not special enough to stay.

"Kay, this is Marilyn; Marilyn, this is my wife, Kay Williams."

The two women shook hands, and Marilyn made several pleasant observations about the house, which Kay batted away, before soliciting a smacking, avuncular kiss on the lips from her husband.

"You'll stay for dinner, won't you?" Kay demanded, arm around her husband's middle.

"That would be wonderful," Marilyn breathed.

"Children, come meet Miss Monroe!" Kay shouted up the stairs.

Their feet thundered across the second story, and then a boy and a girl came hustling down into the foyer. They were handsome children, tall but not yet teenagers, and someone had put a great deal of care into dressing them.

"I like your ribbons," Marilyn addressed the girl, a little shyly.

When she heard the timidity in the movie star's voice, the girl managed to raise her eyes. "I'm Jane," she blurted.

"Well. It's nice to meet you, Jane."

"And this is Bunker," Clark said. The boy flicked his eyes up at her. Though he was as preternaturally blond as his sister, his sapphire gaze was purer and more assertive; he had a bold self-regard that she recognized, and it softened her heart to him. He was so young and beautiful, and it made her realize Clark was old, his skin cracked and his chest thinning; that his body had already absorbed too many blows.

Clark shooed away the children and brought her into the living room. The walls were paneled in pine, and a pyramid of wood had been erected in the fireplace, although it wasn't lit and may have been there a long time already. It occurred to her that movie stars are always their own best customers.

"Why do you call him Bunker?" Marilyn asked as she sank onto the floral sofa and curled her pumps underneath herself.

"Because he's a sadist." Clark's back was to her, focusing on the bar, and she wasn't sure if he was serious or not. When he turned, a tumbler of amber liquid in either hand, he was wearing his Rhett Butler face, and for a moment she felt as though she'd just been told that she should be kissed, and often, and by someone who knows how. "His name's Adolph, after his father—you didn't think they were my children, did you?"

She shook her head.

"I'd have been a lousy father, I guess. But as a stepfather, I think I do all right. Anyway, yes—Adolph after his father, Mr. Adolph Spreckels the Second. You'd have thought the war killed their taste for the name, but no. So they call him Bunker because that's where it ended for the great dictator. Cute, ain't it?"

"I'd think that would be a hard name to hear all the time."

"I suppose." He passed her a drink and sat down, propping an ankle on the opposite knee and drinking long. She waited for him to say more, but he didn't.

"They seem like sweet children."

"Sure."

"And you and Kay, you're happy together?"

"I've been married five times, so I don't expect much from the institution, but yes—we're happy, after a fashion."

"That's nice." She let her lids sink and sipped the whiskey that Clark Gable had brought her. She was beginning to enjoy the faux simplicity of his place, the good-looking children, and the meaty aroma that was wafting from the kitchen. "I guess happiness isn't perfect any place . . ."

"So." She opened her eyes when she heard his voice, newly hard. "You want me to make this picture of your husband's, is that it?"

"That's right." She lowered the glass from her face. "John Huston is set to direct, and . . . we think you're the only one to play Gay."

"Gay?" His eyebrows did a dance. She felt a surge of anger at Arthur for being so stupid and obvious. She'd heard the stories of what Clark had done to get ahead, and knew that when stories like that persisted they were often true.

"Oh, well, you know . . . it's just a name."

He shook his head. "Sure. I don't mind that. Listen, kid, you and me, we're the same, more or less. So you have a pretty good idea what kind of things I did in the early days, just like I know without asking what you've done. And I know all the tricks you use to stay in this business, too, and why you want to. Why you'll never go Garbo. Yes—I can make you squirm, same as you can make me squirm. Only I don't want to. I just want to tell you straight. I'll do the picture."

"Oh." She straightened, pressed her ankles together. "You will?"

"Sure." His left eye twitched, the suggestion of a wink, and she knew what he'd meant when he said they were the same. "So long as the money's right."

"That's such wonderful news!" She touched his glass with hers, and took a sip that reminded her of her insides as it went down scorching. "The picture wouldn't work without you, you know that?"

"Yes, I'm sure everybody will be looking right at me." He laughed and shook his head, his gaze for a moment traveling over the places where her slacks had tightened on her thighs. "You go on and tell your husband you convinced me after a lot of burdensome talking, and let's just have some fun and not worry about that anymore. Okay?"

"Okay."

Kay was calling to them that dinner would get cold if they didn't quit their gossiping and come into the kitchen. They exchanged a glance, and drained their glasses.

"Let's have some chow," he said, and they rose and went ambling, arm in arm, toward his wife's voice.

Dinner was meat loaf, and Marilyn felt lulled by the homeliness, the sitting at table with a family, Kay in her housedress, her blazing smile and warm, direct manner. The adults talked about how each of them had been raised poor—agreeing it was a relief to live for a spell without the extra fuss of a cook and maid now and then—while the children picked at their food. The girl kept looking up at Marilyn—slowly, as though she might thus disguise her curiosity—but the boy didn't bother averting his eyes, which were fascinated and unembarrassed. Children were always interested in her one way or another, and since she liked their company and still hoped to have her own someday, she didn't mind. Kay made them clear and wash their own dishes, and then they disappeared, to whatever dream place children go when they are alone.

"Would you like another?" Kay indicated Marilyn's tumbler with a wave of the hand.

"Oh, sure."

Kay sashayed into the living room and returned with the whole bottle, which she planted in the middle of the table.

"Thank you for dinner, Kay. It was delicious."

"Thanks, honey. Just the same as Ma used to make back on the peach farm in P.A. I know it's not really Hollywood fare, but we like it." She made a show of yawning. "Will you excuse me just a little while, so I can slip into something more comfortable?"

"Of course." As Kay left the room, Marilyn unstopped the bottle and filled her and Clark's glasses. The ice had melted a while ago, but this didn't seem to matter. She sighed, pushing her shoulder blades into the chair's high back and crossing her ankles on the spot where young Jane had lately sat. "What a dear your wife is," she observed, bringing the fresh glass up to her lips.

"Yes." Clark was leaning forward, over the table, his eyes on the ceiling, listening for the sound of high heels above, first on wood and then some softer surface. A door slammed. He blinked, raised his glass, and drained it. "Come on, kid. Let's get out of here. I need to fuck something."

Marilyn heard her own shoes coming down suddenly from the chair, and she must have seemed stricken because he quickly amended himself.

"Don't worry, not you."

"Oh." Her shoulders sloped, whether in relief or disappointment she wasn't sure. "But isn't Kay coming back down?"

"She's taken a pill and gone to bed. She thinks I'm going to screw you, and she can't stand it but she knows she can't stop it, so she figures she'll just put herself down a while."

A sad smile crept onto Marilyn's face. "But you don't want to. Screw me, I mean."

"Oh." His brow flexed and he pursed his lips, sorrow morphing into irony in his washed-out eyes. "Honey, I want to fuck something that doesn't move. Something with big, trusting eyes, something stupid enough to believe I'm going to make their dreams come true. We'll find a nice piece for you, too, all right?"

Her mother really had kept a photograph on her bedside table, a publicity shot of Clark Gable from his early years, and though she had always known he was just a man from the pictures, she felt a swallowing disappointment that the performance of the late afternoon—of mother and father and boy and girl eating meat loaf for dinner while the sun was still up—wasn't true. Her eyes lowered, and she brought the whiskey to her mouth.

"Anyway," he went on with gritty charm, "what if you really were my daughter? We'd have a Greek tragedy on our hands."

"All right." She raised her gaze to meet his, and when she saw his grin she knew this was better. They were the same, like he said, had probably even once upon a time sucked some of the same cocks. She tossed her hair away from her face and told herself to feel careless until carelessness was radiating through her skin. "Let's go. But where to?"

"Mosey Moses is having a party."

Marilyn's eyes got wide, and she rotated her head right and left.

"You don't know Mosey? Well." Clark winked before standing and offering her his hand. They were moving quickly, through the foyer, and outside, where she saw the night sky white with stars. "You *have* been gone a long time. Nowadays everybody goes to Mosey's."

SEVEN

Beverly Hills, April 1959

"DOUGIE!"

At the sound of the diminutive, trilled by his mother, Walls shrank slightly into the lounge chair upon which he had been hiding. It amazed him anew that at this late stage of life, when he was almost entirely emancipated, financially and personally speaking, and when he was, additionally, highly trained in the use of firearms and in a variety of surveillance techniques, his mother's voice should still inject him with such an instant dose of migrainous agony. But he knew that she would find him sooner or later, so he sat up faithfully and allowed her to spot him.

"Yes?"

The tiki torches that had been lit earlier by the Moseses' live-in help waved in the wind, illuminating the figure of his mother, paused on the highest of three long, curving marble steps that led up to the house. She was unspeakably thin, and wearing a tight black top that was cut away to reveal the entirety of her shoulders as well as a good deal of chest, and a full-length black lace skirt, as though she were some sort of Spanish dancer. Her hair was pulled back tightly from her face, and collected above the nape of her neck in a shape reminiscent of an especially large morning bun. Happily for the mood of her party, several guests had already made a big show of acting shocked that she was old enough to have a son of twenty-five.

"Dougie." She lowered her chin and approached along the edge of the turquoise swimming pool, reminding him for perhaps the ten thousandth

time that she was a woman who had taken the advanced class in how to walk. "What are you doing out here? Everyone's gone inside."

"Have they?" he asked, as though that had not been his chief motivation in remaining by the pool.

She sat down next to him. "The temperature drops maybe twenty degrees at night here. You didn't know that, did you?"

"When I came outside it was still warm," he replied irrelevantly.

"That's because it's the desert, darling." She laughed the twinkling laugh that might, to strangers, sound unaffected. "Don't be fooled by all the trucked-in greenery."

She leaned back on her arm, a kind of *Harper's Bazaar* pose, and closed her eyes and inhaled what Walls had to admit—regretfully, and only to himself—was wonderful-smelling night air.

"I'm so glad you've finally decided to come home," she said and sighed. But the moment of contented contemplation didn't last long. With a bat of her eyelashes, she extended her hand for him to take. "Come on in, darling, I want to show you off."

He might have informed her that he was not an accessory, or a dancing bear, or even—in a kinder, more patient tone—the little boy she'd once dressed in sailor suits. But he only said yes, rather affirmatively, and offered her his arm. Anyway, he was wearing the charcoal drainpipe trousers and pink collared shirt that she had laid out for him, so he supposed that in every meaningful way he had already lost the battle.

The best he could do was to perform a small, interior rebellion by reviewing for himself the activities of the day, all in the service of a career choice that Mosey had always disapproved of, and now discovered a fresh reason to dislike: Walls was not only disinclined to discuss what he did professionally but not permitted to by law. In truth, what activity he'd done with regards to his new assignment, he had done grudgingly. This had consisted mainly of reading back issues of *Photoplay* and *Variety*, scanning for the name Marilyn Monroe;

skimming through hefty transcripts of late-night telephone calls between Miss Monroe and her sundry confidantes (chief conclusion: She was an inveterate fabulist); and finally, when she went out, bugging her hotel room.

Inside, a record of Nat King Cole singing in Spanish was playing, muffled slightly by the sounds of collective drinking, and he did not have time to be surprised that the object of his day's labors was approaching from the opposite direction on the arm of Clark Gable. She was just there, quite suddenly and naturally, and white as the moon. Her mouth was a flexed, pink bow, and her drowsy eyes were acknowledging the other guests in as gently swinging a manner as Cole's orchestra. Not only her skin but her clothes were white, and it was obvious that she wasn't wearing anything underneath her filmy shirt. They were casual clothes, in contrast to the gowns the other women had worn to his mother's "evening." But she did not seem to mind, and in fact her presence made the other female garments in the room seem a little hostile, their underpinnings pushing and shoving to create artificially smoothed and excessively fortified peaks and narrows. By contrast Marilyn was so amply feminine that Walls felt overwhelmed, almost nauseous, and had to glance away.

"They're drunk," his mother observed, reminding him of her presence. Of course they were—as soon as Mother said it, he saw that she was right. Clark and Marilyn weren't stumbling, they were just lit up, sailing slightly higher than everyone else, their gestures loose and hungry.

Those others—who had managed to come more or less on time, and were now scattered across several stepped levels of brightly modern décor— were not nobodies. Far from it; and yet they were all staring at the man and woman who had just arrived. Of course his mother had delighted in detailing the density of power in her house—among the assembled were a girl who was up for an Academy Award, a Polish prince, Jimmy Stewart's publicist, a popular science fiction novelist, and a senator who was rumored to be after the presidency, and who was in talks with Lou about turning his book into a picture. (This last one surprised Walls—not the bit about the book, but rather that Kennedy was considered a suitable nominee, as Walls had once observed him at a lawn party in McLean heading for the bushes with a girl who was almost certainly on the wrong side of seventeen.)

Meanwhile, someone had changed the record.

A Negro's voice intoned, "One . . . *two* . . . THREE!" followed by a simple, entrancing beat that was somehow a voodoo incantation and also at the same time a Viennese waltz. The blonde in white slacks and no brassiere who everyone was staring at laughed when she recognized the song, and went slinking away from the man she'd come in with, a theatrical, shoulder-rolling dance. He caught up with her a few steps later, twirled her under his arm, and then they tangoed together across the floor. Those few holders-out could no longer resist gaping at them. The voice on the record spoke, growled, shouted a story of possesive love that appeared to have the two movie stars in thrall.

"That poor girl." His mother shook her head, but she appeared to find the implied misfortune more thrilling than pitiable.

"Why?" Walls asked.

"She's just a little lost thing, that's all."

"Oh."

Soon everyone in the room was keeping the beat with raised, clapping hands, and Clark Gable and Marilyn Monroe were hamming it up for their greedy audience. For a moment Walls wondered if she were having an affair with the old goat, but as the song came to an end he felt a strong instinct that they weren't inclined to each other in that way. Gable was looking down on her rather protectively, and she kept closing her eyes and swaying, slightly off rhythm, almost as though she were dancing by herself.

"I'm going to need your help in a moment," Mosey breathed into her son's ear.

"With what?" He hoped he didn't sound as much like a complaining teenager to her as he did to himself.

"We're going to have to break this up."

"But they're having fun." Walls surveyed the room, the forty or so people entranced by the movie stars making a spectacle of themselves. "Everyone's having fun."

"Yes, but one song's worth of this is enough." She extended an index finger, and after the final chords of the song died out, a new record was put on—four white boys singing in harmony—and the excitement of the previous minutes evaporated. Mosey gave her son a gentle shove, and they both advanced into the room.

Within seconds the hostess had Gable in a loose hold, and Walls, a step behind her, saw that Marilyn seemed confused by the change of music. She was still moving, but her feet were unsure now. He knew the thing to do was just to take her by the waist and start leading, but she looked so out of sorts he couldn't help but handle her gently.

"Miss Monroe, will you dance with me?" he asked.

"All right," she murmured, and fell against him.

The skin between her brows quivered, and her expression oscillated: happy, sad, happy, sad. She was almost humming to herself, and though the song was fast, she kept slow dancing, and he had no choice but to accommodate her rhythm. At close range, the exuberantly curved line of black kohl on her upper lid and the false lashes were brutal against her beautiful, pale, childlike face. Then she turned her eyes up to him and her bottom lip dropped, so that her mouth opened suggestively, and she took a breath that made her chest rise and fall and brush against him. Was he leading at all? He glanced around, embarrassed by her strange voluptuous naïveté and by his unexpected arousal, and saw that luckily for him most of the other guests had risen to their feet and were dancing now; he was not as conspicuous as he had feared.

"What's your name?" she went on in the same breathy whisper.

"Douglass," he replied.

"Douglass." The point of her tongue slid along her upper lip, as though she were tasting the name to see if she liked its flavor. "What a serious name! You don't seem that serious to me, Douglass."

"No, I—" What had he meant to do, correct her? Disown the pink shirt, tell her about his gun, and that he had only a few hours ago violated her hotel room? "Not serious in the least. You must be a pretty good judge of character."

A humorous exhalation through her narrow nostrils. "Yeah," she murmured, but he wasn't sure if she was agreeing with him.

She seemed liable to drift into her own thoughts, so he went on stupidly, "In fact, I'm quite the opposite of serious—I'm twenty-five, and living here with my mother, if you can believe it."

"Mosey Moses is your mother?"

Her eyes were open again, so she saw when he nodded.

"Never been married, huh?"

He shook his head.

"I've been married three times, but it never seems to . . ." She trailed off, but not in the daffy way she had before. A new energy coursed through her limbs—she was lighter in his arms—and her eyes shone at something over his shoulder that he wished to god he could turn and see.

"It never seems to . . .?" he prompted.

She was smiling again, and she had caught the rhythm of the song. Walls felt suddenly as though he had just been given a corner office, a shot of Benzedrine, and the spirit of Fred Astaire. They were doing an effortless Lindy; Walls had never danced so well in his life. When she kicked off her shoes he forgot himself and started smiling. And he was still smiling when he felt the tap at his shoulder, and turned to see Kennedy.

"May I cut in?" the senator asked. Earlier, Walls had spotted him talking up Kim Novak, but Kim Novak was nowhere in sight now. He was smiling, too, but Walls knew it had a different effect than the boyish grin sliding from his own face.

Walls glanced back at Marilyn, as though she might protest that she was enjoying herself with her current partner, and saw that she must have bent down to scoop up her pumps because she was now cradling them in her arms.

"Will you hold these for me?" she asked Walls, as sweetly as though she were telling him she loved him for the first time.

"Sure," he said, awkwardly taking the shoes. With the heels pressed against his chest he stepped back, and then back again, until he was out of the thicket of swinging bodies.

Once he was properly on the sidelines, he realized how dizzy he had felt in Marilyn's presence, how unwieldy she was, and he knew that he ought to be relieved to be back where he could watch and observe. But bitterness tightened his throat. Kennedy had made a pass as surely as he might have ordered a steak. Walls's sense of his own ridiculousness increased when he noted the senator's navy slacks, the fine weave of his white shirt, the narrow black tie, the knot of which he'd loosened but not undone, as though to remind everyone that he was just a visitor in carefree California, and would be going back to the grown-ups' table shortly. Walls did not have the body of a beatnik, and should never have allowed himself to be shoehorned into pink.

In his peripheral vision, he saw the way Marilyn was talking to the senator, and was angry at himself all over again for continuing to feel like a jilted lover. He violently uncorked a bottle of scotch, and poured a double portion into a glass without ice. He took a long pull, and an idea hit him, and he swung his head to look over his shoulder.

At this distance he couldn't hear what Marilyn was saying, but he could see that she was chastising the senator in a flirtatious, joking way. They had met before—it was obvious by the knowing manner in which they were now bantering and moving lightly on their feet. There was a history, Walls was sure of it. He finished the scotch and glanced around for a girl to dance with so that he could get close enough to hear what they were saying.

But he didn't spot one right away, and when he did he wasted precious minutes trying to think of an opening line. In the end he just introduced himself to the brunette in the high-necked black linen dress, and asked if she was enjoying herself. "Very much" was her swift reply. She seemed grateful for his attention, and agreed to dance the moment he hinted that he might be willing. But by the time they were on the floor, swaying to a new record, Kennedy was dancing with Mosey. Walls's gaze went around the room, but he couldn't find Marilyn anywhere, and he knew this wasn't because she had somehow magically started blending in.

"Is something wrong?" the brunette asked. Her ski-jump nose turned a little pink when she asked the question, but she went on looking up at him with those doe eyes. She couldn't have been much more than nineteen, and you could hear the Kansas in her speech, though she was made up to suggest a Smith graduate with a library full of banned books.

"No," he answered, mostly because he realized how rude he had been to ask her to dance and then cast his gaze everywhere but at her. But then he found he was smiling again, and when he said, "No, not at all," he meant it.

"I'm glad." She was beaming.

"Me, too."

In fact, he *was* glad. Of course it would've been better to overhear what Marilyn had whispered so sweetly to Senator Kennedy. But he knew that he had understood the gist of it, even without words, because they hadn't really been using words. That she had disappeared so quickly was yet more confirmation to Walls that he had already procured his ticket out of California. The senator and the movie star had met before, were meeting now, would meet again. This was precisely the sort of blackmail material the Director had built his career on, and if Walls got proof of a senator's dalliance with a movie star, he would be in favored position at the Bureau. Surely they would reward him for this—if he wanted, he could go back to Washington immediately, have his pick of assignments, and finally begin a life of consequence.

EIGHT

Beverly Hills, April 1959

A half mile down the road, Marilyn pulled over and switched off the high beams. The street behind her was invisible around the bend—any drivers coming from that direction wouldn't notice her car until they passed. There were houses nearby, but they were hidden away behind their high purple hedges. Her breath was agitated and music made her nervous, so she turned the radio off. After fixing her lipstick and fluffing her hair there was nothing she could do but recline, put her bare feet on the dash, and wait. He was the kind of man who would lose interest as soon as they finished; if she were wise, she'd guard the treasure box. So she thought about all the tricks she could use to draw it out, keep everything from happening too quickly, make him talk first. Then she heard the sound of a man's dress shoes on the pavement, and knew she wasn't going to use any of them.

His silhouette was visible in the driver's side mirror: hands in pockets, approaching at an easy gait, whistling a melody that sounded like "Summertime." But he stopped whistling when he was almost to her car, and the quietness of the night swept over her. It seemed a long time she had to wait for him to open the passenger door.

The door slammed. After that he didn't take his gaze off her, and she could hear that his breathing was as short as hers. Ever since he had whispered in her ear, in Mosey Moses's ballroom, that she should leave first and he would follow in twenty minutes, she had been imagining the things he might say to her—that he hadn't stopped thinking about her since Chicago, that he had been asking everyone where she was staying, that his wife had had a private detective on his tail, or else he would have found her immediately.

But she liked that he didn't make excuses or tell any stories now. His eyes burned as he took in the length of her, how she was sprawled across the front seat, and she returned his look, steady and unblinking. The line of his shoulders was tensed, but not in a deadened way. There was so much energy about him, as though he were more alive than ordinary people. The tie was gone, and his shirtsleeves rolled to the elbows, so that he seemed not quite so senatorial, more just plain rich. Then his hand had a fistful of her hair, and his strong tongue was opening up her mouth. Her hand fluttered helplessly, landing on the steering wheel, so that the horn blasted softly into the empty street.

They were against each other, pushing and rolling over into the backseat. Already their clothes were in a tangle, her blouse shoved up above her breasts, his belt buckle swinging—then pushed painfully into her belly—her fingers nearly shaking as she undid his shirt buttons. She had his lip between her teeth, and he was trying rather unsuccessfully to pull her slacks down, an effort she would have helped him with if she weren't pulling him to her with such fever.

The slacks were off. He tossed them into the front, and lay her down against the backseat. The fabric of his trousers was rough on the naked skin of her inner thighs, and he fumbled for a minute, and then he was inside her with a thrust that she felt all the way at the back of her throat. A hoarse "Oh, god" escaped her lips. She didn't want to hurry, but she couldn't help it. He had a hand on her ass and one on her neck, and she was holding on to his back for ballast as she rocked against him.

For some moments she moved, her hips locked with his. Then she thought to look up at him, and saw how intently he was staring at her. They gazed at each other, and his mouth came down over hers again, his tongue filling the space around hers, her fingers grasping for the back of his head, pushing through his hair. A quickening that shuddered up through her skull, sending her eyes rolling back into her head, as she shrieked a final "Oh, god."

She was still trembling when she felt his body convulse. Then he collapsed, his full weight sinking down on her. Their torsos were sealed together, so she felt how they both took a long breath at the same time. He lay his face against hers and kissed her cheek. "Christ," he mumbled. "You *are* a fox."

When he lifted off her, she saw the disarray of the car. She was completely naked, yards of exposed flesh, while his clothes had remained more or less intact; her slacks thrown across the front seat, her blouse hanging from the wheel. The balance of the car shifted while he searched for and lit two cigarettes, passing her one. She closed her eyes and dragged, trying to enjoy the protective weight of his hand on her thigh rather than indulging the dismay that she'd given it up so easily, that he would very shortly disappear.

"I'd have you any time." She could tell by the timbre of his voice that he was studying her nakedness.

A prolonged, smoky exhalation. "Is that why you came all this way, Mister Senator?"

"You are definitely California's biggest attraction." He chuckled. "But the real reason I'm here is to talk about a picture deal."

"A picture?" She let her lids lift slightly.

"Yes. Based upon a book I wrote." His hand had drifted to the skin below her belly button, where he began to draw shapes with his fingertips.

"*Profiles in Courage*, is that the one?" She exhaled and gave him a sly smile, as though she were a little afraid of what she was admitting to. "I read up on you, Senator."

"Yes." He grinned. "That's the one."

"I thought it all sounded kind of impressive. In Chicago I had no idea you were an author, too. I mean, a best-selling one. With a Pulitzer Prize."

"Yes, well." His lips twitched, and he took a quick drag. "Father saw to that."

"That's nice," she whispered.

He was gazing at her thighs now, his hand gliding gently over the seam between her legs. "Sure is."

Her eyes fell closed again, and she brought the cigarette back to her lips. She felt empty, and thought how nothing mattered anymore. "What does it feel like? To have a father," she murmured dreamily.

"A father?" In the previous moment his touch had been featherweight, but his fingers became heavy now. Several seconds passed, and then he said, "It feels like never being good enough."

"Oh!" Her eyes flashed open, but he had already opened the car door. As he climbed out he clutched at his lower back, and his shoulders seized as though he were in pain. But then his whole body appeared to lengthen, a show of force, and he took his cock in hand. She listened to him urinating and thought, *Oh, well.* Cigarette fixed between her teeth, she fished for her clothes, pulling on her slacks and shirt and using her fingers to brush her hair. In the rearview mirror she saw what a mess her makeup was, but there was nothing to do about that. She adjusted the lashes on her left eyelid, and sat down.

It was another half minute before he reurned, and by then she was composed. He opened the door for her, grin in place, and she put her bare feet on the concrete. He held the front passenger side door open, closing it once she was seated, and without discussion came around the hood and started up the engine. With one hand he steered the car down the hill, and with the other he drew her to him, so that she could rest her head on his shoulder.

They didn't see another car until Sunset, and even there the passing headlights seemed disinterested and unobtrusive. As they pulled in front of the hotel, she realized how late it was, and knew the good world was asleep.

"I'll have someone drop the car off tomorrow," he said.

"All right." She sat up and took her pocketbook out of the glove compartment. When she put it there some hours ago she'd been drunk, but she wasn't the least bit drunk now.

"I just figured it out," he said.

"Figured what out?"

"What it is about you. You," he said, vibrantly, "are a fox *and* a hound dog."

She smiled faintly, and turned away. Not waiting for him to come around again, she hopped onto the sidewalk and ran on her tippy-toes toward the grass, which was fragrant and pliant underfoot.

"I'll see you soon?" he called out.

She twisted her chin so that it grazed her shoulder when she met his eyes. "Maybe," she murmured.

As she hurried across the lawn, toward the hidden gate that would let her into her bungalow, she said a little prayer that he was lying. That tomorrow Alexei would declare her a failure and dismiss her—she'd never had a father anyway, and never would—that she could forget this brief period of hopefulness, the desperate urge acted on in the backseat. Otherwise, she might grow to want Jack, and then she really would be in trouble.

NINE

Beverly Hills Hotel, April 1959

"NO sleep for the wicked," she said to herself in the mirror with a brazen, lipstick smile.

Frowning theatrically: "Methought I heard a voice cry, 'Sleep no more! Macbeth does murder sleep,' the innocent sleep . . . ,'" but that was all she could remember.

Then, resting her elbows on the sink and squeezing her cheeks with either hand, she let her eyes get empty and her mouth go slack. "No sleep for Marilyn."

So she had room service bring her cigarettes and bourbon and a boy to make the fire. She didn't look at him the whole time he was in the room, and when he was gone she took off her white blouse and slacks and tossed them on the flames. She went into the bedroom and found her lucky bathrobe— she'd had it since before she was famous, and the terry cloth was so worn in places it was almost transparent. The fibers had a sweet, ripe smell—her smell—that no laundress would ever get out.

She lit the first of several cigarettes, and drank the first of several bourbons, and watched the flames grow higher awhile and shrink to embers. Her eyes burned from looking into the fire, but then her insides burned, too, which was the best she could do to keep herself from remembering what had happened with Kennedy, how badly she'd muffed this one, the thing she'd lost by it, which was the only thing she'd ever really wanted.

The embers were finally dying when it occurred to her how long the telephone had been ringing. But it was a ghostly ring—too far away to be the phone in her bungalow. She pressed her fingers to her temples, and wished the sound would go away. But it didn't, so she poured herself another bourbon and went outside.

The dawn was just beginning; it had no color yet. She blinked and tripped forward along the winding path toward the ringing. The telephone booth was obscured by bushes—in all her stays there, she had never seen it before, but she went ahead, opened the door, stepped inside.

"Hello?"

"N.J.," he said. "I've been trying to reach you."

"Yeah, well . . ." She brought the bourbon to her nose, just to smell it.

"We must be careful on the phone now; you never know who is listening."

"Oh?" she replied disinterestedly.

"How was your day, my dear? You sound tired."

"It's over, Alexei. You can snuff me out or ruin my career or whatever it is you've been planning. Kennedy's a dead end."

He took a breath. "Are you sure? What happened?"

"I fucked him. No pictures, no proof, no information. No state secrets, no honey trap. It's over. He'll move on to the next blonde tomorrow, and I'll be useless to you."

"Hardly, my dear. We were never after anything so pedestrian. And you forget: There's no such thing as a next blonde after you."

Ignoring this, she swallowed hard and said: "If you have a heart, you'll tell my dad how badly I wanted to meet him, and that I did my best, but it's hard, when nobody's ever really loved you, to have the confidence to do a thing right . . ." And there she stopped herself, for fear she might cry. She'd been putting it on a bit, but found herself moved by her own performance.

"You made love," Alexei went on, without acknowledging her outburst. "A little soon, perhaps, but not the end of the world. You must have talked first? Or afterward."

"Not really." She squeezed her eyes shut and took a gulp of whiskey.

"Just some nothing flirting at Mosey Moses's, and then we agreed to meet down the road. We didn't talk at all before—and then afterward, I think I offended him."

"How?"

"I asked what it felt like to have a father."

"And?"

"And he said it felt like never being good enough." Suddenly her eyes were open and her heart skidded.

On the other end of the wire, a low whistle. "He told you that?"

"Yeah, well . . . I think it just slipped out."

"Good work, my dear."

"Huh?"

"He's a Kennedy. They are extremely clannish; they never talk about family with strangers. But he did with you."

"You mean, that's good information? Information you can use?"

"Very good." He was speaking to her as gently as he had that first day at Schwab's.

"I'm done, then." Wonder filled her chest. "I can meet my father soon?"

A faint sound, as though Alexei were clucking his tongue. When he spoke again it was still gently, but this time in the way people are gentle when they break bad news. "Oh, no, my dear. You're the girl Jack Kennedy will talk to. This is only the beginning. But for now just try to get some sleep, all right?"

"But I'll meet him soon?"

"Kennedy?"

"My father."

"Soon enough. But in the meantime, proceed slowly, as you would with any man. When you are in New York next we will go over some precautions, some rules about how you and I should contact each other. As for Jack, the best thing you can do now is forget him. Spying is not unlike seduction, which you understand perfectly—if you move too quickly, you ruin the

76

mystique. Always hold the thing your mark wants a little out of reach—a man is never so naked as when the thing he wants is just out of reach—and always let him come to you. Anyway, Jack will be most useful to us if he wins the presidency, and we must be careful that your affair builds slowly, not peter out before he reaches highest office. For now we must play the long game and be patient. Can you be patient, my dear?"

What had she ever been but patient? She'd waited her whole life to meet her father, surely she could keep herself hard and cold a little longer. She was already hard and cold. She couldn't feel her hands, but watched them put the phone back on its hook. Beyond a row of bushes she heard a girl laughing, and then a man calling after her, "Oh, baby, are you gonna get it!" The sound of one body's splash as it broke the surface of the pool, and then a second one. Everywhere across the country, men were chasing women like that, and now she was one of them—a hunter.

II

1960

TEN

New York, May 1960

THE apartment was empty, and the herringbone parquet stretched out from beneath the points of her high-heeled shoes, unprotected by the clutter of real life. Through the window of her taxi she had seen the trees blossoming on Park Avenue, the women strolling in slimming trousers with no socks. She had smelled the air—the dirty sweet mingling of chlorophyll and car exhaust that was the first warm gust of summer in the city. But the apartment was empty—she heard how empty when she set her suitcase down by the front door, crossed to the kitchen, and found the note pinned to the icebox with a magnet: *Went out.*

Arthur had forgotten, or maybe just not bothered, to close the curtains to the daytime sun. The air inside was stuffy and hot, and she fanned herself with his note as she dropped ice cubes into a cut-crystal tumbler and poured bourbon over them. The apartment was not empty of bourbon—so perhaps he did love her a little still.

Her shoes pinched her toes, but she did not want to take them off. It seemed romantic to her, or anyway appropriate, to stand there in the kitchen, the light fading from the day but none of the electric kind turned on, the props that made her legs look so especially feminine squeezing the blood away from her manicured feet. It was her birthday in less than a month, and she doubted she would be celebrating with her husband. Already the lonesome birthday blues played softly in her thoughts. She would be thirty-four—another year gone by, and what had it done, except tire her?

There was no child, and no father, either. And while she still told herself that they would both be hers soon, these bedtime stories had taken on the tone of stale ritual. It had been more than a year since she met Jack Kennedy at Mosey Moses's party, and she had only heard from him a few times since, and Alexei's promise had begun to seem as illusory as the ones she made to herself. She'd had an affair with a costar, and though Arthur hadn't accused her of anything, she had not bothered to hide it from him, or anybody else, for that matter. The movie had been called *Let's Make Love*, and she and Yves had been good little actors and done like the title said, so who could be surprised? Perhaps Arthur truly didn't know, but this was a possibility she shied from. That he was no fool was the reason she'd married him. Meanwhile, she had won a Golden Globe—not the Oscar she deserved, though it nonetheless should have counted for something, some confirmation of her years of slaving—but the award and the ceremony and the press notices scarcely seemed like events in her own life. Had she been happy, clutching her statuette, breathing into the microphone like a grateful idiot the names of all the people who had hindered her? The bourbon was cool down her throat and harsh in her sinuses; for both of these, she gave thanks.

The day had begun in California, where she had briefly forgotten herself in the twist of hotel sheets and hazy morning sun filtering through blinds and the smell of a man clinging to her skin. Her troubles, and her obligations. The man himself had still been there, sitting in the armchair by the open front door of the bungalow, his dark brow in a pensive, Gallic knot. He had been smoking, thinking—no doubt, and also rather predictably—about his wife in France, where he would be landing sometime that night, and how to win her back. Marilyn had pushed herself up on an elbow, a loose, white-blonde curl in her eye and the sheet wrapped girlishly over her breasts.

It would have been easy to bring him back. She'd seen exactly how to play it—with what winks and baby tones she could win his attention, draw him into bed, keep the game going another few hands. But he had never been more than a distraction to her, and in that capacity he was no longer useful.

His mind was already ahead of their fling, and his guilt made him tedious. Anyway, she had mostly pursued the affair in order to distract Arthur, so that if he suspected one infidelity, he would be blind to the other, more consequential one—to the affair she intended to have with Jack, which he couldn't know about.

The phone rang just as she was refilling her glass. Ordinarily this would have been a welcome sound, the insistent trill of someone wanting her. But at that moment, with a fresh drink and the honeyed end of daylight making her loneliness seem almost gorgeous, she would rather have gone on like that forever, not knowing who was on the other line. It might be Arthur; perhaps he had secured a dinner date with someone important and wanted to show her off. Or maybe it was Yves—laid over at Idlewild and weepy with regret—calling for a final reassurance that he was only human and nobody could blame him. In fact, nobody *could* blame him. From the moment she'd seen Yves Montand's one-man show she'd known exactly how she was going to use him, and then had gone about doing it so expertly that everyone was left with the vague impression it was he who had used her. Or maybe the caller was Joe, or Norman, or Marlon, or who knows, maybe it was even Kennedy, and she'd have a reason to roll on after all.

Gripping her glass she went through the apartment, past its white walls and high, grand moldings. *A real intellectual's apartment,* she'd thought when she first saw it, and that was how their parties had been when they were first married, everybody smoking and talking, a pot of something on the stove so that guests could help themselves when they got hungry. Now Arthur had removed much of the furniture, taken it up to Connecticut on some spurious pretext. Something about how it would be good for her to redecorate the place in her own taste, a nice project for her. And why should she care? It was almost comforting to think how she'd never had a home, and that she never would.

The phone was still ringing when she sat down on the kitchen chair where

Arthur must have had his morning coffee. The paper lay beside it, folded neatly and less the theater section, and she picked up the front page. The phone stopped. The headline was about Kennedy—she was only a little surprised to find the name of the person that her mind had been so concerned with of late, there in the news. She skimmed the article, and learned that her mark had won the Democratic primary in West Virginia. So: He had been busy, and she was glad, for the first time in weeks, that she had kept busy, too, with the Frenchman on the Coast.

Suddenly she wanted to know who had been trying to reach her. But before she lifted the receiver, the phone rang again. This time she picked up right away.

"Hello?"

"It's me." The accent was disguised—he sounded jovial and blandly American. "Feel like a walk?"

Her mouth flexed, and before she could help it she was smiling. When had Alexei become so reassuring to her, the placid diction she hoped to hear on the line? Even masked it was familiar and happy-making. There were times, over the last year, when she thought maybe she was getting rather more out of the bargain than he was. Once she'd mused aloud if she should worry about winding up in prison or something, and he had assured her that he would never ask her to do anything dangerous, or even particularly illegal. All he wanted, he promised, was to understand the psyche of the man who might run the country—that was how peace was maintained in a new kind of war, he explained, so in a sense what she did for him would benefit the whole of mankind. She had only to pay attention as she would in any love affair, learn his peculiarities and preferences, and in return Alexei would watch over her, protect her, care for her, and introduce her to the man she had been seeking her whole life. Thus far she'd only had a minor fling like so many others, and here was Alexei, like clockwork, concerned about her welfare.

She was about to ask him if he'd been calling a moment ago, but then she remembered the lessons he'd given over the last year. Never underestimate what an effective tool silence can be was one of them, or what you may inadvertently reveal with even the most casual utterance.

"It's lovely out now," he went on, hopefully. "I'm down on the corner."

"I don't have much time."

"Just a walk."

"Okay." She took another sip of bourbon, in order to more effectively put the smile away, and hung up the phone.

In the shadowy back corners of bars, he'd lectured her on various aspects of the clandestine arts, but she'd needed no lessons in the power game of tardiness. She moved unhurriedly through the quiet apartment, kicking off her heels and unzipping her pencil skirt and dropping it on the floor. Lena, her maid, would pick them up later. In the bathroom, she peeled the false eyelashes from her eyelids and turned the faucet on. The water felt good against her skin, and she lingered there taking off the face that she had put on that morning to say good-bye to Yves. When she lifted her head out of the sink she saw in the mirror—it still surprised her, no matter how much time passed—what they had done. How they had pinched the nose and shaved the chin. She still had fine, girlish skin, and without makeup she saw clearly the remains of her old face, that beautiful child everyone had wanted to touch.

In the dressing room, she put on a loose-knit white sweater and black slacks, shuffled into her driving moccasins, and with her hair pulled back under the black headband she used to wash her face, she left the apartment. It no longer amazed her that people recognized her less, almost not at all, when she looked most like herself.

The sky was turning purple, but the air was warm. She moved up the sidewalk at an efficient stride that did not invite stares. She was as anonymous as the day she was born, and as she came to the corner—to the pay phone where she knew she would find him—the world for once took no notice. They did not need to speak. He saw her and waited, and she managed to keep her smile subtle and mysterious as she accepted his offered arm.

Without discussion they ambled toward the river. His trench coat was open, his blue dress shirt unbuttoned to the neck, and his tie put away. They might have been any couple, so pleased to be in each other's company at the end of day that words were unnecessary. The only sign of their true relationship came when they reached the height of the pedestrian bridge that spanned the FDR and he glanced back. It was a casual gesture, but afterward, as they descended to the promenade, she felt safe in the certainty that they had not been followed.

"Tell me how you've been," he asked, in his real voice. The accent, at once both clotted and lyrical, seemed of a piece with the gleaming lavender surface of the river spreading out toward Queens.

"All right."

"Really?" He nodded at a woman walking a standard poodle on a leash as she passed. When she was gone, he went on: "You seem tired."

"I look that bad?" A sad, soft laugh.

"No."

"I'm done with shooting, thank god. Glad to be away from Los Angeles. I'll have to go back soon—for *The Misfits*, this time."

"How is Arthur?"

She exhaled. "I don't know. We aren't like that with each other anymore."

"Do you want to leave him?"

"Sometimes." She wanted to leave him, but she didn't want to be divorced. "He pretends he's too good for pictures, but really he's jealous of what I can do and he can't. He knows I'm his best bet to get into pictures, and he wants me for his movie. That's all he wants me for now."

"But stay with him."

"What? I'm not some birdbrain twenty-two-year-old who'll take whatever faggot the publicity department assigns her, you know."

"Of course not, but if you stay with him, you'll seem less like the opportunist you used to play, and more like what you are—an artist, the wife of a great man. A woman whose mistakes, whose experience, have only burnished her beauty." He paused, as though to let this flattery hit the bloodstream, and then asked gently if she had ended it with Yves.

But she was still irritated, and spoke tersely. "I doubt I'll see him again."

"And how are things with—"

"You could learn more about Kennedy in the *New York Times* than you could from me," she interrupted and turned her face out toward the water. Alexei already knew everything that had happened between her and the senator since they'd crashed against each other in the backseat of her car up in the hills, way back before he even announced his candidacy. A few missed connections, a voice on the other line for a few minutes after midnight, a wordless encounter one night in the powder room at Romanoff's, from which she emerged without her panties. "He won the West Virginia primary, and they say that if he won there, he can win anywhere. Well, anyway, that being a Catholic won't be the obstacle they thought it'd be."

"You must stop reading the papers. The American press is full of lies, and anyway, it's better if Kennedy thinks you're frivolous."

"Oh." She let out an amused sigh. "Don't worry about that. I've got that routine down flat."

"Have you seen him?"

The question pained her, and she let it show in the twist of her face. Not because of the injury it did her ego, or anyway not entirely. As Alexei said, the great game was a long con, and so was seduction; she knew that she'd get close to Jack again, if only she could better concentrate her whole self on that goal. The pain was because of what it delayed for her. She wanted to rest her head on her father's shoulder, and tell him all the trouble he'd caused her. Eventually she said: "Not since before January. He called once, but we didn't talk long. He only said that he was thinking about me. Something like that, except less nice."

"Good. That's good. He's thinking about you."

"Oh, I don't know if that man can tell one skirt from another. He might've read the wrong number from his little black book, and thought he was talking to some other broad."

"I doubt that."

She shrugged.

"You've done a good job making yourself elusive. When he was less sure he would have been cautious with you—but after he has the confidence of the nomination, he'll view you as his reward."

"Maybe," she evaded. She enjoyed these talks, the careful coddling, the smooth manner in which Alexei discussed her pursuit of the senator. A firm, tender tone from a man always pleased her, especially when it came like this—paternally, without any undertone of a bedroom transaction. Not that she didn't evoke that possibility now and then, in her own ambiguous way, opening her eyes wide, tipping her chest forward slightly, so that it might have been an accident. Sometimes, she almost wondered if Alexei were queer.

"Maybe," she said again, and this time the word had nothing to do with what she might, or might not, gain from the senator, and everything to do with the crumminess of the present moment. The light draining from the day, Arthur out in the city and no longer in love with her, the cruel and pretentious script he was laboring over in order that she might be complicit in her own humiliation, the vast gulf between herself and the still-unnamed man who'd abandoned her a lifetime ago.

"I am sure of it."

They were crossing over the pedestrian bridge at Sixty-Third, she and Alexei, who seemed like her only friend, and she was struck by the desire for them both to have something better than this patient, strategic resignation. "Do you want to see her?" she asked.

A couple was coming toward them, the man in a suit and his wife in a red dress as though they were taking a little stroll before supper at La Côte

Basque or a night at the opera. Alexei flicked his gaze in their direction, and then back at her. "See who, N.J.?"

"Her," she whispered, but it didn't matter what she said, because the gauziness of her voice, the sudden rocking of her hips, was the answer. She gripped Alexei's arm and turned her face up at him and laughed with pure feminine delight. A happy sigh passed through her whole body, as though no one had ever been so satisfyingly alive as she was right then. "Good evening," she said and laughed sweetly to the passing couple.

They stared back at her, the woman's mouth agape, the man's gaze lingering somewhere below Marilyn's neck, as the movie star and her escort glided on.

"Did you see who that was?" the woman whispered, and Marilyn did not have to glance over her shoulder to know that her husband was still looking back, that he had just cheated with his eyes.

Alexei went on holding her arm and though the pressure of his fingertips barely changed, she sensed he was holding her tighter now. As they turned the corner, he put an envelope into her free hand.

"What's this?"

"It's your room key. The key to your room at the Carlyle. Kennedy arrived today, from West Virginia. He is speaking tonight, at the annual Bronx Democratic fund-raiser, which, according to the peculiar custom of you Americans, is being held here in Manhattan, at the sort of expensive address the disadvantaged people of the Bronx will never know. The fund-raiser is at the Waldorf, but he is staying at the Carlyle. Go, find a way to run into him. He maintains a suite there, though it's a well-kept secret. It's time to remind our Jack what he's been missing."

ELEVEN

New York, May 1960

NIGHTFALL did not lessen Walls's discomfort with Sutton Place. Several times, as he loitered across the street from the brick building where Marilyn Monroe lived, he saw a woman with a Pucci scarf over her hair walking a little dog and thought he'd been spotted by the mother of one of his childhood friends. The fact that few of those women were on speaking terms with his own mother would not, he knew, deter them from greeting him with two air kisses and a personal yet detached line of questioning about which firm he was now with, and whom he ought to marry. Children were immune to the social strategizing of these women, or otherwise were regarded as pawns too useful to be sacrificed, and Walls knew that he would still be a child in their eyes, no matter the ominous trench coat he wore, or the low angle of his hat.

When he had filed the travel paperwork, he had not considered that she might live like this, in a doorman building where people he had known in prep school were playing house with the Miss Porter's girls they'd married. New York did not go in for pastel pleasure palaces, and yet he had expected the place where she lived to be some gargantuan, ersatz structure of milky pink and gilt curlicues. The first time she had left the apartment, at dusk, he had almost missed her because she was dressed like any East Side housewife, in slacks and a sweater and proper undergarments. It was only the way she glanced around, as though someone might be after her, that signaled here was the object of his surveillance.

He had trailed her a few blocks to a pay phone where a man, dressed in a coat that might have been the same make as his own, greeted and wordlessly escorted her toward the low roar of the FDR, to a pedestrian walkway where Walls was obliged to ditch them so as not to become obvious. This he did most unwillingly, because he suspected the man owned the voice of the most mysterious character in Marilyn's wide and exotic telephone companionship. Just as Hoffman had jokingly predicted, listening in on her calls had brought Walls into a land of raunchy pillow talk that would have scandalized the housewives who dipped their heads in peroxide trying to look like her. The fights with her husband had more or less put Walls off sex, and he'd stopped listening when Miller was her interlocutor. But of all the men she teased and pleased with baby breath, there was only one who had no name.

Sometime over the last year he had ceased longing for a reassignment, and it was the presence of this nameless man in Marilyn's life that had led Walls to believe that what he had witnessed between John Kennedy and the movie star was more than his ticket back to Washington. That, almost without his noticing, he had finally become embroiled in a matter of true consequence. As far as Walls could tell, she hadn't seen Kennedy since that night more than a year ago, but his hunch was that the man without a name was trying to throw them together again, to some larger purpose. Walls had intercepted only three of their phone calls, in which the man without a name never identified himself, even while knowingly discussing her sundry romantic interests. Of these, there was only one for whom they never used a name recognizable to the casual reader of gossip columns but always referred to, cryptically, as Hal, an obvious alias. Once, when Marilyn sounded a little drunk, Walls thought he heard her replace the usual *Hal* with *Jack*, but she almost might have been saying it generally, a stand-in for all lovers.

The man used an obviously put-on accent that conjured in Walls's mind some wiseguy enamored with the movies—an anglophile from Red Hook. In their most recent conversation, Marilyn had mentioned that she was coming to New York, and that had been the lead upon which Walls had justified his own trip. His conjecture was that the man was using Marilyn to blackmail a presidential candidate, perhaps even force him out of the race just before the election. But maybe they were waiting, counting on him winning the White House, which would mean Walls's assignment was momentous beyond his wildest imaginings. Walls had yet to figure Marilyn's reasons for consorting with this fellow—despite the desperation he occasionally noted in her late-night ranting, she was still famous beyond his own conception of fame, and not, in his estimation, a woman who would be easily pushed around by a smooth-talking criminal. She and Arthur did, to his surprise, fight about their lack of money, but that seemed entirely too neat a motive.

"Want a vacation, huh?" Bertram Toll, the special agent in charge of the Los Angeles Bureau, had razzed him when he filed the travel paperwork, but he had nonetheless given Walls his approval, and had not pushed him to explain a theory that Walls had feared would sound outrageous without solid proof. It was a bitter irony that as his conviction of being on to something grew, so did his anxiety that the Marilyn assignment would come to seem superfluous to his superiors—there had been a moment, back in September, when he was sure they'd shut his operation down, but then Marilyn was photographed shaking Premier Khrushchev's hand, with a big smile on her face, and quoted as saying, "My husband, Arthur Miller, sends you his greetings."

When she returned to Sutton Place alone, Walls cursed himself for having not taken in more details of the man he referred to in his notes as "the Gent." He had been certain they would go up to her apartment together, but this seemed preposterous now, and he could recall curiously little of their meeting. Only that the Gent was tall and slim, that his shirt was blue, that he'd had a courtly way with Marilyn, which most men did anyhow, and that he knew how to look out for a tail. By then the doorman of Marilyn's building had taken notice of Walls, and he was obliged to walk around the corner and get lost awhile. He didn't think this would screw the mission; Marilyn never went anywhere in haste. He found a diner where the waitresses wore mint-green uniforms, ordered steak and eggs for dinner, and returned with a newspaper to pretend to read in the front seat of the rented car he had parked across the street from her building.

Walls chewed his nail, and reviewed what he knew about the Gent. He called Marilyn "N.J.," a reference to her birth name, so perhaps he knew something of her past, and was blackmailing her as well? This didn't quite square, for two reasons: 1) The relationship appeared too cordial to be built on that kind of strong-arming, and 2) Marilyn had weathered a public divorce and nudie photos with candor, so it strained Walls's imagination to conjure a scandal that was both printable in the mainstream press and that she would not willingly admit to.

Darkness fell, and he began to wonder if the paper wasn't a poorly chosen ruse. Then she emerged from her building transformed. The skirt she wore fastened at the narrowest part of her waist and encased the exuberant rump below; the white sweater she'd chosen this time clung greedily to her bosom; the shiny, black sunglasses put sunny California in mind; and the pale yellow of her hair chimed beautifully with the soft peach of her skin. She was unmistakably the woman who once talked, in CinemaScope, of how, during heat waves, she kept her underwear in the icebox. The only aspect of her appearance that surprised him was the girl with whom she walked arm in arm. The sight of her in the company of another female was inexplicably jarring.

Walls stepped to the curb and closed the car door. From the opposite side of the street, and a quarter of a block behind, he trailed the women as they headed north. Their arms were still entwined, and Marilyn seemed to be talking to the other girl in an easy, intimate way. She was also blonde, although her bangs made her seem more innocent, as did the way her ponytail bobbed at everything the movie star said. Was she a friend? Certainly not a relative—Marilyn's claim of orphanhood, while not literally true, nonetheless described her familial status with fair accuracy. And yet, for all the hours of phone calls Walls had listened in on, he could not figure where a pretty, young, fashionably dressed but wholesome-looking girl fit in the dramatis personae of Marilyn's life.

By Fifty-Seventh Street he had closed the gap between them, and then they turned abruptly at the corner and paused, waiting to cross. Afraid they might notice him, Walls busied himself at a nearby newsstand, pretending to study the cigarette selection. In his peripheral vision, he watched them cross toward him and then cross away, so they were again on the opposite side of the street, walking west this time. Though he didn't smoke, he thought it wise to complete the conceit, and purchased a pack of Marlboros before moving along parallel to the women with his hands in his pockets.

This street was wider, and the cars whizzing in both directions separated them. A huge red box of a truck came to an abrupt halt, blocking his view, and began to reverse to enter a garage. He stepped off the curb, watching for the two blondes to emerge. But only one did, and it wasn't Marilyn. The girl was smiling, as though a suave fellow had just complimented her ankles, and Walls began to follow her because he didn't know what else to do. Irritation burned in his chest, and he looked about wildly for Marilyn. But she wasn't behind him or ahead of him, and there was no shop along that stretch that she might plausibly have gone into.

She was simply gone.

Walls was startled out of his confusion by the rude wail of a horn from a car he hadn't noticed hurtling in his direction. He jumped to the sidewalk, so annoyed at losing her that he felt no relief at not being run down, and then, experiencing a premonition of uselessness, the coming weight of a long, pointless evening, made a sudden decision.

"Excuse me, miss?" As he touched the sharp point of her elbow he thought to put on the boyish, eager smile that he usually concealed.

The girl jumped a little. When she was facing him he saw that she had flushed so that her cheeks almost matched her plum lips. "Oh!" she exclaimed. "Do I know you?"

"No. I don't *think* so, it's only that—well, I guess you looked familiar to me, and I was wondering . . . Are you by any chance an actress or something?" He averted his eyes, as though embarrassment had gotten the better of his courage. "I'm sorry, this really is uncouth, I'm sure you get asked all the time. You're probably plenty sick of random men interrupting your day to tell you how pretty you are."

He kept his eyes averted another two beats before glancing up to see her exhale in sweet disbelief and the edges of her lips curl. For another moment she tried to keep away her smile, and then stopped trying. "No." She giggled and pressed the large, black bag she carried to her chest. "I suppose there are times when I daydream about . . . But you must have me confused with somebody else."

"Oh, well." He let his focus drift to the intersection and stepped off the curb. "I'm very sorry to have bothered you, then. Have a nice evening." He strode forward, advancing halfway across the avenue before he paused, put his hands on his hips, and took a deep breath of air—as though it had just occurred to him that it was a lovely evening in early summer, when anything might happen and risks ought to be taken—and turned around. The girl was still standing on the corner, shifting uncomfortably, unsure if she was supposed to wait for him to disappear before she, too, moved on. "Say!" he called out to her. "What are you doing?"

She looked away and looked back at him. "You mean, right now?"

"Yes." He smiled wide. "What are you doing right now?"

"I don't know, I guess."

"Would you let me take you for a drink?"

She glanced right and left, as though for someone to approve or disapprove. Then, when the light was about to change, she called "All right!" as she dashed toward him and, laughing, they ran together to the far side of the avenue.

The elation of running evaporated as they walked to one of the dives on

Fifty-Second Street. Awkwardness grew in its place, which he strategically allowed to remain even as they settled into the bar. He took her black bag from her, noted its heaviness, and hung it on the hidden hook. When he ordered a dirty martini, the girl, who had introduced herself as Anna, asked for the same, and he took sidelong notice of the way she tried to hide her squeamish reaction to the first taste. Their stilted small talk dried up, and she took two big sips of the drink—probably more than she'd intended—and a sheen came over her eyes as though she might cry.

"Do you have a cigarette?" she asked nervously.

His mouth was already forming a "no" when he remembered that, contrary to his custom, he did have a pack in his pocket. Wordlessly he undid the wrapping and lit a match.

The drag relaxed her, and her confidence seemed to improve now that she had an object to occupy her hands. "Aren't you going to have one?"

He was about to inform her that he didn't like cigarettes, but he realized, almost too late, that the person he was pretending to be did. After completing the ritual of lighting and exhaling with what he believed to be convincing smoothness, he began the line of questioning that was his reason for taking her out. "So what do you do with your days, Miss Anna?"

"I'm a makeup artist."

"You are?" He grinned like he'd never heard of anything so enchanting. "For who?"

"Oh, I work at the counter at Bloomingdale's, doing makeovers mostly."

"Is that all?"

"Well, I'm only just starting out," she said, a little defensively, and drained her martini.

Walls, realizing that he had moved unskillfully, signaled the bartender for two more, and asked her instead about her childhood and schooling and what kind of books she read, while the crowd grew around them. The notion that she was perhaps Marilyn's regular makeup artist excited him, and for a while he was certain that if he only got Anna drunk enough, she would spill confidences that he'd never glean listening in on Marilyn's phone. But as the girl's speech got faster, and then slower, and her eyes became unfocused, he began to worry that even if Marilyn *had* confided in her, she was too empty-headed to remember anything of significance.

It was around then that she bit her lip, leaned in close—the divulgence pose—so that he smelled her briny breath. "Remember how you asked if I was an actress?"

He nodded and reached for his glass.

"Well, I wonder if I didn't have some fairy dust on me, or maybe something a little Hollywood that you were sharp enough to pick up on, because—because you'll never *guess* who I met tonight."

His eyebrows drifted upward. "Who?"

She propped her elbow on the bar, brought her nose even closer to his. "Mar-i-lyn Mon-*roe*."

"*No.*"

"Yes!"

"What was she like?"

"Oh . . ." Anna shrugged as her eyes went dreamily to the ceiling. "She was divine. Divine. Just like you'd think, except better. I mean, even sweeter and funnier, and much *much* more beautiful. She didn't even need makeup, she really didn't, which is what I told her."

"Really? My, you're brave. How did she respond?"

"You won't believe it, but she was so humble, she seemed genuinely surprised that anybody would like her better au naturel. But then she told me I was too good at my job to try to put myself out of one like that." She laughed and lifted her second martini unsteadily. "Isn't that clever?"

Walls nodded.

"And after I was done, she said I did such a good job that she would keep my number and call me whenever she was in New York and needed her face done, that she felt I was her friend, and that she would even ask if her usual makeup man needed an assistant on her next picture. I mean, isn't that just *thrilling?* Can you imagine me on a movie set?"

"Yes," he replied with directness that made her blush. "Was she very grand?"

"Oh, no. I mean, her apartment was nice and everything, but it wasn't how you'd imagine a movie star living. Really, she was just like anybody, except of course much more beautiful . . ."

"Did she say where she was going tonight? Who she was meeting?"

"No, and I didn't ask. It seemed rude somehow. . . . I know it's funny, she's so much prettier and richer than I am, and she knows so many more interesting and powerful people, but I felt like I wanted to protect her. Why do you think that is?"

Walls shrugged. "Was there anything else?"

Anna shook her head in wordless amazement, as though the experience was so complete and almost sacred that she might tarnish it by saying any more. "Nope." She sighed happily, and lifted her empty glass to her lips.

Walls rested his hand on her upper thigh, meaning to invite her to talk more. But as she slowly raised her blurred gaze to meet his, he saw that her interest had shifted. That he'd loosened her up, and it would be cruel to go on hammering her for information that she probably didn't possess. Anyway, he'd only been using her to try to salvage his night's mission, which he should have admitted was a bust hours ago. Meanwhile Elvis Presley had started singing "Blue Moon" from the jukebox, and Walls felt tired of pretending, and realized that just for a little while he wanted the warmth of a human body near his. He took Anna's hand, and led her to the back.

Now that they were against each other, he could feel how hot she was, and he wondered if she wasn't used to drinking, if dancing with a strange man in a bar late at night like this was something she might not otherwise have done. If maybe she was acting freer than she really was. Her head was on his shoulder, and she was humming softly. He promised himself that he would offer to call her a taxi after the next song, or maybe the one after that, and then he closed his eyes and put his hands on her waist.

"Oh!" she gasped, and giggled when she realized that her voice was louder than she'd meant it to be. She pointed her small chin up so it almost met his. "I just remembered something. Another thing about Marilyn."

"Oh?"

"When we were coming down in the elevator she said: 'If we're going to be friends I ought to have a nickname for you,' so I said 'all right,' and she thought a minute and then said, 'I'm going to call you Anechka.'"

"Did she?" Walls whispered into Anna's hair.

"Yes! I mean, isn't that something, that Marilyn Monroe has a nickname for little old me?" She giggled again, and pressed her face against his chest happily, and meanwhile Elvis's voice swelled to a hungry, tropical wail. "And isn't that very original of her? Like in a Russian novel, like I was Anna Karenina or something. Anechka," she repeated in wonder, "Anechka."

TWELVE

New York, May 1960

SHE kept the motor running and idled slightly away from the other black town cars that swarmed the street in front of the Waldorf-Astoria. At first she'd found it disconcerting, this killing time out of sight, merely watching the action. In between her second and third marriages, when she'd finally come to believe that she could have her pick of men, she had been in the habit—if a date was late meeting her—of leaving with another man, a lesson no less effective for having led to fistfights. She had labored to make herself the one waited for, waited upon, but as the hours passed she discovered that she rather liked the anonymity of hanging back in darkness, becoming familiar with her own agitated breathing, anticipating any movement under the hotel's pink-and-gold awning. Then he was there, suddenly, a flash of tanned skin and white teeth, and she knew she could not have missed him. A shudder passed through her shoulders (as always when a man came into view she had been with as she'd been with Jack). Otherwise she stirred only slightly, to put the car in gear.

Five minutes of handshaking and drunken congratulation followed, in which she feared he might escape without her notice, but then he parted from the others and, moving to board his limousine, lifted his top hat in a showy gesture of adieu. When the limousine headed uptown, she did, too, lagging at a safe distance. A Cadillac separated them for a few blocks, but she was no longer afraid of losing him. He was going to the Carlyle (so Alexei had assured her), and as she maneuvered the car across lanes she removed the chauffeur's hat and then the oversized black jacket she had used to obscure her appearance and tossed them into the backseat.

The limousine stopped in front of the Carlyle's marquee on Seventy-Sixth, and she double-parked down the block, in a shadow between streetlamps. She did a final check in the rearview mirror—the black cat-eye sunglasses that brought more attention than they deflected, the fuzzy white sweater she'd put in the dryer so that it would stretch just so across her torso—and was relieved she had when she realized a kerchief still covered the high, blonde helmet of her hair. Her blondeness was crucial to the mission. She undid the piece of silk, gripped the canvas tote, and pressed open the car door.

The sidewalk was purple except where it was tinged orange by the streetlamps, and her heels scarcely made a sound as they carried her over its rough surface. Not until she reached the yellow corona of the Carlyle's entrance did she see how perfectly she had timed everything. The scene in front of her was a still life—the liveried bellboy gesturing to the revolving door, Kennedy with his head down about to move through it, the others in the black suits that were their expensive, nondescript uniform. One of the bellboys spotted her and took a step in her direction, but she averted her eyes, as though trying to go unnoticed, and went through the side door. Her agitation surged again, which made it easy to do as she had planned: One pointed toe met the other and she fell forward, stumbling and sprawling on the floor, her bag overturned, its contents spilled across the burgundy carpet. A Graham Greene novel went flying, a lace teddy hung out, an unmarked pill jar rolled, her sunglasses were crushed beneath her weight.

"Oh, damn me," she said in her little broken bird voice as she pushed herself up, so that she was sitting like an odalisque in the middle of the lobby. She whimpered and covered her face with her hand until the concierge came rushing toward her and, with the help of the bellboy, lifted her to her feet. "Thank you," she whispered, keeping her face hidden, as the bellboy hurried to collect the spilled contents of her bag.

"Are you hurt?" the concierge asked. His kindness was professional, muted. In her peripheral vision she could see how he glanced at the well-heeled men who had been coming in through the revolving door, and knew they were watching her.

"No," she whispered. "No!" she sobbed into her sleeve. "I'm fine, I'm fine. I've had a fight with my husband, that's all. I took a room to get away from him and then I went home to get some things and he was there, and we started fighting again, only worse this time, because . . ." She broke off, accepting the concierge's handkerchief and loudly blowing her nose. "Thanks, honey." She laughed bravely, and showed him her eyes, wet with emotion. "Everything'll be okay in the morning, won't it?"

"Yes," he answered, more feelingly this time, as though he'd been swept up, too, and wanted nothing but for everything to be okay for her in the morning.

"I know it will." She smiled, biting her lower lip. "In the meantime, there's champagne. Send up a bottle, will you? I'm in room seven-oh-five." Saying the number, her voice sank an octave and lost its breathiness. "Seven-oh-five, you got that? Thanks, honey." With a shy glance, the bellboy handed her the bag. She patted his cheek as she took it, and sashayed toward the open elevator. As the doors swept closed she kept her hand shielding her eyes. But the unnatural silence that filled the lobby told her Jack had seen her, and that unless the trail was cold she'd be hearing from him soon.

The trail was not cold.

So she told herself, anyway, while she was obliged to wait a little longer. The champagne arrived, and she had a first glass, and a second, and let the tension ebb in her shoulders, before the knock came. A tanned face filled the peephole, but it did not belong to Kennedy. This man had gotten a lot of sun, too, but his grin, especially when distorted by the glass, was more feral than flirtatious, and his hair was gone on top. She'd considered changing into the teddy, or into nothing, but she was glad now that she was still wearing street clothes.

"Can I help you?" she asked, keeping the door between them. The man was half leaning against a room service cart. A domed silver food warmer sat at its center, beside a single pink carnation in a small glass vase.

"Hello, sweetheart." His tone indicated that he wasn't one to explain himself. He was taller than Kennedy, with a barrel chest covered by the tuxedo that he had worn, she assumed, to the Waldorf-Astoria earlier that evening.

"My room service order came already," she said. "Forty-five minutes ago," she added, pointedly.

"This"—he pushed the cart past her and into the room—"is a new order."

"Oh?" Her eyes went innocently from the tray to him.

"Oh, *yeah*," he replied, drawing out the "yeah" lasciviously so that she heard a hint of his Southern accent. He winked at her—a slow, significant wink—and without taking his eyes off her, backed out of the room.

Alone again, she lifted the silver lid and found a folded black-and-white maid's uniform, with a note that read: *Put this on and get that great ass up to the penthouse.* Earlier she had wondered if the champagne wasn't a mistake, if she shouldn't have kept herself coldly sober for whatever encounter, but now she was glad to be slightly numbed as she shook out the uniform and held it in front of her body, checking in the mirror if it would fit.

Another hour had passed, and midnight had come and gone, by the time Marilyn stepped through the unlocked door to the penthouse and asked, in a low murmur that mixed hope and trepidation, disgust and desire, "Please don't tell me *this* is your fantasy?"

She'd worn stupider costumes, was how she tried to think about it while she buttoned the top with the white Peter Pan collar and affixed the doily-like headpiece to her hair. There had been an apron, too, but *that* she had deemed a step too far. She felt even more ridiculous on the threshold of a vast and well-appointed room, all mirror and gilt and marble and walnut, the kind where powerful men did their business.

Jack sat on a stuffed, whiskey-colored leather couch next to the man who had delivered the maid's uniform, whose gaze now settled on the place where the uniform's buttons were having trouble meeting their buttonholes. The apartment was high enough that the tall, leaded windows required no curtains for privacy. They contained only darkness and perhaps, if she used her imagination, a few dim stars. Beneath was a grand, gleaming dining room table cluttered with platters of half-eaten sandwiches, and an ice bucket cradling a bottle of champagne. The coffee table, too, was strewn with folded newspapers and legal pads and beer cans, and both men leaned toward it, shirtsleeves rolled, elbows on knees, regarding her. Kennedy's bow tie was undone, and hung loose around his collar.

"Hey, baby," he said after a while.

She turned one pale, downy cheek to him and held his gaze, showing him how the fire left her eyes and was eclipsed by sadness. "I've already been treated pretty bad today," she said, gesturing at her outfit. "Before you asked me to wear this."

"I'm sorry, baby," he said. "Gotta take precautions."

"You weren't so careful in California." Her tone meant: *I want to believe in you, but I know I shouldn't.*

"That was before I was a presidential candidate." His eyes had a hungry sheen, and his mouth was ticked up on one side as though this were all a little silly and he was sure that she would forget the insult soon and yield to him. "What if someone recognized you? A famous actress, coming up to Kennedy's suite—that'd make headlines for sure."

She stared back at him, summoned emotion. She let her lids close for a long moment and pressed her lips together, before reaching for the doorknob. Holding on to the knob, she moved as though to leave. "I'm not just any actress, you know," she said in a small, soft, brave voice.

For the first time since she had entered, Kennedy glanced away from her, to the balding man, and he jerked his head in the direction of the bedroom doors. "Bill, give us some privacy, will you?"

The man named Bill acknowledged this request by standing and taking a step in Marilyn's direction. He wore an expression that Marilyn knew well and had learned to disregard. His face said: *No matter how this man is about to treat you, we both know what you really are.* She returned his gaze—trying not to show her real anger—and watched him retreat through the vast living room to the back of the suite.

"I've had a hell of a day, too, baby." Jack wasn't grinning anymore—his hands were clasped in front of him, and in Bill's absence his eyes became serious and attentive. "Whatever happened to you today, I wish I could undo it, but see— that's the one thing I can't do. So why don't you come over here and try and forget it, and let's see if I can't make you feel better in the here and now?"

"That's a pretty pitch," she mumbled. It was, too. If she'd heard that one in her own life she probably would have gone along with it, and she wondered that Arthur, who was so clever with words, had never said anything to her as simple and persuasive as that. But this was not her own life, and she could not make the mistake of letting him in too quickly again. Then he wouldn't have to care, and he could put her away just as easily as before. He was a champion skirt-chaser—she had to remember that. Nothing he said was true, and nothing she said was true, either. All that mattered was that she stayed around long enough to get Alexei what he wanted.

In front of the Waldorf she had been agitated, but now she was calm. Her hands were dry as the desert, and she wasn't even dimly aware of her heart. Outwardly her demeanor was helpless, conflicted, but inside she was deathly cool.

"Come on, baby," he urged with a wink, "let's not waste time. I have to go to Washington in the morning, and I'd give just about anything if you'd come over here and sit on my face."

"Huh," she exhaled, the ghost of a sad, knowing smile briefly animating her mouth. "You see, Mr. Kennedy, the thing is . . . ," she began again, in a careful, halting, girlish manner, letting her hair fall forward, so that it hung over half her face. "Well, I read the papers, so I know you had a big week, and I expect you want a little fun. And I think you deserve some fun. I do. But I know you already have a wife, and the last thing you need is to listen to any of my complaining, so . . ."

"What?" His shoulders were gathered around his neck. He spoke briskly but didn't seem impatient. He seemed to want to get at her problem so that he could solve it. "What is it?"

"Well, it's just that—" she glanced down, as though this were some agony for her to admit. "It's just that I'm not your *maid*."

"Oh." He laughed. "Of course you're not. I'm sorry, that rigmarole was Bill's idea. He's here to protect me, is all. Take the damn thing off, if it bothers you so much."

"My own clothes are down in my room. I'll just go and—"

"Oh, come now, don't go and leave me lonesome. I've sent the others to bed so I could be with you—"

"The others?" Her eyes flickered to her left, where the suite receded into opulent shadow.

"Just Bill, who you've met now, and my brother Bobby. He goes to sleep early of his own accord, because he's a real Catholic, you see, and doesn't approve of my hedonism."

Although his hedonism had been on plentiful display already, she was surprised to hear him acknowledge it with words.

"There's a robe in the bathroom." He pointed to the door and—when she hesitated—added: "It'll cover you more than those clothes you were wearing when you walked in."

Each breath she took, as she hesitated some seconds more, worked its way dramatically through her chest, and when she finally let her eyes rise from the ground to meet his, she saw that he was grinning, and she grinned back.

"In this bathroom over here?" She was still smiling as she began to walk—slowly, for his benefit—across the Persian carpet. Watching her, his mouth fell slightly open and the focus of his eyes became fixed.

"Yes. That bathroom over there."

She traveled across the room with exquisite languor, but that was just for show—once she was out of his sight, she moved purposefully. The large mirror over the sink was illuminated by a row of lightbulbs, just like in a dressing room in the movies, and she was grateful for them as she checked the work the girl had done earlier that evening. The girl wasn't as good as her usual makeup man, but she'd been available on short notice. She'd blown Marilyn's hair out into high, golden waves and painted her mouth red and drawn wet black lines on her eyelids, and it had all held, so perhaps she wasn't quite the ninny Marilyn had originally taken her for. When Marilyn was satisfied with her appearance, she leveled her gaze and reminded herself that she was not to give in to any lousy little passions. That was what Yves was for, and the others like him, of which there were plenty, and she could go out searching for that tomorrow if she wanted.

"Hey, baby!"

"Yes?" she called back, rolling her eyes in the mirror.

"Come on, don't make a man wait like this."

Grabbing the robe, she strode back into the living room and found that Jack had rearranged himself, propping his head on the couch's armrest and stretching his legs across its cushions. "But honey, you've waited all year practically. Won't kill you to wait a few minutes longer, will it?"

"Might." He grinned at her. "I've been campaigning so much I've forgotten how to be alone, and anyway, if you think time has made it any easier to be without that ass, there's a thing or two I ought to explain to you."

"Poor Jack," she breathed.

"Hurry up and put that robe on."

"I'll just be a second."

"Don't go."

"What about them?" Playfully, she indicated the bedroom doors where the men who traveled with Kennedy rested, or listened, or perhaps spoke quietly to their wives over long distance. Did Jack get a charge, knowing they were there and might walk in at any moment, or was he merely accustomed to attendants?

"Never mind them."

"Okay." She drew her bottom lip under her top teeth. "Okay, but no peeking."

Obediently he brought his hands to cover his face above his mouth, which remained in an amused configuration as she undid one strained button and then another. She dropped the shirt and was bending forward to roll down her stockings when she noticed that his index and middle fingers had parted. He didn't hide his peeping—and she didn't pretend she didn't know—as she rolled down her stockings and turned to unzip the tight black skirt. Before shimmying out of it, she brought the oversized white cotton robe over her shoulders and glanced back at him.

"Naughty," she admonished.

"Me?" He laughed. "That's a bit of the pot calling the kettle black, isn't it?"

"I'm not black," she deadpanned, eyebrows innocently aloft.

"No," he admitted. "But you are what my people would call a very dirty girl," he went on, grinning at his put-on brogue.

Her lips made a small, surprised diamond. "Irish, huh?"

"My people were. Enough games, now. Bring that body over here, and grab that champagne, too, while you're at it."

She kicked the skirt off and, taking the champagne bottle by the neck, went tiptoeing over to the couch. He didn't make room for her, or move to touch her, and as she stood over him it occurred to her that he might be the one holding out. She swigged from the champagne bottle and handed it over. Watching her, he swigged, too, but remained still. They passed the bottle back and forth a few more times before he put it down on the floor and took her waist. With sure hands he arranged her so that she was on top of him, her thighs parted over his hips.

"So tell me," she whispered. "Tell me what happened to you today that wore you down so bad."

"Oh, I don't have any complaints, really. Just had to talk to a lot of bores over a bad banquet dinner is all, but I'm glad to be in New York. Do you know what a man has to do to win a West Virginia primary?"

"No." Her eyes widened. "What?"

"Well, it isn't cheap, I'll tell you that."

"No?" She smiled sweetly. "Does it cost more than it costs to get me for a picture?"

"Nobody in pictures would ever ask you to eat the slop I've been obliged to eat in the diners of West Virginia this week, and I think they'd cry if they saw a woman like you in person. But I will say this: There are some greedy sheriffs down there who would put your studio bosses to shame."

Her eyes sparkled. "How greedy?"

"Aw, never mind that, baby." His hands were just as firm at her waist, and he looked up at her with the same intensity as when he'd been trying to draw her away from the door. "I've talked politics plenty with the boys. Why don't you tell me what had you running out of the house wearing sunglasses so late at night?"

"Oh." She laughed and tossed her hair. "Who cares about that?"

"I care. Otherwise you wouldn't be on top of me right now." His mouth opened as he lifted a finger to trace the triangular opening of her robe. Her mouth opened, too, and her eyelids sank, as he reached under the robe and took hold of her ribs. Now she could feel him breathing, too, and the quickening where her panties grazed his tuxedo pants, and she was glad of that piece of lace between them. With a sudden push, his hand was underneath her bra, and breath escaped her lips.

"Not yet," she whispered hoarsely. She opened her eyes and looked at him. "Not yet, okay?"

"Not yet," he repeated, confidently, as though that had always been his intention. Was he saving face, pretending that he hadn't been trying to lay her quick and hustle her out? He seemed almost genuine, but then it didn't matter, so long as she held his attention. Meanwhile his hand traveled down her side, his fingertips gliding along her skin, before he took her by the waist again, this time under the robe, loosening the belt. His eyes shone with a quality she might have mistaken for wonder, if she wasn't vigilant to interpret every gesture as carnal. "Not yet. I want to look at you awhile, and anyway, we've got all night."

Morning spilled through high, leaded windows, and Marilyn draped her arm across her eyelids to protect them. She had just been asleep, so asleep that she was hazy on her current location, which was a surprise. She hadn't slept that deep in a long while. Yesterday—she was fairly certain—she'd woken up in Los Angeles, but today . . . Today a little drool had escaped the corner of her mouth, and her face was sealed to a pillow made of leather. Squinting, she lifted her head and arched a brow at the white cotton robe covering her naked body. She pressed the palms of her feet against the opposite armrest of the couch, and made a fist to welcome the day's first wave of dread.

There was no one on the couch with her.

"Good morning."

"Oh!" she exclaimed, sitting up and drawing the robe over her chest. The coffee table was still a mess of newspapers, beer cans, an empty champagne bottle, china plates dotted with sandwich crumbs, although the scene was now completed by her own black lace bra, draped across the wreckage, as though she had slept in the fanciest fraternity house ever. Beyond all that, facing away from her and holding a coffee cup, was the balding man who had delivered the maid's uniform. "Where's Jack?"

"Left, half an hour ago, for LaGuardia."

Shit, she mouthed.

"I had them bring your clothes up," he went on matter-of-factly, indicating the side table by the front door without turning. "There's coffee if you want it."

"I thought you were taking extra precautions, now that Senator Kennedy is a presidential candidate."

"The staff at the Carlyle"—Bill paused to slurp his coffee—"are very understanding of Senator Kennedy's demanding schedule, and incomparably discreet when it comes to his R and R."

Keeping an eye on him, to make sure he didn't see, she felt under her robe and discovered her panties were still in place. The last thing she remembered was being very drowsy and full of bubbles and resting her head against Kennedy's shoulder as he listed the names of his many siblings, and told her how they had driven around West Virginia, shaking hands at churches and diners and coal mines. In dreamland she'd had eight siblings, every one of them with Russian names that ended in –vich and –skaya. If she had her panties on, then perhaps she'd held out too much, and this time Kennedy had left disappointed and without any intention of seeing her again.

"I don't let just anybody see these," she considered saying, as she removed the robe to hook her bra, but was stalled by the fact that, in his current position, he couldn't actually see them. Anyway, it would be simpler to dress and leave. She had pulled on the white sweater and was smoothing the navy pencil skirt over her hips when Bill turned.

"Ready?" He placed his coffee cup on the polished walnut dining table and put his arms over his chest.

She bent to step into her tan pumps without acknowledging him, and paused a while longer to brush her hair out with her fingers before meeting his eye. He didn't flinch at her gaze, and she didn't flinch either, as she crossed the room with head held high. Amidst the abandoned sandwiches were several beer cans, and she took an unopened one, loudly cracked the lid, and swigged. Holding his gaze she swished the liquid over her teeth and tongue before spitting it into his coffee cup. "Ready," she announced with an angelic smile.

She was halfway to the front door when he said: "Not that way, little lady."

Swiveling in his direction, she showed him the face she gave bellboys when they were too starstruck to do their jobs properly. After a silence, she put a hand on her cocked hip. "Which way, then?"

"Allow me." He made a flourish that might have been sarcastic, or might have been chivalrous, and strode past her, grabbed her bag, and headed for the rear of the apartment, gesturing for her to follow. They moved down a long hall, off which were the rooms where Bill and Jack's brother had slept. At the end was a metal door that required some force on Bill's part to heave open, and then, all of a sudden, they were out of the plush part of the Carlyle and in a small, windowless room. Bill pressed a button on the wall, and her heart jumped when she heard a mechanical screech and the floor dropped. "Private elevator," he said with a grin.

"How nice for you."

"Necessary precautions, sweetheart."

"Sure." She kept her expression placid and dewy as they sank through the stories of the hotel, and when the elevator came to a noisy halt, on what must have been the first floor, she kept her relief to herself. Bill smiled and, from his jacket pocket, produced a pair of sunglasses just like the ones she'd broken the night before. They emerged into a large and busy kitchen, frenetic enough that nobody noticed as the big man in the fine suit advanced through the commotion with one arm sheltering the blonde behind sunglasses. They made their way to a dimly lit hall, down a long tunnel, up a narrow staircase, and through another door.

"Good morning, Louis!" Bill called as he ushered her onward. This room was dimly lit, too, but in a way she liked. The man Bill had addressed was pushing a mop across worn floorboards, and he took a while to glance up. He was an old black man with a stooped back, and he exhibited no surprise at this intrusion. The place smelled like spilled beer and rotting fruit, and by the time she saw the letters painted on the transom over the front door she realized that it was the Joy Tavern, where she used to like a beer by herself after analysis. Louis did not reply, but she was too happy to be out on the sidewalk, where people strolled in the cool morning, to worry about that.

A taxi was coming down the avenue, and she stepped off the curb with her arm raised. When the car swerved in her direction, she took her bag from Bill.

"The California primary's in less than a month." Now unburdened, he paused to light a cigarette and exhale. "Can the senator count on your vote?"

"Why not," she murmured, gazing uptown.

"With that and the Democratic National Convention being in Los Angeles this year, he'll be spending a lot of time out in Hollywood." Bill took another drag of his cigarette and removed a card from his breast pocket, which he tucked into her tote bag. "If you leave a message at that number, he'll get back to you soon as he can. That's how you reach him. And he wanted me to tell you thanks."

She glanced at the spot where the card had disappeared into her bag and up at him blankly.

Then, with affected solicitousness, he said: "Miss Monroe, it's been a real honor to meet you," and opened the taxi door for her. While she made herself comfortable in the backseat, he leaned in the driver's window and handed him a bill. "Take the lady wherever she wants."

She was glad of this, not because she cared whether he paid for her ride, but because it meant he missed the smile that darted across her face.

"Okay, mister," the driver replied disinterestedly. As the taxi pulled away she kept her head down and her hand protecting her face the way she did when the press was in a harassing mood. *I'm in*, she thought, as the car hurtled down the empty avenue and her smile flickered and grew, *I'm in*.

THIRTEEN

Reno, July 1960

THE air coming off the high desert was over a hundred degrees, the kind of heat that melts the borders of a girl's body. The girdle beneath her tight, low-backed, black wool dress was already damp with sweat, so she kept still under the shade of a parasol, held by a local boy, while she waited to do the scene for maybe the twentieth time. She didn't focus her eyes on anything in particular, and held the little kernel she had of Roslyn, the character she was playing, in her mind. What Roslyn would feel going to the courthouse to get her Nevada divorce.

Around her people hustled to get cameras in place, dragging thick black cords across the sidewalks. It was the second day of shooting, and already the proceedings had taken on a fractious quality. Huston was shouting at somebody, but she tried not to make out the words. Arthur was also nearby, no doubt waiting with proprietary intensity for her to muff his lines. At the top of the steps stood the man playing her husband Raymond, wearing a slick suit, watching her as though they were playing chess and it was her move. He had been at the Actors Studio when she was first working with Lee, so she was familiar with his disdain. They'd all regarded her with disdain—those handsome, pretentious boys in love with theater, resentful of fame's intrusion in their erudite clubhouse, and yet unable to avert their gaze.

So she didn't look at him, and she put his real name out of mind. He had been gone, anyway, by the time she humbled herself enough that the other students forgot her special aura and realized she, too, just wanted to learn. And she did learn. The things she had learned with Lee she still used and would use every day in Reno. For instance, the way she was going to play the dance scene—the one in which she danced, drunk, alone under a tree. To get herself there she'd mainline a memory of Amagansett, the atmospherics of a night when she and Arthur had invited some fisherman over and she'd cooked spaghetti and they'd played gin rummy and drank bourbon until she'd swayed on the rag rug of the small shingled house they'd rented for the summer. The whiskey burning her tongue, the moldy smell off the cards, the salt wind. She had been happy and sad and luminous with mystery, and she knew she'd made them happy by dancing.

But today, at the courthouse, she didn't have a memory to go by. Instead she had a premonition of some future morning when it would be one too many silent breakfasts, and the sensation of orange juice going down her throat wrong as she realized that her marriage to Arthur was really over. That the house had been sacked before it burned down, and there was nothing to go back for. She was so fixated on the bitter orange juice that she didn't know when they said "action," only sensed when Thelma as Isabelle was ready beside her, and they walked up the steps toward Raymond.

He blocked her way at the top of the steps, cajoling her, as she tried to pass. He spoke words, and she spoke words back.

"You can't have me now, so you want me, that's all," Roslyn said.

Huston must have yelled "cut," but she didn't hear. She only knew they were done because the actor playing Raymond turned his back on her. The spell was broken, and her shoulders sank, and she looked around for an explanation.

"What happened?" she asked Thelma, wearing her costume of housedress and sling.

"They weren't picking you up, honey," she replied wearily and took a step in the direction of their first position marks. "Couldn't hear you. We're going to have to do it again."

But the sun was too bright in Marilyn's eyes, and the emptiness of her life with Arthur too riotous in her rib cage. She followed Thelma in the general direction of the boy who held the parasol, but when she reached him she kept on walking.

"Why is it that sexy women are never on time?"

There were perhaps a thousand answers to this question, and Marilyn—reclined next to a small portable fan aimed at her swampy décolletage—would have liked nothing better than to talk it over with the cowboy leaning against the door of her trailer. *Because everyone wants a piece of her, and how can a girl who's been scattered to the four corners be mindful of a wristwatch?* was the classic explanation. *Because they may be inclined to prove their intelligence by marrying neurotic playwrights who bang on their fucking Smith-Corona all night long, and how's she supposed to get a decent night's rest under conditions like that?* went another. There was also the matter of the juggled lovers, the constant debriefing by Alexei, not to mention the decade of lost sleep. But Clark, not yet wearing his Gay Langland costume of blue jeans and rancher hat, but with the movie cowboy flint already in his eye, was grinning at her with such canny sympathy that she didn't want to risk a bitchy tone. "They can't be ready for me again yet?"

"They say you're hiding out."

"They hate me, huh?" she murmured, removing the damp washcloth from her forehead.

"Nah, just Huston." The two slim arrows of his moustache twitched in amusement. "And don't worry, he's taking it out on that fancy-talking husband of yours."

"Oh, damn me." Since her arrival in Reno, Arthur had been putting on grand displays of doting care. The traveling, and the hurly-burly of life lately, had not been kind—her abdomen was swollen and tetchy with indigestion, and her head split from lack of sleep and too many drinks. But she couldn't lose the good will of the crew by letting him cast her in the role of his unreliable, self-important wife. Too much depended on *The Misfits* being filmed quickly and without the usual incident. That way, she could give herself over to getting Alexei what he wanted. Her marriage was almost nothing now; her loneliness was as searing as it had ever been. She was almost too tired to go on, and needed very badly to put her head against her father's chest and hear that she belonged to someone after all. She scooted forward on the narrow daybed, and moved to fasten her costume—the tight-fitting black wool without much back—which she had half taken off during her break.

"Let me help you with that, kid."

She stood and turned so that he could zip up her dress. They had talked often since the day she drove out to Encino to meet him, and were now close in the loose manner of two tough souls who don't expect very much from people. He had never made a pass, and she liked him for it—liked that she could speak honestly of the men who came and went in her life, liked that he was always ready with some frank, salty, fatherly advice. And yet, when the long, lean body of Clark Gable was close enough behind her that she could smell his cigarettes and mouthwash, and her dress was hanging open, there was a little charge, wasn't there? He had to tug at the zipper to close it over her hips, and she felt the tremor in his hands.

They stepped down from her trailer into the heat. Behind them were the mountains, and in the bright, thin atmosphere she could almost see every rupture and rivulet of the Sierras. The Mapes Hotel, where they were staying, was tall enough to be seen for miles around, but it would not have registered on the skyline of a real city. Huston was sitting under a tent with Arthur, deep in discussion, and assorted crew members glanced up at her resentfully.

Things had gone badly from the moment she landed. This had been on a later flight than the one the studio booked, for reasons she could explain to no one, and she hadn't realized that a welcoming committee was sweltering on the tarmac while she desperately tried to wash out a stain on her skirt, and to dry the resulting dampness with a hair dryer. Jack had been the author of the stain, and she hadn't noticed it at first because they had been in a hurry. When Arthur had gone early to Nevada, checking into the Mapes by himself for a few solitary days of writing before shooting began, she had left Jack a message that she was alone in her Beverly Hills Hotel bungalow. But he must have been tied up in the business of the campaign until the day of her own departure, and had not appeared until right after the concierge called to say that the limousine had arrived to take her to the airport.

"I'm just leaving," she'd told Jack with stage indignation, but he had grabbed her by the wrist and pushed her inside, against the wall, pulling up her skirt and whispering in her ear how he couldn't stop thinking about her, that she'd made him crazy. All the usual lines. Afterward they had agreed to meet again soon, and gone separate ways along the garden walkways that twisted around Bungalow 21, and she hadn't considered a stain until she was descending through the dust clouds. Then she disembarked from the little plane, and saw Arthur standing next to the first lady of Nevada, who wore a dour expression and a pillbox hat and carried a cone of white roses.

Dourness had been the refrain of the past three days. She had seen it repeated in any number of faces. Now, shielding her complexion from the glare of the sun with her fingers, she tried not to recoil at the thought of doing the scene again, of being Roslyn, a character who embodied all of Arthur's false notions about her, walking up the courthouse steps and spouting a lot of self-incriminating gibberish that would create the impression of a duplicitous woman with a child's mind. She watched Huston, perched on his high canvas chair and deep in discussion with Arthur. The director's oversized shoulders hunched, a predator waiting for movement in the bush, the cigar smoke wafting overhead, and she knew that when she went back in he would make her do the scene over and over again until her dress was soaked through with sweat, just so she'd know who was boss.

Clark saw her staring, and draped his arm around her shoulders. "Play hooky with me, kid," he said. "You know that speech you been given is too long, and until Mr. Miller writes it over so it sounds the least bit natural, there's no point in wasting your time or any more of Huston's film."

"Where would we go?"

"How's your luck these days?"

She rolled her eyes, pushed her shoulder into his rib.

"Well, I bet you make men feel lucky even when you don't."

"I guess."

As they walked away from the movie encampment and into town, the script girl came running after. "They're almost ready to shoot again," she called.

"Hello, sweetheart." Clark kept his arm around Marilyn's shoulder and only half turned to look at the girl. "Remind me your name?"

"Angie," she replied. Was she blushing, or was it just the desert heat?

"Angie, sweetheart, you tell the men in charge that once they've figured out how they want their scene Miss Monroe will be ready for them. They'll find her down at the casino. Got that?"

The casino was dark inside and quiet at that hour except for the clank and whir of the slot machines. They chose the darkest corner of the bar, and Clark ordered them double bourbons, ice on the side. He took two quick sips and settled back into his chair, allowing the alcohol to take effect. When he raised his glass a third time, she saw that the tremor was gone. "Script's a mess. I thought your husband had been working on this thing for years?"

"Oh, well. You know writers. Sometimes more time is just more rope."

He was squinting into the casino's gloom, whether because he was anticipating something more from the drink or because a card table had caught his eye, she wasn't sure. "Damn, I'd like to get out of here, go out into the desert, ride some horses."

"You're going to get your wish. I mean, if we ever make it past this scene."

"Come now, you know what I mean. Not with the whole goddamn cavalry, and not in our imaginations, either." He spread his lips back over his teeth, but it wasn't exactly a smile. "Kay's pregnant."

"Oh? She looks well." Marilyn had only seen her briefly, walking to the ice machine last night in curlers, and both women had pretended not to notice the other. If anything, she'd have said that Clark's wife looked thinner than before, and jealousy burned in her chest, although she wasn't sure if it was for his wife or the child they were going to have. "Congratulations, is what I mean."

"Thanks. Drink up, kid, you're looking pale."

"Oh." She laughed and raised her glass in his direction. "That's on purpose, daddy. Do you know how long I sit in that makeup chair to look this white?"

"Even so."

"Are you excited? To be a father, I mean."

"I'm old, honey," he said, and while he spoke in the tone of plain truths, his frame deflated unexpectedly, as though the realization had punctured him. "But Kay's happy, and I suppose she'll worry less about what I do when I'm away from her. I love that woman, but she wears me down with her questions. I am a bastard, but she knew what I was when she married me."

Marilyn rested her chin on the heel of her palm and gazed at her whiskey as she slowly spun the glass. She'd fallen back into bed with Yves over the last few months, while shooting retakes of the last picture. She'd endured maudlin declarations of love and a lot of tiresome regrets, but that had seemed less trouble than ending the affair. Anyway, it was easier to play Jack the way she wanted when there was another party interested, desirous of her charms, and Yves had served his tactical purpose, too—there had been a few times, over the past months, when she was out late with Jack, and Arthur, assuming he knew what she was up to, had looked the other way. Anyway, when *The Misfits* wrapped, and Arthur had what he wanted from her, she suspected that he would be less mindful of her infidelities, and she would no longer need a decoy.

"I'm sorry, kid. That's no way for me to talk. Sometimes I forget that you're just a girl."

Her brows, drawn in darker than usual for the cameras, lifted. She considered sharing with him the complicated shuffling of lovers and husbands upon which she had just been meditating, but instead said, "I wish that were true."

The bartender was approaching them again, carrying a tray with a telephone on it. He had an unsmiling face with low-hanging jowls, and he didn't look up when he put the phone on the bar in front of them. "Are you Marilyn Monroe?" he asked.

His lack of affect amused her—the name really might have signified nothing to him—and she tried to suppress a smile. Her eyes got big and rolled to Clark and back to the bartender. "That's me, I guess," she said finally.

"Call for you. From the Los Angeles Biltmore."

"Thanks."

"I'll give you a little air, kid, but don't talk long." He patted her shoulder as he rose from the cushioned bar stool. "This afternoon belongs to me."

When she was alone, she picked up the receiver and put her bare back against the puckered maroon upholstery of the wall. "Yes?"

"Hey, baby."

"How'd you find me?"

"How should I know? I have a girl for that. I told her there couldn't be that many places in Reno classy enough to host you."

"Is she pretty? Your girl."

"I don't know."

"How is California without me?"

"Lousy."

His directness surprised her, pleased her, especially after the morning's humiliations, and she briefly indulged the illusion that this was like any affair, and she and Jack were simply two people who had more fun when they were alone together, in secret. "They must be keeping you busy."

"Yes, horrifically so. Listen, I'm sorry about last time—that was lewd of me, I know, I just kept trying to get to you and couldn't, and I knew if I didn't see you before you left I'd be agitated the whole convention."

"How is the convention?"

"Terrible. Old lady Roosevelt is backing Stevenson, so she gave a little talk where she said my being a Catholic would be a problem in November, and that I won't win the Negro vote. As if the Negroes want Stevenson, that damned vegetarian. Meanwhile, Johnson has decided to raise a stink even though he knows I have the delegates and he doesn't, giving all kind of hammy speeches, saying that if I get the nomination it will be the fall of Rome. He just loves saying *Rome* and *Kennedy* in the same sentence, that animal. Everybody knows I'm going to get the nomination, but they want to rap my knuckles and remind me that I'm junior, and I haven't put in as many years of drudgery as they have, and meanwhile the Russians have shot down another of our recon planes, over the Arctic this time, and even though Ike is the one currently in the captain's chair this somehow makes everyone nervous I haven't lost my hair yet...."

"But you'll never lose your hair."

This seemed to make him happy, and he laughed a loud, flat laugh. "Can't you come back? I need you."

"I'm making a movie."

"Sounds like you're gambling and drinking to me."

"Well—"

"Just think about it, all right?"

"All right, but—"

"There will be a party, and I'll introduce you to lots of interesting people."

"You will?" The only witness to their affair, besides Alexei, was the man named Bill, and she was surprised that he would risk being with her publicly at a moment when so much attention was focused on him; but then he was probably just saying whatever he thought would make her do what he wanted.

"Hell yes. I want to show off my new baby. Just get on the next plane, will you?"

"Jack, I can't—"

"Tomorrow then," he interrupted, suddenly formal and cold. Wherever he was, he was no longer alone. "Thank you," he said, and hung up.

Carefully she returned the receiver to its cradle. She stared at the shiny black handle a few seconds, as though it might tell her what to do. What would Alexei have her do? He'd told her to play her hand cautiously—for now, he said, the important thing was making sure the affair continued, keeping Jack comfortable in her presence, and observing whatever she could of his character and intentions along the way. Later her assignment could become more specific, he had implied, as though referencing a bill that might never come due. But she was another year older and less girlish every day, and she could no longer convince herself that she had infinite time, even when she was drunk. If she finished the movie quickly and painlessly she would be much freer to spy on Jack. However, she had fixed upon the notion that she might glean information of special importance if she went now, when the convention was on and candidate Kennedy was feeling reckless.

There were only three other people at the bar—a couple who had been pressed against each other since she arrived, and a man drinking by himself, who glanced over at her about the average amount. She could see Clark, beyond them, standing at the craps table. The glass of whiskey was in his other hand, but his grip had become indifferent. His attention was on the dice, and his brow flexed in concentration. The muscles of his face were strong and taut, and they were lit from behind by the ghost of experience. He looked very much like a father, the kind who is slightly beyond the law, especially when it is necessary to protect his family.

Just then he glanced toward the bar, and smiled when he saw how Marilyn had been watching him. With the hand that held the whiskey, he gestured for her to join him. The thrum of slot machines got quiet as she floated through the civilian crowd of afternoon drinkers and hopeless dreamers and risk junkies, to the craps table, where Clark welcomed her by placing a firm palm on her shoulder blade.

"Whoever he is, he'd better treat you nice." Clark's hand slipped to the small of her back, and he leaned in close, so that his whiskey breath warmed her ear. "If he doesn't, you let me know, all right? And I'll sort him out," he told her in a low, gravelly voice, before kissing her softly, not quite on the mouth but not fully on the cheek, either. She closed her eyes to any longing the kiss—or the sentiment—stirred.

"You ever thrown dice before?" he asked. Like that, the sweet haze of intimacy had evaporated, and for a moment she thought she might cry. She wanted to go back, have his protection again, the way his daughter, if Kay carried a girl, would have his protection.

"No," she replied.

"Well, we're gonna see if you're as lucky as you look."

"Okay."

The dealer acknowledged her with a faint bow from across an illuminated stretch of green as Clark took her hand and brought her into the table. The dice were red, oversized like stage props, and as she looked at them she made a private promise that if they were lucky for her, then she wouldn't need to go to Los Angeles, she would stay here, and everything would work out without her chasing around after Jack. Then she reversed herself, and decided that if she was lucky, that was a sign she should follow the lead immediately. But she shouldn't have brought the dice into the matter, because she already knew what she was going to do. That brush of Clark's lips had sealed it—she would go, as soon as possible, to the place where Jack was, to do Alexei's bidding as best she was able.

FOURTEEN

"WHERE is everybody, Charlie?" Marilyn chewed her lower lip and leaned against the small corner bar at the Polo Lounge and tried not to seem like a woman being stood up, despite the fact that she'd been drinking alone for some hours already. She was wearing a simple candy-pink dress with a fitted waist, thin straps, and a U-shaped back that she'd had her dressmaker lower five inches. The bartender—a lean kid with a Latin look who'd been wiping his rag over the bar a few feet from where she sat—came in close. "I mean, it's kinda quiet tonight, isn't it?"

"Yeah." He folded his arms against his side of the bar and gazed at her. "Guess they're all downtown, or watching on the television."

"Think they've made an announcement yet?"

"There's a radio in the kitchen," he offered. And then, more enthusiastically: "I'll go ask if they've heard anything!"

Before she had the chance to tell him she'd appreciate it, he dashed off to procure her information, and she felt a little sorry for him when she saw that his efforts were to be in vain. The concierge appeared just afterward, tucking his graceful hands behind his back as he approached to tell her—so quietly that she might not have understood him if she didn't already know what the message would be—that a man was waiting for her.

"It's Kennedy!" the bartender exclaimed, as he burst through the small door that led to the kitchen. "Kennedy won the nomination!"

"Thanks, Charlie." She smiled and dangled her fingertips as she left.

Outside, the heat of the day had mellowed, and darkness descended over the protective flora that surrounded the hotel. The concierge indicated a silver Mercedes convertible with the top up, idling close to the high shrubbery.

"You will call us if you need a ride home, won't you, Miss Monroe?"

"Yes, thank you, Sal."

The air was perfumed with night-blooming jasmine, and she inhaled and set her hips rocking as she proceeded to the snubbed-nose sports car. She climbed into the passenger seat without glancing at the driver, and from the corner of her eye she did briefly mistake him for Kennedy. When she realized he wasn't, she let the dopey smile slide off her face. "Jack told me he'd pick me up," she said.

The driver's only acknowledgment was a bob in his throat, and he turned his eyes away and put the car in gear. Anyone could see they were related—it was as though Jack's face had been squished between the pages of a book, and come out thinner and slightly deformed. He was smaller, too, and less tawny, but he was also handsomer—the lines of his features were smooth and strong, like a statue, and his eyes were a clear, moral blue. His skin was much younger, except for his forehead, which was prematurely lined. When they took off down the slope toward Sunset, his foot was so heavy on the accelerator that her body got knocked back against the seat.

"You must be Bobby," she said, once it became obvious that he wasn't going to be the first to speak.

"I'm Robert."

"Uh-huh. How old are you? I mean, you're just a baby, it's kinda hard to imagine you're old enough to be his brother."

"I'm thirty-four."

She gasped happily. "How about that, we're the same age. You were born in '26?"

"'I was born in '25."

"Oh."

His gaze was focused on the road, rather fiercely, and he did not seem to think the fact that they were almost the same age was remotely interesting. She didn't either, and afterward gave up trying to make him like her, and instead watched the palazzos of Beverly Hills fall away as they sped west. They drove silently onward, and she wondered where they were going, and if he needed directions, and decided it was too much trouble to offer.

After he'd turned onto the Pacific Coast Highway, he said, "I didn't want to be the one to pick you up, either."

"Then why did you?"

He shrugged. "Jack said you were important, and I'm his campaign manager."

They didn't speak again. Having brought the car to an abrupt halt at a row of beach houses that fronted the highway, he stepped out and tossed the keys to one of the men—they were dressed like the help, but they were also broad enough to be muscle—and strode through the front gate. Marilyn waited in the passenger seat until the man who had caught the keys came over and opened the door for her.

"He's a real charmer," she said.

The man replied with a neutral "Yes, ma'am."

The sounds of celebration were loud enough to reach her on the road, and she was relieved to think that it was a big party. Behind her were the palisades, crowned with a row of gangling palms, and though the houses obscured the ocean, she could already smell its salt.

The living room was crowded, but she saw Jack right away. His magnetism was destabilizing; the whole room bent toward him. There were plenty of movie people she recognized from around town, but there was another element, too—serious, fast-talking men in suits that were slightly too large, and women who dressed primly in red or white or blue and whose small, bright diamonds were only occasionally visible. The gathering possessed a special vitality, as though those present had been party to a momentous event, and knew themselves to be, for a short, blessed while, at the center of everything.

She watched Bobby make his way through the rings of friends and sycophants to whisper in his brother's ear. Neither Kennedy suffered bad tailoring—both wore dark pants and jackets that were fitted to the slim family build. They looked good next to each other, with those faces that had been made from the same stuff, and when Jack lifted his gaze and saw her leaning against the wall on the far side of the room, the smile she wore was genuine.

"Marilyn, I didn't know you were coming." She glanced up at the sound of a lightly aristocratic voice, and recognized the ingratiating smile of Peter Lawford. A long time ago, before she was with Joe, he'd had his agent call her for a date, but she had thought him too pretty, and later she heard he'd married rich. A girl called Patricia Kennedy. Marilyn hadn't known much in those days, and had promptly forgotten all about it. "You look marvelous," he told her, kissing her on the cheek and showing her his hopelessly British teeth. Up close, there was a quality in his heavy brows and drooping mouth that wanted too much to be liked.

"Thank you. It's pretty exciting, isn't it? I guess you're here to celebrate with your brother-in-law."

"That, and this is my house."

"Is it?" She tried not to seem impressed, or to wonder at herself for never being smart enough to marry into money. Real money, not the kind you earn yourself.

"Will you have a drink?"

"Yes."

Peter forged a path through the thicket of bodies, holding on to Marilyn's wrist in such a way that her bracelets were pressed uncomfortably against her skin. At the bar, he ordered daiquiris for both of them. "That's what the candidate is drinking," he said as he raised his glass to eye level.

The drink didn't square quite with her idea of Jack, but when she tasted the first sip of sugary, limey rum she understood. The room was full of people wearing Kennedy boaters at rakish angles, their good-looking faces aglow with inclusion. They had left downtown, the dreary Biltmore, and the homely conventioneers, and found themselves in California, which reflected some inner notion of themselves. "It's wonderful, isn't it?"

"Yes," Peter said.

"I mean for all of us. He looks like us, doesn't he?"

"You mean, he's a star? That's what the old man always says," Peter replied genially as he studied the party over the rim of his glass. "Of course, I'm supposed to stop saying things like that. That's one way they aren't like us, you know. They aren't gossips. They can talk politics till the cock crows, but gossip they turn their sharp Irish noses up at. I keep telling them it's the same thing, and they keep looking at me pityingly and saying, 'Oh, Peter, do shut up.'"

"That's not very kind."

"They don't really care about kind," he replied, and though his tone remained jovial there was a wounded cast to his features that could not be covered over with jokes.

"Where's the senator's wife?"

"Back in Washington. She hates politics—it depresses her, she says, having to listen to all those normal people. She's worse than the rest of them, a terrible snob, likes everything just so. That, and she's knocked up."

"Oh?" *What a bastard*, Marilyn thought, and tried not to feel envious of his wife.

"Yes, and Jack likes traveling as a bachelor. You'd never believe it, from all the photos of them in the press as a perfect family and so forth, but he is *rather* a ladies' man. But there I go again. You know us movie people—can't keep our mouths shut." He gulped his drink, and raised his arm in salute. "Hey there, Jack!"

Jack was approaching them, very slowly, his progress impeded by much backslapping. "Fine party, Peter," he said, shaking Peter's hand and patting his shoulder as though they were only casually acquainted.

"Have you met Marilyn? She's quite a chap."

"Not in person." Jack beamed at her. Even close up he seemed magnified, shinier and more beautiful than everybody else. "Although I feel I know you from your pictures."

"Congratulations." She returned his smile. "Didn't you win some game show tonight or something like that?"

"Yes, something like that. Peter, wasn't there music before? Put on a record, would you?"

Neither Jack nor Marilyn turned to look at Peter as he slinked away. They remained like that, eyes on each other, until a song started, the swelling of strings eliciting delighted yelps from Lawford's guests. The host, despite his babbling, was an expert taker of hints, and Marilyn noted that he drew Janet Leigh onto the dance floor just as Frank Sinatra began to sing.

"Everyone else is dancing; shouldn't we?" Jack seemed to vibrate with the charade—he enjoyed pretending they'd just met, even though they'd been circling each other for more than a year now.

"Your brother doesn't like me very much," she said as he led her down a few steps, into the sunken part of the living room, where the women were kicking off their heels.

"Bobby? Of course he does."

"He's got a funny way of showing it."

"I'm sorry. If he was short, it was nothing to do with you. He's put out over missing a meeting that I couldn't have had him at, anyway."

"But he's your campaign manager."

Jack grinned. "How did a little girl like you learn something important like that?"

She made her eyes like Betty Boop's. "*He* told me!"

"Well, he would only have caused trouble at this one."

"What kind of meeting was it?"

"Oh, god, I'm tired, can't we talk about something else?"

So they talked about Frank Sinatra—the music, not the man—and the beach, and which movies they had seen lately, and other things people talk about when they have just met, or otherwise have known each other so long that there is nothing more to learn. Then Jack was called away to the telephone, and for a while she danced with Peter, and for a while with Jack's youngest brother, who was still rather fat in the face and kept staring at her breasts. The music was rowdier when Jack came back, but it seemed everyone wanted to dance with him, and everyone wanted to dance with her, too, and hours passed where she couldn't even catch his eye. Eventually the living room emptied out, and she saw Peter slumped on one of the couches in alcoholic slumber, and she remembered the real reason that she hadn't wanted to go on a date with him. A party girl she'd been friendly with in her starlet days had been set up with him twice, and never been paid for her services. He was cheap, the girl said, which was captured perfectly by his drunken somnolence in the house that his wife's money had bought. Meanwhile the bartender was cleaning up, and Jack had disappeared, and she wondered if he had gone to bed without saying good night.

She drifted across the various levels of the room toward the heavy, carved wooden door, which was ajar. Outside the wind roughed her hair, and waves crashed in the distance. The turquoise rectangle of the pool glowed like a jewel in those final minutes of darkness—already, the sky was whitening at the edges. Earlier, the kinds of girls who were not quite actresses and not entirely prostitutes had giggled and splashed there, but it was empty now. Peter must have sent them home—it had been a long night.

The tile patio surrounding the pool was separated from the beach by a high glass wall—to keep out sand, she supposed, and riffraff. Beyond that the ocean spread out stark and infinite, and the road north wound its lonely way through the hills toward Hearst Castle. She stepped out of her white high heels, and lay down on a lounge chair. To the south, the lights of the Ferris wheel at Santa Monica were visible against a plum backdrop, and she felt sad, thinking how her mother used to describe youthful nights on the boardwalk in the tough, yearning manner of people whose best days are behind them.

"She's still here," Jack said.

Had she been asleep? When she opened her eyes, he had appeared on the chair next to her. He was wearing the same black trousers and white collared shirt, but his tie was gone and his shirtsleeves were rolled. His hair was less in place than before—it was reddish with the coming dawn, an unruly brush that seemed disproportionate to his forehead. Perhaps he was too tired to speak expressively, for he looked smaller, reduced from his earlier glory, and she could not tell whether he was pleased to have found her or not. She was tempted to tell him that it was always like this—that in the fury of performance, when you are vivid and grand beyond imagining, you believe you will always be so; and that the morning after, when the magic has left your body, is always a cold, desolate surprise.

"I didn't have a way home," she whispered, not reproachfully, as she pressed her head against the cushion of the chair.

"Yes, of course." He nodded. "I'm sorry about that."

"Must have been a pretty busy night for you," she went on, curling onto her side.

"Yes." He seemed to want to say more, but perhaps an actual response would have required too much energy, because he only glanced up at her and stared, his eyes lingering long on the slope of her waist and the rise of her hip.

"Where were you?" she asked, not in the demanding tone of a grown woman but in the small, breaking voice of a girl whose father has gone down to the racetrack for too long and forgotten about her. This was easy—especially late at night, when she was exhausted but trying hard to do the bidding of her father's people, she was that girl.

"Upstairs, with Bobby." He put his face into his hands, which made it impossible to read his expression, although she could see that whatever they had discussed had made him tired, and guessed that it must be something important.

"He's angry that I'm here?" she asked, the wounded worry that this might be true showing through the courage she'd summoned to pose the question. Earlier, she had been insulted that Jack had not picked her up himself, but now she saw what an opportunity it was, how she could play injured, encourage him to talk, press him to tell her what he and Bobby had discussed.

"No. He's angry, but not about you."

"About what, then?"

"Tomorrow the candidate for vice president will be decided, and he's not going to like it. He thinks Symington looks right, but it's not going to be Symington."

"No?"

"Oh—I suppose everybody will know pretty soon, anyway." He sighed and glanced out at the oyster sky. "Johnson's going to get his way."

"But you called him an animal."

For the first time since he'd come out by the pool, he smiled. "You remembered that?"

"I try to remember everything you say," she replied, which was the truth, although not in the way her earnest, childlike delivery implied.

"Well, he is—directly from the barnyard—but I don't have a choice. I don't like it, and I don't trust him. But they got me in a corner this time."

He worked his palms together and glanced at her, his eyes vibrant with mystery. Was he wondering what it was safe to tell her, or how best to have his way with her? Or was she in his thoughts at all?

"Should I go?" she said quickly, before he could think too much. "You must be t-tired," she continued, as though disoriented by her own self-doubt. "Your family, I wouldn't want them thinking that I—"

"Never mind about them, you're staying," he interrupted, not harshly but as though this was the obvious way of things. He added, almost apologetically: "You aren't the first, you know."

If she played wounded by this confession, perhaps he would go on talking, and other details would shake loose, and she could thus please Alexei with all the information she was capable of collecting just by appearing empty-headed. But he had already told her what mattered, and the rest she could piece together. Tomorrow—or later today, rather—when the fatigue had passed and he had regained his strength, he might regret what he had divulged, and punish her or himself by shutting her out. In her interior calculations, she invoked Alexei, philosophizing on the long game. There was nothing she might learn at that moment that was more important than holding Jack's attention, so she let a giggle blow away on a gentle exhalation. She lifted her legs showily and stood to kiss him on the forehead. "Oh, Jack," she gasped, "you don't have to explain yourself to me. *I* know what you are."

Then she darted toward the pool on mincing, barefoot tiptoes, unzipping her dress as she moved, pulling it over her head, revealing the surprise that she had planned for him twelve hours ago—that she wore no undergarments—and pausing just long enough to give him a backward glance that was equal parts mischief and apprehension, threw her arms over her head, and dove in. She was underwater a long time sailing through the dense, silken water, and when she came up for air she saw that he had already followed her lead. He was coming toward her, a dark shadow across the pool bottom's moonlike surface. She took a few easy strokes to the corner, and when she surfaced again she pushed the damp strands of hair straight back from her face. Blinking water from her lashes, she experienced the tingling of being watched, and for a moment she was sure there had been a figure on the second-story balcony. But then a light went out in a bedroom, and she saw that the balcony was empty.

Jack surfaced inches from her, his breath noisy and very close. They stared at each other for a few moments, and—curling her lower lip under her teeth—she wrapped one leg and then the other around his torso and pulled him the rest of the way to her. They had never been like this together—completely naked, their bodies as slick and warm as seals. Her breasts floated between them, almost touching his chest, which was smooth and hairless as a boy's. Then he lowered his head and pushed her mouth open. She murmured when he pushed the rest of the way in, putting her fingernails into the nape of his neck and catching his ear between her teeth, bracing herself as his weight pressed her into the concrete deck, slow and strong at first and then much faster, again and again. They were, however briefly, rather small in that corner of the pool, hanging on to each other, while the glamour of the sunrise broke over the hills and painted the surface of the water a gleaming, peachy orange.

FIFTEEN

Los Angeles, July 1960

FRIDAY morning was as balmy and pure blue as the day before, and the day before, and the day before that, and Marilyn knew that for once she could do almost anything—take her clothes off in the cake aisle of the supermarket, or shoot up on Hollywood Boulevard—and nobody would notice. Kennedy would be accepting the Democratic Party's nomination that afternoon, in downtown Los Angeles, and even the movie stars, who ordinarily were the organizing principle of the place, had been transformed into giddy fans. She took advantage of this anonymity by borrowing one of the candidate's white dress shirts, rolling the sleeves and tying it off at the waist, so it wouldn't be quite so obvious that underneath was the same pink dress she'd been wearing when she left home two days ago.

As her taxi ferried her back to Beverly Hills, she realized how little she'd slept over those days, how wired her mind was and how heavy her bones. She felt anxious and disoriented, the white light washing everything out, but then the car door opened, and she saw Sal, the concierge, and her stomach relaxed. "Miss Monroe," he murmured, taking her hand to help her to her feet. It was a relief, after two days holding herself rigid, vigilant, observant, to see a true friend. He added, a little dejectedly, "We would have sent a car for you."

"I meant to, but I forgot, I guess," she replied sorrowfully. "Next time."

As the concierge took her arm to escort her up the red-carpeted steps, he lowered his mouth to her ear. "Your husband returned this morning."

"Damn," she muttered.

"And another gentleman arrived, half an hour ago, looking for you."

"Oh?"

"Naturally I told him we had no guest registered under your name. He answered that he was perhaps confused about your lodgings, but that he'd most definitely arranged to meet with you here, this morning. Perhaps he is one of your colleagues in the film industry? In either case it is none of my business, but I put him by the pool until I could confer with you. If you want him removed from the property, I would be more than happy—"

"No thank you, Sal. I think I know who it is, and he's okay. Arthur didn't see him, did he?"

"Of course not."

She pressed onto her toes to kiss the concierge on the forehead, patted his hand, and went on by herself through the carpeted halls and garden pathways. A tiny alarm bell rang when she saw Alexei, poolside. He was wearing the usual brimmed hat and sitting very primly at a round table under a striped umbrella, his legs crossed, a teacup in one hand and its saucer in another. The sunglasses he used to conceal the direction of his gaze were white plastic. For the first time in their acquaintance he wore no socks, and the bare ankles more than anything else made it seem off for them to meet this way, in the California sunshine, as they had only once before, a decade ago.

"Hello." She dragged a chair away from the table and sat beside him.

A few other people lunched around the pool, none within earshot. Nobody seemed particularly cognizant of the new arrival. For a few moments they were quiet, gazing out at the tranquil brightness. "It's remarkable," he observed presently.

"What is?"

"They don't notice you."

"They're used to pretty girls."

"Perhaps, but that's not it. You know how to disguise yourself. 'A fool tries to look different; a clever man looks the same and *is* different'—have you heard that one?"

"Guess I didn't need to."

"Apparently not. Tea, my dear?"

She shook her head. "You didn't fly cross country to buy me lunch and give me tips on how to go incognito, did you?"

"Of course not. I heard you were absent without leave from the set, and I was worried about you."

"I see." Perhaps it was sleeplessness, which always leaves the skin a little thin, that caused her to feel irritated, rather than protected, by this evidence of his constant supervision. After all, it was at his behest that she had spent those many hours on edge, manipulating the desires of the most sought-after man in the country. Her clothes were rumpled—a mellowed body smell clung to the threads—and she wanted badly to be alone, and naked. "You're not the only one. Arthur arrived, this morning. Trying to find out why I'd disappeared from his movie, I guess. So if you want to talk, we'd better go elsewhere."

He nodded, left a bill under the saucer, and followed her away from the pool.

"Where to?" she asked as she steered her rented white Thunderbird off the property.

"Don't you want to see what all the fuss is about? Let's go to Pershing Square."

She shrugged indifferently, to hide her true curiosity, and without more discussion headed downtown.

They emerged from the lot underneath the park into a hectic scene: loud and vividly colored as a Disney production, crowds forming in every direction, signs making grand demands in the humble handwriting of romantics and lunatics. The fluorescent-green rectangles of grass were framed by every variety of human: old men in fedoras on park benches with newspapers spread over their crossed legs; lurking teenage girls with greased pompadours and Cleopatra eyes; evangelicals prophesying end times; trim, youthful communists imploring passersby to join the cause of the workingman.

"Did you know that young man?" she asked, as they walked east, away from the Coliseum where Kennedy was to give his speech, against the stream of bodies.

"Which man?"

"The crew-cut one." She showed her annoyance at their drifting, not as she felt it, but as a little girl might, by pushing naïvely for explanations. "Passing out leaflets about the paradise of the proletariat."

"No, my dear. Our cause is great, and there are millions working, publicly and in obscurity—sometimes in total secrecy—to further our aims. It is necessary that many of our comrades remain mysterious to one another, although that mystery does not diminish our brotherhood."

"But you do know *him?*"

He regarded her sidelong, his eyes patient and amused. "Know who?"

"My father."

"Ah. Yes, we were—are—great friends."

"Then tell me something about him," she demanded, as Alexei led them away from the center of things, past towering, futuristic skyscrapers, a landscape that was ready to be done with people. "Tell me where he came from."

"He was born here, in California." Alexei picked up her arm, and his voice rose to a sweet, storytelling pitch. "On a farm, which he left at eighteen when he was drafted. He would have served, except that the Armistice came first. He'd developed a taste for adventure by then, and was no longer suited to rural life, so he took odd jobs around Los Angeles, working in motion pictures mostly. He was good-looking and charismatic, so he tried acting, but he froze whenever the camera was on him, and only managed to work as an extra. In his private life, he was a great seducer. He was floundering when he met your mother and, on a night of passion, conceived you. She was married already, and he had no money to support a wife and child, and so he set off to make his fortune elsewhere, thinking that he could get rich quick in one of the big Eastern cities, and return in time to see you grow up. But New York was crueler than Los Angeles—he got factory work there, which was how he came to understand the worker's plight, and believe in our cause."

"When I was a teenager, I worked in a factory."

"Yes, I know. Funny, isn't it? Our lives have so much resonance, we can scarcely perceive the whole scheme from a fixed point."

"But where did you meet him?"

"Paris, in the thirties. We crossed paths many times—we were both couriers between Moscow and the various movements breaking out across Europe, carrying microfilm in the heels of our shoes across the old imperialist borders. Those were exciting times, my dear"—and she knew, by the way his eyes glazed, that they had been. "Like you, his charisma was his great asset. He was very effective against the Nazis because he was able to make love to some of the most high-born, well-connected women in Europe."

"But when did he tell you about the farm, and the—the factory?"

"Ah. Well, my dear, every story has a low point that must be passed through to reach its happy conclusion—I expect you know that already, from your work in Hollywood. We were imprisoned together, at one of the German camps. All we had was time, and we talked about everything, and he told me about his youth. About you. We were freed by the Red Army in '45, and returned to the same line we had been in before the war. When the order came that I was to go to the States, I went to visit him, and he told me that I should look for you. That he held you in his arms when you were a few days old, and knew you were a good girl, and that you would want to serve the people's cause, too."

She was embarrassed by how this touched her, to hear that a man she could not remember had seen greatness in her infant self. How the phrase *good girl* opened up a well of emotion. "But does he know that I . . . ?"

"Yes. Eventually our cause brought him here as well. He knows you are doing important work for us, though not *how*, of course. Or what kind. He understands that it is better for him to remain in the dark. For now. But he is proud of you, my dear, of that I can assure you."

They were silent a while. She felt curiously privileged to be a part of this narrative of the brave doings of men across continents and at war, and the idea that she, too, was doing something of importance pleased her unexpectedly. She only wished there was a way for the columnists who ridiculed her intelligence, who claimed she did not read the books she brought to set, to know. For the first time in her life it seemed logical that she had not yet met her father—they were destined to meet later, when the work was done.

Eventually they came upon a dim and unremarkable bar, the kind she liked best. All the patrons' eyes were glued to the black-and-white proceedings on a small television set; the light was low, the air smoky, and the furnishings, such as they were, suggested somebody's idea of a simpler time. She and Alexei sat down at a table where they could almost see the screen, and she told the waitress they'd both have Bloody Marys.

He gave her time to take a sip and sink into the faux-rustic wooden chair before asking, "Where have you been, N.J.?"

The drink, and the notion of her father the adventurer who, when they finally met, would have many wild stories to relate over cognacs by the fireplace, made her feel less tired, less irascible. After what Alexei had told her, she was pleased that she had something to tell him, too, and to keep herself from smiling, she bit off the bottom of her celery stalk. "With Hal."

"Oh?"

"Yes—I flew in Wednesday night, and met him out at his brother-in-law's place in Santa Monica."

"How long did you stay . . . ?"

"Till just a few hours ago. I was with him this morning."

"You've been together the whole time?"

"Of course not." Marilyn sipped through her straw, and related the details of the past few days: the party Wednesday night, after he clinched the nomination, which had more or less continued unabated. How the candidate and his people, along with various movieland notables, came and went from the Lawfords' beach house, and how she had blended in with them, reading magazines by the pool during the day and surreptitiously creeping into Kennedy's bed at night. To whom the candidate talked out of obligation, and to whom he really paid attention. The manner in which he conversed with his brother Bobby, who appeared to act as a kind of consigliere—he was the one, Marilyn guessed, who did the tough stuff. How they seemed almost not to need words with one another.

"They're alike, then?" Alexei asked.

"Not really. Hal is always joking. He's intelligent but, you know, kinda profane. His brother doesn't have any sense of humor that I saw. Real serious type. I suppose they must both be pretty serious, but Hal doesn't show it, not when he's away from the cameras."

"Do you think he has it in him to win?"

"How should I know? I'm no newspaperman."

"No . . ." Alexei paused, considering. "But does he seem to want it badly?"

"Sometimes he seems exhausted, but he doesn't show that to everybody. He feels relaxed when he's with me, I think. He must. Yes, he's very driven by something or other, and the strain—" Her eyes drifted from Alexei, to the television. The man they'd been discussing had ascended to his podium, was giving his big smile to an adoring crowd, raising his hands to them, basking in the massiveness of their adoration. "But in the end, the strain'll just make him push harder."

Alexei nodded, lowered the brim of his hat, and went to the bar for fresh drinks. When he returned, the tinny, televised sounds of ecstatic applause had quieted, and the candidate was speaking. In shouted iambs that seemed to require all his effort, he was acknowledging the rival contenders arrayed behind him, interspersed with those thoroughbred sisters Marilyn had seen dancing in their panty hose out in Santa Monica, chatting with each other in their chummy patois.

The man on the television was saying: "I am grateful that I can rely in the coming months on a distinguished running mate who brings unity and strength to our platform and our ticket, Lyndon Johnson . . ."

The row of patrons at the bar was all male, their broad backs turned to the woman in sunglasses and her slim, unremarkable companion, and while some of these fellows watched transfixed, others had begun to grumble at the candidate's lecturing, which was somehow slick and superior and also wooden at the same time. Marilyn's eyes brightened, and her eyes went from the television to Alexei as she switched the cross of her legs.

"I bet you'd like to know why Johnson," she said.

Alexei raised an eyebrow and fixed her with his gaze.

She didn't try to hide her pride as she gave him the information she'd been holding out. It was so much more than he had even asked for. Not just insight into the candidate's thinking and state of mind, but a real secret. What Jack had more or less implied Wednesday night in the pool, and she'd had confirmed that morning, as she lay facedown on the mattress pretending to sleep off the previous night's party. Bobby had come in and picked up a heated conversation that he and Jack seemed to have begun the day before, about Johnson and the director of the FBI being in league with one another and how they'd used it as leverage to control Kennedy's selection for vice president.

"They blackmailed him, you mean? Hoover had something? Evidence of an indiscretion?"

She shrugged elliptically, suggestively. "Why not? Hoover has something on everybody who's anybody. That's what Arthur told me, when he thought our phones were being tapped. He said it's almost like a badge of honor."

Alexei gazed out, his eyes losing their focus as he comprehended this.

"Remarkable, isn't it? Already he is susceptible to blackmail. How did the conversation end?"

"Bobby wanted to talk to their father. He kept saying their father could fix it. Then Hal got angry, too, and he told him they wouldn't be doing that, and that he'd better get out of there and stop wasting his time. That if he didn't get some pussy before the day he was about to have, it was gonna spell trouble for everybody."

"And then what happened?"

"Well."

"Remarkable." Alexei leaned back into his chair and folded his hands in his lap. "Remarkable."

The men at the bar continued in their appraisal of the candidate, and Marilyn and Alexei, coming to the end of their second round of drinks, each retreated into their own thoughts. Her handler seemed pleased, and she was, too, for a little while anyway, thinking about how he could now report to his superiors, whoever they were, that she was a success, that she was even more skilled at their game than they had hoped. That she'd procured intelligence beyond what they'd asked for, and how that might accelerate things, bring her into contact with her father even sooner than promised.

"He looks tired," Alexei said doubtfully.

As though in response, the man on television acknowledged, "It has been a long road from that first snowy day in New Hampshire to this crowded convention city. Now begins another long journey, taking me into your cities and homes all over America." His voice faltered, and she briefly feared it would fail him. That morning it had been scratchy, and like a sweet wife she had urged him to keep quiet. But it became forceful again when he went on: "Give me your help, your hand, your voice, your vote." And the renewed vigor, and the word *your* pronounced by the man whose sweat she could still smell on her skin, made the hairs on her forearm stand on end. "Recall with me the words of Isaiah: 'They that wait upon the Lord shall renew their strength; they shall mount up with wings as eagles; they shall run and not be weary.'"

The speech was approaching its climax, but Alexei appeared to lose interest after the biblical reference. He smirked good-naturedly and said, "We should be celebrating; will you have another?"

"Yes."

"You may learn a lot about Hal in the coming months—I will be watching you, and checking in on you, but if he tells you anything of special importance—anything useful, anything timely—call the Pilar Florist on Second Avenue, and order a large arrangement of purple irises for the children's wing at Memorial Sloan-Kettering. I will get the message, and come to you as soon as possible."

"Okay," she said, pushing their empty glasses in his direction.

As Alexei went up to the bar again, she watched him, the unremarkable way he moved. It was unremarkable with purpose, of course, and she liked him for this ability to pretend, which was her ability, too.

The candidate had finished his speech, and a funny little boyish smile flickered on his face, like he was relieved it was over. The crowd began to cheer and the marching music picked up, and Marilyn smiled faintly at Alexei—who twisted at the bar to raise his glass in her direction, as though the applause from the television were for her—and she felt a spasm of regret over what she'd done. She had explained Jack's weaknesses to an enemy she didn't truly understand, but she must not feel sorry for him. He did not deserve her sympathy. No nation had ever done anything for her—she was, as ever, the only one looking out for herself, and so she would continue until she met the man whose job it really was. That was all there was to do, even if Jack, smiling from the television, was proving difficult to dislike.

SIXTEEN

Beverly Hills, August 1960

IN the one-room guest cottage at the back of the Moses property a telephone was ringing, and Walls glanced up warily from the small wooden desk where he had been transcribing old tapes. He was not a brilliant typist, and now that he was required to type often, he was a little surprised that it was commonly a feminine pursuit. Typing required strong hands and left the fingertips sore, especially today, when the temperature at noon had been over a hundred, and mellowed only slightly since. He was wearing nothing but white swimming trunks and sweating profusely, even though the windows were open, and despite a standing fan a foot from his body. He was annoyed at the phone's intrusion, because he was sure that he had been on the verge of an idea, a perfect understanding of the inner criminal life of Marilyn Monroe—but whatever had been in his head a minute ago was gone now. He threw himself onto the floral bedspread and plucked the receiver from its resting place on the nightstand.

"Walls," he said.

"Douglass?"

"Oh." He pushed up onto his elbows, and silently cursed himself for answering in his curt office manner. The heat was making him stupid. "Anna. How are you?"

"I'm *hot*, but what does that matter? I'm on a *movie* set! I'm meeting all kinds of people, really interesting people. It took a month, but I'm not so afraid of them anymore. I'm almost one of them now—they treat me that way. It's not like New York. I mean, it's different here. Slow, kinda Western,

I guess. And movie people are sort of loose and odd, but in a good way, I think."

"How is Miss Monroe treating you?"

"Oh, she's nice. She looks after me. You know, always asks how they're treating me. I always say wonderful, of course. She's gone missing from the set a lot, which has caused trouble. Some resentment, you know? But I always stick up for her and say that it must be hard, having the whole picture depending on her looking her best and understanding every word in those long speeches. It's true, too."

"You think so?"

"Yeah. Hey, Doug?"

"Yes?"

"Do you think about me?"

"What? All the time."

"Good! Because there's something special I want to invite you to."

"What is it?"

"This weekend. In Lake Tahoe. Frank Sinatra is performing there, and he invited the cast—you know, Miss Monroe and Mr. Gable and Mr. Clift and the rest of them. But Mr. Gable said he wouldn't go unless the whole crew was invited, so we're all invited now! Can you imagine that? Frank Sinatra invited us to his very own resort. It's called Cal-Neva, because it's right on the border between California and Nevada. Isn't that clever? I've never even been to California."

"That's swell. Real big of him."

"Will you come?"

"Me?"

"Yes, you. Who else would I be talking to? It'll be romantic, don't you think? You could stay with me. In my room, I mean. I mean: if you were worried about the resort not having any rooms left. Or—anything like that."

He sighed, not meaning to do so audibly. Then he felt even worse for his partial attentions to this girl over the past few months, since that night in New York in May when he'd carried her, drunk, up four flights to her Yorkville apartment. The poor thing, offering to let him sleep in her hotel bed, when her whole life she had been taught not to do that sort of thing. "It sounds nice," he said.

"Oh, *good*. You'll come?"

"Let me see if I can manage it." He didn't have the heart to ask her if Marilyn was going, and thought, not for the first time that day, that what he really needed was a tap on her phone in Reno. Then he would already know whether it was worth it to go to Tahoe or not.

"Doug?"

"Yes?"

He listened to her unsteady breath. "I miss you," she said, reminding him, for some reason, of a three-minute egg broken open with the blunt edge of a spoon.

A fist sounded on the other side of the door to the cottage, splitting his attention. "You, too. Listen, I have to go now, but I'll call you tomorrow, all right?"

"The show is on Saturday. Saturday the thirteenth of August. You got that?"

"Yes. Bye now."

A washcloth lay on the nightstand, and he used it to wipe the sweat from his brow. He was still holding it when he opened the door and saw the special agent in charge of the Los Angeles division, Bertram Toll, a bear of a man in an unbelted trench.

"Agent Toll."

He turned, his eyes traveling from Walls's face, to the washcloth, and back again. "Taking it easy, Agent Walls?"

"No. Working, actually," Walls said, putting the washcloth behind his back, wishing he could cover up his bare chest and tight-fitting shorts. The

California sun had bleached his hair white-blond, which reminded him of the summer he turned twelve. "How'd you get in?"

"Your mother let me in." He grinned. "I guess she liked my look."

There was no explaining how little this kind of ribbing troubled Walls. "But why?"

"You forget you were invited to dinner tonight?"

"I was?"

"Gretchen made pork chops."

"Oh." Though he tried hard, Walls could surface nothing from his mental swamp regarding an invitation to dine with the Tolls. But he was feeling rather unlike himself—maybe the weather was getting to him, or maybe he was spending too much time trying to comprehend a woman who was routinely hours, even days late, and often forgot to put on underwear when she left the house. "I'm sorry—was she angry at me?"

"Nah. No such luck, kiddo—she's been so pissed off with me for so many years there ain't any left over for anybody else."

"Oh, well . . . come in, then?"

"Thanks."

Walls went to the tiny galley kitchen and fixed them each a gin-and-tonic—opening the door to the icebox only narrowly, so that his boss wouldn't see that gin-and-tonics were pretty much the only thing he fixed there. When he came back, Toll was inspecting the detritus of his desk—the tangle of cords, the tape machine, the back issues of *Movie World* and *Life*, from which a blonde stared up at them, wearing an expression somehow sly and guileless at the same time.

"You're not in love with her, are you?"

"Who?" Walls handed the drink to his boss, hoping that it didn't slosh noticeably with his discomfort. For a moment, he felt sure everybody was listening in on everybody, and that he was about to be reprimanded for toying with the affections of a simple-minded girl who did makeup for a living.

"Marilyn." Toll picked up one of the magazines, the cover of which offered her in a particularly cheesecake pose, and sipped his drink.

"Oh. No, no," Walls replied quickly. "How could I? I don't even know her. I don't think anybody does."

Toll shrugged, put the magazine down, and sat on the metal rolling chair, which forced Walls to perch, uncomfortably, on the corner of the bed.

"She's not really Red, is she?"

"Don't think so." It pained him to say this, as he knew it was the main rationale for keeping a file on her, and his desire to understand what she and the Gent were up to had transcended some notion of how the case might bolster his own glory, and taken on the pure force of a desire to learn that which others wished him not to know.

"That bit with Khrushchev? Miller says 'hi'?"

"She's sort of a genius at being provocative—I don't think it matters to her whether she means it. I'm fairly certain Mrs. Miller wasn't sending a secret message to the Russians. I don't think she's even going to stay Mrs. Miller much longer. In either case, she and Arthur, they don't think alike."

When Toll laughed, his mouth went lopsided. "Is that what dooms a marriage? You should write a romance advice column, kid."

Uncertain whether this was meant as a compliment or an indictment of his work for the Bureau, Walls said the only phrase that came to his mind. "Excuse me?"

"Listen," Toll went on, crossing his legs and disregarding the question. "There's a rumor going around town that she and the Kennedy kid are having a little fling."

"Really?" Walls's disingenuousness was a surprise even to himself, and he was suddenly unsure why he had been keeping his suspicions regarding the presidential candidate and the movie star a secret. Perhaps it was that, having felt so sure that he had witnessed something consequential between them, and then having seen so little evidence of it for so long, he didn't now want to spook her before she revealed her motives to him.

"Do I gotta do everything for you? Your mother is Mosey Moses, for chrissakes, she's probably over there yakking about it right now."

"Oh, I . . ." This was not the time, he knew, to be indignant, or point out that he was not paid to have chatty, alfresco lunches. "It makes sense," he said cautiously. "Kennedy always struck me as a skirt-chaser."

"God bless him. I'd sleep a little easier thinking that the man in the White House was getting laid, wouldn't you?"

"Yes, sir," he replied, not agreeing but not wanting to argue, and immediately wishing he could unsay the subservient phrase.

"Anyway." Toll put aside his empty glass and shifted as though preparing to leave. "The Director is interested in anything to do with the Kennedys, so pay attention for once, would you?"

"She's going to Tahoe this weekend."

"What?" A moment before, Toll's attention had been anywhere but on Walls, but he assessed him with a sharp gaze now.

"Frank Sinatra invited her. He's performing at some lodge," Walls began slowly, as though putting the facts together as he spoke. "Isn't he campaigning for Kennedy? His whole crew is. I mean, they're friends, aren't they?"

"Ah, yes." Toll interlaced his fingers and cupped his knee. "The Rat Pack is now the Jack Pack; I think Gretchen mentioned something like that."

"Well, Sinatra invited the whole crew of the movie she's making. But that's strange, when I think about it. Doesn't that make it seem like somebody's trying to cover something up?"

"You mean, it'll look less like Jack Kennedy's friend invited Marilyn Monroe to Tahoe for the weekend if it's Frank Sinatra inviting the whole crew of some movie to see his show?"

Walls nodded. "Odd, too, that Sinatra invited her. She must know him, they've both been in the business so long. But he's friends with DiMaggio, and back when she was divorcing Joe, it was Sinatra who found him a private dick, helped him break into the apartment where he thought she was with another man. Of course, they got the wrong place, that's why it ended up in *Confidential*, and later in front of a grand jury." He was getting excited just talking about her, lining up the facts he'd collected, fitting them together. "They aren't close that I know of, and she doesn't have much reason to like him, so there must be something more to the invitation."

"Agent Walls." Toll paused and lowered his chin so that it doubled. "The Director is interested in *anything* to do with Kennedy. If this man could be the next president of the United States, it's the Bureau's business to understand any threat to him. And if he's having an affair with a woman who may have communist sympathies, however unlikely, we must endeavor to keep ourselves informed. It will be good for all of us at the division if you can get something definitive. Do you understand me?"

"Yes, sir."

"Tell me you're going to Tahoe, Agent Walls."

"Yes, sir," Walls replied, more energetically this time.

"Good man. Call my girl, have her set you up with plane tickets, equipment, whatever you need."

"Thank you, sir." Walls walked him to the door, and for a moment they stood on the threshold, gazing into the volatile atmosphere. The Santa Anas had picked up, knocking palm fronds from their high perches, so that they lay like Paleolithic wreckage all over the deck. A member of his mother's staff circled the pool, scooping them up. "Tell Gretchen I'm sorry about dinner."

Several seconds of silence followed as Toll gazed out at the property—the rigidly rectangular lawns, the white gravel, the aquamarine pool, the statuary, and the pergolas. "So this is how Lou Moses lives," he said eventually, as he drew a cigarette from his jacket and tried—vainly, at first—to get it lit. Whether this comment was irrelevant, or a kind of answer to Walls's apology, was unclear.

The smell of Toll's cigarette smoke lingered even as he crossed the patio, and Walls, invigorated despite the humiliation of having had to play dumb for his superior, returned to his cottage, made himself another gin-and-tonic, and sat back down at his desk. The first sound that came through the headphones when he pressed PLAY was high, slightly cracked laughter, and then he heard Marilyn saying, "I've never fooled anyone, darling. Sometimes I've just let men fool themselves."

SEVENTEEN

Reno, August 1960

"THAT sounds wonderful." Marilyn wrapped the coiled telephone cord around her finger and gazed out at the Sierras, which had been purple and green when she first saw them a month ago, but now in mid-August were ablaze with forest fires. "Absolutely wonderful. Thank you, Frankie."

She half listened to Frank as he continued to tell her about his Lake Tahoe resort, how much she'd like it, and what she should wear. With the receiver tucked between her shoulder, she left the bedroom of her suite in the Mapes Hotel and returned to the living room, where Arthur was pretending to write for one of the Magnum photographers Huston had hired to document the making of the movie. Not Cartier-Bresson, but the other one—the woman with the Freudian accent and boy's haircut. Arthur was wearing black-rimmed glasses, not his usual ones, and using a pack of cigarettes as a prop.

"Thanks," Marilyn said again. "See you tomorrow."

She hung up and took a step toward the bedroom.

"Marilyn."

"What."

"Call him back, and tell him you're not going anywhere."

Her hand was on the doorframe, and she paused to stare at Arthur, who half turned in the chair with his long, slender arm draped casually over the chair's back. This easy posture enraged her almost as much as his paternalistic command.

"You've made the crew wait around for you enough already." His tone was as equanimous as his posture; it was the way he spoke to his children on the phone when they wanted something frivolous for their birthdays. "You've got new lines to learn. When the crew comes back from Tahoe, you're going to be ready to work."

This interest in her weekend plans took her by surprise, and she wondered if he was truly concerned about her showing up Monday morning, or whether he was finally getting a little jealous of what she did without him.

"I've been slaving all week in hundred-degree heat, and I'm going to go swim in a lake this weekend, and hear some music."

"I was talking to Dr. Kurtz earlier. She suggested that your procrastination might be closely correlated with your impulsivity—could it be that this fleeing the set on a whim is due to your fear that you won't be good enough? Are you avoiding showing Huston, and all of us, what you are really capable of?"

"What do you care?" Marilyn said, her eyes focused furiously at the place on his oversized, birdlike skull where the hair had started to thin.

"I care because I am your husband," he replied evenly. "And I gave Huston my word that I'd get you through this."

She rolled her eyes and crossed toward the curving bay windows on the far side of the living room, rocking her hips for the benefit of the trim, androgynous person who crouched on the far side of Arthur, in a black sweater that covered her collarbones and her wrists. If Arthur wanted to make a power play when they had an audience, she was game. "I shot pool with Huston last night," she said to the windowpane. "He doesn't give a shit what I do when I'm not on set. I'm going to Tahoe, and you're coming, too." This had not been her plan, but as soon as she said it, she wondered why she hadn't thought of it before. If Arthur came, then Kennedy would have to work to see her. Alexei had been right; someday it would be advantageous that she was married to a big-time playwright. His presence would stir Jack's jealousy, make it a hunt again, remind him that he wasn't the first Pulitzer Prize winner to share her bed.

"Why would I come?" He stood up, pushing away the chair. His height no longer impressed her much, but it did now for a flickering second. "Isn't your lover going to be there? Isn't that why you want to go, so someone else's husband can make love to you in French? Or is Jersey Dago your new flavor?"

The photographer stood up suddenly, as though in support of Arthur's assertion. Her hands clutched the camera that hung around her neck.

This belated acknowledgment of adultery, of all the betrayals and dis-appointments, did cut at her, and she let it show, let her mouth hang open wretchedly as he came toward her through the boxy furniture. She watched how his anger calmed him, amplified him, and she let him see how it did the opposite to her, how it shrank her down to a delicate and lovely nothing. "Yves is in France," she said, neither admission nor denial, just the plain fact.

He took a cigarette from behind his ear and put it in his mouth. "Then why?" he asked as he felt in his pockets for a light. The fumbling alerted her that jealousy had finally done its work on him. "Why do you want to go?"

There was wetness on her eyes, and she didn't wipe it away. Her face twitched, rabbit-like, and the tip of her nose went pink, and she coaxed her red lips into a brave smile. The smile that was slow and hopeful as the dawn, despite everything her life had been. The one the camera loved. "Because I want to have a little fun, Poppy. Don't you want to have a little fun? Even now? Or maybe, I don't know . . . maybe *especially* now."

His hands were still groping in his pockets for the matches, and she could see that she almost had him. He was softening to her, remembering that she didn't know any better, how she more than made up for it by brightening a room. His head lolled slightly to the side while he assessed her, the cigarette hanging from his full, damp lips. She smiled a little more before letting the smile fade away, letting her posture fall apart, as she revolved away from him, putting her fingers up to the window glass like a child at a museum. It was not difficult for her to conjure a wounded emotion. She had been summon-ing it all day, in order to do the scene that Arthur said was a metaphor for the whole damn story. A scene in which she half fell out of the little desert shack, was almost kissed by the character named Guido, and then broke free into a strange, drunk dance that culminated with her embrace of a tree.

"The tree symbolizes life," Arthur had explained to her, sitting under the white umbrella that morning on set, gesturing with his long fingers as though he could thus convince himself that he was actually saying something. "Roslyn is clinging to life."

You think I need that spelled out for me? she'd wanted to reply. But she hadn't. She had done take after take instead, falling out of the shack in the same black dress she'd been wearing for weeks, the one with the cutouts around the chest and the low, scooped back, tripping over the grass, showing her ass to the cameras, throwing her arms wide and shaking.

She was about to turn to him and ask him please when she heard the shutter. Such was her habit that she couldn't help but adjust herself, lengthen her spine so that her shoulder blades emerged to cast cinematic shadows over her pale, naked back, waiting for the camera to click twice more before she broke the pose and twisted to face Arthur. "What is she doing here?"

Inge was the woman's name, and she had conferred with Arthur a great deal while Huston was shooting that morning.

"Are you fucking her? Is that why she's here?" She had intended the accusation strategically, to put attention off her own infidelities. But as soon as she said it—as soon as Inge lowered the camera from her face, revealing the thin lips beneath the dark, focused eyes—she knew that it was true. Maybe they had already started sleeping together, or maybe she was as yet only enthralled by his genius, and had not yet committed anything in body. In either case, Marilyn had an unexpected glimpse of what was, and her face went numb with shock. They were all quiet for what might have been a long time, and then Marilyn's nostrils flared and her lips pulled away from her teeth. "Get out! You fucking cunt, get out of my house, get out!"

With infuriating dignity, the woman collected her equipment, swung her canvas bag onto her shoulder, gave Arthur a pregnant look, and left the room. He closed the door gently behind her and turned slowly back, wearing that mask of poorly contained exasperation Marilyn knew so well.

Then the shouting.

They shouted and shouted, shouted themselves hoarse, and all the unsaid resentments and accusations accumulated over years came tumbling down. As always in these situations, she had little idea what she said, and for once Arthur didn't, either. His usual command of words was broken, but not his anger, and she saw finally the seething cuckold she had made of him. They stopped only because they finally exhausted themselves, and by then a lamp lay sideways across the floor, its neck broken and its bulb shattered, and there was a dent in the plaster where a hurled ashtray had made its mark. In the aftermath she felt too weak to stand, and sat heavily on the couch with her face in her hands, further muddying the mascara tracks on her cheeks.

Without looking at her, he said: "I will go to Tahoe. I will put on a good show. We will get through this movie. But it's over. You know it's over. You know."

"I know." She was very tired. "Once the movie is over, we'll make an announcement."

He was right. They had not acted like husband and wife for years, and she would have left him already if Alexei had not persuaded her otherwise. But now, in the dying light of the thing, she remembered how important he had once seemed. How, as Mrs. Arthur Miller, she had imagined that her life would be always protected and precious. She could not pretend with herself that she had even been trying to keep him; and she could not pretend anymore that she might someday have his brilliant babies. But even the fiction of a marriage gives some comfort, and she shivered, thinking of the stark road ahead.

EIGHTEEN

Lake Tahoe, August 1960

SINATRA had done his thing. He'd crooned, and told off-color jokes, and given the girls that criminal, azure wink, and everyone in the wigwam-like banquet hall had been left in a drunken, roguish mood. He'd sat the Millers to his right, for the supper that followed the show, and a long way from Kennedy, who was surrounded by a squadron of powerfully built men in black tie. Big Bill of the maid's costume was amongst them, and Marilyn thought she recognized the mobster from Chicago in the entourage as well. Earlier she and her leading man had done as the publicity department wished, and danced with the local bigwigs and their wives, but Clark had since escorted his pregnant wife back to their cabin, and for Marilyn the night was just beginning.

She was in fine, glowing form. Several times she'd caught Jack staring at her, and when the waiter appeared at her shoulder, proffering a note on a tray, she figured it was from him. Only after she read the note and understood it was from Arthur—informing her he had writing to do, and was driving back to Reno for some quiet—did she realize he was gone. But the party was in full swing, and she didn't wonder if he'd noticed the vibration between her and Kennedy, or pause to feel much at all about her husband's departure. Instead she smiled at the waiter and asked him if there was any more of that good French champagne on ice close by.

Once her champagne glass was replenished, Frank leaned in and said, "Hey, sweetheart, the old man wants to dance with you."

"What old man?"

"You know. Ambassador Kennedy."

"Oh!" She rested her teeth against her glass and inhaled in a way that brought attention to her décolletage. "Which one is he?"

Frank came closer so that she could smell the cigarette smoke that clung to his hairpiece. "The one with the little glasses, over there with the low-rent Liz Taylor."

"Isn't he a Nazi or something?" she asked ingenuously.

"What? No! Why would you think that?"

"Oh, I don't know. I guess I heard Arthur say something like that once."

"Nah. He's just tough old Irish Boston. Now come on," he said, standing and taking her arm. "Don't say anything dumb like that to his face, all right?"

Frank led them through the crowd, his shoulders hunched and his nose alert and charging as a bloodhound, pulling her after him and not noticing how she had to hustle in her tight-fitting dress to keep up. The bandleader spotted his boss on the floor, and started in on a new song, slow and sultry, as Frank led her into the dance. They both smiled like they had been taught to in the old days, big enough so the people in the back row could see all the money the studio had put into their dentistry. *Poor Frank*, she thought. He wasn't meant to age, or else he was trying too hard not to.

"How's Joe?" she asked, as Frank twirled her out and reeled her in so that her shoulder blades pressed against his chest. During her second marriage, she'd realized that there was a part of Joe DiMaggio that was the same as Frank Sinatra—the worst part—and she'd learned that the nights when they'd been drinking together were the nights she could expect to get it.

"Still likes it better up in San Francisco." That smile, it could have withstood a hurricane. "Says the pizza dough rises better there."

"Does he still miss me?"

"Sure. All the time. I tell him not to. But I understand, I'm the same way about Ava. Doesn't make any sense, but that's love, right? The thing that doesn't make any sense."

This sounded to her like the sort of pedestrian sentiment that worked only when you had a really good melody to float it over, but she just said, "Yeah, I guess so," in a vague, sleepy voice.

"Perk up, sweetheart, here he comes."

The old man and his brunette sidled up next to them, and Frank and Marilyn beamed their glistening, show business smiles. All four kept their feet light and laughed at little nothings. Flattering observations of the women's clothing were exchanged, and playful put-downs were made regarding the appearance of the men, after which the blonde was transferred to the Kennedy patriarch. He was taller than Frank, and his sun-speckled skin, close-cropped white hair, and round glasses gave him the appearance of a college professor. But the way he carried himself was not remotely academic.

"Marilyn Monroe," he said, the same way his son once had, as though he was beholding a national treasure for the first time and had to step back to appreciate the whole view.

"It's a pleasure to meet you, Mr. Ambassador."

"Believe me, the pleasure is all mine." *Pleasure* he pronounced with an emphasis she couldn't hope to miss. "My son told me you were a fine bit of stuff."

"Did he?" Her smile must have been blinding.

"Yes." Joe could dance, but not as well as Sinatra, and he compensated by keeping their bodies close. "He said you were just a sweet, innocent, really beautiful girl."

"Well, isn't that charming?"

"Indeed it is." He lowered his mouth to her ear, and a surge of volume from the orchestra gave him the excuse to jerk his pelvis against hers. "Of course I don't believe one damn word of that."

She had moved in the world of men, played the desire game, long enough—she had heard put-downs that were come-ons and come-ons that were put-downs, she'd had her hair pulled and her head slammed against walls—so there was no chance that Joe's snarling comment, as blunt and incestuous as it may have been, could rattle her. It did provide good cover, however, for the surprise she experienced a moment later, when she spotted a familiar but unexpected face at the edge of the crowd, and the rhythm of her heart became agitated. "Excuse me," she said, and half ran from the dance floor, knocking Alexei's shoulder with her own as she left the room.

Once she was in the halls of the resort, she relaxed her stricken expression and began to walk at a more controlled pace, her ears alert to any noise behind her, her breathing quiet and steady. She heard the footsteps in her wake, and matched her own to his, letting him almost catch up to her. She turned abruptly into the men's room and walked down the aisle of stalls, where she positioned herself in front of the mirror on the far end. Although she kept her gaze steady on her own reflection, she noted from the corner of her eye how Alexei casually bent to see if there were any shoes beneath the stall doors as he approached. Satisfied, he placed himself at the sink next to her, turned the faucet, and let the water run.

"What are you doing here?" she said evenly.

"Why wouldn't I be here?"

She lifted her chin and opened her mouth to laugh. "Everyone likes a little song and dance, you mean? Okay. But how am I supposed to make this whole scheme natural when there's someone always watching me? He's going to notice, you know, if you keep breathing down my neck. What's next? You going to jump out from under the bed with a camera?"

"N.J., I am sorry if I've made you nervous. That's not why I'm here."

"Then what?"

"Our girl in Giancana's organization, she told us he's meeting with the old man this weekend. There are all kinds of Mafia about—it could be dangerous. Not for you, perhaps, but—in a general kind of way. And I wanted to be here. To watch over you. To make sure you're safe."

"Oh." She nodded, taking this in, experiencing in the same moment that shivering comprehension of a danger she hadn't known herself to be in, and the relief of learning that someone else was taking care of it. "Clark's here," she said sharply. "He looks after me."

"N.J., he's not a *real* cowboy."

"You didn't worry before. In Chicago, I mean—"

"Of course I did, N.J. Of course I did." He sighed, shutting off the water and picking up a cloth. Once his hands were dry, he put them reassuringly on both her shoulders. "I always worry about you. But you were less involved then. And of course you are much more valuable to our operation now, to the Party. To the people . . ."

Their conversation was interrupted by the sound of an object hitting the tiled floor, and they both turned to see one high heel under the door of the last stall. There were no feet visible—the woman must have been crouching on the toilet. A trill of feminine laughter followed, and Marilyn realized there were two people in hiding, because a man's voice said, "Come on, let's get out of here."

A moment later the stall door was flung back, and by then Alexei had moved to shield Marilyn from view. Two people ran for the far side of the men's room, and Marilyn glanced up in time to see the assistant makeup girl—wearing one high heel and holding the other, her crinoline bouncing as she pulled a man with light-colored hair in a black jacket into the hall—before quickly pointing her face in the opposite direction. The door sounded shut behind them, and Alexei moved to pursue the couple.

"Don't worry," Marilyn said. "That girl's an airhead. She was so excited about seeing Frankie she couldn't stop talking about it all week. She was probably caught unawares by the news she'd be sleeping in a bunk bed, and her boyfriend is trying to get what was promised him where he can."

Alexei glanced in her direction. "Are you sure?" His blue eyes gleamed with urgency.

"Yeah." Marilyn was calm now, and she took the opportunity to fix her lipstick with the tube she kept between her breasts. "I'll make sure she gets more drinks, and then she really won't remember anything. Meantime, would you get lost? I appreciate your concern, daddy, but you can't make love with three people in the room."

Lipstick nestled back in place, she put a red kiss on Alexei's forehead—it was going to take him a while to get *that* out—and swerved back toward the banquet hall, or wherever Jack was.

The telephone in cabin 3 tried to ring, but she answered before it got the sound out. In dreamland a private detective had been following her through the barracks of a dusty Southern California military compound—she had been wearing magenta, and holding the hand of an Iowan private first class—but she should've known that wasn't real. Arthur would never send a detective, as Joe had, to prove what he could figure out on his own, a characteristic she knew she ought to admire. "Yes?" she whispered, curling away from the man who lay beside her.

"Mrs. Miller?" said a bright, inquisitive, female voice.

"Yes," she answered, more tiredly this time.

"Your husband ordered a wake-up call. Good *morning*! Would you and Mr. Miller like breakfast in bed?"

She twisted, pushing a fistful of blonde fluff away from her eyes to glance at the sleeping man. "No." She gripped the phone with both hands, becoming aware of the unease in her stomach, the drumbeat at her temples. Then she remembered the many drinks she'd had last night, which had obliterated several haphazard trains of thought and given her a clear picture of how to use Sunday morning. "No, but uh—could you fix us a picnic?"

"A picnic?"

"Yeah, you know, lunch in a basket. Sandwiches and coleslaw and potato chips and maybe a few cans of beer. My husband and I—we're going canoeing today."

"I'll call the kitchen and see—"

"Good. Just have them leave it outside our cabin when it's ready."

"Yes, ma'am."

"Thank you."

If she were wise, she would have tried to rest a little more, but she knew sleep would only elude her, and anyway the pillows in that place were cheap. The agitation of her stomach, the discordant title *Mrs. Miller* ringing in her ears, the memory of the eyes on her last night—watchful Alexei, leering Joe Kennedy, menacing Giancana—kept her mind alive. She lit a cigarette and pulled a sheet over her nakedness, exposing the body beside her. Jack had not slept in the nude, as she had, but even so she could make out the morning wood through his striped boxer shorts, and she was not quick enough to banish the thought that he was rather beautiful in repose.

"What are you looking at?"

She tried not to seem surprised that he had been conscious all this time, and quickly put out the cigarette. Smoking did not fit with the girl she intended to play for Jack today, which was the sweet ingénue who shows up with a package full of good, simple things, and no thought in her head but how to make her man happy. A relaxing August interlude, before the campaign resumed its relentless pace. "At you."

"You're taking me canoeing, huh?"

"Well, I'd like to." She put a hand on his tanned torso. "If you've got time."

He leaned away to check his wristwatch on the nightstand, and disappointment rose in her, displacing the nausea. She reminded herself that it didn't matter. If not today, there would be another day to coddle him into a chatty stupor, another day to impress the unknown men Alexei reported to. "Okay," Jack said, putting down his watch and rolling over so that she was pinned and the mattress groaned, and she couldn't lie to herself that she wasn't relieved. "Take me canoeing. But we had better go before Bobby figures out where I am."

So they went, with their wicker basket, across the deep brown forest floor, fragrant with loam and pine, and out onto the placid sapphire surface of the lake glistening in the morning sun. She paddled lazily, and Jack lay down at the head of the canoe, removing the dress shirt he'd put on and closing his eyes to the sun. There were no other boats at that hour, and they glided away from shore, so that the lodge looked like the silly little toy that it was, and she could see a long way through the clear water to the lake bottom.

"Think I can touch the bottom?" she asked.

Jack glanced over the edge of the canoe. "Must be a hundred feet."

She grinned and pulled her white cotton sundress over her head and dove in. The water was bracing, and as she plunged down she realized he was right, the bottom was much farther than she'd guessed. When she broke the surface again it was with a girlish *"Brrrrrr!"* of shock.

"Pretty cold, isn't it?"

She swam back to the boat, and folded her arms against its edge, affecting a smile of unself-conscious delight. "Come on in, honey. Water's fine."

"No thanks—I'd rather watch you."

"Don't you remember last time we were in the water together?" she asked with a wink.

"I think about it all the time. But my back's killing me. There's no way I'd be able to get myself out again, and I'll not have a woman pull me."

"Oh, all right." She threw a leg over the side, and hauled herself up. When she dove in she had not considered that they hadn't brought towels, and for a moment she sat opposite him, shivering in the clear sunshine. Then she knew she'd miscalculated. She had thought he would follow her in, but now she was the only one naked, dripping, her skin chilled and her hair bedraggled. She had made herself too vulnerable, and could not play the geisha now.

Meanwhile Jack whistled, reached into the picnic basket, cracked a beer. Closing the lid, he saw the tag that read *Mr. and Mrs. Miller, Cabin 3.* "How'd you manage to get rid of your husband, anyway? If I were him, I wouldn't let you out of my—"

But he broke off. She hadn't meant to respond, but the truth must have been in her face briefly. How it had choked her to be called "Mrs. Miller" that morning when the name no longer meant anything, or how ugly it was to be replaced so quickly after four years of marriage. Alexei had warned her to keep Arthur, that Jack would grow leery if she was just another desperate, unattached actress, but she had no choice except to play the situation for sympathy now. "Oh, that didn't take any doing," she whispered, making her voice small and sad. "He doesn't care anymore, you know. It's over. Once we finish the picture, everyone else will know, too."

The boat rocked under her, and for several seconds Jack said nothing. She wished she could take it back, erase any mention of her own troubles, but it was too late. In a little while he would make an excuse, and she would bring him back to shore, and that would be the end. Perhaps she had done enough already, and Alexei would not deprive her further of the man she'd waited so long to meet. Perhaps. A few seconds passed, and she saw how Jack was watching her. She watched him back. She watched him as the fragile woman she was pretending to be, and also as herself, and they briefly became one and the same.

He didn't speak. Only pushed himself up, took the dress shirt from where it lay, and carefully drew its sleeves over her arms and buttoned its buttons over her chest. Then he pulled her to him, so that he lay again in the curved bottom of the canoe, her body nestled in the crook of his arm. "Don't worry," he said eventually. "You'll find another husband. Any man would have you."

The sun was strong against her eyelids, and her hair was half dried already. Jack placed a hand on her head protectively, and for the first time she was able to imagine him as the father of a little girl, and knew that he had experience reading a child to sleep.

NINETEEN

Up in the air, October 1960

FLYING no longer troubled Marilyn. Especially this morning, when she left her bungalow and went, not to the United Artists lot as she was scheduled to, for reshoots of the movie that ought to have been finished by now, but to the small airport in Burbank, where she paid cash for a seat on a New York–bound flight.

What did it matter now? The movie would not be finished on time, and everybody already blamed her, with some reason. At the end of August she'd claimed exhaustion, been flown from Reno to Los Angeles where she checked into the Westside Hospital for a rest, only to use the medevac helicopter to return to the airport and catch a flight to Bangor. A blissful week had followed of meeting Jack in fusty New England hotels while he campaigned throughout Maine and New Hampshire. Shooting was shut down for ten days, after which her only friends on set were Clark (who enjoyed his vacation) and the simple-minded makeup girl.

The country passed beneath her in all its rough, gaudy texture as she traveled away from the life that had come to seem like a dream and to the place, and the person, that absorbed her true attention. She was not, she knew, the only one—the networks had put the presidential debates on television this year, and so sixty million or so souls had now seen for themselves, and in the comfortable privacy of their own homes, how much better that handsome face made them feel than the bushy brows and sweating jowls of the vice president. But the necessary secrecy about who she was to the candidate, and her own private motivation for keeping close to him, electrified the whole enterprise. As the airplane descended over the marshy, broken coast of the west end of Long Island she experienced the same thrill she had occasionally experienced at work, when her whole self meshed with the role, and she no longer had to strategize, or even to think.

She crossed the East River in a taxi and found Bill, as promised, at the far end of the bar at the Joy Tavern. His eyes scanned her from head to toe, and she was gratified to see that he approved of her appearance, even though her simple black crewneck sweater and slightly A-line skirt covered more skin than usual.

"Allow me," he said. She handed him her suitcase and followed him underground.

The Carlyle suite was changed from May. The smoke of many cigarettes, the volume of competing conversations, obscured the Victorian opulence, and the Oak Room atmospherics were further effaced by the extreme youth of the men who occupied the couches, clustered in corners, worked the phones. Bill disappeared into the crowd, leaving her alone amidst the hubbub. She clutched the wrist of one arm behind her back with the opposite hand, until one of the young men drinking Schlitz came to her rescue.

"You can't really be Marilyn Monroe?"

She glanced over her shoulder, as though he might've been talking to someone else. "Oh, yes," she said after a moment, letting the blush highlight her cheekbones.

"Will you have a seat?" He shooed another young man from one of the leather armchairs by the fireplace. He was long and gangling as a farm boy, and his lips and nose seemed too large for his face, even in dress shirt and suit pants. Despite his slender arms, he exhibited sudden, unexpected strength as he maneuvered the ponderous chair.

"Thank you." She beamed at him as she arranged her legs, knees close together, one bare calf draped over the other, high heels crossed.

He stared at her quite openly until embarrassment got the better of him and reddened that funny face. "Can I get you anything? A beer, or a sandwich?"

"Oh, I don't know, I—" Her lips were painted deep fuchsia, and she let them quaver over the words as she considered her reply. "Ordinarily I don't drink beer, but—if that's what everybody else is drinking, I guess it sounds kind of nice."

By the time he returned he was only one of many young campaign workers surrounding her, some sitting on pilfered couch cushions, others crouching excitedly nearby. "Yes," she said, as the farm boy worked the can of Schlitz with a church key. "Isn't it really exciting? That somebody so young and attractive and full of energy is going to be president?"

All around, heads bobbed in agreement.

"Thank you," she whispered, giving the farm boy a private, bashful smile for having procured her beer.

"But what are *you* doing here?" he asked, emboldened by the smile.

"Oh, well, we're old friends, Jack and I," she improvised. "We met through Frankie—Frank Sinatra? My home is here in New York, and I'm just back from the Coast, and I got a call from somebody in Jack's organization asking if I could give him a few tips for his debate. You know, like acting tips. Not that he needs it. He was wonderful in the first three. Don't you think?"

They all nodded.

"Yes, I thought so, too. But maybe I can help a little. I *do* work in a business where appearance is everything. And like it or not, that's true in the rest of America, too—appearances, I mean, they're so much more important than we like to think."

Hours passed without a sign of the candidate, and the boys explained various political matters to her—about the electoral college, and what genius it was that Kennedy had chosen Johnson, who would deliver Texas, about how their man didn't need makeup but Nixon did, and other political details to which she nodded along, assuming an expression of grave concentration even while seeming slightly mystified by their fast speech and rapid recitation of facts. When Jack walked in, the whole room sighed in happy relief, and as she watched him, walking amongst his acolytes with a blazing smile and focused eyes, his light blue shirt in high contrast to his sun-darkened skin, she found herself wondering why she'd been so silly as to think that she could be with a man because he was merely very intelligent, or merely very strong. That any of her husbands could possibly have been enough for her. Of course, Kennedy was both intelligent and strong, but he was so hungrily alive besides, and she thought that if she ever remarried, it would be to someone as restless as she.

"You should have seen the parade yesterday," the farm boy said. He wasn't looking at Marilyn anymore, and she didn't care.

"Must've been something, huh?"

"Hundreds of thousands of them. In downtown Manhattan, all the way to Yonkers. Oh, boy, did the women swoon . . ." He cut himself short, and perhaps it occurred to him that this was not a dignified observation of a presidential candidate.

"I'll bet." She winked to show him it was all right.

Beyond the fortress of shoulders surrounding the candidate, Marilyn saw Bobby, how his eyes roved over the scene, how he barked orders. After that the crowd thinned—the young men were ushered out the door, sent home or wherever they were staying, until only ten or so lingered on the stuffed furniture, drinking scotch out of cut-glass tumblers. Bobby was among them, and she kept overhearing little snippets of conversation, the word *revolution* a refrain in his conversation. She tried to look sleepy while she wondered if he were referring to Cuba, but then she realized that he was actually talking about television. The candidate was nowhere in sight, and none of the men in the room seemed particularly interested in her presence, and she was beginning to wonder if it was going to be another long night of waiting when the man named Bill appeared at her shoulder.

"Miss Monroe, the candidate is ready for your little seminar." His voice was glazed with a formality that might have been Southern, or might have meant to mock; and if he was being cute, she couldn't be certain whether it was to her, or the other men in the room. She collected her stole around her shoulders and stood up, proud and blank. To the rest of the company she may have seemed like a woman about to be led to a married man's bedroom, but she knew from long experience that when she appeared clueless, that made it difficult for others to sit in judgment. Yet as she passed out of the room, the quality in Bobby's eyes was like fire on a lake.

"Here," Bill said at the door of the bedroom, handing her a stack of pink index cards that had been softened by much shuffling. "These are prompts for the debate tomorrow. See he does some work, too."

She took the cards and slipped into a spare, masculine bedroom. The low rectangle of the bed was the main attraction, and adorning that was Jack, who held a newspaper over his face and wore nothing but checked blue boxers and a strange white contraption over his midsection. His clothes were in a pile on the floor, a navy suit jacket laying on top with its yellow silk lining exposed, so that she could see its print of tiny golden chevaliers.

"What is that," she asked, "some kind of corset?"

He put aside the paper and folded his arms behind his head. A lit cigarette wagged between his teeth. "Let's have a look at you," he said.

"Because I saw you on television. If you ask me, you're perfectly trim already."

"It's for my lousy back," he said, and when she raised an eyebrow, he waved away her concern with an open hand. "You didn't know? I'm the sickly second son, the understudy who got lucky." She must have appeared stricken by the gallows humor, because he laughed and said, "Don't worry, I have more fun than Joe Jr. ever did, god rest his soul. But don't you go gossiping about it with your hairdresser—if the Republicans find out, they'll smear me as a crip. Anyway, never you mind. Seems a lifetime since I saw you. Where was it? Houston, Miami? Come here to me."

"Oh, no." Her painted index finger tick-tocked. "You have work to do, and I'll not be the reason America has to be lectured by Nixon's grim mug for four more years."

"You're worse than Bobby. But at least I get to look at something pretty while I answer the same damn questions. I'll do whatever you say, baby, only take those clothes off first. You're dressed enough for Georgetown."

Her lips pressed together and her eyes shone and she did as he said. The sweater came over her head, the skirt down her ankles, and then, wearing only her black slip, she perched on the edge of the bed. Close to him, but not close enough to touch. She made a show of getting comfortable, summoning seriousness, and cleared her throat. "Quemoy and Matsu." She pronounced the two words unsteadily before breaking into giggles. "What are those, Mrs. Nixon's lapdogs?"

Jack laughed and collected himself, made his face unsmiling and presidential and adopted the clipped diction he used when giving speeches. "As I have stated several times, this is not an issue in the campaign. My view is in line with the administration's policy, and differs from the vice president's only in regard to his assertion that he would defend these islands, only two miles off China, from a threat even if the threat did not include Formosa and the Pescadores . . ." She nodded, seeming not to understand, as he listed with bland confidence his congressional voting record on the matter. "How was that?" he asked, breaking character.

"Oh! Well . . ." She bit her lip to summon the blush and turned the card over. "It says: *Nonissue* and also *Senate Foreign Relations Committee* and also *1958*, whatever that means. Anyway, you sounded convincing to me, and I can tell you from experience that half your audience will just hear a confident man saying big words."

He grinned. "Good. Next?"

"Fi-del Ca-stro," she enunciated carefully. She had meant to seem not quite sure of the name, but in fact her unsteadiness was more a hesitation to prompt him on a matter of such international intrigue. Any casual reader of the newspaper knew that Khrushchev had taken an interest in the Cuban revolutionary's nascent government—but then Jack's answer would also be pitched to that casual reader, to anyone with a television.

"Castro," Jack repeated, switching to his speechmaking timbre. "Castro is not just another dictator, another petty tyrant bent merely on enriching himself and a few cronies. He represents nothing less than a threat to the whole Western Hemisphere!" He increased his volume as he went on: "Why, the administration has allowed a communist satellite to gain unprecedented power a mere ninety miles from our shores. Cuba under his control is not only a potential site for enemy missiles or submarines but a base from which Marxism may spread like a contagion through all of Latin America. The current administration did nothing to combat the bloody and corrupt regime that ruled the island previously, and they have done nothing to support those freedom fighters who even now are ready and waiting to take their country back and make it safe for democracy!" He unclenched his fist, and a dimple appeared in his cheek. "What are you smiling about?" he asked in his own voice.

"Oh . . . it all just sounds so *serious.*"

"Don't tell me you like Castro."

She lifted her shoulders toward her ears. "He's kinda cute, don't you think?"

Jack pushed himself up on his elbows, and with mock jealousy exclaimed, "I certainly do not. You'd better not, either. Not while you're with this fellow. You made me sweat enough with Khrushchev."

She lowered her lashes. "You read about that?"

"Of course. That old peasant! Why'd you say that stuff anyway, about your husband sending greetings and so forth?"

She laughed. "He was on a tour of the United States, and wanted to see a film studio, and I guess I happened to be there that day, so the publicity girl had us take a picture together. And he was looking at me the way a man looks at a woman, you know? And I felt sorry for him with that big, bald head of his. I could tell he'd suffered in this life, and I thought he probably deserved to have a pretty woman flirt with him, just for a minute. And I don't know, Arthur was being a bastard probably, and I figured maybe the FBI would shuffle things around in his office if I said something like that. Anyway, my name ended up in the paper, didn't it? You're not the only one who knows how to get headlines, you know."

"I do know."

"Anyway," she went on, trying to strike the naïve chord again, "don't you think there ought to be more understanding between our countries? I thought you were the candidate who stood for peace and all that."

"Sure, of course I am."

"Then why all this big macho talk?"

The grin was back, and she could see that he was pleased about something and couldn't help himself. "It's a trap, baby."

"A trap?" she repeated innocently.

His eyes shone as he explained it to her. How the current administration had planned a secret operation to take Castro out and save the island from communism, and since it wasn't strictly legal they'd hired the boss of Chicago for the job. But the boss of Chicago was Sam Giancana, and he'd told Jack all about it, and Jack as a candidate was free to call for just such a strike, while Nixon, who had been officially briefed, was forced to remain silent on the subject. The end result (Jack told her with boyish glee) was that Nixon would come off soft on communism, while he looked tough, and meanwhile Giancana had delayed the operation until after the election.

"And then," she asked, eyes wide, "once you're elected, you'll call it off?"

The joking light had disappeared from Jack's eyes, and they became miserable as he said, "Well, one way or another, Castro's got to go." The quality in his face just then was as complex and inscrutable as a sky threatening to storm, and her stomach dropped when she realized that, for the first time, he had told her something Alexei might truly value. Not something that he would have found out sooner or later from another source, or in the news, and not just insight into the candidate's character. This was what he'd meant by *timely*, when he told her about Pilar Florist, the arrangement of irises, the children's wing at Sloan-Kettering. What Jack had just told her was crucial to the cause Alexei had given his life to, the cause his masters waged war for, and she felt crushed by the weight of this knowledge. But Jack, meanwhile, had brightened. He reached for her ankle, encircled it with his fingers. "So don't get attached—that bearded oaf can't be your boyfriend long."

"Oh!" she exclaimed, finding herself incapable of responding in flirtatious kind. When he revealed himself to her, her heart had gone quiet as a winter dawn. She felt suddenly protective, wanted him never to tell her another secret—wanted never to repeat his confidences to Alexei again—and without thinking she ripped the cards in half, and then in half again, and tossed the pieces in the air like confetti, laughing while they fell around them as though none of it had anything to do with her. Then she lay on the mattress, facing Jack, on her side. "You ever been to Cuba?" she asked, not as though she was curious about Cuba but as though she was curious about him and the things he'd done before he met her.

His hand was low on her thigh, traveling toward the hem of her slip, his fingertips gliding along her skin, creeping under the silk. His eyes were focused there, but they weren't really focused at all. "Sure. You?"

Hair fell into her eyes when she shook her head.

"It's paradise. At least it used to be. Those Spanish mansions in Havana, the narrow streets of the old town, the nightclubs, the way they dance. It's so humid at night the women wear hardly anything at all. You know I met Meyer Lanksy there, in '57, at the Montmartre? City smells like sex and money. You'd love it."

"I wish I could've seen it," she whispered.

His hand and eyes meandered upward, to the narrow of her waist, along her shoulder, where he toyed absentmindedly with the strap of her slip. "If I lose this thing, I think maybe I'll kidnap you. We'll go to Cuba and live in the mountains and wear fatigues and smoke cigars, and when we get bored of that we'll get dressed up and go to the Hotel Nacional, or look for Papa Hemingway at the Floridita, or listen to hot music and drink rum with sugar and mint on ice. I'd like to show you off for real, you know, in a country where they know how to appreciate a woman's figure."

All of a sudden his gaze met hers, and she returned it with a fearfulness that was genuine and an imitation at the same time. "But you are going to win this thing."

He blinked, nodded.

His eyes stared into hers just as intensely, and for a few moments she thought he might confess to her things he'd never admitted even to himself. Her heart was a hammer, comprehending what he might unburden to her, and she was relieved when he instead spread his fingers under her hair, against her scalp, dragging her face to his. Whatever frightful realization or desperate thought had been in his mind a second ago was in his tongue now. She felt it and forgot the reason she had flown to New York, and—greedily, and quite simply—kissed him back.

TWENTY

New York, October 1960

THE day she was to return to California she was awakened before dawn by the sound of an ambulance down on the street, and couldn't fall back asleep. Instead she waited for the deep blue of her bedroom wall to become diluted, and knew that though she was scheduled to fly west that afternoon, she'd be there only temporarily. The city was where she wanted to be, and once she realized that, she wrapped an old fur around her body and went walking. The predawn air chilled her cheekbones and enlivened her mind, and it made her happy to see, just by glancing at the windows of the apartments above, how many other insomniacs had given in and turned on their bedside lamps. A corner newsstand beckoned her with its neon glow, and when she picked up the early edition she understood why. She paid for a cup of coffee and the paper with Jack's face on the front page, and as she turned away she was reading about his campaign stop in Ohio, and didn't notice the cab trailing her at a slow roll.

She remained oblivious until Alexei called out to her, using his customary nickname, and she promptly dropped her coffee on the sidewalk.

"Never mind about that," he said, stepping to the curb and holding the door open. His shirtsleeves were rolled, revealing ropey forearms, but otherwise he was dressed as usual—elegant in a way that no one would remember once they were no longer in the same room. He made a graceful gesture ushering her in, and waited patiently until she'd done as he wished. Less than an hour ago, she had been asleep. Her limbs tingled like they weren't quite real, and she climbed into the cab as though still in a dream. "We'll go get you some more."

There was no meter in the cab, and the driver appeared in no hurry to arrive any particular place, and these facts dimmed the pleasure she had lately taken in her restless, yearning, all-night city. They were heading crosstown, and the streets at that hour belonged to delivery trucks, and she wished that she had thought to put a real dress over her slip before she went out walking.

"If I had known you were in town, I would have come to you sooner," he said eventually.

"It was a last-minute invitation," she replied, too quickly. "Spur of the moment."

"But you saw Jack before the debate." He glanced at her sidelong, warning her not to pretend otherwise. "And yet I haven't heard from you since. Did you forget what I told you? About Pilar on Second Avenue, the arrangement of purple irises for the children's wing?"

"No, I didn't forget."

"Why do I feel that you're avoiding me?"

She shrugged and looked out the window, at the heaps of last night's garbage outside restaurants waiting to be taken away. "*Do* you feel that I've been avoiding you?"

"You're leaving today, aren't you? It does seem likely you would have returned to Los Angeles without seeing me. Without informing me of your doings at all."

"I guess I might've," she answered carefully. "Nothing much has happened. Nothing of note."

"The big event is less than a month from now, and Hal had you fly all the way to New York to be with him, and there's nothing to report?" He exhaled, a sharp dismissal of everything she'd ever done for him. The driver pulled over—it was still dark out, and she hadn't been counting the streets, but she guessed they were in Hell's Kitchen—and Alexei's tone changed suddenly. "Ah!" he said brightly. "Here we are. Come up, I'll make you coffee, and we'll get to chat a little before you go."

Nervousness dampened her palms, the skin behind her knees, as she climbed the stairwell of a tenement building that smelled of cigarette butts and rotting trash. Alexei was close behind her. She listened to the heels of his shoes against the metal steps, sensed the width of his shoulders, and knew that if she fell, or switched direction, he'd block her way.

On the fifth floor, he unlocked the apartment on the street side of the building and stood aside for her to enter. "I'm sorry for not inviting you here before." He kept his voice casual and flipped on the lights. "Perhaps you will feel more comfortable, find it easier to talk, in my home . . ."

"Thank you," she said, stepping inside the small studio apartment and glancing around. The Murphy bed was down, unmade, a thick volume of the complete Shakespeare spread open on the sheets. Where a kitchen table might have been, there was an easel instead, and the air in the room was sharp with turpentine. "Are you a painter?"

His face slid into a self-effacing smirk. "Once, perhaps. I studied life draw-ing when I was a young man in Paris, and it was said I had great potential as a draftsman. That was a long time ago, of course. During my first years in the States, when I worked with Johnny Hyde, I posed as a backdrop painter at Metro-Goldwyn-Mayer, and when it became necessary to run my operation out of New York, I found that being an artist is good cover. Neighbors are never surprised when an artist keeps odd hours, or is gone for long stretches of time, or disappears for walks to nowhere."

"I see." Inside her coat pockets she made fists as she crossed the bowed, paint-splattered floorboards to look at the canvas up close. It was medium in size, all salmon-colored abstractions, the paint so built up that it made a kind of knobby landscape, although somewhere in the middle she thought she saw a nose, lips, heavy shrouded eyes. "It's nice," she said after a while. "Is it a self-portrait?"

"I suppose you could say that." The floor creaked as he approached, and came to linger at her shoulder. "I've been working on it for decades. But of course I have more important things to occupy me now."

"Oh?" She spoke breezily, but she knew what he meant, and her throat closed at the prospect of what came next.

"Yes. Let's have some coffee, see if we can't help you remember if Hal did—or said—anything of special importance. Wouldn't you like some coffee?"

"No thank you." She turned suddenly and walked across the room, almost to the entrance. She liked him, even after everything. Liked that he lived like this, and anyway she was accustomed to his protective shadow. But she reminded herself that he had not so much brought her close to her father as used the idea of him to steer her, and by then her heart was thudding, the blood coursing with such fury that she barely heard the words she did finally manage. "I don't have time," she blurted. "I can't stay. There really isn't anything to tell, anyway."

"What a shame." He flinched, and it seemed the color of his eyes changed as he studied her. "I was sure there would be. Nonetheless, I am glad you're here. I've meant to tell you how much Moscow appreciates your work. What you have learned about Hal, what you will yet learn of him, promises to unite our people. Strengthen our resolve. When the world sees that such a man—callow, corrupt, susceptible to blackmail, a hoarder of wealth earned on the backs of others—is so close to being elected leader of this country, it can only reveal our system as the more just. The system that shall prevail, and bring peace to the world at last. Already your intelligence has done so much, my dear. It is only the beginning."

"No—" Her voice faltered, and she wished she was gone already from that place. "It's not the beginning—it's the end."

"What?" He stepped toward her, his chin lifting to the left.

"I won't be telling you about Jack anymore," she blurted. There was no going back now, she told herself, no matter the consequences. "What he tells me he tells in confidence, and I won't betray that. I can't because—because . . ."

"Because?" His face was twisted at an odd angle, and his eyes were bright. Watchful. That pale blue you could almost see through, fixed on her, not exactly angry but no longer patient, either. They were eyes that didn't miss much, but she supposed his perspicacity didn't really matter. The way she was smiling, even through her fear—the sort of natural, dopey smile a girl just can't help—would've made the reason she couldn't betray Jack obvious to anybody.

"I'm sorry," she said, as she put her shoulder into the door.

"Oh, N.J." He sounded weary, and she knew he'd taken her meaning. He put his hands in the pockets of his slacks and looked away. Was he warning her, or overwhelmed with disappointment that he had to let her go? In either case, he didn't chase her when she passed into the hall and ran down the five flights and into the street. Outside, dawn had broken, and the puddles were iridescent with the first rays of morning. The cabdriver without a meter was gone, and she felt relieved to have made it through the night. The difficult part was over. As she pulled the fur tight to her body and walked fast toward the avenue to find a real one, she found that she was wearing the same wide, involuntary smile.

TWENTY-ONE

Los Angeles, November 1960

MARILYN had forgotten what it felt like, or otherwise she truly hadn't ever known. How the world yawned gently open; how delicious almost any kind of food tasted, so that just a bite or two was completely satisfying; how she could subsist on late-night calls and sweet water from the tap. It was in this state of grace that she lost twenty pounds almost without trying, and in the first week of November, when filming in Nevada was finished and she owed *The Misfits* only a few more favors, she went to have still shots taken for the publicity department, and her costumes had to be pinned. The wardrobe girl asked her how she'd managed to reduce so quickly, and Marilyn replied in the frank, tough-gal manner that had been in vogue with all the big actresses when she was first coming up, "Same old studio regimen, iceberg and uppers." But privately she thought: *Honey, there's never been a diet to beat falling in love.*

She cleared out the bungalow, packing only a few of the dresses that she'd bought or been given during her intermittent stays in California. The rest she sent to Anna, the makeup assistant, who had moved to Los Angeles with the idea that she'd keep working in movies but who had found herself rather adrift in a new city. Apparently her boyfriend had grown distant, and she was finding it difficult to get around without a car, and Marilyn—who knew the girl had remained loyal and defended her during the long months of shooting, even after every other member of the crew had turned against their star—thought that a box of hand-me-down gowns was the least she could do.

Even Arthur—who was taking a road trip through the Southwest with his photographer friend—no longer troubled her. They had mistaken each other, that was all, and she hoped that his life would be better now, as she knew hers would be. She figured it would be better to remain married until after the picture premiered—there would be fewer messy scenes that way, and she was less likely to encounter emotions that might dim her euphoria— and he had agreed to go along with the charade. On her last day in California she stopped in at a jeweler on Rodeo she liked, to buy Clark an engraved cigarette case, a thank-you gift for the patience he had shown her during those frustrating months when she had tried to make a movie and seduce a busy man at the same time. Later she was going to send a telegram—she didn't want the jeweler to read her private note—with the message: *Who needs a daddy when I've got you? Love, Marilyn.* She had called the ranch last night, and Kay had said he wasn't feeling well enough to come to the phone. A little gesture was the least she could do. But when she saw how beautiful and sleek the cases were, she knew she'd order two.

"And will you have it sent to the Carlyle Hotel in New York? Just mark for the penthouse, they'll know. As quickly as possible, please."

"What initials shall I have engraved?"

"Oh." The election was less than a week away, and she didn't think that anybody in America could see the name Jack, or the initials JFK, without thinking instantly of Kennedy the candidate. "Will you just have it inscribed *To Johnny?*"

At the hotel she went to thank Sal, who insisted on accompanying her out to her car, and she kissed him on either cheek and said, "I might be gone awhile, but don't forget me, promise?" He made a sad, earnest face and told her she could come back anytime. And as she rose through the clouds and drifted in and out of sleep, she knew from the way the other passengers kept glancing at her that even when she nodded off she was beaming. Ordinarily, strangers stared at her in curiosity or jealousy or desire, but now they just beamed back, as people do when they see a woman who glows.

"Isn't it wonderful?" she asked, gazing at New York from the backseat of a cab.

"What is?" The driver glanced at her in the rearview.

"Seasons," she said, as the East Side, in its crisp, autumn wholesomeness, flew by.

"And right you are."

For a few days this seemed to be all she needed. She walked alone in Central Park examining the leaves, the garnet and the ochre and other shades she'd never noticed leaves could turn, and listened to Ella Fitzgerald albums at home on Sutton Place, and smoked a single cigarette at dusk. She had never felt less lonely, and anyway, Jack was everywhere—she could find him in the newspaper or on the television whenever she wanted.

Watching the debates back in October, the day after she had gone up to his Carlyle suite on the flimsy pretext of helping him prepare, she had known already what this feeling was. She had known, too, that it was inconvenient, but the notion that she was in love with Jack had by then become fixed, bringing with it a pleasant gust of delirium, and she was certain that no matter what happened everything would be all right. It was good to know this feeling, even if it couldn't last. The way he had prodded Nixon into saying that an invasion of Cuba was not tenable, that the United States government could not support the overthrow of a Latin American government even if its leader was communist, seemed almost like a private joke between them. That was how he had told it to her, and she was glad that it was a confidence she had not betrayed, even if it had meant cutting ties with Alexei. Even though it had meant giving up her old, best dream. If she thought about that, she began to wonder how it might have gone differently. What would have happened if she'd called Pilar and ordered the irises, if that might not have given her sudden advantage, if Alexei wouldn't have finally rewarded her subterfuge. But she didn't think about it much—she tried not to, and anyway her pining for a father had lost much of its power when there was the promise of Jack on the line.

A delicate snow fell on Election Day, and she walked aimlessly just to feel snowflakes melting on the tip of her tongue. As she descended into the school basement, she thought only of Jack. How his every gesture seemed to say *Oh, what the hell*. Of Jack handsome in his suit across a room, of Jack's carnal gaze as he watched her through a car window and pronounced her both fox and hound dog, of Jack lying down in the hotel room wearing boxer shorts and his funny corset, looking like the prep school student he must once have been, dreamy in his weakness, yearning and a little goofy for everything there is to know. She imagined him like that, eating toast in bed, leaving crumbs in the sheets, and she loved them both, the sick boy and his vibrant creation; she even loved him for choosing a woman of such rigid sophistication and relentless chic to play his wife. Like a hundred million others she went into the booth to make her secret choice, and when she pulled the lever she thought *for Johnny*. The phone was ringing as she came through the front door, and she felt sure it was him.

"I've missed you," she said straight away, not wanting to waste breath on *hello*.

"Miss you, too," Jack replied. "Thanks for the case."

"It's a good-luck charm! For today."

"Boy, did I want to bawl when I saw it."

"Oh, I'm sorry, I didn't mean to . . ."

"Don't be sorry. It's just that nobody's called me Johnny in a long time. Not since Kick."

"Kick?"

"My sister, Kathleen. She's dead now, but she was my—everybody's favorite, I suppose."

"How did she—?"

"In a dinky little airplane, trying to get to Cannes. Right after the war. They were in a hurry, because they knew they were going to have to rush back to see the old man. She wanted his approval, you see. The fellow she was going to marry was divorced. Or would've been if he'd lived. Anyway, I'm sure you know pretty well we're all Irish Catholics here, and what does any of it matter now—she always knew how to make me laugh, is the main thing. If she were here now—" He interrupted himself with a sound that was like laughing but which held no humor. "Goddamn, am I nervous about this thing."

"I wish I were there. To make you laugh."

"Will you call tomorrow? When it's all over, I mean."

"Yes."

"I should go—I only had a minute."

"I know. Jack, I—"

"Yes?"

"Nothing, I . . . I just wanted to wish you all the luck in the world."

"Thanks." His throat had been worn down by the speeches and the late nights, and even through that, or maybe because of it, she heard emotion in even his blandest words. "Good night."

"Good night."

November ninth woke Marilyn to the soft hiss of a radiator and a flood of anxiety not her own. When she'd gone to bed the night before, the election had been too close to call, and the newsmen on the television had gone back and forth. At first it had seemed Nixon would win easily, but she had reminded herself how most people lived—that they had to wrench themselves from bed too early, that their days belonged to someone else, that they had to wait until the workday was done to exercise their own will. Those were her people, and she knew their votes would pour in for Jack as the night rolled on. The back-and-forth on the television made her nauseous—they seemed almost to be saying that nothing could ever be known for sure, and she was confused and annoyed by the numbers they kept repeating without meaning. So she'd gone to bed and slept a long time, but in the morning she was as nervous for Jack as she had been the night before, and didn't want to leave her warm sheets.

Then she heard footsteps in the kitchen, and went toward the sound. She hadn't heard from Alexei since the night he'd taken her to his studio, and this made her believe a little more each day that he really had let her go. But her faith could slip late at night or early in the morning, or after her maid had gone home, when every noise from the apartment above, every groan of the radiator, made her brittle with fear that he had come to mete out punishment for disobeying him.

"Arthur." She leaned against the doorframe, relieved, and pushed her unkempt hair away from her face. "What are you doing here?"

He glanced up from the kitchen table where he sat, legs crossed and absorbed in the *Times*, and she thought how though he was barely older than Jack, he seemed of another generation. "Just came to bring you the paper, and some coffee, and to get a few things from my study. I'll be driving up to Roxbury this afternoon."

She suspected that when he said *I* he meant *we*, but even this could not unsettle her, with her heart so otherwise occupied.

"I hope that's all right," he added indifferently as he returned to reading.

"Of course." She crossed to the table, picked up the *Post* and one of the two steaming paper cups. "They still don't know, huh?"

"No. It's going to be very close, but I'm sure that crook Joe Kennedy paid off the right people—enough of them, anyway—to get his boy into the White House."

"But you must have voted for him?"

Without moving any other part of his body, Arthur let his eyeballs roll upward, assessing her. "It didn't seem to matter much this year," he replied eventually.

"You can't want Nixon." She wasn't sure why she cared, but she heard herself going on: "When Nixon would have hung Dr. King out to dry, and it was Kennedy who lobbied for him, got those ridiculous charges dismissed? He would have gone to the penitentiary otherwise, just for exercising his rights as a man."

"And John Kennedy saved the day?" Arthur sighed tiredly and switched the cross of his legs. "If that's true—*if*—I'm sure he'd already tallied how many Negro votes it would net him, long before he acted."

"Does it matter why he did it? Dr. King might have been lynched if he went to prison down there. . . ."

Arthur folded the paper, put his chin on his knuckles, and narrowed his eyes at her. "Don't tell me you have a crush on him."

"A crush on Kennedy?" A murmured laugh escaped her lips, and her body softened. "So what if I do. I mean, what woman in America doesn't?"

"Are you done with that?" He indicated the *Post* and, without looking at her, took it from her hand. "Well, my money's on him, so you'll probably get plenty more of that matinee idol face on your television. But he's a political animal, a real chameleon—he'll say or do whatever garners the most votes, so don't get it into your pretty head that he *stands* for something now."

She nodded, but Arthur's focus was on the paper, so he wouldn't have noticed how this affected her, anyway.

"Perhaps he stands for himself," Arthur allowed. "Perhaps."

"Maybe you need some time alone here." She stepped away from the wall as she changed the subject. "I'll give you a little time," she went on briskly. "Enjoy the drive up to the country."

"Good-bye, Marilyn," he said as she whisked down the hall.

"Good-bye," she called. But already she was busy getting dressed, in a clinging black sweater dress and a fur coat.

She went to the Joy Tavern, because it held pleasant associations, and though she knew Jack's man Bill would not be there waiting, she still found herself rather disappointed that he never materialized. There were many reasons to feel agitated that day, and when she came home after two drinks she was glad to find Arthur gone, because there was no one to look disappointed when she poured herself a double scotch and sat down next to the phone to dial the answering service number her fingers had learned to do automatically some time ago. It did not matter that Alexei would not introduce her to her father now, she told herself—not when the thing she had gained was so much greater. She left the usual cryptic message—that he should call Miss Green at the New York office—and tried in vain to sit still. She crossed to the window and watched the street, expecting to see Alexei in his trench coat, or some associate not yet known to her, loitering on the sidewalk or peering through binoculars across the way. But there was no one—only a family eating breakfast in the apartment opposite, and housekeepers walking dogs in the late morning. A half hour passed, maybe a full one, and by then the scotch had slowed her pulse. She went to pour herself another and put the needle on the Ella record, which was the only music she had listened to in days.

She closed her eyes and let her shoulders keep time with "Mack the Knife," and danced with an invisible partner. Moving felt good, and it shut out thoughts of old hopes she'd let go forever. The music swelled, and Ella's voice with it. Marilyn didn't hear the telephone until its third ring, and she stopped dancing suddenly and glanced around as though someone might have caught her acting strange.

"Hello?"

"I have Hyannis Port for you," the girl said.

"Oh, thank goodness." She curled into the armchair and closed her eyes.

"Is this Miss Monroe?" She was startled to hear Jack's voice like that, so formal after everything they'd done together, but then she thought he probably couldn't find a moment alone, yet hadn't been able to resist calling her even if it meant pretending.

"Hey there," she whispered, her words like melted sugar.

On the other end of the line, the sound of a throat clearing. "Miss Monroe, this is Robert Kennedy. Do you remember me?"

Her back got stiff as she comprehended that the voice had only been very like Jack's. "Well, yes, of course I do . . ."

"As of this morning the Secret Service assumed responsibility for the safety and protection of my brother John. Do you know what that means?"

"Yes."

"That means he is the next president of the United States. Any number of security precautions have been, are being, implemented. Certain ties, certain activities, must be severed forever. Do you understand?"

Her head bobbed helplessly, though of course he wouldn't hear that.

"You're not to call anymore, Marilyn. He can't see you anymore. Good-bye."

Before she managed to say anything the line went dead. Very slowly, because she didn't trust her fingers to do as she instructed, she replaced the receiver. The white walls closed in around her, and her arms and legs were too heavy to move. There was nothing to do but sit, and reflect on the utter predictability of this denouement. The only thing that surprised her was how stupid she could be, after so much living, and how prone to believing in things she could not see.

TWENTY-TWO

New York, November 1960

A long day passed in which Marilyn did not bother getting dressed in any-thing more than her old bathrobe, and the whole world seemed to forget her. Then the telephone did ring, and she was so relieved by this proof that somebody out there knew she existed that she picked up straight away.

"It's me," Alexei said. When she heard his voice so brusque like that, she knew she hadn't ever really believed he'd stay away. But her mind was too sluggish with sorrow to register a threat. "Are you ready? To put this foolish-ness behind you, and get back to work?"

"No. I'm sorry," she replied, with as much emotion as she might have given an encyclopedia salesman, and put the receiver back in its cradle.

Another day passed in much the same way, except she thought a great deal about what she might say to Alexei when he called back—messages for her father, questions about where he was located. If her father was as Alexei had described him, if he was worth meeting, he must have some power, and surely he would eventually come looking for her. But none of that really mat-tered. Even if Jack didn't care anymore, still her heart wouldn't let her spy on him, although that seemed too tender to share with the member of a shadow organization, whose real name she might not even know. But when he did call back, she felt no desire to explain herself, and hung up the moment she heard his voice.

Then it occurred to her that, while Jack's victory meant he would no lon-ger see her, it had at least put the rest of the country in a jubilant mood, with an infinite appetite for news about the magnificent Kennedys, and how they'd pulled this miracle off, and what it portended for all America's futures. Nobody cared particularly about an aging movie star, and she might as well get the divorce announcement over with now, while the world's attention was elsewhere.

So she called her friend Earl at the *Post* and gave him the scoop, and then sent a telegram to Arthur that read:

Happy Armistice Day. Best of luck with your German. She certainly knows how to take a picture. Love, Marilyn

Afterward, she closed the blinds and poured herself the last of the scotch and got back into bed. She did little, and ate nothing, over the weekend, and might have gone on that way had her maid Lena not arrived with groceries on Monday morning. By then Marilyn had remembered how it was—falling in love will slim a girl down, but nothing finishes the job like getting dumped. Lena stood in the doorway, matronly forearms crossed over her cotton housedress, and sniffed the room—which did, by then, have the ripe odor of depression—and declared that she was going to make egg salad sandwiches.

"You know you got company downstairs, don't you?" she called as she retreated to the kitchen.

"What kind of company?" Marilyn pulled the sheet from her face and shivered, even though the radiator had been going for days.

"Bunch of reporters and photographers. They want a statement, about your divorce."

Marilyn drew her hands down her face, pulling the skin. Of course. Now she saw how badly she'd misstepped, how uncharacteristically witless she'd been. Love and shrewdness rarely go together; at any other time she would have known better than to make the statement before she was ready to put on a happy face, for the press never passed up an opportunity to see her sad. And then she realized something else.

"Lena?" She threw back the sheet, and tied the robe over her nakedness.

"Never mind about the sandwiches. I'm going out to lunch. Can you help me with my hair? After that, you can take the afternoon off."

An hour later she emerged perfectly made up, her skin powdered, her lips frosted red, her hair blown out and covered with a kerchief, wearing a black seal coat and no stockings, so that she could really feel the cold, channel that discomfort as distress. When she saw the photographers, she let her mouth open and she clutched her coat self-protectively with one hand, and with the other she feigned covering her face. But she didn't try too hard. The face was what she had come down to show them, and the whole newspaper-reading world, which, if she were lucky, tomorrow would include Jack. Once she knew they had their shot, she pushed through the clutch of reporters, flexing her brow and telling them, in a barely audible voice: "I'm sorry, I'm sorry." That low mumble forced the hubbub down, and then she added, "I am sorry—but I have nothing to say about my personal life."

There were so many of them, and they were so frenzied in their attempts to record anything else she might say, to capture any shed tears, that she had to force her way through, and on the other side she was grateful to see a taxicab idling.

"I hope you don't have anywhere to be for the next two hours," she said as the driver pulled away from the curb. "I just want you to drive."

But when she returned, in the middle afternoon, the crowd of reporters had only grown. There were maybe thirty of them clustered just beyond the awning. When they saw her approaching they began shouting questions, and she put her hands over her ears and ran past them into the building. The doorman held the door for her, and she made it halfway across the lobby before she saw the red lacquer vase full of what appeared to be two dozen black roses on the marble front desk. "Those are peculiar," she said, pausing by the elevators, to the doorman stationed behind the desk.

"They are for you, Mrs. Miller." He stood and lifted them in her direction. "A man dropped them off an hour ago. I am afraid I didn't get his name . . .

there was a commotion outside at the same time—one of the photographers was pushed, and his camera fell and broke, and it seemed likely to come to blows, so I went out to defuse the situation. In the confusion, I didn't see the gentleman leave. But they came with a card."

The envelope was ominous black, and her fingers trembled as she ripped it open. The sense of dread had already spread through her belly by the time she saw the simple ivory card stock with the thick black border of a mourning card. In elegant cursive—she did not recognize it as the handwriting of anyone she knew—was scrawled the message: *I am deeply sorry for your loss.* Her eyes were shiny with terror, her feet lacked sensation, as she turned from the desk and walked resolutely back to the front door, allowing the man in the dark green livery to hold it open.

"Miss Monroe! Miss Monroe!" they all shouted.

"Who brought the flowers?" she demanded. When nobody answered she shouted, "Who's dead? Who died?"

"Miss Monroe, will you give a statement about Mr. Gable?"

"What?" She had to grab one of the reporters by his jacket for balance, and she saw in his face that she had gone pale. "Not Clark."

The reporter related the news quietly. "He died this morning, in the hospital, of a heart attack."

"But they said it was just a little one," she protested, as though this were some trick that she could fix simply by pointing out its unfairness. She had heard about the heart attack from the studio, and had sent Clark flowers and a card telling him that he had better get well soon, because she expected him to take her dancing when she was back in California, but those had been the heady days before the election, when she had floated on thoughts of Jack, and the message that it was minor, and that he would make a full recovery, had been her excuse not to think much of it. But she could no longer pretend that those excuses justified her not calling immediately. "They said he'd be all right."

"I'm sorry," said the reporter whose lapel she was clinging to.

She leaned more heavily on him, and put her mouth close to his tape recorder so that it would have a chance of picking up her statement. "He was an excellent guy to work with and one of the few really decent human beings I have known. He was my friend." She would have said more, but she was afraid she might begin to sob, and she had to cover the gaping of her mouth with her hand.

The incessant clicking had ceased, although she couldn't be certain whether it was out of respect for her or Clark. Then a disembodied voice, somewhere deep in the crowd, cried out: "What do you say to those who believe his heart was strained by the prolonged shooting schedule of *The Misfits*, and that he might still be alive had he not been forced to endure long hours in the desert heat, waiting for that film's leading lady. . . ."

"Oh, god," she muttered and, fearing she might be sick on the sidewalk, rushed back into the lobby, grabbing the vase as she went, and jamming her finger against the button for the thirteenth floor until the elevator began, mercifully, to rise.

"Ah. There you are, my dear."

The vase slipped through her already unreliable fingers and smashed on the floor, shiny red shards scattering across the parquet, the necks of the black roses snapped pathetically, their water splashing her naked calves. She thought of demanding how he got in, but that would have been wasted breath—he had watched for Lena to leave, instigated a ruckus, slipped up the stairs, picked the lock.

"Oh, no—your flowers," Alexei said. There was nothing ironic in his tone, or anything to suggest that his concern was not real, but in the past he would have come to her aid immediately. Instead he remained in her wingback chair, his legs crossed, his hands calmly folded in his lap. "Now look what you've done," he went on, and though he spoke in the same level manner, she sensed the subterranean implications.

But the world, at that moment, was too meager and nasty a place for her to heed threats that did not possess the simple decency of making themselves obvious. She pushed the door closed behind her, and let a silent sob heave through her chest. "He's gone," she said. "Clark Gable's gone."

"Yes."

"They think it's *my* fault."

"But N.J.," Alexei said, leaning forward now and summoning the old, soothing way, "it *is* your fault."

"Why? Because I was late to set? Because I was off chasing Kennedy for you, and missed shooting days? Believe me, he was happy to be out of the house a little and stretch his legs before . . ." And then she realized that there was going to be another baby born without a father, and she couldn't hold back her tears. They came fast and salty, streaming unprettily over her ruddy cheeks.

Alexei smiled, but there was malice in his eyes, and a kind of satisfaction when he said, "You really liked one another, didn't you?"

"Oh, god," she muttered, comprehending what that smile signified.

"He had a minor heart attack a week ago, and was taken into the hospital for monitoring. But you would be amazed how dangerous American hospitals can be. Practically anyone can get in, and they are so full of medicines that, in the wrong dosage, are quite fatal."

"Oh, god." It was lucky there was nothing in her stomach, because she wouldn't have had a chance of keeping it down. "Oh, god, oh, god."

"It is time to get back to work, N.J."

"I can't." She was begging now, between the sobs. "I can't."

"I told you not to fall in love with Hal."

"Even if I wanted to, I can't spy on Jack anymore. There's no way back in."

Alexei scratched the skin behind his ear with a crooked index finger and regarded her, the way a teacher might regard a favorite pupil who has turned rebellious. "You will spy on him. You will find a way back in."

For a while she thought he might be preparing to say something kind, but eventually he just stood and walked into her kitchen. He returned with the broom and dustpan and carefully began to push the broken pieces of the vase into a small pile. While he cleaned up the flowers she remained planted, shoulder blades against the wall, afraid that otherwise she might collapse. Once the mess was put away he came toward her. She winced, her muscles frozen and her eyes clouded with fear, sure that a blow was finally coming.

But instead he scooped her into his arms and carried her to the bedroom, where he laid her down. He lifted her head to arrange the pillows, and then brushed the hair off her forehead. "N.J., my dear, you have no idea what you are capable of. Rest a while. You'll get Jack back—for you it will be easy. Things are so much easier for you than you believe."

She closed her eyes. Her mouth was dry, her throat constricted, and it required everything she had to say, "Why did you have to kill him?"

"Ah, my dear. To warn you. To teach you that your actions have consequences."

A small sob escaped her lips. "It was me you should have killed. Oh, god, just kill me. Please. There's nothing left for me now, anyway."

"Don't talk that way." Finally she did hear the anger in his voice. She blinked at him as he picked up her hand with both of his. "You are too important for us to—harm you in any way. But you must see that we are serious. You see that now, yes? And you cannot go on behaving like a child any longer. This is the real world, and you must sometimes do things you do not like. It is for the greater good."

She listened to the heels of his shoes as he left the room. Her eyelids sank shut—she was tired and stunned enough that she thought perhaps she would be able to sleep a little before the nightmares began. Then she heard him coming back, and though she told herself to rise, to summon some dignity, to at the very least sit up, none of her limbs obeyed.

When he returned he was wearing a long fur coat with a high collar, which somehow accentuated the dramatic curve of his nose, the cruelty of his lips, and she saw for the first time that he was a foreigner, that he came from a land of hail and wood smoke. They were not friends, even if he was carrying a fresh bottle of scotch. She could smell the liquor when he poured it into a low, round glass, within her reach on the nightstand. "If I leave this for you," he asked with exquisite patience, "can I trust that you will not drink the bottle too quickly, that you will not harm yourself?"

She nodded mechanically.

"No, I did not think so. Despite what you have sometimes implied to your friends in the press, I do not believe you have that in you. Now, mourn your friend, and remember that he was not your real father. Get some rest. Soon you will be going back to work. You understand what is at stake now, yes? And you—we have only glimpsed what you are capable of. If you put your mind to it, you can do anything, my dear. You can certainly win Jack Kennedy back."

TWENTY-THREE

Los Angeles, November 1960

AS yet Walls had resisted all his mother's exhortations to "smoke grass" with her and her coterie of bored, gorgeously put-together women friends. He had in fact never done any kind of drug. But he thought that maybe he knew what it felt like already, as he drove to work, merging from one surreally broad freeway to another, everything very fast and somehow also very slow. He was high on an idea that had first occurred to him in a bar in New York last May but had since coalesced and hardened and was now as simple and complete and gleaming as the truth. Marilyn Monroe, whose likeness his prep school roommate had pinned to the wall upside down, so that her bare legs were spread toward the ceiling, and whom he had thus for many years associated with the Clorox-like odor of that young man's side of the room, was an agent. She was an agent of the Soviet intelligence apparatus, and she was an intimate of the next president of the United States, and as far as Walls could ascertain, he was the only G-man who knew.

To think of himself as a G-man, even in the privacy of his own mind, had always seemed ridiculous and slightly embarrassing to Walls. It was an appellation of movieland. But, pulling into the Bureau parking lot on a cloudless November day that was just cool enough for him to comfortably wear the slim-fitting black wool suit and narrow black tie that his mother had given him for his birthday, he thought that it did have a certain hammy appropriateness. He strode across the asphalt, for once pleased by the sentry of palm trees, the convertibles in shades of yellow and sky blue, the Technicolor California-ness of it all. He had smiles for everyone. As he passed his own desk and proceeded, with two fresh cups of coffee in hand, toward Toll's office, he even winked at his boss's secretary, Susanna—whose legs were a frequent conversational topic, and whose eyes he had always found especially pretty—and decided that later he might ask her for a date. Then he would be remembered, at the Los Angeles field office, for two coups.

"Special Agent Walls." Toll's displeasure at this intrusion appeared to decrease when he saw the coffee in his subordinate's outstretched hand. "Thank you. Although I must say Susie Q over there looks a whole lot better bringing my coffee."

Walls glanced over his shoulder, showing his grin to the back of Susanna's shellacked, mahogany bob. "I'll bet."

"Glad to see you, anyhow. I imagine you must be a little bored with nothing but Marilyn to do—I have a new job for you."

"What?" Walls's grip on the paper cup loosened, and he was lucky to catch it before he made a mess on the wide metal desk, which was also a burial ground of paperwork. The venetian blinds behind Toll cast bars of sunlight across this immense bureaucratic topography.

"You'll be working for Special Agent Harvey. There's some organizing down on the docks in Long Beach that smells wrong. Here." He held out a folder for Walls, his eyes already shifting to whatever came next. "Your homework."

"But sir, I—"

"Yes?"

"What about Marilyn?"

"Walls, don't you read the paper?"

"Yes." This was the moment he had been waiting for, and he didn't hesitate in removing the folded New York Times from the crux of his armpit and placing it in front of Toll. "Do you see this?"

"See what?"

Walls leaned his hip against the desk, so that he could view the paper from the same angle as his superior. A story about Marilyn's divorce from Arthur Miller, with a shot of her looking lovely and distressed, ran beside a big picture of Kennedy, en route to Palm Beach, making a stop in Washington to drop his wife and daughter at their Georgetown home. The picture was of Kennedy deboarding his plane, his daughter in his arms and his wife ahead of him wearing a cloth coat that revealed her advanced pregnancy. The presence of these two items on one page of newspaper had seemed, to Walls earlier that morning, all the proof he would ever need.

Toll appeared less impressed, but Walls persisted. "I'll bet she's going to Florida, too, only there's no way for me to know that because I don't have a tap on her New York phone—"

Toll was shaking his head slightly, as though trying to knock water out of his ear. "Listen, kid, the thing I was hoping you had noticed in the news is that Kennedy made some announcements this week regarding his administration. He's keeping Hoover. So we don't want to ruffle any feathers just now. The Director doesn't need to apologize to the president if his girlfriend finds a wire in her chandelier, got that? We're friends for the time being— who knows what will change, and you've done good work, and I'd appreciate a detailed report with everything you have on Miss Monroe and John Kennedy. But let's just let this one rest awhile, you understand?"

"But sir, it's so much more than an affair—" He was furious with himself, almost disbelieving, that he hadn't managed to get the story out yet.

"Oh, yeah?" Toll had switched to heavy irony, never a good sign. "What are they—deeply, *madly* in love?"

"Toll, she's a spy."

"A *what?*"

"She's a Soviet spy. Did you know her first agent in town, Johnny Hyde, was Russian? He discovered her, got her nose and chin fixed, made her first big deals, and then he died. *Mysteriously.*"

"And he was KGB?"

"I don't have anything conclusive on that yet, but the Gent has mentioned him a few times, and the Gent is working for them. Of that I'm certain."

"The Gent?"

"Don't know his real name yet, but he's the one running her. I saw him in New York, at a distance, and closer in Tahoe, just for a minute. He was telling her how important she was to the people."

"The people?"

"Yeah, you know, the people of Russia. The workers. The proletariats."

"Maybe he just meant people who go to the movies?"

"No, no, I'm sure of it. If you had heard his tone, you'd be, too. And there's more. The analyst she sees in New York, Marlene Kurtz, studied in Berlin before the war with a group of Freudian-Marxists, and to this day she's on a list of analysts approved by the Communist Party. Marilyn met her through her husband's analyst—*also* a Communist. And you should have heard this thing she said to Anna once: 'A wise girl kisses but doesn't love, listens but doesn't believe, and leaves before she is left.' Don't you understand? She's leading a double life. That's what the Gent told her, or maybe even Hyde. How she has to behave in order to do what she does with Kennedy . . .'"

"Who is Anna?"

"Oh, this girl I went on a few dates with. She works as Miss Monroe's makeup artist sometimes. Anna is her real name, but Marilyn calls her—get this—*Anechka*."

"You dated her makeup girl?"

Walls—who during his morning drive had rehearsed a line of argument that was by turns exquisitely witty and daringly cogent—found his conviction badly eroded. He did manage an affirmative head bob.

"Agent Walls, this is the FBI," Toll said, hitting every syllable with weary exasperation. "It is standard procedure, when you are working on an assignment, to check in every two hours, and if you are at a lady friend's house, to leave her name and number with your supervisor. I saw no mention of any

'Anechka' while I was reviewing your file for Agent Harvey this morning. I am further alarmed—if what you are saying is to be believed—by your failure to file timely paperwork on the object of your surveillance, as much of what you are alleging does not appear in your weekly reports. But I am mostly alarmed by the fact that you might actually believe that Marilyn Monroe is capable of infiltrating the highest office in this country on behalf of a foreign enemy, when everybody in this town knows she is a bimbo who can't memorize a simple page of dialogue." Toll sighed and drained what was left of his coffee, before handing the cup over to Walls. "Throw this out for me. And don't share any of that with anybody else, kid. I'll just chalk it up to you losing sleep listening in on breathy nonsense, but others won't be as kind, you understand?"

Words had abandoned him. He wasn't even sure he could recite his theory now if asked—all he had was a seething desire to put his fist through plaster. "Yes," he did finally manage.

"You got that folder? The Long Beach one. And remember that this is Special Agent Harvey's job; you're just the office boy on this one." Walls saw the folder in his hands, nodded, and focused on the floor as he retreated, quickly as possible. His chest burned with shame, and he couldn't tolerate the possibility that if he lingered he might actually go red in the face. He had almost succeeded in leaving the scene of his humiliation when a sweet, feminine voice stalled him.

"Hey, Doug?"

He turned, nearly dropping the file. The two coffee cups, one full and one empty, were awkward in his hands.

Susanna was smiling at him with glossed, darkly pink lips.

"Yeah?"

"I just wanted to say you look good in that suit."

III

1961

TWENTY-FOUR

New York, February 1961

SNOW was falling, a white coverlet over Manhattan, turning back time so that cars stalled and disappeared and the skyline might have been a ridgetop through the blur. The city appeared for once a simple, old-fashioned place, but for Marilyn the weather only made her think of skiing, sledding, snowball fights, and scenes of happy childhood that belonged in the life stories of other people, and she took no pleasure in it. She sat with her feet on the windowsill in the room that had once been Arthur's study and watched it coming down, hoped it would go on and form big, impassable banks, so that finally the reporters who loitered outside her building would be forced to go home. They had abandoned her briefly over Christmas, but when she returned from her trip to Mexico (the purpose of which had been to obtain a hasty divorce), they had smelled blood and flocked back. In fact, there was blood everywhere. That same week, Arthur had attended Jack's inauguration with his photographer friend, and she'd had to marvel at this almost unconscious ability to go on spitting in her wounds.

"Telephone for you."

Marilyn glanced over her shoulder at Lena, eyebrow raised. She no longer hoped Jack might call, and she and Arthur had lawyers to communicate whatever needed communicating. Alexei she had not heard from since the day he'd come to tell her he'd killed Clark Gable. She wore black as she had every day since Clark's death, black slacks and a black turtleneck, and thought of his widow, who by then had made it obvious that she was not interested in Marilyn's condolences. "Who is it?"

"It's Alan Jacobs's office. They say it's important. Mr. Jacobs himself wants to talk to you."

Marilyn slowly put one foot and then the other on the ground. She had hired Alan Jacobs as her press agent because she trusted that he had her best interests at heart, but she was currently so indifferent to her own interests that talking to him struck her as a waste of both their time. "Okay," she said finally, and followed Lena into the living room. The furniture was new, hers alone, and looking at it made her sad.

"I have Miss Monroe," Lena told the girl.

"Hey, Al," Marilyn said as she took the receiver and moved to the window to see if the snow had thinned the crowd below.

"How are you, sweetheart?"

Marilyn rolled her eyes. "Grand, Al. I'm just grand."

"Those boys still hounding you?"

"They can't do much hounding if I don't leave the apartment."

"Sweetheart, that's no way to live. You're a young woman, at the height of her powers. Don't let old Willy Loman get you down. He's a bore! You were too much for him, that's all. We both know you're only getting started. Romantically, professionally . . ."

"I need a job."

"Yes, dear. But in the meantime why don't we give those boys a happy story, so that they'll leave you alone awhile?"

"What did you have in mind?"

"Sinatra's called you, hasn't he?"

"Once or twice." In fact, it had been more than that, but she had felt a little sick just hearing Lena say the name of Jack's drinking buddy.

"He's interested, Marilyn. He knows it would be a boon for him to be married, and he thinks you're the only one big enough for him."

"Oh, wonderful. That's swell. Really romantic."

"Marilyn—I'm not saying you have to marry him. Just go on some dates.

210

Get photographed looking lovely. Have some fun. You know what they say about his—*you know.*"

"About his cock? Yeah, Al, I've heard what they saw about his cock."

"It is supposedly very large."

She was silent awhile contemplating what, in the vast spectrum of her displeasure, she should articulate. "But he himself is an odious little man."

"Yes," Alan allowed. "But he's very romantic with the ladies, especially leading ladies. And there's none like you. So why not let him show you a good time? No strings attached. Just some nice stories in the columns, some pictures in the magazines, both of you looking sexy and smiling and happy. And if you don't like him, you let him go."

"I'll think about it."

"Did you get his gift?"

"The doorman called up about something, but I didn't really care that much, and Lena's been busy all morning. It's from him?"

"Yes."

"Well, okay. I'll have Lena bring it up before she goes home today, and if he wrote the note himself, and if it's not totally moronic, maybe—maybe—you can set up a date."

"I'd go get it now."

"Who gives a shit, Al? I've had roses before; if they die before I get to them, then it was their fucking time to go."

"It's not roses. Just go get it now, all right? And call me once you have."

"Jesus, okay."

Lena was in the kitchen, involved in the preparation of an elaborate lasagna, so Marilyn pulled on the first coat she saw—a white beaver that Arthur had given her when she first moved to the city—and went down to the doorman herself. She felt irritated and was already planning to call her P.R. man back and tell him that the gift had been inadequate, that she wasn't interested in Sinatra. The more she thought about his solicitations the more repugnant she found them. Did he want the reflected glory of laying the president's most recently discarded piece of ass? Or were he and Joe not getting along—was she a pawn in some ornate Italian pissing contest? But these thoughts melted away, and her heart fluttered despite itself, when she saw the wicker bassinet on the marble desk, from which emerged the floppy white head of a little French poodle.

"Hello there, friend," she cooed at him. To the doorman, she said: "How long has he been here?"

The doorman came toward the desk, and the dog scuttled around and let out several high, sharp yelps. "Three hours, I'd guess."

"Oooooo, the poor thing!" She lifted him out of the bassinet and blew him a kiss, but he only kept staring at her with those giant helpless chocolate eyes, his small body shaking slightly. "He must be terribly uncomfortable," she said, narrowing her eyes at the doorman. "Imagine if you were trapped like that for hours."

"I'm sorry, I— "

"Never mind." With the dog in her arms she proceeded across the lobby to the front door. The rabble of reporters lurched into motion when they saw her, and she paused for a moment, smiled brilliantly, and held the dog up for them to see. "May I introduce my new friend—a gift from Frank Sinatra— isn't he darling?"

The photographers raised their cameras. The flashes singed her eyeballs. Her smile went on and on. "What'll you call him?"

"Well, since he's from Frankie, how about Mr. Mafia? Maf, for short. Because everybody knows how good Frankie is at playing tough guys."

"Are you and Sinatra the new item?"

"Oh, we're just friends." She laughed suggestively, and the reporters, taking her meaning, scribbled on their little pads. "Okay, now you boys have something to print, how about giving this old girl a break? I'm going to take my new friend for a walk, and when I come back, I'd just adore it if none of you were here."

The poor dog was trembling in her arms, and she was sorry for having used him in this way. She pushed through the reporters, glaring to show she wasn't kidding around anymore. The ground beyond the awning was dusted white, and the streets were caked with the new-fallen snow, and she half ran across the street to get away, seeking some partially protected place for the frightened creature to relieve himself. "That's okay, darling," she whispered. "Tonight you're going to have real steak for dinner."

By the time she had walked around the block the little dog had calmed down and begun to trust her. She'd only said the thing about the Mafia to make the story juicier in the hope the reporters would be sated awhile, but she was beginning to think the name Maf did sort of suit him. In fact, the dog had cheered her up, and she was wondering to herself if maybe it wasn't such a bad idea to go on a date with Frank, just for show. Even if he was an unpleasant man, Alan was probably right that he'd be gentlemanly. Seeing him would mean a lot of slick parties, and perhaps it would be good for her to be out in the world, shake off her blues, have a few drinks and laugh some. These were the thoughts that absorbed her when the black car pulled up and caught her attention with a faint honk.

She bent and peered through the passenger window. As soon as she saw Alexei's face, she knew she ought to have been better prepared for this moment. He was smiling at her, gesturing for her to join him. With the dog snuggled under her coat, she opened the door and got in. "I thought you'd forgotten about me."

"How could anyone forget you, my dear? I've been keeping an eye on you, of course; I just wanted you to get some rest. But you've had it, and now it's time to get back to work."

"Look." She pulled back her coat, showing Maf. "A gift, from Jack's friend

Frank Sinatra, who apparently has the okay to make a pass. I've been handed down. It's over. There's nothing I can do for you, even if I wanted to."

"So you won't do it? Go back to work, I mean."

She shook her head. "There's nothing for me to do."

"All right, my dear," he said, slowing to the curb. They were arriving at a street corner, the car at a slow roll, when two men rushed toward them from a candy store and climbed into the backseat. The light was turning yellow, and she glanced around frantically, but by the time she realized that she should try to get out, Alexei had put his foot on the accelerator. She considered jumping, but one of the men in the backseat held down the lock as they sped through the intersection.

"She says no." Alexei addressed the rearview mirror and gripped the wheel.

Marilyn opened her mouth, ready to rage at them, to tell Alexei to pull over immediately, to scream for help. But that only made it easier for the man behind her, reaching around, to stuff a cloth doused with cloying liquid in her mouth. She struggled against him, but he held her face with one strong arm and pinned her to the seat with the other. Her heart raced, and then it slowed. Suddenly her shoulders felt heavy, and after that very relaxed. The dog was barking, high and sharp, and clawing at her chest while the world went dark. She started to tell Maf that everything was going to be all right, but then she remembered the rag in her mouth, and that seemed kind of funny, and also exhausting, and she decided that in a minute she was going to summon the strength to break the man's hold, but first she was going to close her eyes and get some rest.

Just for a second, or maybe two.

TWENTY-FIVE

New York, February 1961

THE dog was barking, and her heart was slow. The air was dense with the kind of cleaning product that is used in reform schools and DMVs and abortionists' offices, and other places people do not go by choice. She had to will her eyes open, but the glaring fluorescence punished the effort. Blinking, she took in the room, white and windowless, and knew precisely where she was. All psych wards, she guessed, look pretty much the same. She imagined her mother pacing in one of these, and wondered if they might seem rather comforting to somebody truly insane. Whatever they'd given her had put her out a long time; she wasn't completely back yet. Once she was, those walls were going to close in on her fast.

Was there also the smell of urine? Maf barked again, and she let her head loll in his direction, and she saw that he was sitting, primly, a little nervous, on a heap of white fur. "I'm sorry," she mumbled. Her throat was dry and chalky, and her tongue was swollen like she'd had a Novocain injection. "Ima gonna get you outta here."

A headache speared her forehead. She winced, and forced herself upright. The sudden movement upset her stomach, and she cupped her mouth but heaved only air. She took a breath, and put her hands on her chest, her middle, her thighs, as though to reassure herself she'd lost no limbs. The clothes she'd left her apartment in were gone, replaced by a mint-green hospital gown. Her toes were red, and this seemed a possible good omen, and she remembered that it was Lena who had painted them, the day before yesterday, assuming it was yesterday that she had gone out for a walk and been snatched by Alexei.

When she banged on the metal door it reverberated like a drum. "Help!" she called, but her voice was small and feeble. "Help me!" She rested her forehead against the door, and waited, but no one came, so she began to use both fists. As her panic escalated, her voice came back, and soon she was beating against the door with strength and volume she hadn't known she possessed. Time passed, and she had no way to mark it, except that she strained her throat and became hoarse. Finally the slot in the door opened, and a pair of kohl-rimmed eyes appeared. The nurse stared at her, and Marilyn's body sagged with relief over this proof of another human being. She put her palm against the door for support, and said, "Help me, please."

The slot closed with a bang.

"Oh, shit, Maf," she murmured, resting her cheek against the door. Then she raised her fist, slamming it repeatedly against the door. "Help me, you motherfuckers, help me!" She wasn't sure how long she went on like that, but she didn't stop screaming until the slot opened again.

"Marilyn." It was a woman, patient and detached as a physician, and Marilyn—hearing a voice she recognized—began to cry.

"Oh, Dr. Kurtz, thank god," she wailed. "Thank god, thank god."

"Step back from the door, so I can come in, all right, dear?"

Marilyn did as she was told, and Dr. Kurtz pushed her stout body through the partially opened door, which was closed and locked once she was inside. Her frizzy hair, a mahogany streaked with gray, was done in her customary pincushion style, but she was wearing a white lab coat, which was unlike any clothing Marilyn had ever seen her analyst wear before. She smiled with half her mouth and frowned with the other, and sadness passed through her eyes.

"Sit down, dear." Dr Kurtz arranged herself on the metal chair by the door as Marilyn retreated slowly to the cot she'd woken up on. "Now tell me, how are you feeling?"

"Like hell." The initial relief ebbed, unease taking its place. "I don't know why I'm here. But I don't belong here. You've got to get me out."

"That depends on you. Doesn't it?"

"On my being sane? I am sane. Sane enough to want out."

Dr. Kurtz crossed her legs and cleared her throat. "*Sane* is such a complicated word, isn't it?"

"No."

The analyst sighed. "I want to get you out of here. We all do. But first I need you to answer some questions."

Marilyn nodded, stared fiercely.

"Where does your mother now reside?"

"In the Rockhaven Sanitarium, Verdugo City, California."

"And how long has she been institutionalized?"

"Eight years, maybe. I'm not really sure." This line of questioning unnerved Marilyn, but she tried to remind herself that Dr. Kurtz was someone who had helped her—someone she had paid extravagantly to help her—and if she could just play along now, maybe Dr. Kurtz would get her out of this prison. "She's been in and out of mental hospitals for the last twenty years."

"And where are you now?"

"I don't know. New York, I guess."

"And how long have you been here?"

"In New York?"

"In this hospital."

"A day, maybe?"

Dr. Kurtz scribbled on a clipboard, met Marilyn's gaze. "When did you last speak to John F. Kennedy?"

Marilyn's eyes flashed. In her analytic sessions, she had spoken of lovers, but never of Jack. But she wanted to comply—wanted only to do what would free her. "November eighth, 1960."

"And what was the nature of your conversation?"

"Oh, it wasn't much. That was Election Day, and he was busy, of course, and couldn't talk long. We just sort of talked around things—he thanked me for a gift that I had sent him, and asked that I call him the next day."

"Is that all?"

"He said he was nervous."

"But you didn't call him the next day."

"I did—he never returned my call."

"And how would you describe your feelings for President Kennedy?"

"Oh, I . . ." The headache reasserted itself, and she began to massage her temples. There was nothing to say but the truth. "I was—am—was—in love with him."

"Ah."

"But he doesn't love me back. It's not my fault, I tried to keep him, but he's on to the next, or otherwise he's playing it safe now that he's elected. I don't know. He's married, obviously, and his life is so public. I was stupid to have fallen in love. Anyway, I should try to forget him now. He's forgotten me."

"We doubt that."

"We?"

"In fact, we know that is not the case. He has had dates with a woman who is also an occasional lover of Sam Giancana—our Chicago source told us. If she can get to him"—Dr. Kurtz paused to snort—"surely *you* can. Unless you refuse. Unless you've lost your charm."

Marilyn put her knees together and let her torso hang pathetically. The information that Jack had a new lover cut her, and the realization that Dr. Kurtz, in whose Upper East Side office she had replayed the story of her orphan girlhood, spilled her misery, was one of the people who had been manipulating her in secret, made her feel woozy and wretched.

"I won't," she muttered. "I can't."

Taking a fistful of hair, Dr. Kurtz yanked her patient's head back so that their faces were inches apart. Marilyn smelled the sea breeze of a tooth gone bad. "You will," Dr. Kurtz commanded with sudden, shocking violence.

A tiny, spiteful smile played at the edges of Marilyn's mouth. "Can't do much from here, Doc."

Dr. Kurtz released the fistful of hair disgustedly. "I will take that to mean you are at least theoretically open to behaving."

"Take it any way you fucking want."

Dr. Kurtz's thick, pudgy fingers reached out, grabbing Marilyn by the ears and slamming her head hard against the brick wall so that the world went black.

Marilyn dreamed.

They were the variety of dreams that announce themselves as such but are too viscous to rise through, out of, into waking life. And so she was held there, underwater, unable to breathe. She was trying to swim upward, but the surface kept receding, and somehow or other she reached the shore first. She dragged herself from the bloodred sea onto a beach. Purple seaweed was tangled in her hair, and the sand scalded her hands and knees. The shade was close, but also unreachable. Then she saw Jack, under swaying palms, wearing horn-rimmed sunglasses flecked with gold, his chest bare. Was he sleeping? She called to him, but there was a wound in her throat. Did he see her? Perhaps he sensed her presence but couldn't move, because of those flesh-colored snakes winding around his body. Then she saw that they weren't snakes. They were two lithe women, with strawberry blonde hair blown out and styled in high bobs, caressing him with their mouths.

When she reached him, he grabbed a fistful of her hair, and pushed her face into his lap, and she was grateful for the steadiness that came when he stiffened against her tongue. Seconds passed, or maybe hours, and when he pulled her head back they weren't on a beach anymore but in a dimly lit nightclub, and Frank Sinatra was on stage, wearing a fedora, snapping his fingers. And she, and Jack, and the two girls, were lying at the center of the dance floor upon a pile of mirrored and tasseled pillows. He pushed her away, into the arms of one of the girls, who wrapped her legs around Marilyn and began to run her fingers through her hair, to whisper in her ear: "You're so pretty, you're so pretty, you're so pretty."

But Marilyn couldn't hear her. She was choked with horror. The other girl was on hands and knees, and Jack gripped her hips, pounding her from behind, causing those big breasts to swing like water balloons. All Marilyn could hear was that girl's extravagant moans, the way Jack kept encouraging her, their ragged panting. Marilyn tried to cover her ears, but the girl whose thighs clenched her own body kept begging Marilyn to touch her. And the other girl kept wailing, "Fuck me, Jack, fuck me, Jack, fuck me, Jack!"

"Make it stop!" Marilyn cried.

Fluorescent light burst through her eyelids.

She blinked, lurched. But her hands were fastened behind her back, and she lost balance. The concrete floor met her face like a punch.

The sound was piped in from somewhere, filling the already claustrophobic room with "Fuck me, Jack, fuck me, Jack, fuck me, Jack!" And though he said nothing, she could hear him grunting and exhaling. There might have been a second girl, breathing heavily on the recording, but the one saying *fuck me* had decent range, so it was impossible to know for sure.

"Make it stop!" she screamed.

The door opened. Two sets of feet came toward her, and she was lifted backward onto the cot. The recording stopped.

"What the fuck is this?" Not in the orphanage, not even when she worked in an airplane parts manufactory, had her skin been exposed to fabric this abrasive. Of course she knew what it was without being told. Her arms were wrapped around her middle, tied in the back, and the garment was fastened with a crotch strap.

"You objected to our entertainment." Alexei was wearing the same clothes as when he had picked her up off the street—the slacks were rumpled now, his shirtsleeves rolled to the elbows—although he was clean-shaven.

"You had to be restrained," Dr. Kurtz, at his shoulder, put in.

"Your *entertainment*." Marilyn bared her teeth. "Where'd you get that recording anyway? Some rotten little shop in Times Square? You really think I'm dumb enough to fall for that trick?" She wasn't sure if she believed this or not, although her intuition was to argue with whatever her captors told her. Once she said it out loud, she realized it could easily be the truth. "How many whores in this town have pretended to beg some guy calling himself Jack to fuck them?"

"Does it matter where we got it?" Alexei replied. His soft chin was drawn back into his neck, and he was bending toward her, examining the part of her face where she'd hit the ground. It stung, and she knew there'd be a bruise. He knew, too.

"It was easy." Dr. Kurtz smirked. "He's a womanizer, you knew that."

"But why did you have to—"

"We don't want to hurt you." Alexei stepped back and crossed his arms over his chest.

"But we don't want him to hurt you, either." Dr. Kurtz came forward. "It is necessary for us to show you—remind you, actually—what he is really like."

"I don't like seeing you like this. So unlike yourself. So . . . disheveled." Alexei was speaking to her in that low, sweet manner, and she hated how she wanted him to go on, stroking her with kind words like he used to. "We want to get you out of here."

"But first you must see things as they really are."

"Oh?" She looked up blearily. "How are things, really?"

"John Fitzgerald Kennedy is corrupt, a womanizer. The figurehead of an imperialist government. You cannot be blamed for being won over by his charm—charm is his most finely honed skill. But you are too good for him, and we are here to set you right."

"N.J.," Alexei purred. "Don't you want us to get you out of that thing?"

This question provoked so many reactions. She wanted to spit on him, hurl herself across the room, tear at the straitjacket with her teeth. But a fear was taking hold that the only asset she really had, her beauty, would be ruined in this place, and she knew she couldn't go on lunging and screaming without doing herself harm. In the end she just said, "Yes."

"Then show me. Show me you are willing to cooperate."

"If you'd just let me out of here, I promise, I'll . . ."

Alexei strode toward her. "We are not just going to *let you out of here.* Some proof, an act of good will. Show me you no longer harbor these feelings of 'love' for the president."

She swallowed and closed her eyes. Panic seized her throat. If she stayed another night the dreams would get worse, and who knew what would become of her face. "All right," she whispered hoarsely.

"All right?"

"If I tell you, will you get me out of here?"

"Tell me what?"

The need to be free of the straitjacket was making her feverish, but she tried to keep her voice steady as she related what Jack had told her, the night she'd ripped up his flash cards. "This was before the election, a few weeks, I think, and Jack told me about an operation that they were planning for Cuba. We were, I guess. America. Or the former president's people. The mob was in on it, Sam Giancana and the Chicago organization. They're going to invade the island, assassinate Castro—"

Alexei snorted. "I thought you meant information."

"But that's—"

"The Giancana plot is off. Our source in Chicago, she says that—"

"Oh, your source in Chicago says it's off!" She was angry again, angry in a way she had no chance of controlling. "It's not off!" she screamed. "They were only delaying the operation until after the election. 'One way or another, Castro's got to go,' that's what Jack said. So maybe your Chicago source is bullshit, consider *that.* Who is she anyway, Giancana's third favorite Russian hooker?"

Too late, she realized she was right. Not only was she right, but the operative in Giancana's organization meant something to Alexei—he hated hearing her called a hooker. Then she saw the strap. An oily terror spread in her stomach. But she had been hit before, so she held his gaze, curled her lip into a snarl, braced herself for the blow and the darkness that followed.

"Wake up!"

A slap across the face, and she gasped and sat up fast into Alexei's arms before she could stop herself. She was shaking with fever and could not feel her extremities.

"There now," he said, patting her arms after she realized her mistake and stiffened. "Here, have some water, some food."

Her eyes rolled to him. His lips pulled back from his teeth, and he nodded reassuringly at the standing tray that had been erected by her cot, a glass of water and a plate with saltines and slices of orange cheese. She picked up the glass of water, took a tentative sip.

"Have something to eat."

"I don't want it."

"But you must. You need your strength. Come." Alexei took her hand and stood, pulling her gently to her feet. "Come, I want to show you something."

At first she couldn't believe that he really would take her with him, didn't want to let herself hope. But the door was opening, and he had her by the hand.

The hall was even brighter than her cell, and it seemed to go on forever in either direction, with metal doors like the one that had trapped her lining the institutional pink walls. A stern-faced nurse passed them, her square paper hat pinned in the curve of her chestnut hair, leading a patient the same way Alexei was leading Marilyn, with an iron grip of the wrist. The patient's hair was also brown, and might once have been neat and glossy, too—she did not look so old, or beyond vanity—although it was limp and stringy now and hung in her face. Her head was cowed, and her eyes were dead. She wore the same green hospital gown as Marilyn. As they passed, Marilyn glanced over her shoulder and saw the patient's robe was open in the back, and in horror she glanced down and saw that her bare ass was equally exposed.

With a shudder she turned, looked resolutely forward. No matter what they did to her she could not go dead in the eyes like that.

"Where am I?" she whispered.

"You're at the Payne Whitney Psychiatric Clinic at New York Presbyterian."

"You had me committed?"

"Your analyst thought it best."

Meanwhile Alexei had chosen a door, and with a gallant gesture urged her inside. Her throat closed at the prospect of entering another small room, but there was no one in the hall—no one to hear her scream, or object if he forced her—so she did as he wished. But the room was not a cell. In fact, it was decorated rather like Dr. Kurtz's office, with a Persian rug, two velvet armchairs, and a low walnut table where someone had left a carafe of water and two silver-rimmed glasses.

"Sit down, N.J."

She did as he instructed, trying not to flinch when the door closed.

"Have a glass of water." Dutifully she poured a glass, drank, and then refilled the glass. Opposite the chairs was a window covered by a curtain. "It's a mirror on the other side. To observe," Alexei explained when he saw her staring.

The chill started at the nape of her neck and traveled down her spine. "Who's in there?" she demanded.

Alexei gave her the faint smile—the one that mixed affection and amusement—and turned away. He flipped a switch on the wall, which pulled the curtain to the right and revealed a brightly lit room. Not the dim, warm light of the room with the armchairs, but rather the fluorescence under which she had passed—how many days now? There was a cot in this room, too, and a man sitting on it, his legs spread, his elbows resting on them, his head bent, his hands clasped together as though in prayer. He was not wearing a hospital gown but rather a denim shirt and denim pants, like a chain gang escapee. She rose unsteadily as Alexei knocked on the glass.

The man glanced up. He pushed his overgrown gray hair back from his face, and stood. He crossed the room tentatively, and his tentativeness created the illusion that his face was coming slowly into focus as through a camera's lens. She was glad of this—she would not have believed it otherwise. The face was so like hers she felt dizzy, as though she were uncovering some ancient evidence of herself, and couldn't comprehend having the mystery solved so suddenly or completely. His skin was thick, worn and creased with age, and his hair was in truth a light blond chased with silver, especially at the temples. The narrow button nose, the wide eyes, the cleft, well-defined chin were her own. When he reached the glass she saw that he was tall, much taller than she, so that she had to gaze up at him. His eyebrows twitched, and his brow folded, as if glimpsing someone he longed for in the distance. Then he began to smile. She watched that smile grow, like a piece of music that she was conducting. His lips quavered, struggled, and opened—that brave, hopeful expression of yearning to be loved that she'd perfected long ago.

"It's him, isn't it? My father."

"Yes."

"Can he see me?"

"Perhaps he can make out a silhouette. He knows you're on the premises."

"Can he hear me?"

"No."

"He looks tired." Inside she was soggy with tears, but she had a reason to be tough now. "Did you hurt him?"

"He has been awake a long time, but no, we haven't hurt him. Not yet."

"Please, can't I talk to him?" she asked.

Alexei was not smiling now. He flipped a switch, and the curtain was pulled quite suddenly over the window. With patient fingers, Alexei rolled down the sleeves of his shirt, buttoned them at the wrists. "That depends on you, as it always has."

Her eyes were bleary with hope, but he only stared at her impassively. "Tell me his name, at least."

"William," Alexei said. "Your father was born William Summers."

William Summers, she thought to herself. *William Summers, who are you?* It sounded just like the kind of man who would father a girl like her. If she were writing a novel about her life, that's what she would call the character who disappeared before she spoke a word. What she mostly noticed, through the one-sided window, were the features that were hers. The tip of the nose, the lantern jaw. But those were the parts of her face that had been improved a long time ago. And the way he smiled—it was as if he'd learned to smile from watching her in the movies. He was a fiction, which they had used to control her, and she was cold with the realization that he had never existed, and she was, as ever, the only one who could look after herself.

She clasped her hands together, to show Alexei how moved she was. "Don't hurt him, please."

"It all depends on you."

"Okay." She nodded, swallowed. Summoned that old determination, a little girl refusing to die. "Just let me out of here. Give me some time, a good pair of high heels. I'll find a way. I don't know how, but I'll find a way."

"Good." Alexei took hold of the doorknob. He inclined forward in a courtly bow, and she was suddenly afraid of being left alone, locked in a room, maybe forever.

"But you've got to get me out of here!"

"We have done so much for you. It's time you help yourself," he said, pointing toward a telephone on the far side of the chairs. "The nurse will be here in a few moments, and if you are good, perhaps they will put you in a room with a window next. Don't forget that we are watching."

When he was gone she sat down, tried to forget the days she had spent in the cell, the poor state of her skin and hair, the indignity of the hospital gown. Alexei had killed Clark, there was no reason he wouldn't kill her, or lock her up again. She would have to seem to go along with him, for a little while. Until she got her wits together, until she had her strength back. What had Kennedy ever done for her, anyway? She reminded herself of that girl saying *Fuck me, Jack, fuck me.* She told herself: *Honey, don't trust a soul.* Then she dialed the number that she used only when she was in real trouble.

"It's Marilyn," she told the housekeeper at the DiMaggio residence. "Can I talk to Joe, please?"

She felt a little better, knowing that in a few seconds she'd hear her ex-husband's voice and that soon afterward he'd come to her rescue. What a rage he would be in when he heard how they'd confined and humiliated her, the hell he'd give her captors. Or those who remained on the scene, anyway. If only she had been a little smarter or a little dumber, she would have stayed with him and been safe forever. But the anger always came for you, too, eventually, and you had to make yourself small to stay out of its path. You had to numb yourself pretty good to be a woman who belongs to that kind of man, and numbing agents only worked on her so long. As she clutched the phone and waited for the housekeeper to locate him, she began to cry, softly at first, and then with the sorrow of all her years.

TWENTY-SIX

Los Angeles, March 1961

NEITHER father nor son had spoken in a while. It was a cool, moist morning, the world sunshiny and shockingly green, and they stood in adjacent stalls at the driving range, careful not to observe each other's swing. They let the whoosh of the clubs, the hard thwack of iron against ball, the crisp whistle of white arcing through the atmosphere, talk for them. In fact, they hadn't spoken in years, and it was just occurring to Walls that they might have forgotten how, that they might never manage it again, when his father observed, "You know, I've always hated golf."

"Then what are we doing here?"

"Ah." Whoosh, thwack, whistle. "But I do enjoy *hitting* things."

Walls swallowed as he watched the ball soar over the markers, beyond the fence, disappearing against the backdrop of the hills. The elder Walls struck a match and exhaled smoke into the clean air.

"Cigarette?"

"Thanks." Since last May, when in the line of duty he had found it necessary to smoke, Walls had learned a lesson about habits, which is that even when they begin in fakery they often become real soon enough. He would have accepted the cigarette even if that were not the case. He was a natural athlete, possessed of a powerful, precise swing, but he found himself childishly averse to the possibility that he might not be able to hit the next ball as far as his father had, and was grateful for the excuse of a break. He considered asking his father what had brought him west, how long he had been there, if this visit was the main reason or an afterthought, but instead took a silent drag.

"Mo's husband has some fancy gear." Jutting his jaw, the older man indicated the borrowed clubs.

"He never uses them."

"Ah." The elder Walls leaned against the concrete partition that separated the stalls, his strong shoulders covered in a collared shirt made from a thin, embroidered white fabric. The shirt seemed to indicate a life of travel, a penchant for taking it easy, but there was a twitching, unsettled quality in the veins of his neck. "Think there's someplace to get a beer around here?"

The son, relieved, answered that indeed there was.

"So," the father said, after the girl had delivered their second round, "how are things at the Bureau?"

That he had held this question until the first beer had time to hit the bloodstream made Walls believe that perhaps they might understand one another after all. "Not good," he answered simply, having concluded that there was no manful way to evade the question.

"No?" His father sipped his beer and squinted. "Why is that?"

"I'm on some other agent's case, and I just get in the way. He'd happily be rid of me; they all would. The case I was working before—I had the wrong idea about it, and I made a fool of myself."

"How's that?"

Walls sighed. "I got the Marilyn beat—"

"Marilyn Monroe?"

"Yes." Walls tried not to cringe when he saw how his father took this. "The Director likes his Hollywood gossip, I guess, and there was the pretext that her last husband was a leftist. I thought it was pretty weak myself. But then once I'd listened to god knows how many hours of her phone conversations, observed the way she comes and goes, I started seeing patterns. Thought I figured something out, I guess. You'll laugh, but my theory was she was working for the Russians. Spying."

His father did not laugh. He took a pull of his beer, and glanced at the waitress, who was across the room, flirting with the youth behind the bar. "What made you think that?"

"Little things at first—in hindsight, too little. She used a Russian diminutive for her makeup girl, and she sees a Marxist psychiatrist. But it was more than that. It was the way she talked about herself, like she was two people almost, one of them steering the other. Anyway, she was having an affair with Kennedy, and the way she described the affair, it was like a military campaign. That much calculation, that much precision."

"She talked about the affair with her friends?"

"Just one—a man I call the Gent."

"What's his real name?"

"No idea. I saw him once in New York and again in a men's room in Tahoe. They were together, in a heated discussion, and he kept talking about how important she was to 'the people.'"

"Do you have a picture of him?"

Walls regarded his father a few moments before shaking his head.

"You should try to get one."

"But it was all just a lunatic theory I had. She's not a spy, she couldn't be. She's insane."

"What makes you think that?"

Walls swallowed some beer before relating a story that he still found inexplicably painful. "She was committed—just spent twenty-three days in a psych ward in New York. Had to call Joltin' Joe to spring her. She just likes talking nonsense. Or talking about herself. Which is the same thing. And I was just the unlucky man who tried to piece it together."

During the ensuing silence, Walls had time to contemplate his father's success at cards and with women; even his pauses were only blank invitations to second-guess oneself. Eventually he said, "Is she still seeing Kennedy?"

Walls shrugged. "Hard to tell—I don't have any evidence that the affair continued after the election."

"If you were Kennedy, would you still want to see her?"

Walls stared into his beer, considering the many ways this question might be answered, wanting to be professional, and instead saying, "Yes."

The elder Walls sighed, as if this somehow solved the riddle, drained his beer, and waggled it at the waitress. "You always liked secrets, you know."

"Me?"

"Who else would I be talking to? When you were little, I mean. You used to collect things—do you remember that trip we took to Montana? To hunt elk."

"I was ten."

"Yes, you were too young. I see that now. In any case, Claudette, who was my lady friend that year, she met us at the lodge, and her things kept disappearing. Old theater tickets, lipsticks, panty hose, that kind of thing. For a while, I was afraid you were queer."

"I am not—"

"Oh, I know." His father chuckled, looking at him significantly while the waitress arranged their fresh beers on the table and removed the old glasses. "You just wanted to know what other people did behind closed doors," he went on, when they were alone again. "You might have gotten that from me. Or from your mother. It occurs to me that you were not born to particularly loving parents," he went on, irrelevantly. He said this without apology, as though informing his son that he had not been born to parents who were particularly mathematical. "D.W., I've been pondering something."

"Yeah?"

"Why did you join the Bureau?"

Walls could have spoken, not dishonestly, of the desire to keep innocent people safe, or the wanting to belong to a fraternity of able-bodied men of purpose, but that sort of talk did not seem to belong in their afternoon, so he shrugged and gave his father a sly smile. "Well, Dad, I do enjoy hitting things."

"Oh, sure. Sure. But what made you choose the Bureau? Rather than the Company, I mean."

Walls tried to shift his gaze to his father without moving his head. Men of his upbringing with a mind for clandestine doings did usually end up at the CIA, and he liked to tell himself that this was why he had been attracted to the Bureau. "Well, to begin with I wasn't recruited," he said instead.

"Ah." His father lit another cigarette, and stretched his legs out on an adjacent chair. "Have you read the James Bond novels?"

"Lou has them all."

"Roguish Brit agent jets to exotic locales, does battle with the unspeakably evil, has much fun, beds many beauties."

"I skimmed them," Walls conceded.

"Yes." The elder Walls knocked the ash from his cigarette. "Then you are no doubt aware the author, Mr. Ian Fleming, knows a little of what he writes. Worked for British Naval Intelligence during the war, et cetera, et cetera. As it happens, your new president is a fan." Walls wasn't sure why Kennedy should be his president and not his father's, but he could see the old man was waxing into the warm timbre of expertise, so he only nodded subtly for him to go on. "Such a fan that he invited him to one of his swanky Georgetown dinner parties. Fidel Castro was in the news at the time, and Senator Kennedy—this wasn't long ago, but he was still Senator Kennedy—was fascinated by the rebel leader, wanted to know everything about him. Asked what Fleming would do to depose him. Well, Fleming was rather drunk, and never passes up a challenge, and he floated several highly literary ideas, ideas quite worthy of his Bond character, in fact. Operation Ridicule, he called it—they'd slip him an explosive cigar, for instance, or convince his mistress to rub depilatory lotion in his beard so that it would fall out, revealing to the Cuban populace what a boy he was, and thus undermining their faith in him. The Georgetown set enjoyed the show quite a bit. The next day, when Fleming was packing for his flight to Jamaica, he got a call from one of the guests—a crony of Kennedy's, one of those Skull and Bones types who came up through OSS—who wondered if Fleming wouldn't come out to Langley and go over the details of some of those plans with him."

"How do you know all this exactly?" Walls asked, breaking the unspoken contract that he listen to his father's tales without drawing attention to their more elliptical points.

"Ah, well." Walls's father got another cigarette going with the butt of his last one. "Fleming and I have known each other a long time, from here and around. He's quite a card player, as it happens. But you understand what I'm saying, don't you?"

The beer was making Walls feel good finally, and the shame over his bold failure with the Marilyn file was ebbing. What he had once regarded as his father's elegant reticence was, in light of day, just overblown romanticism. "What *are* you saying?"

His father waved his hand, as though the people they had been discussing were arrayed before them on the golf course, and were only awaiting his cue to begin acting out the scene he had described. "The mechanism by which nations hold and exert power is more bizarre than you could possibly imagine, and at the same time simpler, smaller, stupider. It would not surprise me in the least if Marilyn Monroe were a spy. For one thing, it would explain how she manages to be so famous while making so many fewer movies than all the other voluptuous blondes in Hollywood. The Nazis tried something similar, you know, and with the same man—sent over one of Hitler's girlfriends on the hunt for naval information, and guess who she goes to bed with?"

Walls's mouth was dry. "Kennedy."

"Right—of course, he was only the second princeling in line for the throne then. Most spies are idealists, rogues, showmen, or some mixture of all three, their schemes far more outrageous than the stuff you find in novels. The outrageousness of an operation, in my experience, has nothing whatsoever to do with its success or failure."

Both Wallses glanced up when a group of men fresh from a game came into the restaurant and began a flirtatious exchange with the waitress about which of the many unoccupied tables was the best. The son was thinking how little he knew about his father, and was trying to figure the best way to begin asking him where his information really came from; but the father drained his beer and stood to leave.

"I should be getting back," he said, turning toward the waitress and motioning that he was ready to pay.

Get back where? Walls thought. But he said only, "This one's on me."

Wes Walls smiled and clapped his son on the back as they made their way to the parking lot. "Thanks, D.W. We'll do it again soon."

The sun was at its highest point, and they stood awkwardly for a moment on the asphalt, squinting. "It was good to see you, Dad."

"You, too, D.W."

Walls slung his stepfather's clubs into the trunk, and turned to shake his father's hand. They shook, smiled at each other, and then the older man began to amble back to his own car, his limp slowing him only slightly. The sky was an unyielding blue, the parkland spread around them, birds sang to their fledglings. At that moment it was hard to believe that somewhere out there in the vast unknown people were listening in while other people made adulterous love or agitated for social upheaval. "Thanks, Dad," he called as he put the key in the ignition.

His father paused and glanced back at him. "Of course, son. Oh, and D.W.?"

"Yes?"

"Don't be embarrassed to use your mother's connections." His mouth twitched mischievously, and he shrugged and opened his palms as though to say, *who can blame me for being just as I am?* "I never was."

TWENTY-SEVEN

New York, April 1961

MARILYN sprawled across the couch in the Copacabana dressing room, the spaghetti straps of her black dress doing their best to contain her décolletage. She hadn't bothered with a bra that evening, and she had a few drinks in her already, and she was feeling loose. Frank, seated at the dressing table mirror, his pockmarked skin forgiven by that row of sweet, soft bulbs, was being attended to by five or so hair and makeup people. He himself was wielding the comb, so fiercely that she feared for the rug he wore. No one was paying much attention to her, happily, and she surreptitiously refilled her champagne flute with the champagne-colored combination of bourbon and soda water. Tonight was a night to be well oiled.

An assistant rapped on the door and poked his head in. "Five minutes," he said.

"Okay, sweetheart." Frank met her eyes in the mirror. "Get out there where people can see you."

A daffy, indistinct smile wavered on her lips as she draped her long white fur around her shoulders, plucked her champagne flute from the glass table, and brushed a few strands of peroxided plumage out of her eyes. "Play 'Luck Be a Lady,' for me, will you?" she asked as she moved to the door.

"You got it, baby," he said, twirling in the chair to admire her and letting his hand land with a smack on her black-silk-encased ass.

She waggled her glass at him, and allowed his valet, George, to take her arm and guide her through the wallpapered corridors and into the main room of the nightclub. The table Frank had reserved for her was just under the lip of the stage—he'd planned that, so that people would see her, right in the middle of his swinging tableau, and wonder whether she slept in his bed. She knew she should oblige, especially since she had gone along with Alan Jacobs's proposal while thus far managing not to put out. She had waited until Joe returned to San Francisco, but he must know by now with whom she was being seen around town, a lousy reality that she tried not to dwell on. These days she was only trying to survive, anyway—trying to get close enough to Jack again that Alexei wouldn't lock her up—so who cared what anybody thought of her.

She knew George had been instructed to deposit her at the front and center table, but when she saw the crowd she tugged at his arm and gave him a shy, fearful face. This wasn't difficult—she was afraid all the time, and she knew she was being watched by Alexei's people, and so appeared always tentative, out of it, lost. She hoped that Alexei noticed that she was clearing a path back to the president, too, and that this would buy her time to figure out her next move. That he wouldn't hurt her, or anybody else, as long as she was hanging around Jack's people. "George," she whispered, "sit me over there with the Lawfords, would you? I can't stand being alone tonight."

He hesitated a while, but she clung to his arm so desperately that he had no choice. "You better make him happy later, so he forgets to fire me." He gave in, and led her to a less conspicuous table with a white tablecloth and a small lamp at its center. As she followed along, Marilyn dangled her finger-tips at people she didn't know, and smiled her red smile, giving them what Frank wanted, which was the illusion that a Sinatra concert meant entrée into a special realm of nicotine and liquor and midnight urges, where goddesses might show up unannounced.

"Mrs. Lawford—" George began.

The woman with the russet hair glanced up at the valet, revealing a face more handsome than pretty. At the party she had hosted—for her brother, after he won the nomination last summer—she had seemed only one of many sisters, but Marilyn had since singled her out as a likely friend, the best way back into his life. Just looking at her conjured Jack: the arrangement of her features, the aristocratic mouth and the short, unobstructed forehead, the easy way she had of hanging expensive clothes on a slim frame. Like Marilyn, Pat wore a black cocktail dress, although hers involved a great deal more fabric in the skirt and at the neckline. "George, must we continue with this rigmarole? I've told you a thousand times. Call me Pat, darling."

"Pat, may I introduce you to Miss Marilyn Monroe? She's Frank's special guest this evening, and he was hoping you two would look after her."

"Of course, George." A scarlet, thin-lipped smile came and went from Pat's face, seemingly without the effort of any other facial muscle, and then she shifted her attention. "What a pleasure to meet you! I can't tell you how excited Peter and I are to see *The Misfits*. Please, won't you join us?"

"Thank you," Marilyn replied tentatively, lowering herself into the chair that George held out for her. On Pat's other side sat Peter, his dark brows knit together, mouthing to himself, an anxious concentration freezing up his features, which was an expression Marilyn knew well. "Hello there, Peter," she called, and he glanced over, as though surprised, and quickly grabbed her hand to kiss her knuckles.

"Stage fright." Pat rolled her eyes. "Don't worry, he'll be better company after he does his bit."

"Oh, well . . ." A smile flickered at one corner of Marilyn's mouth, and she exhaled a melancholy breath. "*Salud*, I guess." She raised her champagne flute, and Pat met it with her old-fashioned, and they both drank. "Actually, you've hosted me before," she went on, as though just remembering. "I should probably thank you for that, too. Last summer, out in Santa Monica, during the convention. What a party that was."

"Oh, yes." Pat hooked the elbow of her slender, freckled arm over the backrest of her chair, twisting to face the newcomer more fully. "I remember seeing you across the room. I would have loved to talk to you, but that was quite a week for my family, as you can imagine. I was barely home myself—Mother and Father had a place in Beverly Hills, and of course we had rooms downtown, too. The party went on at the beach pretty much all week, and I confess I had to go elsewhere just to get some rest. Quite a few people drank too much to get home and had to stay the night, and the next night, too. But that's why we keep that house, you know. Peter and I, we love company."

"It's a beautiful house," Marilyn whispered, as though a house were a wonder not quite to be believed.

"Thanks, darling. You should see the one my family keeps in Palm Beach. Have you ever been to Palm Beach?"

Marilyn shook her head.

"You must come sometime." If Marilyn had believed this, then she might have taken it as a sign that her troubles would soon be over, but the way Pat shrugged and glanced away, removing a cigarette from an ivory case and fixing it into a silver cigarette holder, made her think that this was just the sort of empty invitation she issued to let people know that she liked them. It made sense that she alone amongst her siblings had married into Hollywood. Her regal posture, the way she inhabited her surroundings, her unconcealed indifference to the nervous husband beside her—now being called onto stage—suggested a proclivity for contentment.

A smattering of applause traveled across the nightclub, and then the lights dimmed, and everyone hushed while the cone of the spotlight illuminated Peter's charming, rueful face. "Ladies and gentleman, welcome to the Copacabana. I am here to introduce a man who needs no introduction. And yet I will say a few words . . ."

Marilyn focused her attention stageward, as she assumed Pat would until her husband stepped down. But Pat, uninterested in the mild palaver Peter was warming up the crowd with, inclined her head toward Marilyn and said, "I'm so awfully glad you sat with us. You know these boys can be such a bore when they get together; it's nice to have another girl along for the ride."

Marilyn beamed and snuggled against her fur. "Well, it's nice for me, too."

"Are you and Frank the new item?"

"Oh, I don't know about that, we're more just like—"

"I don't care what goes on behind closed doors, darling, I really don't. I'm sure Frankie is a terrible pain. But stick around, would you? We'd have *such* fun."

"Thanks." Finally Marilyn was beginning to relax, and when the waiter came by she didn't bother explaining what was in her glass, and whispered, "Just a little champagne, if you have it, please."

The room had meanwhile applauded as Frank swaggered to center stage, and he and Peter began laughing, shifting on their feet, lightly snapping their fingers, ribbing each other in a way that she supposed was meant to be good-natured. After a while Peter retreated to a stool in the shadow, and Frank advanced toward the microphone with his boxer's intensity. For a moment he gazed steadily into the far back reaches of the club, and then he cleared his throat and said, "This first number is for a good friend of mine who just so happens to be gracing us with her presence tonight, Miss Marilyn Monroe . . ."

A drumroll sounded as he gestured toward the empty table in the front row, and the spotlight drifted in the direction he'd indicated. His upper lip tensed when the spotlight showed only an empty seat. Marilyn, swallowing her dismay, put two fingers in her mouth and whistled. "Frankie!" she stage-whispered. "Over here!"

The spotlight found her, and she stood and lifted her white whip of an arm so the audience could see her figure, which inspired much clapping and cat-calling. Once she sat down, and the attention of the room was focused once again on Frank, he chuckled as though her unpredictability hadn't bothered him. "That dame's never where she says she'll be, but who can blame a guy for following her around. Am I right?"

The room noisily agreed, and then the string section started up, and

Frank leaned into his microphone, stretching out the syllables of the half-sung, half-shouted opening line of "Luck Be a Lady."

The music washed over Marilyn, who was glad that neither Sinatra nor anybody else was looking at her any longer, and she sat back and happily accepted the champagne that the waiter brought. There was another old-fashioned for Pat, too, and this time it was the Kennedy sister who offered her glass to cheers. Then she draped an arm over Marilyn's shoulders, and Marilyn realized she was shaking with silent laughter. "That was to die for," she whispered, between giggles. "Did you see the look on Frankie's face?"

"He's gonna be mad later," Marilyn whispered back.

"Who cares? Stick with me, darling, he won't show his temper when I'm around. He's too proud of being the president's friend to be a bastard in front of anybody who's got Jack's private line."

Up on stage, the rhythm had picked up, and Frank's singing had grown full and flowing. He blew on a fistful of imaginary dice, and tossed them into the audience—it was one of those theatrical moves from the big band days. But she couldn't really laugh at him, only reflect that he was lucky to have that voice.

He was singing about luck as though luck were a woman, and Pat was still giggling, although Marilyn wasn't sure if it was because Frank's feathers had been ruffled, or because she was pondering what the lyric about some other guy's dice really meant, and Marilyn was glad to be out in the world, and beginning to think she might have some luck left, too.

"When are you coming back to the Coast?" Pat had eased away slightly, but her arm rested protectively on the back of Marilyn's chair. "Say it'll be soon. I think you and I are going to be fast friends."

TWENTY-EIGHT

Santa Monica, May 1961

"WHAT are you doing out here all by yourself?"

"Oh, I . . ." Marilyn glanced up from her lounge chair and watched Pat descend from the brightness of the house to the unlit place on the patio where she had been listening to the Pacific crash up against the rim of the continent. There were several truthful answers to this question, none of which she found advantageous to share. She was tired, was the simplest—in the months during which her friendship with Pat had blossomed, she had been happy to fulfill the unspoken expectation that she brighten up the dinner parties the Lawfords hosted, doing a sweet little drunken dance, or spilling some movie gossip, or murmuring a naughty bon mot so that their guests would have an anecdote to take home about what Marilyn Monroe was *really* like. Of course she had filled the same function before, but always with a larger goal in mind, and she had been performing in this capacity for a few months now without even a glimpse of the thing she was really after: Jack.

And, too, she had been pondering the news out of Cuba. What the president called an episode, and Havana called an invasion of a mercenary army, at a place vividly named the Bay of Pigs. Perhaps Castro had received advance warning of the operation by some other avenue, but Marilyn couldn't help but feel sick over what she'd told Alexei during those bleak days in Payne Whitney, and wonder if she weren't to blame for the fighters who had been shot up on the beach, or executed in the ensuing terror, suddenly and without trial. It made her almost nonchalant about what he might yet do to her. But mostly she had been staring at the spot in the far corner of the swimming pool where Jack the senator had given it to her, at dawn, almost a year ago now. She shouldn't miss him, but she did. "I just wanted to say hello to the ocean, I guess," she said eventually.

Pat paused with her hand on the back of the lounge chair and gazed out, as though just remembering about the ocean, and that it was so close to her house. "It's a pretty night, isn't it? The way the moon paves the water silver."

"Yeah . . ." Marilyn murmured vaguely, her gaze shifting to the moon, which was where Jack wanted them to go. For a moment she was with those men, one Russian and one American, who had looked down on Earth from space within weeks of one another, wondering if they'd been lonesome up there.

But it was not in Pat's nature to stand around in reflection, and before Marilyn could drift too far into her own mind, she said: "Come on, Blondie, I have a surprise for you."

Dutifully Marilyn stood, slipping her feet into high-heeled mules. For a few moments her vision was splotchy from staring at the moon and at the ghostly underwater illumination of the swimming pool. Then it came back: the palm trees, the lavender sand beyond the glass walls spreading out to the shore, the manicured lemon trees of the Lawfords' garden. And amongst those shadows, behind the broad tree trunks, she saw men wearing suits creeping toward the house. Her breath shortened, and she was afraid she was hallucinating, as she had frequently since her days of confinement.

But Pat tilted her head back, shaking her hair out with her fine, rippling laugh. "Don't be scared, darling, they're here to protect him."

"What?" She hadn't known she'd seemed scared, and was more concerned with concealing that than parsing the word *him*.

The hostess didn't bother responding, and laced her arm through Marilyn's and drew her toward the party. "You've never met a president before, have you?" she went on teasingly.

Too late, Marilyn realized what the surprise was and regretted the clothes she'd chosen for the evening. If Pat had told her, she'd have put on a dress, not the yellow slacks and white blouse she'd worn for what she'd imagined would be another casual, intimate gathering of the Lawfords' close friends and allies. She was about to say that in fact she *had* met Pat's older brother, but of course that had not been the question. "No," she said. "I've never met a president before."

"Be nice to him. They really gave him hell in Europe, and he was lucky to get a few days out here to relax while Jackie and the children are in Middleburg, doing whatever horsy stuff she does out there." Pat was talking low and conspiratorial, her nose at Marilyn's ear. "Lord knows there's no rest when that woman's around. He had to marry her, you know. Without her he'd never have been really class, and I guess he got served exactly what he ordered up. She's so stiff it's *absurd*, runs the water whenever she's in the bathroom for fear somebody'll hear her doing what everybody else does, you know."

Marilyn was only half listening to this commentary. Her mind was occupied with her appearance, and she was hoping that she would manage to slip away to fix her lipstick before Jack saw her. They had come up the steps, through the heavy Spanish door, into the large open room where the Lawfords' guests had been served digestifs, and she saw that she was too late. Jack was entering from the opposite side, handsome in his navy blue suit, tie loosened. His eyes met hers automatically. The whole time his gaze was on her she couldn't breathe, and though she told herself to smile, she had no idea whether or not she managed to. He did seem fatigued—the skin under his eyes was purplish, and his expression communicated the variety of displeasure that comes from lack of rest. There was a blink of recognition, after which his gaze shifted. A moment later he saw someone he knew, and gave them his dazzling, toothy smile, and Marilyn, now feeling much farther than a room away, experienced that weightlessness of having never existed at all.

"Poor Jack, he must have had a long flight," Pat went on in the same manner, not noticing how thoroughly her friend had been cut. The mood of the party had been languorous before, but it perked up now. The twenty or so dinner guests were standing, talking over each other while they watched the most important person in the world make his way across the carpet. "Come. They'll be sucking his blood in a minute if we don't save him."

"Oh, but everybody wants to say hello . . ." Marilyn began to protest, hoping that if she had some time to recover, she'd be better prepared to meet him.

"Of course they do. That's exactly why we have to save him." Pat's arm remained interlaced with hers until they reached her brother and she let go. "Here you are at last!" she cried, embracing him. "Have you met our Marilyn?"

"Marilyn Monroe." He pronounced the name, not as he once had—like he could not quite believe he was beholding her with his own eyes—but as though she were a person he had grown bored of, and was annoyed to find hanging around.

"This is Prez." Pat had not taken her eyes off her brother, so she would not have noticed how Marilyn's face fell.

"Hey there, Prez," Marilyn murmured, trying hard to conjure the shy flirtatiousness that used to work on him.

"Ah yes. Nice to meet you. I believe we're both acquainted with Mr. Frank Sinatra," Jack said flatly before turning his attention back to his sister. "I'd clear a small village for a drink about now. Tell me where, I'll fix it myself."

"What'll you have? I'll get it for you, darling," Pat replied, her eyes focused, brilliant with adoration, on her brother.

"Just point me in the right direction," he said, squeezing his sister's waist. "It'll be the only five minutes I get alone all month."

"I'm so glad you're here," Pat said with a sigh, before pointing out the bar and moving on to greet her younger brother, Robert, who had arrived in the president's wake. Marilyn smiled bravely for whomever was watching, and then found an inconspicuous couch. The way Jack had said *Frank Sinatra* bruised her; it had seemed to suggest she was that man's problem now. Not that this wasn't somewhat true. Luckily, Frank was away doing a show in Honolulu that weekend, but he had helped her in many ways over the last few months, setting her up with an apartment on Doheny, finding her a new analyst—his, in fact, a Dr. Ralph Greenson, who saw her in his own lovely house with a view of the sea, and had no compunction about prescribing her enough pills to get to sleep. Which was a lot, considering her dreams these days. Frank was protective, and made sure she wasn't too alone in Los Angeles, offerings she wished she didn't need. He would have liked bedroom favors in return, she knew, but he had plenty of other girls and did not seem to mind letting their attachment be mainly for publicity. Of course, that explanation never satisfied anybody, and anyway, Jack's indifference to her seemed entirely more complete than that.

She did not sit in quiet contemplation long. The conversation swept around her and picked her up; Jack was the star of whatever room he was in, but her aura was strong, too, so she did not have the chance to wallow in the awkwardness she felt. After a while the president went for a swim—which incited some animated, admiring chatter—and when he came back he was wrapped in a towel, and he sat down next to a film producer's wife who wore a turban and smoked a Kent. Out of the corner of her eye, Marilyn monitored him, and when he rose—saying he wanted to fix himself a drink, and repeating the line about it being the only five minutes he'd get alone all month—she, too, made an excuse.

"Hey there, Prez." She had come up behind him at the unmanned tiki-style bar, her lips already quivering. She made herself think about that high-pitched groan—*fuck me, Jack, fuck me*—so that her fingers trembled as she took the shaker from him and began to fix his daiquiri, and she wouldn't have been able to meet his eye even if she wanted to. It was an impression of hopeful weakness that only a very cruel person could have shut out entirely. Of course, she had told herself not to hope, but there hope was, anyway. They were out of earshot, but even so she let her voice burn down to a whisper before going on, "You forgot about me, huh?"

"Forgot about you." He exhaled dismissively and put his elbows against the bar, showing her his profile.

She thought he was going to say something more, but when he didn't she went on in the same manner, as though every syllable required the marshalling of her whole spirit. The tremble in her fingers was too strong now—she set the shaker down, drinks unmixed. "I mean, I understand. I do! There must be all sorts of important things you gotta see to now. Maybe I never thought you'd stay interested in me very long. But I miss you. I'd like to say I didn't care anymore, but there doesn't seem much sense in lying, you know?"

"Some girl." Jack shook his head, keeping his gaze on the window, at the illuminated jungle plants outside, vivid against the black night. "You get me choked up on the most important day of my life, so that the only thing I wanted on this green earth was to listen to you say a few words to me over long distance. I made all those speeches, kept myself upright through those uncertain hours, and then what do I discover? The thing I'd been counting on was a lie."

Marilyn had never been a shy girl at a high school dance—she had already been married off, to a merchant marine, by the time she was old enough for that—but for a moment she thought she knew what it was to be a wallflower who finds herself unexpectedly in the arms of the most popular jock in school. The trembling routine was forgotten, and—slowly, cautiously—she put her fingers against his wrist. The words coming out of her mouth were not very intelligible, but they were sincere. "But I—why?—Bobby . . ." She closed her eyes, swallowed. "Bobby said you wouldn't see me anymore."

"He said—?" Jack turned toward her suddenly, and there was his torso above the towel, the bare chest and still-damp hair, and the gravitational pull made her seasick.

"When I called that day, he—"

"What are you two on about?" Pat called out as she approached, and Marilyn swerved in her direction, hoping that her face wasn't quite so spread open with longing as it had been a moment before. "Our Marilyn's an actress, you know; we don't let her do this sort of plebeian thing." Wearing a broad smile, she picked up the shaker Marilyn had set down. "Can't cook an egg, but of course she was built for better things."

"We were talking about Lincoln." Marilyn's blood had become cooler; she had a clear vision of her play. "Pat, sugar, do you have a pen? I want to be sure I write down the name of this wonderful book about Lincoln that Jack has just *got* to read before I forget."

"Yes, darling, in the credenza over there," Pat said, in a tone that implied, *Go ahead and write the title of a book Jack won't have time to read.* She had come around behind the bar, tossed the contents of the shaker, and gone about remaking the drinks.

Marilyn winked at Jack and went to the credenza where she found a piece of paper that she ripped in half, writing on one *Abraham Lincoln: The War Years by Carl Sandburg* and on the other *882 Doheny off Santa Monica.* She returned with a pack of cigarettes and a lighter, and she placed one piece of paper next to the cut-glass ashtray on the bar in front of Jack, and the other one inside it. "Care for a smoke, Mr. President?" She delivered the line Lauren Bacall style, so that he would know it was a ruse.

He glanced up from the scrawled address in the ashtray. "Sure."

She inhaled, lighting the cigarette for him and dropping the match into the ashtray without blowing it out, so that the paper curled into flames. "There you go," she said. "Oh!" she exclaimed, in her own persona, bending and blowing out the mini-conflagration. "Damn me!"

Pat turned around, wrinkling her nose at the smell of burned paper. "See? That's why we keep her out of the kitchen," she said, lining up three glasses, pouring the drinks.

"Oh, not for me." Marilyn let her eyelids droop and smiled wistfully. "I'm exhausted—I think I must still be on New York time! I should probably head home."

"Don't go. We're only just getting started."

Marilyn was afraid that if she so much as looked at Jack she would reveal herself to Pat, so she only batted the request away with her hand and said, "You enjoy your brother, sug, and I'll call you tomorrow."

"All right." Pat leaned across the bar, kissed her on either cheek, and then shouted: "Bobby, you ready for another daiquiri?" by which time Marilyn had already drifted to the margin of the room.

She glanced back once, at those nicely tanned people arranged in clusters on the low, buff-colored furniture, the men with their collars open and the women with their hair down. Jack's naked back was to her, but even that felt like a secret message, and she stepped out of her shoes and picked them up, so that she could exit quickly and quietly. The adrenaline was making her feel weightless in a different way, and as she darted through the hall into the interior courtyard, she wasn't certain whether she was more excited that Jack had been thinking about her all this time—that he had thought it was she who had forgotten him—or because she finally had a way back in, and could stop being afraid that Alexei would arrive to punish her further. Anyway, Jack would be coming after her soon, she was sure of it, which was perhaps why she was not surprised by the footfalls that sounded behind her as she passed through the portico adjacent to the street. Trying not to smile, she asked the butler if he could bring her car around.

Her chest was airy with expectation, and she could almost already feel Jack's hands on her as she waited, watching the traffic zoom by on the highway. And then, almost as if she had conjured him, his fingers dug into her wrist and he dragged her backward, into the darkness of the portico.

"Where do you think you're going?"

She could smell his eagerness as he shoved her into the wall. "Home, where I was hoping you'd . . ." But she trailed off when she realized that she'd been fooled by this voice before, and experienced the dreadful current through the skull of apprehending a carnal embrace's true violence. Bobby didn't loosen his grip on her wrist, and with his other hand he grabbed a fist-ful of her hair, pulling her head back so that she could see a glint of reflected courtyard light on his eyeballs. His whole body tensed, pinning her against the brick. Her chest heaved, and his eyes traveled very slowly down, to the place where her blouse revealed the parting of her breasts.

"I told you to stay away from my brother," he hissed.

Every attempt to break free only brought him more forcefully against her, his hipbone sharp at her belly and his breath hot on her face. The darkness was all around them, but she could see his fierce blue irises. She was caught, and for several seconds neither of them knew for sure what he was going to do. Then the headlights of her car swept over the gate, blinding them both long enough that she was able to break free. "I think Jack's the one you need to talk to, if you want him to stay away from me," she said over her shoulder, before he could grab her again. *You better calm down,* she told herself, *or you won't be able to drive away.*

TWENTY-NINE

Los Angeles, May 1961

AS she waited at the window she became alert to all the night sounds, a car engine blocks away, a drink being shaken in the next apartment, palm fronds brushing against each other. Every sweep of headlights was a kind of heaven and then a kind of hell. When Jack did come, she was relieved to see that he had Secret Service men with him, and she realized belatedly that Alexei could now use her in a different way, to put Jack in danger. The Secret Service men took up posts at the corners, and Jack stepped out of the car and came toward her apartment building and whistled, and she leaned out and pointed the way in.

They didn't speak, and she didn't switch on the lamp. The room was full of lavender light from the street, and she brought him to bed and murmured as he put his mouth between her breasts. He didn't seem to be in a hurry, and time passed before she unbuttoned his shirt and he pulled off her slip. For months she had moved through the world in a numbed, listless manner, doing just enough to avoid being locked up again, perhaps forever, but now she was glad that she had succeeded in working her way back into Jack's arms. Even if Alexei came for her tomorrow for the last time, she thought, this night made it all worthwhile, and as long as Jack rocked her she forgot to worry.

But morning broke with the usual acidic rush of anxiety. She wanted to slip back out of wakefulness, to be conscious only of the rumpled sheets and Jack next to her, to cling to him as though there were nothing else, two entwined bodies, pliant with sleep like newborn animals. But her mind wouldn't shut up, and after a quarter hour trying to lie still—chasing away restless thoughts of Alexei, and how long she had before he came for her again; of Bobby and what he would do to separate her and his brother; of those fearsome, barrel-chested warlords, oceans and continents away, whom Jack was charged with keeping at bay; and inevitably of mushroom clouds unfurling over the Nevada Proving Grounds—she found her eyes irrevocably open. Quietly she withdrew from the bed, tiptoed to the window, and parted the blinds. The sidewalks down below were broad and empty, and the hedges artfully concealed the entrance to her two-story apartment complex. His guardians were in position—one across the street, and one perched on the fire hydrant on the corner, a newspaper spread over his knee.

"I've missed that view." She started to turn, but Jack went on: "Come on, stay that way. I want to look at you."

Over her shoulder she regarded him. In that barely furnished white box of a room—with nothing to obstruct the early light, just a mattress, boxspring, folding side table, lamp, and partially disemboweled suitcase—there was no sign of the puffiness she'd noticed last night. Only the tawny leanness, the indefatigable grin. "Did I wake you? I'm sorry, I was hoping you'd get some rest."

"Never been particularly gifted in that respect." He reached for the gold cigarette case on the nightstand and lit a cigarette. "Anyway, why would I want to? I should just have your ass declared the Eighth Wonder of the World and stop worrying about my legacy so much." He whistled low, and in an after-hours voice remarked, "I could spend all day watching you walk across the room."

"I would've thought the president of the United States has better things to do."

He shrugged, leaning over to tap his cigarette against the ashtray. "I guess that all depends upon your definition of *better*."

"Your friends are downstairs."

"Oh?"

"Doesn't it make you nervous?"

"It would make me nervous if they weren't there."

"Why?" Now she did revolve, picking up her halo of messy hair with two fists and pausing dramatically—knees kissing, feet arched, elbows up, breasts free, the hint of a smile telling him she was half in jest. "And here I thought everybody loved you, Mr. President."

He winced, revealing the worry lines between his brow and around his mouth, and toyed with his cigarette as smoke streamed from his nostrils. "Not everybody, baby," he said after a while.

She put her forearm over her nipples, her other hand in the fig leaf place, a burlesque of modesty, her mouth open in surprise. "Who could help loving you?"

"Lots of people. The Cubans, for starters. That mess down there—it would be a mystery if Castro *didn't* know how we wanted that caper to end. And if we can try to take out their leader, nobody should be surprised if they try to take out ours."

The force with which her own brows drew together almost shocked her. She'd meant to show concern, but the actual feeling was more than she could possibly have anticipated, dread spreading through her veins as she saw clearly that she'd never cared so much before. She wanted Jack to go on forever, just as he was, and the idea that he might not was too ugly to contemplate. "Don't talk like that." Her voice had gone dusky, and she wanted to feel his skin against hers. His gaze was steady on her as she made her way to the bed, walked on her knees across the mattress, hovered above him with a wing of wan hair shrouding half her face.

"Why not talk about it? I'm not afraid. I've been read last rites four times, you know. Not to mention, it requires a whole damn pharmacy to keep me propped up all day. Anyway, those men down there know what they're doing, and Castro can't hold on to power forever—"

"Don't . . .," she said again, lowering toward his chest, bringing her hungry mouth to his.

"Don't what?" Their lips parted briefly, which did nothing to cut the humidity.

Meanwhile his fingers had begun a survey of the skin along her inner thighs, which was only one reason she didn't want him to tell her anything more about Castro or the Secret Service or anything else to do with the office he now held. "Don't *bore* me."

"All right. What are you doing today? I have the sudden notion to monopolize your time."

"I have a lunch."

"A lunch? Call and cancel."

"It's with my publicist!"

"All right, you have my permission. What else?"

"I have an appointment with my shrink, Dr. Greenson. And I thought maybe I'd have my nails done. And then buy some flowers, get some color in this place."

"It could use it." His teeth were grazing her neck now, making her breath short. "Looks like a bachelor lives here."

"It's only temporary. I don't have a home in Los Angeles anymore. I have the place in New York, but I can't stand it now. Frankie knows the manager here—it's where he always puts his girls."

"Oh?"

With his hands on her, she was becoming a little stupid. "But I'm not, you know," she said quickly. "One of his girls."

"I know." His mouth was making a slow migration over her abdomen. "But I still don't see why you don't buy your own house."

Suddenly her nipple was between his teeth. She was still hovering over him, but her entire musculature had gotten so heated, melting almost, so that she wasn't sure how much longer she'd be able to hold herself up. "Would you come visit me there if I did?"

"Yes."

As though sensing the pleasurable disintegration taking place above him, he took hold of her ribs with both hands, while her nipple swung to and away from his half-open mouth as she inhaled and exhaled.

"What are you doing today?" she mumbled.

"Spending time with Pat and her children." He spoke straightforwardly, his voice brawny as usual with extra vowels, but his words were divorced from the happenings of his physical self. "Getting ready for a fund-raiser tonight."

"Oh, yeah?"

"Yeah. You should come."

"Come with you?"

"It's a thousand dollars a plate. I'll get ten thousand if people start thinking they might meet Marilyn Monroe every time I have a dinner. In fact, I got fund-raisers like this coming up all across the West. Why don't you ask that publicist of yours if you don't have a reason to be in Washington, D.C., or Houston, Texas, or Seattle . . ."

"Enough talking."

By the time she rose above him and fixed him with her gaze her patience was gone, and it took everything she had to wait for him to respond in kind. "Enough talking."

"I must say, you are looking very well," Alan Jacobs observed as their salads were cleared from their shady table on the Polo Lounge patio, and Marilyn waved off the suggestion of a second Chablis. His hair was as polished as a crook's over his tanned forehead, and his collar was unbuttoned to the sternum.

"Better than expected? That's what you really mean, isn't it, Al?" she asked with her singular quivering, brave candor. She didn't mention the real reason she looked healthy, which was that her cheeks had the ecstatic color of a morning in bed.

"Well." Alan glanced at her pointedly over his black sunglasses. "Let's not bullshit one another."

"A girl has to get away from everybody sometimes. That's why I needed that hospital visit. And when I get back to work I'll be able to give it my all."

"Which will be this project with Cukor."

"Yes."

"And that begins shooting in the fall?"

"In the spring. They need to fix the script first—it's kinda screwy now."

"Well"—Alan paused long enough to dispatch the check with his signature—"in the meantime we'll get you a few appearances and magazine placements and such. Maybe sing the National Anthem at Dodger Stadium. You're at fighting weight, I see, so we've got that going for us."

"Oh, I'm not sure . . .," she whispered, smiling dreamily and rising to his arm. As they crossed the red patio she waved at a few of the others doing business over luncheon, and though she had a flash of encountering Alexei there a year ago, how disturbed she'd been at the sight of his bare ankles, now she saw nothing ominous, only names she knew, the taut, envious, admiring, gossiping faces of her friends and compatriots. "I think I might travel some this fall."

"Oh—where?"

"Well, Peter Lawford's doing the next Otto Preminger picture, which is filming in Washington, D.C., and you know Pat and I are thick as thieves these days, and I've never been to the capital. And then I thought—oh, I don't know, maybe see a little bit of this great country. I've spent too much time in this sort of joint," she said, indicating the white starched tablecloths, the floor-to-ceiling pink drapes, the swirling pattern of the carpets of the restaurant, which they were passing through on their way to the lobby. "Too much time with showbiz folks."

"Whatever you say, gorgeous," Alan said, batting away the comment. Perhaps he had heard actors talk like this before, and knew to treat it as a phase. But her life, now that she'd let go of the fantasy of meeting her father, felt unreal, futureless, and she saw no reason not to spend her days as the president's mistress. How many days did she have left, anyway? "I'll send someone with you, make sure you have your picture taken on set, maybe get you an interview or two while you're there. Look after you."

"Oh, please, I don't need looking after."

"Sweetheart, listen to me. This is why you pay me. You are newly divorced. You spent three weeks in a psychiatric hospital. The press is in love with pictures of you in distress. Puffy, or worse. You should have someone with you, just to see that those sharks don't take advantage. And see if we can't get a little coverage of the opposite kind."

"Well, all right. But not Nan." Marilyn briefly put aside her gentle mumbles and spoke sharply. Nan Pettycomb was one of Alan's subordinates, and she had worked with Marilyn in the mid-fifties, when things had been changing for her for the better. Nan had been good company, but she had clung too tight—she had wanted to be a real friend—and Marilyn had had to shake her loose. She certainly couldn't have anyone that nosy around now. "I won't do that again."

"As you wish." They were out of the lobby, descending the carpeted steps under the porte cochere, and Alan handed a bill to one of the uniformed valets. "Bring Miss Monroe's car around, would you? And let my man know I'm ready for him, please."

They stood silently posed, Al in his navy blazer with gold embroidered insignia, and Marilyn in her tight white linen and cat-eye sunglasses. Their cars arrived at the same time, and the man driving Al's cream-colored Bentley was around the hood with his hand extended to Marilyn with a swiftness that struck her as comical. His light hair was slicked back, too, and his expression was so serious she wanted to laugh. Then she realized he must be nervous, and smiled instead.

"Marilyn," Alan said. "This is my new protégé. His mother sent him over. Mosey Moses? Surely you've been to her parties."

"It's a pleasure to meet you . . ." Her voice trailed off with a question mark.

"Doug Walls." His sweaty palm encased hers, shook hard. "At your service."

"Thanks, honey. I think I'm gonna enjoy that service."

A grin spread over his face, and she saw that there was nothing to worry about with him. He was only a boy.

"You resemble someone I knew once," she went on, and though it was the kind of thing she said to make people feel special, she meant it, too.

"That's because we have met before. At one of Mother's parties. I asked you to dance, in fact. I mean, we did dance, but I— it didn't last long."

"Story of my life," she laughed, and for a moment she was sure she'd made him blush.

"Dougie, Miss Monroe is considering a trip to D.C. Don't you have family there? Perhaps you could give her some tips."

"Yes—" For a moment she thought he might stutter, but he got a hold of himself and went on smoothly. "I'd be happy to. In fact, I know the town pretty well. If someone is escorting you, I'd like to recommend myself. It would be an honor."

The skirt she wore was mid-calf and tight, so that her thighs were almost bound together. When she tried to move forward it was a funny, off-kilter prancing, and she almost fell against Doug Walls trying to give him a kiss on the cheek. They were so close that he must have caught a whiff of her body, which had the smell of sex in the morning and drinking wine in the sun. "Thanks," she whispered, biting her lip. "I'll be looking forward to it."

He continued half supporting her until she had slid behind the wheel.

"Thanks for lunch, Alan," she said. "I'll call you when I know my plans."

And, happy to think that there would be a man to protect her while she traveled, she put the car in gear and went in search of a dress for Jack's dinner.

THIRTY
Washington, D.C., October 1961

THE sloped bronze bowl of the concert hall was warm with the reflected light of the stage, where a cellist cradled his instrument. The faces of the audience were cocked at all angles, wearing grimaces of reverence, impatience, preoccupation, or trance. They were dressed in their finery, teardrop-shaped jewels hanging beneath the lower curl of the women's coiffures, the men's cuff links gleaming when they rested their chins on the heels of their palms. The music seemed to invite Walls's emotions to take wing, sinking and soaring by turns. He was briefly distracted by the idea of returning to live in Washington, perhaps marrying some brisk, clean-smelling girl who understood Bach and knew how to host a cocktail party, and he almost didn't realize that the blonde sashaying up the aisle was the one he was now charged by two masters with watching.

Or one and a half, as he had taken a leave of absence from the Bureau in order to work for Alan Jacobs. He had not been able to shake his conviction that the Gent was a Soviet spy and that Marilyn was his operative, but neither had he chased away his anxiety that this was a lunatic theory, the pursuing of which would lead to his professional undoing. Yet he felt duty bound to either uncover, or definitively disprove, her traitorous secret self, and he feared that he would never know peace again if he did not learn the truth.

His right foot came down to the floor. He was seated, according to his station, in the recesses of the hall, and so there was no one to notice how his eyes scanned the rows of the concert attendees to the box where Jacqueline Kennedy, in a sleeveless column the color of Key lime pie, was watching the performer with the same placid, aloof smile, even though the seat next to her was now empty. When had the president left his seat, and how had Marilyn managed to walk up the aisle and right past Walls without his taking notice? During dinner she and Pat kept slinking off to the bathroom together, not bothering to be discreet, and returning with the giggles and a strange quality in their eyes, big and black like porcelain dolls. Neither had subsequently seemed capable of keeping her voice down or walking a straight line. And so Walls, with some reason, had allowed his vigilance to lapse. He rose, irritated with himself, failed to notice the outstretched leg of the man next to him, and nearly wound up splayed across the aisle.

"Pardon," he muttered, before hurrying to the exit.

For a moment she was there—the strapless red floor-length dress, the naked scapulas of her atypically covered-up back, the pouf of white-blonde hair reminiscent, from behind, of a giant speech balloon—and Walls relaxed. Then she disappeared around the curvature of the hall, and he saw the mistake that he had made in believing her to be as drunk and helpless as she appeared. He jogged the length of the hall but found it empty, the only evidence of her a faint trail of Chanel perfume.

He hurried down the stairs, into the auditorium's empty lobby, where there was not even the receding click of high-heeled shoes to guide him. Through multiple glass doors he could see that outside the world was slick and dark with rain, so he turned instead and headed deeper into the building, where the music reverberated through the floorboards. He quickly determined that she was in neither bathroom (he was so relieved that he had not met there with the shocked and disapproving face of some social doyenne that he almost didn't mind the fact that Marilyn was on the loose). The coat-check room was unmanned, but he saw the boy who was meant to be guarding it halfway down the hall. His head, the close-cropped hair gone white in dramatic contrast to his black skin, was pressed to the wall listening to the concert on the other side.

Inside, row upon row of furs greeted him, more mink, sable, otter, and ermine than he'd ever seen before. He was a little shocked by this display, by all those beautiful pelts. The sounds brought him back—a woman's sigh transmogrifying to moan, the rustling of clothing, a man saying *baby*. Walls froze, not sure what to do. Of course, wasn't this what he had been hoping for, definitive proof of Marilyn and the president? But he wasn't really in doubt about that, and if she saw him now she was unlikely to want him near her again, which would make it difficult to find out what he actually needed to know, which was how she met with the Gent, who he was, and what they planned. On the other hand, his official reason for being here was to ensure that she received some positive notices in the press, and to keep her out of trouble. And trouble this certainly was—he would only be doing his job, and if she was irritated, he could always plead inexperience, good intentions, and the negative consequences of being discovered in a compromising position with any married man, much less the one whose job it was to safeguard the free world.

With caution he approached the coupling, stepping around the last standing rack, his heart skipping when he saw that head of chestnut hair buried in her neck, how her stockinged legs wrapped around his black trousers as he kneeled on a sealskin. Three things happened very quickly: He saw the woman's expression, rent with gratifying agony; it occurred to him that she was not the woman he'd been attempting to locate; and the man's face turned up to him, his pleasure becoming fear. In the previous moment they had been people older and more sophisticated than himself, but now he realized that they were actually just kids in slightly disarranged ushers' uniforms.

"Oh, crap," said the girl. Her moan had been throaty, but her speaking voice had the high pitch of a bobby-soxer.

"We weren't—" the young man started.

"Terribly sorry." Walls backed away.

As he left the coatroom he saw that the attendant was no longer trying to feel the music through the bones of the building. He was returning, but with a quality of circumspection in his worn features, and when he met Walls's gaze he held it apprehensively. From the opposite direction, and at a much more confident gait, came Patricia Lawford.

"Well, hello there, mister," she said, lowering her chin and raising her emerald gaze to meet his. The eyes were still rather dazed, and her lips had a lurid twist. "I was wondering where you'd gone."

"I was looking for Miss Monroe. Do you know where she's run off to?"

"Home. I expect she had a little too much, the poor dear."

"I should go check on her . . ."

"Nonsense. If she wanted that, she would have asked." Pat winked and interlaced his arm with hers, drawing him back up the stairs. He couldn't tell if she wanted only to flirt with him, or something more, but he resented her attentions and how they stalled his progress. "Anyway, don't go, it would make me *so* sad."

When they reentered the auditorium, the orchestra was in the midst of a passionate movement, and he felt that he was trying to contain a wild impulse to go where the action was, to catch Marilyn and Kennedy in the act. That if he had that information, maybe he'd at last be able to force her to tell him what she was up to. Her empty seat taunted him as they approached and Pat sat down, and he realized that he was meant to take Marilyn's vacated spot. Scowling, he did as she wanted, and did not even try to conceal the jerk of his head when he glanced in the direction of the president's box. His scowl dissolved in surprise when he saw that Kennedy had returned and was sitting beside his wife, her gloved hand rested affectionately upon his shoulder.

The music no longer captivated Walls, and when the concert finally ended it took another twenty minutes to extract himself from the Lawfords. Pat kept holding on to him, and Peter, who appeared even drunker than she was, had eyes for every woman who loitered in the lobby while plans for the rest of the evening took shape. She kept insisting that Walls should come with them to the Virginia estate—her brother Bobby's place—where they were staying.

"Jack won't be there," she said sadly, to nobody in particular. "That nag he's married to insisted he accompany her back to the White House tonight."

Walls, disappointed by this information and disgusted by the prospect of a country game of musical beds, insisted that it was his job to locate Marilyn as soon as possible and make sure she was all right, an assertion which nobody seemed to take very seriously. In the end he slipped away without saying good night, after Pat was drawn into conversation with a Floridian senator she appeared to know well.

Their hotel was quiet when he arrived, and the Victorian furniture, the large hydrangea arrangements, and the gilt-framed portraits of American heroes from the last century showed no traces of the woman he was seeking. He went to her room first—the larger of the two adjacent rooms he had booked himself as an employee of Alan Jacobs's public relations firm. When she didn't respond to his repeated knocks he glanced up and down the hall, with its striped gold-and-robin's-egg-blue wallpaper, removed the pick from his tuxedo jacket pocket, and went to work on the lock. His fingers were jumpy with adrenaline, but the mechanism gave before he was discovered. He entered Marilyn's room and closed the door behind him.

A lamp glowed pinkly. Her red dress was thrown across the bed, and the rest of the contents of her suitcase were strewn on the floor. He proceeded to the bathroom, which was also empty despite the plentiful evidence of her recent presence, then crossed to the window and took in her view of the Potomac, moody at that hour with the reflection of midnight clouds, before cursing and leaving the room somewhat less carefully than he had entered it.

In his own room, he undid his shoelaces, paced, poured a whiskey, drank it angrily, and then poured another before admitting to himself that he was not going out to find her. She might be at the White House for all he knew, which was the one place he had no chance of getting into. Or she might be at Hickory Hill with the others, and he had foolishly rejected the invitation to go along. There was nothing more to be done tonight, he told himself, and he sat on the bed and spread the afternoon edition of the paper over his outstretched legs.

The news out of Berlin was as dreary as the day before. Ten U.S. tanks were still facing ten Soviet ones across the Friedrichstrasse checkpoint, the American soldiers with their guns pointed at the wall that had gone up in August to keep the young and bright from defecting to the West. The pictures depressed Walls—they reminded him of the Big War, which mostly seemed to him like a long-ago event with no relevance to his own life, a tragedy now suitable for movie entertainments. But he felt obligated to read on, and did so, wondering all the while whether Kennedy really could go to war, or whether he was bluffing, and what he was doing at this exact moment, whether or not he and Marilyn had managed to find each other.

With a jerk he was awake again, followed by the sluggish comprehension that he had nodded off. His mouth was foul with the aftertaste of whiskey, his bow tie constrictive around his swollen neck. Somewhat slowly his attention moved on to the sound that had woken him—out in the hall a door was being jiggled, and a small metallic object had just fallen for the second or third time to the ground. For more than two years he had been following this woman, and he had a strong instinct that she was nearby. She must have returned from gallivanting with Kennedy. He threw aside the newspaper, and rushed into the hall.

But she was not as he expected her to be. Instead of the low-cut dress he had anticipated, she was wearing a fuzzy white robe with the hotel's insignia on the breast and her hair, though still high and white, was somewhat wilder. The red tint on her lips was faded, and the black eyeliner was smudged. One of her hands was splayed against the wall for support, and she was half bending to pick up her key from the floor, where she must have dropped it. He guessed she was pretty drunk—her movements were slow, and she seemed to waver like a puppet on strings.

"Oh!" she exclaimed. Her voice became slurred and mumbling as she said his name twice.

"Are you all right?"

"Think so." She straightened suddenly, and, afraid she might fall backward, Walls took her by the arm. "I had a bad dream and I couldn't fall asleep again and I thought I'd have a little nip of something, to knock myself out, and I went to the ice machine, and it's sort of silly I guess, but I can't seem to get my key to go . . ."

Walls felt almost sorry for her, catching her in so obvious and pathetic a lie—she didn't have an ice bucket—but even worse for himself when he saw it there, a few feet behind her, sweating on the oak floorboards. Was it possible she had been in the hotel all along?

"Here, let me help you," he said. As he bent to grab the key, he realized what had happened—he must have screwed up the lock earlier, while picking it, and if not for this she might have crept into her room silently and without his notice. He squeezed his eyes shut, trying to think fast. When he righted himself, he put his body between her and the door, so that she couldn't see his hands—it was lucky for him she was drunk—and, quickly and subtly as he could manage, removed the pick from his pocket and leaned in to the lock. When it gave in a matter of seconds he was so relieved that he almost forgot to slip the pick under his sleeve, and out of view, before he swiveled and gestured for her to enter. "There! Just a sticky lock, that's all. I'll call down to the front desk and have them give it some oil tomorrow."

"Silly me." She gave a frail laugh and made her unsteady way into the room.

The light was on, and Walls peered over her head, looking for evidence that the room was as it had been earlier. But the door closed on him fast, and with surprising force. She stared at him through the crack of the doorframe, and for a second it was impossible to think of her as helpless in any way. He was stunned by this glimpse. Her eyes shone with the fierce, multifarious spirit that must have been within all along. Then the view was gone, her lids drooping to obscure the glare. "Thanks, honey. I'll be seeing you in the morning."

She pressed her fingertips to her lips, so that a diamond bracelet he hadn't noticed earlier caught the sconce light, blew a kiss, and shut the door. Walls remained in the hall a few moments staring at the place where she had just been, cold with the conviction that she was not only capable of treason but possessed a malignant intelligence he could not previously have imagined.

THIRTY-ONE

Miami, November 1961

"MISS Green?"

Being addressed in this way provoked a ripple of pleasurable associations in Marilyn, for Jack had given her the alias, and it was the one she still used when she called the White House switchboard. Of course, she'd told Alan Jacobs to reserve her suite at the Fontainebleau under the same name, so its use now might indicate any banal interruption. A waiter hovered at the bright edge of her cabana with a note perched on his silver tray. Behind him were the raked beach and the lazy clouds and the Atlantic Ocean gently lapping in every variety of turquoise.

After she read the instructions, she folded it twice and tucked it down the front of her navy tank swimsuit. "Thank you," she said, reaching for her robe. "Is there a dress shop on the ground floor? I'm late, and I don't have time to go all the way up to my room."

This wasn't entirely logical, as her room wasn't far, and finding new clothes that fit right was never a swift proposition, but the waiter either saw it as part of his job not to question her or he was used to beautiful women and their elaborate justifications for shopping. The real reason was that she didn't want to alert Douglass Walls, whose room was next to hers, to her excursion. His crush had seemed unremarkable at first—he was tongue-tied around her, and obvious about staring down her blouse—but she had been unnerved in Washington, the night she'd come back from taking a midnight dip in the White House pool, and he had leapt into the hallway wearing that expression of bizarre intensity. They had been regarding each other warily ever since. Alexei had said he'd be watching her, and yet she found it incomprehensible that Mosey Moses's son would be with the Russians, too. Even so, she was taken with the notion that he wasn't really a publicist—he was too disdainful of fame for that.

In any case, he had no reason to doubt her stated purpose for traveling to Miami, which was to visit with her ex-father-in-law. Isidore wintered in Florida, and they'd dined together last night, at the hotel restaurant where everyone could see them, and afterward they'd watched a show at the Club Gigi. But if Alan's boy had any suspicion regarding her and Jack, it would have been easy for him to discover that the president was in the vicinity— the *Herald* had run a large picture of the Kennedys descending *Air Force One* in Palm Beach yesterday evening, for a weekend away from the capital—and she didn't want to risk his following her when she left the property. As it turned out, the dress shop carried an easy pink Pucci that she already owned and knew to be flattering, with a narrow waist and fitted below-the-knee skirt and a sleeveless, slightly blouson top with the sort of low back that worked especially well on her. She told the shop girl to charge it to her room, and changed in the bar bathroom on the first floor.

She left her bathing suit with the front desk clerk and asked her to have it laundered, adding—almost as an afterthought—that if her assistant called down wondering about her, they should say that she'd gone out for a walk. As she sashayed past the valets and the topiaries, the high hedges that did their clever work of disinviting ordinary passersby, she had a thrilling, reckless sense of being out in the world without anyone knowing her whereabouts, her face barely made up, her hair tousled from the wind and salt water, her feet strong against the asphalt in the flat, strappy sandals that she had worn to the beach in the late morning. For a few moments together she found it possible to forget all the fatal complications of her life. She lived for the hours she had with Jack now, assumed she was safe when she was in his orbit, and tried not to think too much the rest of the time.

The streets were full of rich men from the Northeast in tropical shirts, and Spanish boys with greased hair, and for a moment she thought she heard someone speaking Russian, but she twirled, as though overjoyed by the balmy breeze, and didn't spot a tail. With her hair not blown out, and walking in a sure, fast manner unlike the one she used in movies, in a city teeming with women in low-cut dresses, she was not the object of any special notice. She found an empty side street, and reached the end without anybody following her. A few more blocks along the bay and she saw the boat docks she'd been told to look for, with a place called Earl's—the kind with a thatched roof, and no walls, just hurricane shutters—overhanging the water. It was empty, except for a man in a nondescript black suit, sipping water at a side table. He responded to her arrival with a neutral glare, and led her out to one of the boats bobbing along the worn plank pier.

"That way," the man said, as he helped her onto the waxed deck. She made her way around the cabin, holding on to its roof for balance, and found Jack arrayed on a blanket on the bow, wearing swim trunks and with his arms folded behind his head. He seemed so comfortable and relaxed in this posture that she almost didn't want to disturb him, and stood watching while the current lifted and lowered the boat under her feet. Another vessel floated slightly farther into the bay, holding two men also clad in black suits incongruous to their surroundings. They were here to protect Jack, and she wondered what they would do to her if they knew what she really was.

"What are you gawking at?" he asked without opening his eyes, and she realized that he must have felt her shadow crossing his torso. *Well, at you,* she wanted to say, but even this felt too poignant to say out loud. She shouldn't be there; she almost wished he would get tired of her already; she wanted to be brave enough to tell him how poisonous she was, with what duplicity she had started their affair, the betrayals already committed. The best she could hope for was that he would end it quickly—for Alexei would make himself known again, soon enough, and she would have to reveal things she didn't want to, or else risk being put away permanently. This was borrowed time. "Well?" he prompted.

"I was just wondering if your goons are going to follow us all night."

He sat up, propped his elbows on his knees. The curve of his back was so tanned it appeared almost black in that light, except where the sun's reflection made it white. His hair, too, was a summer color, except at the base of his skull, where it was recently trimmed and dark brown. "I wish I could stay all night."

"Oh. I'm sorry, I didn't expect . . ." She hadn't expected to spend the night with him, but hearing that she wouldn't put a knot in her stomach. "Of course."

"Aw, don't be like that. We only have a few hours before I have to get back, and I want to enjoy them."

"Tell me." She gazed out, above the heads of the Secret Service men, at the wide, gentle surface of Biscayne Bay. Everything appeared perfectly tranquil, but she no longer believed in appearances. "Tell me how we're going to spend them."

"Was there anybody in that restaurant up there?"

"They must've cleared it for you."

"Good. We're going to go sit there like two ordinary people and drink some beer while the sun goes down, if that suits you. I'd like to take you to a fancy place, or a big gala, but that's impossible, and besides I'm rather tired of them."

"Oh, I like the first story fine."

"Good. But first I have to get this damned coconut oil off me." He swung his head around to look at her, removing his dark sunglasses with sudden energy. "Fuck me, are you a happy sight."

With an awkward, wincing motion he was on his feet. After that he moved quickly, pulling her behind him along the side of the cabin, up onto the pier. The men in the motorboat out in the bay shifted position, as she followed

Jack past idle boats and the occasional fisherman to the end of the dock where a wooden structure, grayed by the elements, housed a showerhead.

"Take that dress off," he said when they were inside and he'd latched the door.

She turned away, showing him how she pulled at the zipper. Holding on to the straps, she stepped out of the dress, carefully so as not to dirty the hem in the drain, and hung it over the high wall. He grunted faintly at the revelation of her lack of underwear, and came up behind her, while turning on the shower, reaching around and grabbing her by the belly. The water broke over them from the side, the same temperature as the warm air, and as her hair got heavy and damp he put his face into her neck and she smelled the suntan oil he'd been wearing. She'd thought he was joking, but in fact he was fragrant with the stuff. The skin of his chest was slick against her back, pushing her into the wall, his hands sliding over her waist, one hand taking hold of a breast, the other gliding down her abdomen. Her own hands went up against the worn wood for ballast, and she pressed onto her tiptoes. They exhaled sharply, as one, when he nudged closer, and they hovered there for an exquisite, oxygen-deprived second before he slid the rest of the way in. Overhead, the sky was pure blue, and the mountainous, dramatically shaded clouds migrated south.

They were both quiet—they were very much in the world, but at the same time apart, and could hear the lap of waves, the snap of fishing line, the occasional shouting of one sailor to another on the other side of the shower wall while they went on silently moving into each other, against the rickety wooden structure, trying not to shake it too much. Light was refracted through the drops of water spilling over them, and she could sense how close they were to everything. When her mouth gaped she felt those droplets on her tongue, and shut her eyes to what waited outside.

Neither spoke for a while afterward. They turned to each other, and let the water wash over them, before drying off with the same towel. She put her dress back on, and he his swim trunks and a blue dress shirt and the black sunglasses, and they held hands and went barefoot into the place called Earl's at the head of the docks. Without being asked, the man in the black suit brought them two beers and then retreated to the doorway. They sat at the edge and looked out over the water. From behind, she thought, they probably appeared, in his blue shirt and her pink dress, like any wealthy couple who had left the children with their grandmother and gone in search of the slums of their youth.

"Did you know you can sail all the way down, to the tip of the state, without having to go onto the open ocean?" he mused. "All the way to the Keys. All the way back up north, too."

"Uh-uh."

"Ever driven down that away, through the Keys?"

She shook her head.

"Papa Hemingway has a house there. Or had, rather." He sighed, let his fingertips drum against her knee to the Judy Garland tune playing faintly on the radio. "I suppose we'll never go looking for Hem at the Floridita now."

"I guess not."

"I still can't believe it."

"That he's dead?"

"That a man who could write like that would want his head blown off. I suppose I mean I don't *want* to believe it."

"Well, maybe he didn't mean to. Maybe he was just trying to scare himself and went too far. Maybe he was thinking about death, and wanted to see death's face, you know? Just out of curiosity, kinda. About what he had coming. But then death called his bluff."

Jack glanced at her as he pulled on his beer can. "What's all this mystical mumbo-jumbo? Please don't tell me you know of what you speak."

She shrugged, and squinted at a sailboat out in the distance. "I didn't grow up like you, you know, surrounded by people who care what happens in your life. When nobody but you cares whether you live or die, you spend a lot of time thinking about death. But I wouldn't be here now if I hadn't chosen living."

"You said you had an analyst." He shook his head. "I usually don't go in for crazy broads."

She laughed. "Sure you do."

"I like good-looking broads; is it my fault so many of them are off their rocker?"

"Well, Mr. President, it just *might* be your fault, at least in a few dozen cases in the New York and Washington areas. I bet you've messed with their pretty heads plenty."

"Oh, come now. There haven't been *that* many—"

"We were born under the same sign, did you know that? Gemini," she told him. "So I understand. There's a half of you that you show the world, and another half that's yours alone. One part of you just wants to be loved, and the other part wants to know everything. But those impulses don't go together very well, do they?"

He put his arm around her neck, spreading his hand over her breastplate, his teeth cold from the beer against her warm ear. "More mumbo-jumbo," he muttered.

"All I meant is that sometimes the nicest things are the ones that can't last."

"I don't like the sound of that very much."

They had wandered dangerously close to her actual feelings, and her heart was as light and unmoored as a balloon loose in the atmosphere, and she changed the subject in the first way she thought of. "It's that way, isn't it?" She pointed south, across the water. "The little island that's caused all the trouble."

"Less than a hundred miles." He drew away from her to reach for his beer. "It's too bad. In a funny way I rather like him."

"Like who?"

"Castro. Not his policies, of course, but he's got wonderful flair. Under different circumstances, I think he and I might stay up all night arguing history. And his people actually matter to him; he's not like Khrushchev. Khrushchev can talk about detonating a hydrogen bomb—about the possibility of a million fatalities, say—as though it's totally acceptable to him. I don't think he'd bat an eye. I used to think all people could be reasoned with, if you only figured out how to talk to them, but I don't think that anymore. There have been times this year, I swear to you, where I just want to get out."

"Get out of where?"

"This planet."

"Well, couldn't you just talk to him?" She glanced down, into the amber bottom of her beer can. She ought not to have asked. It was better for her not to know. But the rest of her life—the nightmares, the wired, paranoid days, the specter of Alexei, her face more etched with wrinkles every morning—none of that seemed real. The only thing that seemed real to her was this moment, this place, sitting with Jack, discussing the fate of the world. She liked talking to him like this—not probing him but actually curious—and couldn't help lifting her gaze to him, and going on, "Castro, I mean."

"No, no, too late for peace and love." He waved off the suggestion, his troubled eyes focused out on the water. After a few moments of silence, he went on contemplatively: "I don't want a war, nobody does. But we can't look weak. We have to keep reminding them we're stronger—that's the only way another horror doesn't happen. Anyway, Castro's with the Russians now. It's one thing to let them put up a wall—it's not very nice, but that wall across Berlin is better than World War Three. It's another thing entirely to let Khrushchev have his own satellite a hundred miles off the coast of Florida."

"Don't!" she gasped. Once he said *Khrushchev*, it was impossible for her to go on in this manner, as though her curiosity were innocent. "You said if we took out their top man, they could take out ours—so if that's the case please don't tell me about it, it'll only make me worry!"

"We have to . . ." His gaze was fixed out on the water, and he seemed not to have registered her plea to change the subject. "The old man says he made us look like fools. Like little boys. He's right, too. And we *are* trying it. Every night, out of places like this, in boats smaller than mine. To get intelligence, lay the groundwork. There'll be another coup, there always is. Has to be." He spoke with worried excitement, and it was in that spirit that he drained his beer and put it down, hard and dismissive, on the ledge. She was relieved that he seemed to be through with the topic. "Anyway, enough about all that. I love this song, don't you? There's only a little time left, and I'd rather spend it dancing than talking about things that keep me up at night."

"I do worry about you . . .," she murmured as he took her by the hand and into a slow sway. The radio was playing Sammy Davis Jr.'s rendition of "September Song," a sorrowful saxophone accompanying the mellow vibration of his voice.

She thought Jack might brush off her worry. Tell her how the men in the black suits were highly trained, that this was his job, that the American people were who he worried about, or any number of courageous, campaign-trail pronouncements. But instead he surprised her by singing along, in a clear, accentless voice, to those melancholy show tune words about a year falling away, days becoming short, and realizing who he wanted to spend them with. His voice was low so that the bartender and the Secret Service man wouldn't hear, and his cheek pressed against hers. They were very close, barely moving, and the salt-eroded floorboards creaked under their shuffling feet. As he repeated the refrain, the surface of her eyes got moist with the pure joy of being held like this, and sung to.

THIRTY-TWO

Miami, November 1961

MARILYN walked back along the beach holding her sandals by the straps, and let the waves wash over her toes. The big hotels towered to her left, some with rounded, white edges and their names proclaimed in neon cursive, others with glass fronts that reflected the changes of the seascape. The places on her body where Jack had touched her tingled, and she thought she would be happy forever so long as she could conjure the memory of sitting with him at the edge of that ramshackle place over the bay, talking about life and death. This uncharacteristically serene mood lasted all the way to the crescent moon spaceship of her own hotel, and she was smiling as she crossed the boardwalk onto the property—illuminated at that hour by torches—and didn't think to disguise herself in any way.

A man's voice called to her—"N.J.!"—and put a swift end to her bliss.

She turned, trying to locate the source of a nickname that now filled her with dread. He was behind her, and she felt his hand on her arm before she saw him. When she glanced up, Alexei's lips curled. She pulled away, jerking her arm out of his grip and almost colliding with an older couple strolling toward the beach.

"Sorry," she muttered, as they hurried on.

"Come." Alexei took her arm again, and though his posture was casual his fingernails dug into her skin.

She'd known this moment would come, had never successfully put it out of her mind long. But she had not imagined how completely the sight of him—even dressed, in panama hat and brightly printed shirt, to blend in with vacationers—would flood her with the vile hopelessness of being locked up in the psychiatric hospital. The loss of Clark, too, cracked open again, and she couldn't help but see Alexei's features, however currently benign, as those of a murderer. Her breath was short, her stomach full of ice, as he pulled her along the hotel's garden pathways.

"Have you eaten?" The old silken manner of address was gone—just a clipped request for information.

"No." It was the only word she wanted to say to him.

"Where are you coming from?"

"Just a walk."

"So you had the front desk tell the young man traveling with you," he said, and did not have to add that he knew she was lying.

Her gaze flashed over the lawns of the Fontainebleau, its manicured trees, the fat, polished people eating alfresco, the pool illuminated at dusk, up along the curving wall of hotel rooms, some with their lights on and some abandoned already, trying to guess which one was hers. But she didn't have to guess. It was the room next to the deck where the young man Alexei had just mentioned was standing, watching them through a pair of binoculars he was now pretending to look out to the sea with. *My god*, she thought, *they can get to anybody, even a hunky California boy, even the stepson of a studio boss.*

Alexei must have sensed her tension, because he softened his tone. "Let's have a drink, a little something to eat. You'll tell me what you've been up to."

"Was Arthur in on all this? He introduced me to Dr. Kurtz—did he know who she really is?" She spoke with her true hostility, but followed his lead, walking easily arm in arm like any two people enjoying the night air. If Alan Jacobs's protégé was in Alexei's camp, then any of those darkened balconies might be the place she went to die, and she knew she had better think quick and make no sudden moves.

"No, no. Of course we knew some things about you, and were able to steer you in the right direction, because of his sympathies. But he did not

276

know of Dr. Kurtz's other role, about me, that you were of any interest whatsoever. He was just a useful idiot."

She'd never heard anybody call Arthur an idiot before, and was a little embarrassed to find that it relaxed her some, even at this moment of panic, when it seemed quite likely that every person she had ever been close to was in on a conspiracy against her. "How can I trust you?" she said instead. *Go along,* she told herself, *but don't seem too easily won over, or he won't believe you.* "That you won't lock me up again."

He did not answer, and she wondered, as they approached the maître d's lectern at the outdoor restaurant, if his silence was an answer. If he was about to veer unexpectedly, then a bag over her head, her body shoved in the trunk of a car.

"Good evening, monsieur, madame. A table for two?"

"Yeah, thanks," Marilyn answered.

"But of course, madame." The maître d's voice had changed, and she knew he had recognized her, which was a small comfort, to know that if she disappeared there would be someone to report her final sighting.

"You have no reason not to trust me," Alexei said when they were alone. He picked up his dinner napkin and arranged it on his lap, not meeting her eye, as though he were disappointed, but willing to explain to her, one last time, the order of things. "I have always taken good care of you. I was the one who told you not to fall in love with Hal, and you see how he hurt you." He looked up at her suddenly. "You can't be in love with him now, can you?"

"No," she said. The word stuck in her throat, as if she were wounded, and she summoned the sound of *fuck me, Jack, fuck me, Jack,* her emotions upon hearing that recording back in the wintertime. Of the cleaning-product smell in Payne Whitney, just like she would in Lee's class, summoning a sense memory to deepen performance. "How could I? I mean, I knew he was a womanizer, but . . . I guess for a minute there I thought I was different from the other girls. I learned, though. The way he dropped me—I saw what I was to him."

"So you *haven't* seen him?"

The waiter was approaching, and Marilyn was grateful for the opportunity to collect herself. "Just bring us a bottle of something white and expensive—this fellow is paying—and we'll both have steak tartare," she said and dismissed him with a wave. She wished she could tell Alexei she hadn't seen Jack, that he was more guarded now he was president. But she thought of Doug up there on the balcony, what he must have gleaned from traveling with her, and decided it was best to stay close to the truth. "As it happens, I was just with him. Took a while, but you were right—I found my way back in."

"And?"

"Well, he hasn't forgotten me exactly. But it doesn't mean it's easy, now that I know how he—that stupid girl you recorded him screwing—and who knows how many other—"

But Alexei was no longer concerned with the charade of caring about her emotions. "What did you talk about?"

"Oh, you know," she stalled. "How nice it is to get away a little, that kind of thing."

"What is he doing here?"

"In Florida?"

Alexei cleared his throat and removed his panama hat, revealing the gray hair pushed back over his skull.

"His family has a place, in Palm Beach. I guess they come down on the weekends sometimes."

"He didn't say anything about Cuba? Perhaps something is under way. Plans for an invasion, or—?"

Marilyn leaned back into her chair and glanced across the other tables on the patio. "If there were, I don't think the top guy himself would be here overseeing it, do you? I imagine he'd be in Washington, if there was something big going on. My guess is they've decided that there's nothing to do and they'll just let Castro be."

"Why would you think that?" Alexei sneered, an expression she'd never seen him make before. "If he didn't talk to you about it."

"Well, he talked about his worries in a general kind of way." She spoke slowly, as though it were all very complicated and a little difficult for her to recall. "Berlin, and how deadly everything has gotten. He seemed exhausted to me, and he said something about wanting the situation to work out peacefully."

"Oh?"

"I did say that I thought that wall in Berlin was pretty hideous, and I asked him what he thought about it. And he said that it wasn't a very pretty solution, but that at least it wasn't a war."

The waiter returned, made a grand gesture of showing them the wine. Marilyn saw that he had taken her at her word when she said "expensive," but Alexei appeared untroubled by the excess, and after the waiter poured out their glasses and absented himself, he raised his in toast.

Marilyn did not touch her glass to his. She took a gulp and turned her gaze out again, at the white tablecloths and candles, the way the restaurant's glow turned the underside of the palm fronds orange. An orchestra played somewhere, but the musicians and their instruments were hidden by hedges. He didn't trust her, and she didn't trust him, so there was no sense in trying to seem cooperative.

"Come now, don't pout. This is a celebration." He was acting kind again, but she suspected this was an attempt to disorient her. "I'm not disappointed—you are only just starting over. Now is the time to concentrate on getting close to the president again, and you must not worry about whether or not he is telling you anything of particular importance."

"I wouldn't call it pouting." She took another gulp and put her glass down on the table. "Pouting is what children do when their toys are taken away. You hit me."

"That was only to put you out. You said yourself, he is a cad—and it is almost impossible to talk reason, to change the mind, of a person deluded by love."

"Yes, but—"

"You must trust me. And you will again, in time. Come, let's drink to him."

"Him?"

"To your father."

"Oh." She winced at the old trick, picked up her wineglass, swallowed. She hadn't thought much about the man in Payne Whitney, but she found now that Alexei was not entirely foolish to have used him. Even if he wasn't her father she was still fond of him, wanted no harm to come to him, just because he looked like her. "Is he all right? That day, in the hospital, he was so . . ." She sipped again, as though overwhelmed with all the things they might have done to the actor they had hired to play her father. "So broken, I guess. You wouldn't. You won't? Like with Clark."

"Of course not. He is one of ours. So long you behave, all will be well."

"William Summers," she mused. "Where is he? Where do you keep him? Tell me."

He shook his head—a show of kindly vacillation—and she saw how the greater the lie, the more gentle his manner became. "I cannot tell you that. Not yet." Alexei inclined his head reassuringly, and this time when he raised his wineglass in her direction, she mimicked the gesture and met his eye. "To your father—who is very proud of you and is, I know, so eager to introduce himself to you."

She summoned a dreamy, far-away expression, like an unhappy child imagining a fairy realm. "I hope so," she said and refilled her glass. She wanted to seem, and be, very drunk, very fast. Then she might actually sleep, and wake up tomorrow to some new idea of how to get out of this alive. "But he can't possibly be as eager as I am," she went on, closing her eyes and thinking of the only man she felt any loyalty to now. The one she'd watched the fading of the day with from a seedy joint on the bay side.

"Soon we will all be together. In Moscow, perhaps."

"Moscow?" Her eyes were open, and she gave a sharp, dismissive laugh. "Honey, have you *seen* me? I wouldn't last a week in Moscow."

"But you're a traitor. You can't stay here forever; you must know that. They'll find out eventually." He shrugged in a manner that would have appeared, to any of the other diners, quite casual, like shaking off a blanket when it is no longer necessary, but as he held her gaze she saw the hostility behind his eyes. "We have papers made up for you, my dear. You see? We do still need one another after all."

IV

1962

THIRTY-THREE

Palm Springs, March 1962

"YOU really love him, don't you?" Marilyn whispered.

Bobby glanced up from his deck chair, and was obliged to lift his hand to protect his eyes from the sun. His hair flopped over the creased forehead, and his lips pursed, forming a diamond shape around his slightly askew teeth. Although they were by the pool, and it was a Saturday morning in the desert, he wore pants and a long-sleeve, button-down shirt. "Oh," he said. She and Jack had managed to meet pretty regularly for over six months, so he must know by now that she had not done as instructed and stayed away. "You."

"Can I sit with you?" she asked.

He did not answer either way, so she lowered herself into the chair next to him and crossed her ankles. Under her robe she wore a bathing suit, but she had no intention of swimming. Stragglers from last night's party were swimming lazily, or else positioned to best absorb the rays of the sun, or drifting in and out of the main house of Bing Crosby's place. Marilyn herself had slept in one of the small bungalows, on the other side of the property, with Jack, who had escaped for a weekend while his wife made a state visit to India. Jack must have got up early—the bed was empty when she woke. Now he was sitting on the diving board talking with a California businessman she had met the night before, wearing swim trunks, his toes skimming the pool surface. Both men glanced in her direction while the businessman made an observation that she was too far away to hear.

"When did you arrive?" Bobby returned his focus to the bound report he was reading. Either it contained very fascinating information, or else he wanted badly not to look at her.

"Last night. It was kinda late, I guess. Your brother-in-law brought me in by helicopter," she explained, thinking how long ago that seemed now, driving to the Lawfords' as she'd been instructed and boarding a helicopter with Peter on the beach behind his house.

"Oh." He turned a page. "That must have been after I went to bed. There certainly was a lot of noise into the early hours. Anyhow, to answer your question—Jack's my brother; of course I love him."

"I just meant that I can see why you might not like me very much. You want to protect him. From scandal. And I understand that."

Bobby closed the report and dropped it on the pool deck. He leaned back into the chair and rubbed the heels of his palms against his eye sockets. "Scandal," he repeated irritably.

"I mean, you're doing important work out there in Washington, you don't want a little love affair getting in the way, and . . ."

"I never said I didn't like you."

She laughed quietly and wrapped her robe tighter around her body. "It wasn't anything you *said*."

"Did you know the FBI has a file on you?" He straightened, and his tone became sharp with accusation.

"Oh?" Her breath was short. For much of her life she had felt hunted, but it wasn't just a feeling anymore. She had woken up happy, but the dire trouble she was in turned her stomach sour now.

"I guess they started when you were married to that commie playwright, but they seem plenty interested in you, too. Thing's thick as the Bible, and full of characters just as colorful."

"How do you know?" she whispered. She closed her eyes and pressed her palms together. "I mean, what does it say?"

"The Director brought it to my office, gave me a little peek. Pretended like it was a friendly gesture, just letting me know the president was having an affair with a movie star, in case I might be interested. That you two went on a canoe ride in Tahoe during the campaign, and afterward lay around in bed talking political strategy. Must have had a bug in your room. If they have that, who knows what they have?"

"Oh, dear . . ." Her face was slack, and her eyes darted to Jack. "He's blackmailing you, isn't he?"

"Hoover? Fuck him. I'm the attorney general of the United States—I'm his goddamned boss."

"Then what does it matter?" she prodded, not wanting to know, and needing to know, how deep it went.

The fury of the previous moment now dissipated with a sigh. "It's all so much more complicated than that. The problem isn't just that you're screwing, though that's inconvenient, I'll allow. Jack must actually like you, the way he talks to you. He talks to you too much."

"Yeah?"

"Yeah," he repeated sarcastically. "Maybe you relax him, I don't know. But apparently he's saying things to you he should only say to me."

"Shit."

"*Shit* is right. And that's not the worst of it."

"What's the worst of it?"

"Hoover's not going to do anything with that information. He just wants me to know he has it. But there are some other people interested in who the president is going to bed with, who he's loose-lipped around—people who don't have to worry about their future in politics."

Marilyn glanced at her feet—they were still there, relaxed against each other, the toenails painted coral—but she couldn't feel them anymore. Beyond the white brick walls of Bing's compound were the folds of the hills, gray brown with scrub brush, and above them the limpid blue of the sky going on forever, over the whole world. Which was a world she'd never move freely in again. Here she had come prancing up to the most important lawman in the country, thinking she could make him like her, convert him to her cause. Now she'd be leaving this place in chains. They were going to fry her on the chair. Could Bobby know everything? Alexei, what had really happened in Payne Whitney, that the mess in Cuba could be traced to her? "What kind of people?" she finally managed.

"Mafia" was his brusque reply. Her lungs filled with the dry desert air. The word had never been so beautiful, and she thought perhaps it was in anticipation of this moment that she'd bestowed her little poodle with the name. "Sam Giancana kind of people, good pal of Mr. Frank Sinatra, who you seem to be awfully close with. That's why I made Jack change his plans for this weekend, why we're here and not at Frankie's."

"Oh, poor Frankie. So that's why. You know he had a helipad built for this visit? Peter said he took a sledgehammer to it when he found out we—I mean, you—were staying at Crosby's instead."

Bobby tried not to chuckle at this, and failed. "Good riddance," he said, once he'd managed to banish the smirk from his face.

"Anyway, I thought Giancana was on your side?"

Bobby exhaled in exasperation. "How did you know that? There you have it—he's too chatty with you. Anyway, Giancana's not on *our side*. The old man always knew how to talk to him, but since the stroke he can't talk to anybody. *I* can't talk to the boss of Chicago. I won't. So it's all a lot more complicated than it used to be, to say the least. And I can't have my brother sleeping in a house where Giancana sleeps, where he might easily put a bug, especially not when he's sharing a bed with a movie star who likes to ask him about world affairs—"

"You know I'd never repeat anything Jack tells me," she said quickly. *Not anymore*, she equivocated silently.

"I know that. It's not *your* big mouth I'm worried about."

"Then—?"

"It's all just awfully complicated, aren't you listening? And I wish you would have stayed away like I asked you to."

If I could, I would have, she wanted to say, but that was more than she could explain to him, so she just nodded sadly and changed the subject. "I was sorry to hear about your dad."

"Thank you." Now it was Bobby's turn to glance away toward the landscape, for his eyes to become obscure.

"I make him feel good, you know."

"Yes, I'll give you that," he conceded. His eyes roved, almost shyly, to the place where her robe parted over her thighs, though his mouth remained tight as a fist. "And that's important, too, I suppose. Just be careful, all right? He can be reckless, but I bet he'd be less so if you—tried to keep him in line. Don't have him at your house, or any place they might get a wire in."

"I think I could do that," she replied, letting her fingers linger tentatively on the armrest of his chair. She'd have to, she knew, although the disappointment was briefly overwhelming. This realization that the little Spanish-style house she'd bought in Brentwood, gone all the way to Mexico for, to buy furniture that matched the rough-hewn beams in the sitting room and the curved red roof tiles, fantasizing that Jack would come and visit her there and maybe she'd roast a bird for dinner—something simple and wifely like that—was a place he'd never see.

Bobby had been studying her fingers, and when he spoke again he was friendlier. "So you're in the vanity business. Tell me something." He shifted in the chair, making it squeak. "Who's the handsomest guy you've seen in Palm Springs this weekend?"

She gasped, bit her lower lip, let her eyes scan the scene innocently. There were twenty or so people around the pool, all of them slender, tanned, easy in the quiet California splendor. "That would have to be you, Mr. Attorney General," she said slyly, grateful for the opening he had given her, the chance to charm him, make him think of her as something other than a threat.

"You tell all the fellows that?"

"Maybe." She removed her hand from the armrest and met his gaze. "But I always mean it."

A Secret Service agent was escorting a man with glasses and an old-fashioned leather doctor's bag along the shaded arcade. The moment of flirtatious levity had passed; Bobby's body stiffened and then hunched forward, his eyes metallic as he watched the newcomer. Meanwhile Jack had left the diving board and was ambling across the grass, in the direction the man with the doctor's bag had gone.

"Some quack who shoots Jack up." Bobby shook his head and cursed under his breath. "Dr. Feelgood," he added sarcastically.

"Shoots him up with what?" she asked.

"*That* I am pleased not to know. Something like cocaine, I would guess, but the doctor doesn't give away his trade secrets, in any case. It's unbecoming, if you ask me. Of the office of the president. Of a father." He clasped his hands, worked them against each other. "But of course, he didn't ask me."

"I wonder . . ." She squinted at the copse of orange trees where Jack had disappeared.

"Well, as long as you're here, go make yourself useful, would you?" She looked back at Bobby, and after a minute his mouth cracked open, and he gave her something akin to a genuine smile. "Make him feel good, if that's what you do so well, so he doesn't need those damn shots."

"You got it," she said, rewarding him with a wink as she put her feet on the hot concrete.

"Marilyn?"

She had darted onto the grass, but turned at the sound of his voice. "Yeah?"

"You know Peter is planning entertainment for this big fund-raiser for Jack's birthday in May, don't you?"

"Yeah."

"It's going to be at Madison Square Garden. They say they're going to charge a thousand dollars a ticket, and he wants you to sing 'Happy Birthday' to the president for the finale. Well, you have my permission."

She smiled, straightened, and gave him the silly little salute she used to give the boys in Korea after the USO shows. "Yes, sir," she said, and hurried across the lawn.

"Hey, baby, you want a shot?"

Jack was lying facedown on the bed in the bungalow, and the fidgety man who wore glasses was already putting his equipment back into the worn brown leather bag. He paused, regarded Marilyn, and removed a glass syringe worthy of Mengele from his bag in the manner of a sommelier proffering an elegant vintage.

"Oh, no thanks. I like the other kind. If you give me that stuff, I'll never get a good night's rest again."

The doctor shrugged—*suit yourself*, he seemed to mean—and zipped the bag with an efficient, Teutonic tug.

"Thanks, doc." Jack was up, his hair standing high and brushy and wild, his pupils big and black. The doctor nodded and left, but Marilyn did not see him go, because Jack had her in a waltz hold and was moving her around the room with sudden, fluid energy. His nostril grazed her nostril; his mouth was open an inch from her open mouth. She was pretty sure he hadn't slept at all the night before, but he showed no sign of fatigue. Every gesture was boundless.

"You don't need that stuff," she murmured.

"Bobby put you up to that?"

She gave him a knowing smile, thought what a dupe she was. All her life she'd just wanted to find a man who could give her a little shelter, and here she was in the arms of the most powerful man in the world, tall and handsome, rich and educated, and her strongest impulse was to love him and love him until he never felt bad again.

"Don't you want to get off the compound?"

"Sure," she murmured. He didn't seem less like himself, now that he was flying; he seemed to pulse with all his matter, and she saw the blood coursing through him, how it throbbed beneath the skin.

"Think you can get me past those Secret Service men?"

She grabbed his hand, twirled away from him under the arch of his arm, twirled back so that her shoulder blades pressed his chest. They swayed like that. "I do enjoy a challenge."

"Come on. Let's go."

In fact, that part was easily done. She made a spectacle of herself when she returned to the house—fixed a Bloody Mary, asked the hostess in a stage whisper if she had any reds lying around, and announced she was going into town for a while. A small pile of joints were displayed in a cut-glass bowl on the bar, and she put one behind her ear before draping a Navajo throw blanket, which had adorned a sofa, over her shoulders. She walked through the front door as if she wasn't precisely sure which town she was in, then veered toward the garage. By then she'd lost the robe, but added only rolled dungarees to her outfit of white bikini, and she imagined she must be quite a sight. She got into the cherry-colored Mustang convertible that Jack had lain down in the backseat of, found the key waiting in the ignition, tossed the blanket over so he could cover himself, and sped off the property with her morning cocktail held aloft and a brilliant smile for the guard at the gate. When she stopped at the first streetlight, Jack climbed over the seat.

"That was well done."

"You see? I'm smarter than I look," she said, shifting as they sped along the flat, wide desert road. "Take that, would you?" With her chin she indicated the Bloody Mary she was clutching between her knees. "It's freezing."

"They'll soon realize I'm gone," he observed genially as he took the cocktail and sipped. "Come after us."

"Well, we're free a little while anyway, right?"

"Sure." He winked and reached over to undo the top button of her jeans.

Her voice was lower when she spoke next. "You really don't need that stuff, you know?"

"Believe me, I wouldn't take it if I didn't need it. I'm broken in about a hundred different ways. But I get that shot, there's nothing I can't do."

The morning had been cool, but at midday the atmosphere was dense with heated particles. The temperature, and Jack's hand under her bikini, caused her eyelids to droop a few seconds, for her to relent on the gas pedal. When she opened her eyes again she saw the chase car in the rearview. "Shit," she said, batting his hand away.

They were out of town, everything flat and barren for miles, the same simple landscape rolling out forever with nothing but a few bare-bones structures to interrupt the strange midget trees and sand-colored stones. She was getting close to ninety when she realized she wouldn't lose them. Then she saw it—a dirt road that snaked out from the highway, through a sculpture garden of rusted cars and tractors, old doors, and other detritus held together with disintegrating rope and homemade nails. A Model T glinted, its wheels half sunk in earth. At the center was a shack of sun-bleached wood with a roof rigged from corrugated plastic and a hand-painted sign that declared it The Sacred Church of the Yucca and the Halleluyah. Below that was a message exhorting weary travelers to heal their souls. The wheels shrieked when she took a hard right, and the dust was still waist high when they reached the shack.

A man emerged serenely from behind the sheet that served as a door. He was tall, with bulbous shoulders and nose, and he wore blue jeans but no shirt or shoes. His gunmetal hair fell down his bare chest, tangled up in the heaps of turquoise beads hanging from his neck.

"Hello, strangers." He raised his hand in greeting, and if he recognized them, he didn't show it.

"You heal people?" Marilyn called.

"Occasionally," he replied, sounding amused, as though he'd told the beginning of a joke and was already enjoying the punch line in the privacy of his own mind.

"You some kind of Indian shaman or something?" Jack asked as he climbed out of the car. His hands were in the pockets of his plaid shorts, and he wandered off to examine a totem pole constructed of several dusty television sets.

"Mother was Norwegian, father of German descent. I came out from Oklahoma during the Depression. Used to do a pretty good business, too." He held up his big hands to examine them and wiped whatever sweat or dirt he'd found against the thighs of his pants, and she saw that he was missing his left middle and ring fingers. When he smiled, his two front teeth flashed silver. "Guess people aren't quite so desperate for guidance as they used to be."

"My friend needs some healing." Marilyn slammed the door behind her and advanced toward the shack. "You're a holy man, right? Anything we told you would be in confidence, wouldn't it?"

This seemed to amuse him. "I'm holy as anybody" was all he answered.

The Secret Service car was at the turnoff, and the one behind it was speeding toward them along the highway.

"Come in," the man with the turquoise urged them.

They followed him under the sheet, into a room cast a rose color by its temporary roof. It had all the parts of a church: simple wooden benches for pews, a raised platform of pine boards, a music stand for a pulpit, a clawfoot bathtub full of holy water.

"This is some place you've got," Jack said as they walked up the aisle to the front of the church.

"Thanks. Built it with my own eight fingers. Now tell me. What needs healing?"

She wasn't sure if Jack would say what really ailed him or not. His hands were in his pockets, his sunglasses covering his eyes, and he had the appearance, especially in the surroundings, of a person whose privilege has set him above the abject needs of ordinary folks. "Bad back, mostly," he said after a pause.

"First, you must purify yourselves. Wash your hands and mouths." The man with the turquoise indicated the bathtub, and when Marilyn hesitated, he explained: "Don't worry, it's rainwater. I have a basin on the roof, and it comes down through that pipe. It's all perfectly clean and fresh."

A ghost of mirth passed over Jack's face, but he went along as Marilyn brought the rainwater up with the copper dipper and poured it over their hands—the runoff made dark rivulets on the dirt floor—and then used more to rinse their mouths. They were completing the ritual when one of the agents pushed aside the sheet and started up the aisle.

"Mr. President—"

"This is a house of worship," interrupted the man in turquoise. "You can't charge in here like that."

"Agent Schiller, will you wait outside, please?"

"Sir, I don't think . . ."

"I am being healed," Jack announced and, with a wicked smile, turned his back on the agent charged with his protection. "It will take only a minute or two."

The agent retreated reluctantly to the doorway, where he remained, the sheet pulled to the side so that the agents who had followed him could observe the doings within.

"Please, both of you, kneel down."

Marilyn took Jack's hand, and knelt in the dust before the raised platform, where the man in turquoise had arranged himself cross-legged. After a few seconds Jack followed her lead.

"So. How long has your back been giving you trouble?"

"I suppose I was born this way. Crooked. Then things I did as a young man—roughhousing, in the navy—they didn't help it any."

The man in turquoise did not hesitate. "No doctor will ever be able to heal that back."

Marilyn glanced at Jack, afraid that he would be angry, denounce the man for his obvious fraudulence, or be irritable with her for half believing in his racket. But the answer seemed to please him. "Finally, a man who speaks the truth. That certainly seems to be the trend, though nobody ever wants to tell me straight."

"But can *you* heal him?" Marilyn asked.

"You two are a sight to behold. I must say, it is a pleasure just to look on you. So I'm going to tell you the secret." He extended those big hands, pressing his palms against their foreheads, and let his voice wax grand and lyrical. "All sickness is homesickness."

"What?" Jack said.

"Do you feel at home when you're with this pretty lady?"

He coughed and laughed. "Yes."

"Well! You're healed. Go on your way, now. I can see your friend Agent Schiller has an itchy trigger finger, and I don't cotton to firearms in my church."

Marilyn stood first, helping Jack to his feet. The manic energy had left him, and he stared for a moment at the preacher, as though he might be able to tell by looking whether or not he was a sham. But the preacher didn't meet the president's gaze. Instead he reached for Marilyn's hand, bowed his head, and brushed his lips over her knuckles. "It's a real honor, honey. You take care of yourself, hear?" And Marilyn, bewildered by his tenderness, could only nod yes, take Jack's arm, and lead him up the aisle toward Schiller and his three fellow agents, who had been waiting anxiously for the president to quit indulging in foolish displays so they could bring him home safe.

THIRTY-FOUR

New York, May 1962

WHOEVER was on stage must have come with good material, because every ninety seconds or so a fit of hilarity seized the audience, setting off foot stomping and uncontrollable quaking in the rickety old seats, which reverberated all through the building, even in the walls of Marilyn's dressing room, causing her reflection in the mirror to blur. She hadn't been put together like this for years. The premieres for *The Misfits* and *Let's Make Love* had both been sad affairs, a whiff of failure about them, and though her loyalists in the press had described her dress and hair on those occasions with the customary hysterical adoration, she had seen to her appearance with an indifferent, partial attention, and known the effect to be short of magical.

Tonight her hair was freshly dyed—one shade closer to white—and styled in the high, side-swept bouffant she was wearing for *Something's Got to Give*, the Cukor picture, the set of which she had abandoned to be at Madison Square Garden. Her dress had been created especially for the occasion. It was *her* dress, not just literally, but because she had asked Jean Louis, *The Misfits* costume designer, to come up with something only she could wear. In this he had not disappointed. No other actress would have dared. Even referring to it as a dress was off—he'd created a costume exactly suited to the performance of femininity that she had honed one movie at a time. Beyond that it barely existed—skin and beads, a woman-shaped nude stocking encrusted with rhinestones, the total mass of which was so insignificant that she'd brought it east in an envelope clutch. The first rush of nerves had come earlier that day, when she climbed on stage in loafers and slacks—to rehearse a song that she, and everybody else, had sung a thousand times—and she felt like a miniature creature at the center of a dark cavern, and realized how many years had passed since she'd performed live.

The nerves had not abated. She assessed the face she had built, its slender form and voluptuous features, the false eyelashes and line of kohl capping the sedate smolder of the gaze, the parting of the painted lips. Did the face even belong to her anymore? It impressed her, the way she might be impressed with a picture someone else had drawn.

A fist sounded on the door, which opened before she could answer. "Marilyn?" Nan Pettycomb peered in, her smile rigid, her eyes eager, her bob stiff. "How we doing, baby?"

"Oh, I think I . . ." Marilyn twisted in her chair, her posture soft and her voice fragile. Then she saw the man behind Nan. "What's he doing here?"

"Who?"

"Doug." When she had requested Nan as her escort on this trip, she had hoped to get rid of the young man watching her for the Russians. "What is *Doug* doing here?"

"Well, you know it's going to be a lot of press, and Fox is worried that you'll miss more days on set, so Alan and I thought it would be a good idea to have an extra set of hands. Just in case. Just to be sure everything goes smoothly."

"I'm here to assist you. In any way I can." Doug hovered, pushed his head beyond the barrier of the door. That earnest expression! It was hard to believe he was Alexei's eyes and ears, that he was part of an operation that would use a psych ward as an interrogation room. But he was; and this only made the earnest gaze that much more insidious. "Is there anything I can get you, Miss Monroe?"

"Yeah, a shot of something." She narrowed her eyes at him. "Whiskey, vodka, I don't care. Not champagne. You got that?"

His head bobbed resolutely, and then she heard the heels of his dress shoes as he went in search of her drink. Nan approached, keeping Marilyn in her sights, moving cautiously, conscientiously inward. "You ready for this?" she asked, as one asks a child if he is ready for the first day of school.

Marilyn turned back to her own reflection, which was as it had been before, and also at the same time astonishing. "Ready for what?" she asked. When she was having the dress made, when she was arguing with the studio about allowing her to travel, she had been thinking only of Jack, celebrating him, being close to him. What it would mean to perform for an audience this big occurred to her later, not just movie fans but also the evening news, the whole world, serious people, and people who disliked her—as well as those whose interest in her doings was of more catastrophic consequence—and these elements had crept slowly into her consciousness throughout the day.

"Here you are, Miss Monroe." Doug was back, his sturdy, tuxedoed body all the way in the room, and there was nothing she could do to prevent it. He had a highball nearly full with brown liquor, so she decided to drop her outward opposition to his presence.

"Thanks, doll," she replied, looking at the glass, not him, as she took it from his hand. The whiskey sent a comet down her throat, burned off the seasickness, granted a reprieve to the many extraneous transmissions of her consciousness.

Nan's smile was blinding, forceful. "Mr. Lawford is about to introduce you, honey." Then she snapped her French manicured fingers in the direction of the mink that Marilyn had borrowed from the studio, and which was hanging by the door. Doug lifted the fur for Marilyn to step into, and when the weight of the coat fell against her shoulders she knew that if she was able to hide, it was only going to be for a little while. They were moving through the dim corridors of the Garden, the odor of stale sweat from fighters long forgotten, toward the noise. Nan up ahead, her arm extending backward with a reassuring grip on Marilyn's hand, and Doug behind, as though to protect her, but in fact to monitor her every gesture, search out the signs of her disloyalty. They were, briefly, a single organism—Nan the shepherd of everything she had ever worked for, Doug representing her most secret dealings, and in the middle the mortal body that had carried her so many miles, to this place.

On stage, Peter was massaging the crowd, getting them ready for the finale. "This lovely lady is not only pulchritudinous," he was saying, "but punctual. Mr. President, Marilyn Monroe!" It was not her cue; it was the penultimate beat in the long lead-up to the joke of her entrance, which was a joke on her famous tardiness. All night, her name had been accompanied by an empty spotlight. The laughter surged and simmered, and Peter went on, as though at the beginning of a bout of windbaggery. "But I'll give her an introduction, anyway. Mr. President, because in the history of show business, perhaps there has been no one female who has meant so much, who has done more . . ."

The spotlight reached for her at the top of the stairs, and Nan and Doug pushed her up into its illuminated cone. The dress encased her so completely that her legs almost couldn't part, and when she reached the stage, with the help of their hands, she had to scamper to the podium on her tiptoes. Peter kept his back to her, so the audience had the pleasure of spotting her themselves. A little applause set it off, then the whole room roared. Peter turned just as she was reaching the podium, and extended his arm. "Mr. President," Peter intoned into the microphone, "the *late* Marilyn Monroe."

Then he stepped aside and reached for her coat; she moved toward him, so that the podium would not obstruct the audience's view, and allowed him to disrobe her. They saw her dress, which concealed so little and attracted so much light, and she heard the sound of thousands of mouths sucking in smoky air. Someone laughed, and a cheer went up. Her hands shielded her brow, and she located Jack, whose smile and bow tie were askew. Nakedness had been her intention, as always. Over the years she had shaved layer after layer from her persona, until here she was, on this stage, where everything she felt, the current giddiness, the old sorrow, the places on her body where his hands had been, were on display without even a shadow for protection. The audience knew it—they were hooting; and the stage lights knew it—they illuminated every rise and fall of her figure, the vibrations of breath. There would be no hiding, so she drifted back, tapped the microphone, and opened her mouth.

Darkness enveloped her. Music surged from the orchestra. Now the spotlight was on the towering birthday cake, which was being carried into the crowd. She could hear whispering, and she knew what happened next, that the president would be coming to the stage, and that his people didn't want him photographed with her. She felt nauseous over what she'd done. She wanted to move quickly, to accommodate their desire that she not say a personal happy birthday to the president—if she shook his hand up there, she would be able to conceal even less than she just had—but she couldn't remember in which direction she was supposed to exit. A hiss cut at her eardrum, a voice called *"Get her off!"* and before she could move arms were underneath her, scooping her up and carrying her away.

They descended a staircase into the recesses of the arena, and she was obliged to hang from the man's neck so as to not be jostled. They were coming into a harshly lit corridor, where long catering tables covered with red paper were laden with coffee urns and pastries. As the man put her down she began to coo her thanks, but the dress was too tight, it left her off-balance, and she had to fall against him for support. That was when she recognized Alexei, in a cheap tuxedo that created a glancing impression of any other stagehand.

"What are you doing here?" she managed.

Someone passed them briskly, paying no attention.

Jack was at the microphone, his voice amplified throughout the arena. "I can now retire from politics," he was saying over the crowd's laughter, "now that I've had 'Happy Birthday' sung to me in such a sweet, wholesome manner . . ."

"We don't have long." Alexei's gaze flicked about—the coming and going had not stopped, and he assisted her to the red table, where he made a show of pouring her a coffee. From his breast pocket he removed a flask, tilted it toward her cup. But he left the cap on, and afterward handed it to her. "Keep that, and whatever you do, don't drink it."

"But why—?" The flask was made of antique silver, and cold to the touch.

"Summer is coming. Slow months in Washington—you'll be able to see a lot of Hal. Your affair will never be so regular as it is now. What you'll need to do is get a few drops of that in his drink once a week. Ten or so. Twenty, if you are only able to manage it every other week."

"I can't," she gasped.

"I thought you saw him clearly now."

"So? I couldn't kill a fly, much less—"

"My dear, it won't kill him. No, no. Not unless you gave him the whole bottle at once. In little doses, it is designed to make the teeth rot, blacken, fall out."

"But why go to all the trouble then?"

"Things have gone too far. It doesn't matter how many mistakes he makes, how inconsistent he is. Despite everything he is a hero figure not just to Americans but to the whole world. Because of you, we know he is an invalid, unfaithful, materialistic. We have spread these stories widely. It makes no difference! His image is too strong. He is beloved, the whole world over. We are losing our best minds—they're willing to die crossing that wall. You Americans worship perfect teeth, and you childishly associate dental decay with moral decay. They must be made to *see* his dereliction."

"But he tells me what he's thinking, isn't that more important? What if I fail?" she went on wildly. "You'd lose all that."

"Already he is giving you bad information, false information, lying to you," Alexei hissed. "What you told me in Florida, none of it was true—"

"But maybe time will prove it is?" she interrupted. She felt desperate, she wasn't even sure what she was saying. She didn't remember what she'd said in Florida, only that she hadn't wanted to repeat anything Jack had told her.

"We can't wait that long."

She shimmied goofily, indicating the tightness of her dress, a garment with no place for a hidden compartment. "But I've got no place to put it," she tried to joke. But the joke was lame, and when she heard it out loud she knew she'd reached the end. She had just told the whole country she was in love with Jack, so Alexei must know, too, and she couldn't pretend anymore she was seeing the president on his behalf.

He pursed his lips and paused, as though trying to decide what to do with her. She heard a shuffle, a mechanical click, and revolved to see Doug, high on the balcony above them. "Miss Monroe! There you are," he called.

She glared at him as he jogged down the stairs. Of course—that was why Alexei had been so brazen, talking to her in public like this. He'd had a look-out the whole time, the man now descending to provide the one item missing from this latest plot. Once again Doug held the mink so she could slip under its silken wing, dropping the flask into the hidden interior pocket. Alexei was gone like a ghost, and she turned all her dread and fury on his underling. "Where's Nan?" she demanded. "I've had enough. I want to go to the party now, be around people for once."

The journey to the party, and the party itself, were as swirling and grotesque as a nightmare. Her spangled form floated through the elegant apartment detached from consciousness, wielding a champagne glass, laughing at jokes, blushing at compliments. Bobby was there, hovering around her, as though he might thus contain the memory of her carnal rendition of "Happy Birthday," her unsubtle declaration that she'd made it with the president. Or maybe Bobby wanted only to be where she was. She could not seem to drink enough champagne to keep Alexei's face from appearing in the windows, amongst the millionaires eating blue cheese in endive and leering at her. Occasionally a peculiar sensation would bring her back into her body, and she would see Jack across the room with a new quality in his gaze, something like possession.

Life had not been easy on her—it had pinned her to the mattress with a pillow, depriving her of oxygen, often enough—but she had never been so trapped as this. That she had already committed crimes for which she could be executed seemed the least of her predicament. They wanted her to poison Jack; the poison itself was in the pocket of the fur she now wore. She had few moves, all of them unspeakable, and still the worst outcome she could imagine was the one in which she was alive and couldn't have Jack—couldn't see him, feel his appreciative eyes on her, listen to him talking about the world. That, as Alexei had said, their affair would never be so regular as now.

"Hey, honey," she said to the host, a movie producer who had the block-like head of a pugilist. "Where's the ladies'?"

He indicated it with his fat finger, and she hurried in that direction, trying to conceal her distress as she made her way through the big men in their dark suits. Alone again with her reflection she was neither impressed nor astonished. She leaned heavily against the marble sink, and stared into a stranger's face. It would be easy—Alexei had said only the whole flask would kill him. Surely that much would kill her quickly, end the game. She could escape, tonight, not just the impossible situation her relations with Jack had become, but the awful maze of her self. To die sounded sweet almost—a reprieve from wanting.

The door opened and closed in an instant. Jack did not look at the knob as he turned the lock. She couldn't smile as she watched him advance across the room in the mirror, couldn't change her horrified expression. But he wasn't smiling, either. In fact she had never seen him so serious. He jerked the fur down from her shoulders, apparently not noticing the clanking of the flask on the bathroom tile when the coat hit the floor. He tugged on her wrist, spinning her around so that she felt the heat of his breath on the tip of her nose.

"At the Garden," he said. "When Peter took your coat. There was a moment—I was convinced you were nude underneath."

The corners of her lips darted unhappily.

"I was so angry. Not because of the potential embarrassment. It didn't even cross my mind what a clusterfuck that would have been. But because they'd all see you. And I was so relieved when I knew I was wrong."

Her mouth softened open. When he heaved her onto the sink her dress split across the thighs, and he did not hesitate putting his fingers through the rift, tearing it completely. Rhinestones popped from the fabric, scattered on the floor, as he parted the legs that had been pressed together all evening, and wrapped them around his torso.

"They'll hear . . .," she protested, not forcefully, as she leaned against the mirror.

"I don't care." He was trying to undo the buttons of his shirt while burying his face in the skin below her ear. "I love you."

The whole evening seemed imagined, and she almost couldn't believe he'd said those words she'd thought so often while in his presence. He had. He must have. It was her only chance. He was saying it now with every gesture. So as she helped him with his shirt she arched her back, encouraging his mouth to move down along the neckline of her ruined dress, and said the phrase back.

THIRTY-FIVE

Brentwood, June 1962

MAYBE, just maybe, she had been born under a lucky star after all. Maybe the decades of struggling and confusion were necessary pieces of a grand scheme. So she tried to tell herself, in the final weeks of her thirty-fifth year, when the words *I love you* recurred in her thoughts every quarter hour. When her anxiety became too great, she'd close her eyes and conjure the ruination of that sparkling, skin-colored dress, and for a moment be flush with emotion. She began to think of the age she was about to become not as old but auspicious, so sweetly square and divisible by two. And she was lucky also to have work, which filled her days and blocked out fear and left her tired at night, without the energy to wonder what Jack was doing, or whether he'd really meant what he'd said to her in that penthouse bathroom.

Not that it was easy to be back on set. She hadn't worked like this in a year and a half, and the script was flimsy, and she had no idea how she was going to make many of the lines sound the least bit natural. But she was looking good, everybody said so, and on Friday afternoon they had Dom Perignon, and the crew toasted her thirty-sixth birthday. Driving home, in the limousine the studio had hired for her during filming, she felt jittery with hope. If Jack loved her, then maybe she'd be saved after all. It was miracle enough to make her believe in more miracles. Anyway, Alexei had told her that the poison could be administered over several weeks, so there was time. She had a little time; maybe there was a way out.

"Rudy, will you wait until I lock the gate behind me?" She leaned in the window, smiling but with the gleam of fear in her eyes, too. Because she could not tell him what she was really afraid of—and because he would not believe her if she did—she added: "Never know what fan has gone bananas, you know?"

"Sure thing, Miss Monroe." He grinned back at her and kept the limo idling in the cul-de-sac while she walked up the drive, and she rocked her hips extra, to reward him for protecting her in this way.

"See you Monday morning!" she called out, before locking the gate behind her.

The palms swayed in greeting, their shadows long across the grass at dusk, the smell of jasmine on the evening breeze, the flora thick and fortress-like around the property. The low, fat sun blazed on the windows of the small hacienda-style house, with its white brick walls and red tiled roof. It was the first house she'd ever owned by herself. That it was charming without being ostentatious, and that it had a fireplace, pleased her immeasurably, and she wondered at herself for having thought she needed more, or less, than this. She put her handbag down on the table by the door, and felt for the light switch.

"Hello, N.J." He was leaning against the wall next to the fireplace. His arms were crossed tensely across his torso, and his eyes had that waiting quality.

"I was wondering when you'd show up," she replied, evenly as she could manage. His eyes followed her as she made her way across the terra-cotta tiled floor. She affected a sedate, unhurried manner, and when she reached the far side of the room, leaned her hip against the small, polished teak desk where she kept the telephone. "What can I do for you?"

"You haven't been following orders," he said.

"Excuse me?"

"The formula you were to give Hal—you haven't done with it as I instructed."

"What makes you think that?" She tipped her head back, showed him the point of her chin. "You said a few drops over several weeks. Nothing should've happened yet, right?"

For the first time since entering the room, Alexei took his eyes off her. His gaze fixed on the Moroccan carpet that spread out from the hearth, but his attention seemed to be on some long-ago event. He shook his head and cursed in a foreign language. "Why are you so useless?" he demanded with sudden rage.

"I know how you know I didn't give him anything out of that flask," she replied, stringing the words together with frightened precision. "If I'd done as you asked, he'd be dead. That was all a story—a few drops, the rotting teeth. Wasn't it?"

She knew already Alexei was not shy of violence, that he had no scruples about the murders carried out on his orders. But she hadn't witnessed it in him until he stepped away from the wall and his arms dropped from his torso so his hands could form fists. His shoulders seemed to grow and spread, and his mouth twitched with fury. "Why couldn't you just do as you were told?" he barked.

The telephone was inches from her hand—she had been trying to get close without his noticing, and now wrapped her fingers around the receiver. Her movement was quiet, but her voice was loud: "But you're the liar," she shrieked. "I *told* you I couldn't kill him."

"You wouldn't have killed him!" He advanced across the room with patient menace. "You would only have been following orders, nothing more."

She plucked the phone from its cradle, her fingers trembling but strong as she dialed the police. A whole epoch of terror passed as she listened to the ringing, but the operator answered before Alexei reached her. "Hello, this is Marilyn Monroe," she said quickly. "I'm at 12305 Fifth Helena Drive in Brentwood. There's an intruder in my house."

The operator sounded giddy with the notion that a movie star was on the line—a movie star in distress!—but she did her job, said a patrol car was on its way.

"Now why did you go and do that?" Alexei's aspect had changed again. His voice was lower, but that only made him more frightening. The fact that she'd called the police didn't seem to worry him—his posture suggested that he had already decided her fate.

Fear had her now—she wasn't sure she'd be able to move, if indeed that was advisable. "I thought you might hurt me." She managed to step away from him, and the realization that he still might, that he could kill her easily before the police arrived, sent a fresh dose of terror through her veins. She tried to back away as quickly as he was now advancing, get up the three steps into the next room, but instead stumbled on an umbrella stand, lurched haplessly, and cried out in shock and pain.

Then he was on her. He had her by the throat, pinned her against the wall, her head knocked against the plaster, his elbows shoved against her ribs. "You idiot!" he hissed. "You dumb fucking bitch."

She couldn't breathe. His hands gripped her neck, squeezing the air out, and her eyeballs bulged. Desperately she tried to get air into her lungs, kicking at his shins with the pointed toes of her high heels.

"It's not as though you've changed anything. There will always be another pretty girl who can whore her way into state secrets. They'll kill him anyway. Your replacement is already on his way. But now you'll have to die, too. And I could have protected you! I, who was so proud of you. I'd have made sure you had a long life. But *you*—you had to be an idiot sentimentalist. You had to fall in *love*." His words seemed to deplete him, and when his hold on her throat loosened they slumped against each other, he enfeebled with the apprehension of a great loss, she gasping for air. "Goddamn you," he said, with profound regret. "Goddamn you."

A distant siren rose over their noisy breathing, and she watched him, never believing in her safety, as he backed away, withdrew into the solarium. She heard him open the door onto the rear patio and followed, apprehensively at first, and then with greater urgency. She was still afraid of him, but more than that she wanted to know why he'd left her alive. What he meant by "her replacement." The door stood open, but in the evening light she couldn't see much. What she did make out seemed to be a figure skirting the swimming pool and pulling his weight up over the wall at the edge of the property. Then he merged with the gloaming.

THIRTY-SIX

Los Angeles, June 1962

TWILIGHT played its usual trick of reminding Walls that he would like a cigarette; it was at the intersection of day's expectations and night's anxieties that he most wanted to singe the delicate tissue of his lungs. He smoked one after another as he drove through the clotted streets of Los Angeles toward her house. The tie he'd worn for the flight from D.C. was thrown across the passenger seat, and he felt jittery and roguish. No one else in the world knew what he knew, nor could they do what he was about to do, and he felt justified in taking matters into his own hands, and about six foot ten. Only a man keeping his own hours, acting on his own instincts, and answering to his own conscience could take down as cleverly disguised a plant as Marilyn Monroe, and he found, in the event, that he was rather looking forward to forcing her confession.

This despite the dismissive parting observation his father's friend from the Agency had made last night. "That is one hell of a story," the man—who called himself Hollis—said, not admiringly, as he stood to leave the bar off Connecticut Avenue where they had met. Walls had understood immediately why Hollis chose the bar—it was not a place where he could imagine encountering anyone he knew. "If it was me staking my name on that theory, I'd want to have all my ducks in a row before I told it to any of the big boys." Hollis—Walls reflected, while waiting another twenty minutes so they would not be seen leaving together—simply lacked vision. But vision was not required for the favor Hollis had done him, which was to use the picture Walls had snapped of Marilyn and the Gent backstage at Madison

Square Garden, deep in conversation, to match her handler to the file of "Bill" Fitin.

"Can't let you keep it," his father's friend had informed him as he ordered a rum and Coca-Cola and eyed the working girls. "I'm seeing the secretary who guards that cabinet, but I'm not dating her, if you know what I mean."

Then he'd leaned against the jukebox and let a girl who looked about sixteen rub lethargically against him for the next hour while Walls committed to memory the CIA's file on William Vladimirovich Fitin (known aliases Aleksei Swift, Billy Sumners, and Felix Markin). Born out of wedlock, Paris, 1905, to a former Irish lady's maid and a dilettantish revolutionary descended from a line of minor St. Petersburg nobility, who after the dissolution of the affair ran guns for the Bolsheviks and was executed in 1917. Fluent in Russian, French, German, English. Fled Europe at onset of First World War with his mother for New York, where she briefly attempted to get by as a mother-son vaudeville act but ended up working in a munitions factory and marrying her foreman. Young William ran away to Europe at fifteen, where he worked as a pimp and petty criminal, leading a wild, impoverished, international youth before proving himself with the Soviet secret police by luring prominent anti-communists into Russia, and to their deaths. Active in Berlin, 1930s. Instrumental in counterintelligence schemes in the Soviet occupation zone, founding of Stasi. Thought to have run an espionage cell in New York in the 1950s with the intention of stealing nuclear secrets while using Markin alias. Currently believed to have retired from fieldwork, holding high post in Moscow, running operations from an office in the Lubyanka, perhaps including the recruitment, brainwashing, and attempted repatriation of members of the United States Marine Corps, along with their new Russian brides. An addendum noted that most of the file was based on the information of an OSS man with whom he'd been on drinking terms during the war, and that even he allowed much of Fitin's biography might be fabricated.

Surely the FBI had a similar file, which Toll would be able to summon once Walls brought Marilyn in. But first he wanted to interrogate her himself, fit together the basic elements, in what manner Fitin had recruited Marilyn, how many state secrets she had managed to pass on while sleeping with the president, their end game. Get all his ducks in a row, as Hollis said. Walls was not so brazen as to think that he could complete those maneuvers on his own. At that point, he'd go to Toll, and they could run the operation together—using Marilyn to locate and entrap the Gent. Afterward they'd turn him over to the Director for a lengthy interrogation at headquarters that would surely prove an unprecedented windfall of information on the Soviet intelligence apparatus. It was going to be a big case. Perhaps even someday—Walls permitted himself the vanity—a movie, in which a young special agent brings down the enemy using his own, unorthodox methods.

There was, additionally, the matter of the old-fashioned flask Marilyn had left in a wastebasket in her hotel room in New York, which Walls had managed to surreptitiously collect (in truth, he found it only because Nan said Marilyn was forgetful, and ordered him to check her room for important items left behind). He had noticed Marilyn putting a flask into the coat of her mink after she talked to the Gent, and he was sure there had been nothing in the pockets earlier, when he helped her into it before she sang "Happy Birthday." On his way from the airport he had dropped the flask at the Bureau, with a lab technician he knew from his morning trips to the shooting range, and asked him to have the contents tested.

"I thought you'd taken a leave from the Bureau," the technician had replied, looking uncomfortable.

Walls had slipped him a fifty and explained that he was doing some private dick work on the side. That he'd appreciate it if the results didn't get around to anybody else. The technician claimed the lab was pretty backed up, and Walls, figuring the case would have progressed dramatically by tomorrow anyway, told him not to rush.

He parked his car on a stretch of Carmelina Avenue, off which budded several short streets called Helena—just south of Helena's fifth namesake—and lit a final cigarette. The street was empty and almost dark, and he wanted to collect himself before he strode to her front door and showed her his badge. Instead his thoughts drifted, and before he could help it he was wondering what she was doing in the small house at 12305, how she was spending her final moments of freedom. Then he saw the studio's limousine turn up the block, and ceased his manic speculation.

He stubbed out his cigarette and pulled his holster out of the glove compartment, fixed it in place, grabbed his black jacket from the backseat. He waited until the limousine departed, and proceeded up her driveway at a near run, pulled himself over the high wall that surrounded her property, and jumped to the brick patio. The grounds were quiet and the house mostly dark, and he moved stealthily along the wall toward the back, barely breathing. Surprise was crucial, he had decided—he wasn't sure how much training she had, if she would resist him, what kind of weapons she might have hidden in the house. He'd have to get pretty close before he alerted her to his presence, and from outside, he couldn't even determine what room she was in.

Minutes passed when he began to wonder whether she had come in at all, or if the limousine hadn't been another one of her tricks. By then he was around the house, on the pool deck, and he finally glimpsed a sign of life within. A woman cried out—she was close, but inside, and the sound was muffled so that he wasn't sure if it had been a cry of pleasure or pain. He moved hastily to a high window, climbing onto a piece of deck furniture to get a better view. What he saw shocked him—the room was dark, and they were halfway into a corridor, and the man embracing her, pressing her into the wall, was the same man he had glimpsed at the Garden. The Gent was not only her handler but her lover, and as Walls took in the full depravity of Marilyn Monroe, he felt rather disgusted and had to step down.

But he did so ungracefully, and the footstool slipped and clattered against the patio tile. They must have heard—he couldn't really make out what they were saying, but it was rushed and urgent, like people who have just been found out. A siren wailed, somewhere nearby, further startling Walls, and then the Gent burst onto the patio and his silhouette emerged at the edge of the pool.

Walls gave chase. His breath was short, the light murky and the shadows long, but the Gent could be only a few lengths ahead of him, and the yard wasn't big. Walls was a good runner, more powerfully built—it wasn't even a contest—and he could scarcely believe that he was going to be able to arrest the infamous Fitin so quickly and easily. There was a wall at the rear of the property, and he hauled himself over. But when he landed on the other side there was no sign of the man he'd been chasing. Walls was at the edge of a vast lawn with no place to hide, and besides the burbling of a fountain in the middle of much statuary, there was no movement, no trembling of leaves, to indicate in which direction the Gent had gone. Walls ran through several yards, jumping over gates stealthily at first and then not trying to go unnoticed at all. But the Gent had evaporated into the night, and eventually Walls was left with no choice but to return to Marilyn's from the front entrance.

A police vehicle was parked in front of her house by then, its red lights swirling hellishly against the white walls that encircled the houses at the dead end of the street. Her gate stood open, and as he hurried across the lawn he saw the police officer in his black, short-sleeved uniform, standing in the open door and surveying the property.

"Is she all right?" Walls asked, hoping the urgency in his voice would be interpreted as concern. He ought to have been more careful—his first guess was that Marilyn and Fitin were simply using the police to their own purposes, to chase him away. But it was possible that they were impostors, and he was walking into an ambush.

"Whoa there." The officer put out one hand as though to stop traffic, and showily rested the other on his holster.

Walls was glad he'd had the instinct to replace his own weapon under his jacket.

"I'm Douglass Walls, Miss Monroe's public relations man. I just had some negatives that need her approval . . . and I saw your car out there. What's going on?"

"You got any identification on you?" The cop looked about twenty-two, the baby fat still hiding his man's face, and he appeared reluctant to give up his post. Either he really was a greenhorn cop, and American, or he was a better actor than most movie stars.

Wall paused long enough to remind himself which pocket held his FBI badge, and which held his civilian wallet, before producing his driver's license. The cop examined the license and returned it. "Stay here a minute," he said, before closing the door. Walls stepped away from the entry, to the picture window onto the front salon where she sat on a hassock, wearing a fitted skirt and high heels, her torso bent forward and contracting with sobs. There were two policemen, one of them crouching beside her and massaging her shoulder. The other cop said a few words, and then Marilyn glanced up. Her face was wet with tears, and her mouth hung open with an emotion he couldn't identify. Idiotically, he lifted one hand and waved. After she looked away he realized that he was standing on a flower bed, crushing her begonias. She spoke a few, terse words to the baby-faced cop, who returned to the front door and took Walls's arm to lead him from the property.

"There's been an intruder, Mr. Walls. She's awful shook up. Says she'd rather not see any 'Hollywood vultures' right now. Her words, not mine."

"Listen, my boss will have my head if I leave when she's in bad shape. Are you sure she has everything she needs? I mean, what if the intruder comes back?"

"We'll stay with her and make sure. She's called Joe DiMaggio, and he's on his way here to make sure everything's safe and sound." The way the cop said her ex-husband's name implied that *he* wouldn't want to be an unwanted guest on Marilyn Monroe's property when Joltin' Joe showed up. "So you can tell your boss that she's being well looked after."

In the years to come, he would castigate himself for not driving to Toll's house then and there. But as he lingered outside her gate, the cop car's light oscillating on the neighbors' homes, his pulse breakneck, he thought how she could only put him off with such tricks for so long. That he'd have her cornered soon enough.

THIRTY-SEVEN

Santa Monica, June 1962

"I guess my time must be up by now." Marilyn shone the sad, brave smile for Dr. Greenson's benefit and put her toes into the high-heeled pumps that she'd let slip from her feet during the session. She hadn't slept last night, tormented by the memory of Alexei's suffocating grip on her neck. Every creak of the house seemed to be one of his henchman coming after her, and she was in a hurry to fill her Nembutal prescription and go home. One of Joe's boys was at the house—perhaps the combination of watchman and barbiturate would allow her a few hours' rest. "Thanks for—"

"You've already told me that one."

"Excuse me?"

"Twice."

"Oh . . ." She had filled the last hour with memories of the orphanage she'd been sent to after her mother lost the house on Arbol Drive, how she'd bathed in water that had already been used by five or six other children, and how she knew it was wasteful and selfish to soak in baths perfumed with Chanel No. 5, but she couldn't help indulging in such luxuries after the lean years. "I'm pretty forgetful these days, aren't I?"

Dr. Greenson switched the cross of his legs and made a hut with his hands. For a while he was silent, regarding her with his hooded, ocean-deep eyes. "Are you?"

She cast her gaze out the window, at the jacaranda, which grew all over his property. She planted her palm against the leather couch and leaned her weight onto her extended limb. "I already told you I couldn't sleep. I mean, doesn't that usually make a person forgetful?"

"Marilyn." He inclined his torso toward her, his eyebrows pulling together in sympathy and consternation, forcing her to return his gaze. "Are you all right?"

"Sure. But if I *really* were, don't you think I'd be able to sleep through the night?"

"I'm here to help."

"Oh, yeah?" Her smile became brilliant and ironical. "You got something stronger than that?" she asked, indicating the prescription that peeped from her handbag.

"It is 1962, my dear," he replied gravely. "There are always stronger drugs. I could make you sleep like the dead for twenty-four hours, or stay up for three days straight." He cleared his throat into his fist. "That was not what I meant by *help*."

The sense of peril she experienced in the next moments, as his gaze grew fierce while revealing nothing, was impossible to pinpoint. She made sense of it only when he reached out and put his hand on her knee. This was not a touch of seduction, nor compassion—its intention was to control. She stood abruptly and thrust his hand away. "You're one of them. Aren't you?"

She had never seen Dr. Greenson perplexed before. "One of who?"

"You're with Alexei. You're in on the plot."

"Plot?"

"You and Dr. Kurtz. Oh, fuck, this was all part of the plan, wasn't it? Does that stuff you give me even help with sleep? Or is it designed to keep me up, keep me always off-kilter, make it easier to push me around, get me to do what you want?" She was shrieking now, and her eyes had dilated with rage. She took a forceful step toward the door, but he grabbed her wrist.

"Sit down," he commanded.

Her gaze flashed to the place where his fingertips dug into her skin. "Or are you the one who kills me? Is this how it ends?"

He loosened his grip, giving her the chance to leave, or try at least. But something in the way he looked away from her, his posture slumping into the back of his leather chair, made her pause. "My god," he muttered, removing his hand. "My god."

"Oh, now don't *you* go to pieces," she said angrily. "I mean, I'm the one who's going to be tortured—isn't that right?"

"Dr. Kurtz, your previous analyst?" he went on, almost to himself, ignoring her dramatic line of inquiry. He couldn't so much as glance in her direction. "She's threatened you? Or made a proposition of some kind?"

"Yeah, you could fucking say that."

"What did she propose? What exactly? You haven't—*conspired* with her? Dear girl, tell me you haven't."

Dr. Greenson no longer appeared composed, but he was as tweedy as before—his frayed jacket rumpled on his soft body, the weariness in his eyes somehow enhancing their power of observation. He knew so many intimate details of her life—had vouched for her with the studio, which was paying his bills. And yet she'd never really needed to trust him until now. "How do I know you're not one of them?"

He shook his head slightly, lifted his open palms to her. "You can't. You'll just have to make your own decision about that. Either I am—in which case, you are in no worse a situation than you were when you walked in today. Or I am not, and might actually be of assistance to you. If you are involved with the people I think you're involved with, you are in bigger trouble than I ever imagined. You'll be needing all the help you can get."

"Fucking *hell*. Are you with the Russians, or aren't you?"

"No. I am not."

"Okay." He was right—there was no way to be sure, but the way he was watching her, the urgency in his gaze, made her want to believe him.

Right then, that and his word seemed enough to take a chance on. As she returned to the couch, she asked: "How do you know Dr. Kurtz? What she really is."

"Ah, well. We have been in the same field a long time. And when I was a younger man I had what you might call socialist sympathies. That was how we grew up—my parents were Russian Jews, born under the tsars, so they saw firsthand the real horror of this world. Growing up in Brooklyn, Lenin was a hero in my family, and later I studied Marx as I studied Freud. It was a different time . . ." He trailed off. "I first met your Dr. Kurtz when I was studying in Vienna, and saw her at conferences and cocktail parties over the years. I had a vague sense of what she was involved in—it was generally known in psychoanalytic circles that the Party intelligence apparatus liked to have analysts as cell leaders, for the twin reasons that their training gave them insight into the psyches of the members under them, the ability to spot disloyalty and doubt, and that it provided perfect cover. They could meet in the privacy of their offices, receive information from their agents and give new instruction, all under the guise of an analytic session."

"And you knew that Dr. Kurtz was a Soviet agent?"

"No. I couldn't have imagined it. Most of us who leaned that way in our youth were disillusioned during the atrocities of the thirties."

"Have you met Alexei?"

"Not that I know of. But I am sure that is not his real name. Why don't you start from the beginning? Tell me who 'Alexei' is to you, everything that has happened."

An old instinct rose in her—to tell a half-truth, to make herself a sweet, clueless heroine lost in a bleak fairy tale—but as soon as she began talking, the need to unburden herself was too great, and the whole ludicrous story poured out, from that sunny day at Schwab's, to the hoarse *I love you* on a bathroom sink in Manhattan, to the near strangulation last night. When she finished, her throat was wounded and dry. Dr. Greenson slouched in his chair, his hair more disordered than when they had begun, as though he, too, were exhausted by what had transpired and could muster none of the usual empathy.

After a time he straightened, and with his eyes focused on the thread-bare carpet underfoot, began to speak. "You can't go home. It won't be safe, even with your ex-husband's employee there. You'll stay here, for the time being. We'll call the studio—they have much better security, I'll tell them it's important to your mental health, for the completion of the picture. And you have a way of contacting the president? A private line, you said?"

Even now, this fact gave her a twinge of pride. "Yes."

"You've got to call him right away and tell him he's in danger. Don't tell him everything, but tell him about Alexei, what he asked you to do. That you suspect there may be other plots afoot. If he meant it when he said he loved you, then you might come out of this all right."

Marilyn nodded mechanically. He was right, and anyway she had no energy to argue. The way she had dressed herself that morning felt silly, the open neck of the peasant-style blouse tucked into the fitted navy skirt, the high heels, and the big hair, as though her feminine beauty would ever do her any good again, if indeed it ever had.

"There's a telephone in the living room," he went on, not meeting her eye. "I'm going to think through what you've told me. Then you'll have dinner with my family, and we'll put your troubles aside until tomorrow."

The living room was paneled in dark wood and built-in shelves stocked with books that looked much handled. It was like her house, or how she hoped her house would someday be—lived-in and warm. She could hear the sound of a radio somewhere, Dr. Greenson's wife and daughter talking to each other in a nearby room. Marilyn set her jaw, picked up the phone. He answered right away so she didn't have time to fortify her resolve. There was Jack's voice, as forceful as ever, and before she could help it her right foot was girlishly twisted around the back of her left ankle.

"Goddamn, do I have a hankering for you," he said, in the sure manner that could make her forget everything.

"You miss me?" she whispered.

"Hell yes. I've been in the office burying myself in paper just so I won't go crazy thinking about it."

"I know." She glanced up at the wood beams of the ceiling. A smell of onions turning sweet in a frying pan wafted from the kitchen. "Listen, Jack, I need to talk to you—"

"Me, too, baby."

What was that in his voice—all of a sudden he sounded far away, short of breath, distracted. "I mean it's kinda serious. I need to tell you that—"

"You thought I meant the usual talk? No. No—I have something serious to say to you, too." He cleared his throat, and she realized that the thinness of his voice was actually nerves, and her heartbeat began to make itself known. "I can't stop thinking about you. I can't stop thinking for anything. I might be going crazy, I don't know. But what that phony shaman said out in the desert—what he said about feeling at home—that just keeps repeating in my head like a skipped record."

"Yeah?" Her voice had gone reedy, too.

"Yeah. Listen, I don't want you to belong to anybody else. I want you to be mine. I know it doesn't make any sense. But if the world can blow at any minute—and believe me, that's about the size of it—seems to me we might as well be as happy as we can until then. Don't you? Marilyn, would you marry me?"

"But you're already—"

"I know, I know. Maybe it couldn't be right away. But you know that's all for show, don't you? And I can't live like that. Not forever. So say you will, and we'll figure everything else out tomorrow."

"Yes." She had never been so keenly aware of the blood traveling through her body, how it pulsed between her toes, up the backs of her knees, in the tip of her tongue, to the rhythm of her heart. Her own aliveness had never been so vivid. "Yes, yes."

"When can I see you?" he went on, forceful again. "Tell me tonight. Get on a plane tonight? I've got to see you."

"Yes."

"Go now. I'll meet you at the Carlyle."

"Yes."

"You remember the procedure? How to get to me at the Carlyle?"

"Yes."

"Marilyn—I love you."

"I love you, too."

Through the glass of the front door she could see the Greensons' yard, the overgrown garden, the daisy-dotted lawn stretching out toward the westernmost point of the property, where you could see all the way down to Santa Monica, the vast blue sea beyond. The old green Dodge that she'd bought last week at a garage for fifty dollars was parked in the shade of an oak tree. In a nearby room Mrs. Greenson was saying something that made her daughter laugh, and Marilyn silently placed the receiver in its cradle. There was no sound from his office. If he saw her, he would ask her how the conversation had gone, how her confession had been received, and she couldn't answer that.

Jack was going to marry her, he wanted her always, which was what she'd been seeking her whole life. A man like that to give her always. The reason she'd gotten close to him in the beginning was too complicated to tell him over the phone. She couldn't risk telling him over the phone. She was too afraid he'd take it all back. When they were together she would explain the whole thing from the beginning, the very beginning, the original hurt of her father's leaving, and why she'd gone to such insane lengths to find him. But just now she wouldn't be able to make any of that come out right. Her head was too scrambled, and her heart too sure. In the meantime, he was the president. Surely Jack was well protected already, and as soon as she was with him she'd be well protected, too.

Her handbag was still on the couch in the office, but that didn't matter. She'd managed to board planes with just her name before. Very quietly, she stepped out of her shoes, picked them up by the ankle straps, and tiptoed for the door.

THIRTY-EIGHT

New York, June 1962

IT was morning when she arrived in Manhattan, but she was not the first customer at the Joy Tavern. A cabbie in a dirty blue jean jacket was discussing the vicissitudes of the stock market with a genteel housewife whose diamonds refracted brilliantly but whose wig sat at an off angle. Both appeared deaf to the yips of the Pomeranian in her lap. Marilyn had telegrammed the Carlyle before boarding her flight, saying that Miss Green would arrive at eight A.M., but she was early, so she ordered a screwdriver and daydreamed about a time when she wouldn't need a pseudonym. "Say, aren't you Marilyn Monroe?" the bartender asked.

She placed her finger perpendicular to her smile. "But don't tell anyone, okay?"

He winked, and let her be. She knew when the hour changed because a church bell began to sound. The car came to a sudden stop outside the bar a few minutes later, reminding her that haste and agitation still existed in the world. A man in a black suit climbed from the backseat, pushed through the bar's front door, let it bang shut behind him, surveyed the scene, and approached Marilyn at a purposeful gait. "Miss Green?"

"Yes?"

"This is for you."

The man was young and had an arrogant, unsmiling face. He held out a green leather jeweler's box, which ought to have pleased her, but there was something in his insistent presentation that made her want to refuse. As soon as she took it from his hands, he nodded his good-bye and departed, more rapidly than he had arrived.

Inside, on a bed of red tissue paper, was a gold cigarette case engraved *To Johnny.* The case had been cleaned, although inside was a folded, typewritten note that said *We cannot possibly accept this lovely gift. All best wishes. Robert F. Kennedy*

"Oh, shit," she muttered.

The bartender's eyes darted in her direction. "You all right?"

"Got a telephone?"

He indicated it by lifting his chin. "Pay phone in the back."

She tried to keep herself steady as she dialed the number. Tried not to assume the worst. Yet there it was, the shrill bleat of a disconnected line. She closed her eyes, put the listening end of the receiver against her forehead. A hundred voices clamored within her, in fury and disappointment, but she took a breath, tried again. The air was thin, as though she were at a high altitude, and the result was the same. Her agony did not make it less obvious what had happened. Somehow Bobby knew what Jack had said to her last night; he had made Jack think better of it; they'd have changed the number she used to contact him before she even landed in New York. "You're crazy," Bobby must have said to Jack. And probably: "She's crazy, too."

The bar had no gravity. Patrons, bar stools, bottles of booze, mirrors—the earth had no hold on them. These seemed off-kilter, one second from flying at her. She was furious at herself for not listening to Greenson, horrified that she had selfishly believed in everything turning out all right.

She had the operator connect her to Pilar Florist on Second Avenue. "This is Marilyn Monroe," she said. "I'd like to order an arrangement of purple irises for the children's wing at Sloan-Kettering."

"Marilyn Monroe?" the woman said, and made a sound like spitting. "Never heard of her."

The line went dead, and Marilyn didn't call back. Instead she tried Jack's private line at the White House again and again until her fingers went numb and she had to admit that it was no mistake, not some error of dialing. By then, her heart felt like a little mouse that had been shot up with amphetamines and left to run in a ball till dawn. The elation of the last twelve hours had been cut down clean, and in its place was the stark lonesomeness of all her years. *He meant it*, she wanted to tell herself, but the other feeling was so much stronger. The feeling of lying awake on a hard orphanage cot, another girl's feet shuffling against her pillow, and knowing that if she died there would be no one in the world to care. She had only a few minutes to allow the devastation to come and go. Afterward there would be so much else to see to, and no time to waste on self-pity. *You'll get him back*, she told herself and, trying hard to believe it, left the Joy Tavern with what dignity she could summon.

You'll get him back, she mouthed to herself as she rode in a taxi across town, and as she climbed the five tenement flights. She would get him back, but in the meantime she had to find Alexei, make him tell her what he'd meant when he said her replacement was on the way. She had to, and anyway she wasn't afraid. She had seen that Alexei couldn't do the job himself—if she found him alone, she'd be all right. Her heart was broken, anyway. How could they harm her now? The door to the studio apartment was already open, and she could see through it to the old floorboards, which were shiny where they had recently been mopped.

"Hello?" she called.

A few moments later a woman in a beige housedress and mules appeared from the back of the place. She flinched in recognition when she saw Marilyn but, out of politeness or maybe resentment, gave no other sign that she knew who the visitor was. "Can I help you, miss? You here to see about the apartment or something?"

"No—I was looking for the man who used to live here. A man named Alexei Lazarev. Do you know where he is?"

"He's gone. That's what men do, girlie. They go."

"When did he leave?"

"I haven't heard a peep from him in weeks. Then a couple of gentlemen cleaned out his things—they must have come in the night and been careful not to make a sound. Creditors maybe, or the bookie. I didn't hardly realize anybody was here until they were on their way out—but they paid through August, so I don't complain."

"Do you know where he went?"

She shrugged. "Don't know, don't care. Only way to get by in this mean old world."

"I've got to find him—do you understand? It's more important than I can possibly explain. Do you have any idea where he might have gone? Did he leave a forwarding address? Is there anyone who'd know? Anyone who visited him, knew him?"

The landlady put her hand into her lower back and observed Marilyn. After a silence she shook her head and went back toward the kitchenette, where the mop was stuck in its bucket. Over her shoulder she said: "Only person ever visited him was that Russian lady. Big black hair, long nails, enough perfume to drown a cat. Looked like a whore to me. I suppose she'll be taking a pay cut now—maybe you'll find her bawling her eyes out down on Tenth Avenue."

"Well—thanks all the same."

"Yeah, yeah." The mop was in the woman's hands again, and she didn't glance up to acknowledge Marilyn's parting.

THIRTY-NINE

South of Los Angeles Airport, August 1962

THE bungalow was on a street that sloped toward the beach, five blocks or so from the boardwalk, and the yards nearer the water were decorated with the pastel colors of surfboards and bathing suits left out to dry. She supposed it was a temporary neighborhood where people rented for the season. That it was the kind of street where nobody took particular notice of strangers. For a few days she drove by the place, saw the lights on and the car in the driveway, and gleaned that he never went out except for a walk in the evening. She had been hunting Alexei for two months, and in that time she'd grown surer of her hunch: He would never hurt her.

On Friday, when he returned from the daily walk, the strained six o'clock light was filtered through blinds, painting gray and yellow bars on the bedroom floor. By then she had entered the house, by forcing open a bathroom window, and prepared herself for him. She lay on the bed—or rather, the mattress on top of the box spring on the bedroom floor—partially covered by a sheet, her face mostly denuded, just a little lipstick and mascara, her hair pushed back from her forehead and gone wavy after days in which she had neglected the rituals of physical appearance.

She listened as he closed the front door, took three steps inside. Paused. He seemed to quickly realize he was not alone. The slow crinkling of the paper bag he was carrying, as he placed it down, suggested a sudden instinct for caution. The glasses of water she had positioned, on either side of the bed, were still there—a glance reassured her of their presence. To let him know she knew he was listening, she lit a cigarette and let its smoke waft through the rooms.

She almost couldn't believe Alexei was there, in the next room, after searching for so long with a doggedness that had left no time for yearning. No dwelling on Jack, what could have been or might yet be. The White House switchboard was under strict orders not to take her calls (as a sweet operator explained to her one night, before identifying herself as a fan). Bobby had stonewalled her, and Peter and Pat had remained friendly in a distant way, inviting her over less, handling her in such a manner that she knew one false move and she'd be dropped. So, Marilyn had kept moving.

She'd taken to carrying a large change purse and placing her calls from pay phones, never using the same one twice. The studio had fired her after a week's absence (she claimed exhaustion, but nobody believed that one anymore), and she'd taken advantage of the ensuing controversy by giving as many interviews, posing for as many photographers, as possible, figuring that the Russians wouldn't dare have her killed in front of a member of the press. Plus, the wild look in her eyes seemed to turn the photographers on. She'd told Alan that Douglass Walls had made a pass ("In my own *home!*")— that once rejected, he had become violent—and insisted he be fired. Alan didn't believe her, but he did as instructed. After that she'd tried to be in the orbit of either Joe or Frankie, who always had a small army of toughs. Each could smell the other's recent presence, and disliked it, but they were of that old school of masculinity, and couldn't resist a damsel, especially when she meant a competition.

It was through Frankie that she eventually discovered Alexei's whereabouts.

In the final week of July, she'd flown to Tahoe in Frankie's private plane, mostly because he mentioned that Pat and Peter would be staying at the Cal-Neva that weekend as well. But Pat told her flatly to stop asking if any of her brothers would be visiting California soon ("Forget them, darling, that's just what they do—Jack passes his girls down to Bobby, and Bobby to Teddy, so unless you want to go to work on *him*, you had better move on"). *So,* she thought, *the rumor is I've been with Bobby, too.*

Marilyn had been trying to kill time without letting down her guard when she spotted Sam Giancana entering the ballroom. He'd been flanked by a large entourage that included a pale, voluptuous woman whose black hair was wound in an elaborate pile on top of her head, and who possessed a stare of blank, continental indifference. There was something gorgeous and secretive about her, and with a flash of intuition, Marilyn saw what had happened—that Alexei, when recruiting a source who was most malleable when she was loved, had become attached. Attached enough that he was furious when Marilyn guessed her real profession. But, as she was to discover over the course of a long and lurid evening, Alexei's source in the Giancana outfit was in fact his number one Russian hooker—not, as she had angrily declared in Payne Whitney, his third favorite.

The hooker's name was Vera, and Marilyn had cornered her in the ladies' lounge, where they quickly bonded over their portable medicine chests and the technical difficulties of fellating Frank Sinatra. By the time they returned to the party, arm in arm and plenty looped, Marilyn had the situation pretty well figured: Giancana's main mistress—a singer whose fame must have seemed sparkling enough when the actress who played Lorelei Lee on the big screen wasn't hanging around—was unwilling to perform the kind of tricks a professional would, a fact which guaranteed the coexistence of these two women while cooling their mutual resentment not at all.

"He used to love me, before *she* came around," Vera confessed, in her slurred, muddy accent, when Giancana and Phyllis (the official girlfriend) were on the dance floor. "Now he only brings me out when he thinks there might be an orgy."

That she was fast friends with an even bigger star made Vera bold, and then chummy, and then intoxicated, and by the time Marilyn dropped that she knew Alexei—musing first that *she* used to have a Russian friend, and explaining, once it seemed safe, that she had worked for him, that they had cut ties when it seemed the FBI might be on to them, but that she had some big information now and needed to get in touch—she was sure Vera would help her any way she could. The idea that she and Marilyn Monroe had been secretly connected all this time seemed to fortify her, imbue her with fresh importance. She was certainly willing to whisper the address of the bungalow, south of the Los Angeles airport, where Alexei had told Vera he could find her, if she were in trouble.

Marilyn closed her eyes, took a breath, listened to him crossing the bungalow's main room, approaching her. Everything came down to this.

"I've missed you," she whispered, opening her eyes. There he was, filling the doorframe, his features in high relief with the end-of-day shadows. He was dressed to blend with the summer population, in blue jeans and a white T-shirt and a bomber jacket, but this only made him appear old. The translucent blue eyes watched her and revealed nothing as she took a last drag of the cigarette and put it into a tea saucer on the floor. "Isn't that the way? Soon as you start looking out for a man, he's nowhere to be found."

He glanced at the water on the far side of the mattress from her. "Poison?"

She gave no sign of surprise at this turn, that he had so easily read her plan. It was only half her plan—the backup, in case her hunch was wrong. Instead she let her mouth quiver open, her eyes become wide and vulnerable. "Don't you like talking to me anymore? Can't we talk a little?"

"You thought you would seduce me, and afterward, when I was spent and thirsty, I wouldn't think before I drank. That I'd just reach out, and take the nearest glass."

Marilyn pushed her head into the wall, so that her back arched slightly and the shape of her breasts showed through the sheet. "There must be something you want? Something I can do to make things right between us."

Her knees swayed together and apart, and she let her hand slide down the inner slope of her thigh. She stretched her naked toes, held his gaze. "Let me repay my debt. I'll show you what a good girl I can be. All this time we've spent together—you must have thought about it. Imagined how it would be. Tell me what it is. I'll give you everything, anything you want. Only, let me try it my way—you don't have to kill Jack, I can convince him of anything you say. He loves me, you know. He said he wants to marry me."

"Oh, N.J." Alexei's head swung disappointedly, and he could not meet her eye. He focused on the ground as he slipped his hand under his jacket. The gesture made her heart tick faster—but after that, she knew where to find his weapon.

"You're going to kill me?" Her voice broke over the question. She didn't believe he would—his lack of desire told her he couldn't—but saying the word let the fear in. Her breasts rose and fell with her frightened breathing, and for several seconds his hand remained invisible, inside the jacket, somewhat below his heart. "I didn't think you had it in you. After you came to my house. When you had your chance, but didn't take it. I thought you'd never. Not after all the time we spent together. Not before we—"

"Can you even imagine a purposeful life?" He spit the words, but still didn't lift his gaze off the floor. "Do you know the training I've had, how long I've been at this game? And you, you *stupid* girl—you thought you could climb in the bathroom window and put an end to me, just like that. After all I taught you—and you didn't even remember to close the window behind you. Anybody could see it from the street."

Her face went white, and her heart beat a furious tattoo. "You really gonna snuff me out, then?"

The room had become murky with sundown, but this only made the whites of his eyes, not directed at her, that much brighter.

"You can't, can you?" she went on. "I knew you wouldn't. I know the reason why." The tremble was still in her voice, but she was growing sure. She saw it all, the whole conspiracy—not what they had planned for the country, but what they had planned for her. He had known, before he ever spoke to her, the way her heart softened when someone called her *my dear*. The odd, far-away tenderness she held for the child Norma Jeane, whom she must once have been. How she reacted when someone said Norma Jeane's name, seemed to care for the girl. She was almost sure now, and really he'd been telling her so all along, lodging the idea in her subconscious from the beginning. He knew how to pronounce those syllables better than anyone who had ever lived. "It's the same reason you don't want to fuck me. You're my father. Aren't you? That man, in the hospital, he was just an actor. An image, to give me hope. This whole time, it was you who was my real daddy."

He did not reply, but his gaze migrated slowly to meet hers. The grip he had on whatever was inside his jacket relaxed. She could see the vein in his neck, his blood pulsating.

"It's true, huh? That's why I'm not like the others. Why you can't kill me as they told you to. Or I guess maybe as you'd like to. That would be too cruel, even for you. I mean, to kill your own daughter."

"Yes, my dear." A sigh worked down his torso, distending a belly she hadn't known he had. He released the grip on the hidden gun so his hands could clasp together as though in prayer. After a moment, he spread them over his face. "I've wanted to tell you for a long time. But I ought to have known you wouldn't need me to figure it out."

Tears surged unbidden to the rims of her eyelids, and she did not have to remind herself to make her voice girlish and scrubbed of guile. "You know how long I've waited? For—this?"

"Yes." His head tipped compassionately, and he opened his arms, beckoning her.

With an arm across her chest to hold the sheet in place, she stood unsteadily. She kept the sheet up, but didn't try to hide her nakedness, which she hoped would make him uncomfortable, make her seem delicate and hapless. "Do you know how hard it's been?" she said as she approached. "How lonely and lost I've always felt deep down?"

"Yes," he said. He was watching her with a sympathetic light in his eyes, and when she reached him she found there was some part of her that wanted an embrace, and that made it easy to throw her arms around his middle, rest her cheek against his chest. One of his hands rested on the small of her back; the other stroked the crown of her head, and she turned her face to gaze up at him, just as she'd always imagined she someday would. He smiled at her, sadly, with half his mouth, and she smiled back.

"I had it all planned, just what I'd say when I finally met him. You."

"What was it?"

"I'd say . . ." She let her eyelids sink a little, and sighed as her fingers tip-toed down his chest, *da da da da.* "I'd say . . ." Without changing her soft, contented expression, she thrust her hand into his jacket, grabbed the gun, cocked it, aimed for his knee. Pulled the trigger.

There are some things that happen in life, no matter how young, which the body does not forget.

The force of the bullet knocked him backward, onto the floor in the hallway. He shrieked, a moan of pure agony that began high but soon became low and guttural. The sheet had fallen to her feet, and she stood, naked, every muscle tensed with the gun. For another minute Alexei screamed in pain, grasping at the place on his leg where his blue jeans were torn open and soaked with blood. Then he went quiet. His breathing was still ragged, but he had put the pain away somehow and focused his attention on her. Despite his injury, he appeared more wary than angry. "I'm sorry," he managed, through heaving breaths. "I'm sorry."

"Fuck sorry." She cocked the gun and pointed it at his face. If he moved fast, he could grab an ankle; he was stronger than she, and surely he knew the best way to take her down. The sheet had fallen to her feet, and she hoped that her stark nakedness would unnerve him, give her some advantage.

"Let's talk. Don't you want to talk? Remember how much you wanted to talk? I'm your father, N.J., isn't there so much more we need to tell each other?"

She regarded him down the shaft of the gun. "You're going to tell me what they have planned for me. What they have planned for Jack. That's all I want to know."

"N.J., don't be a fool. Forget about that. Here I am. Don't you want to know how this came to be?" The blood was spreading across the beige linoleum. He leaned forward, on his elbow, as though testing how close he could get to her.

She stepped away, jerked the gun to show him she meant business.

He nodded that he understood and drew back. "Listen. Be reasonable. I can help you, my dear. But I've got to call a doctor—I'm bleeding too much. Call him, all right? I'll give you the number. After that, we'll figure everything out. We'll take care of you."

"Take care of me?" She exhaled sharply from the lowest point of her exposed belly. "I'm not calling nobody. Anyway, how can I trust you? What if this is just another lie? A lie you've trained me all this time to believe in."

"N.J., you don't have any choice. If you kill me, I can't shield you anymore. They'll find you. You won't last long on the run, you know that, don't you? I'm your father—you were right, you sensed it. I could never harm you." Again he reached out, the same tentative gesture, resting his hand on her foot. It was a gentle touch, protective, neither menacing nor carnal. "Think about it. How many men have had the opportunities I've had, and haven't made a pass at you?"

The metallic odor of blood was strong, and Alexei had begun quietly to stroke her foot. She relaxed her arms slightly, so the gun was no longer aimed at his head but a few feet away on the floor. He marked this change, and his hand on her foot became more reassuring, more intentional, as though he believed he had her.

"N.J., my dear, give me the gun."

But the nickname, the "my dear," had lost their magic. They made her sick now. She tightened her grip, narrowed her eyes, pointed the gun at his face. Fast as a cat, he yanked her leg out from under her, and she fell hard on her tailbone. She gasped in shock. For a moment they breathed in tandem, both watchful, making their own calculations. She had the gun, her only power. Another moment, and she wouldn't have that. But if she killed him she'd never hear the story, how she really came to be. All her life seethed in her, every neglect, humiliation, every moment of desperation and of hope, the inescapable wound of her origin, which had led her here, to this forgotten bungalow. If he was her father, still he wasn't, for what kind of father would do what he had done? And yet even after everything, she wanted to know. The who and the why, how he had become the person sprawled before her, about the blood spreading over linoleum, which was her blood, too. What he thought when he first saw her mother, the color of the dress she was wearing when she smiled at him that long-ago day. Then everything got very quiet, and her lungs ceased their fluctuation, and she heard the clear, high, determined voice of a child saying: "But I don't *want* to know."

She braced herself and fired. The first thing she felt was how her palms burned. That part she had forgotten. Alexei was splayed on his back, arms like a cross, mouth ripped open, a smash of matter and bone at his temple where the fatal bullet had entered his skull. *It's over*, she thought, aware that she could only afford to believe that one a few minutes longer.

FORTY

Los Angeles, August 1962

THE gun went off once more before she left—to break the lock on the suitcase in the bedroom closet—and then she dressed quickly in the black slacks and loose black sweater she had left in the bathroom earlier. There was nothing else in the house: The cupboards were bare; the closet held only three pairs of pants and three white dress shirts. The shopping bag Alexei had returned with—a carton of milk, a dozen eggs, a loaf of white bread, the afternoon edition—remained on the built-in hutch by the entry. She plucked the newspaper before knocking over the other contents as she left, thinking that would give the impression of a struggle, a story for the investigators to chew on. She stopped at a pay phone a half mile down Highland, to call the police and report that while walking her dog down to the beach she had heard shots near the bungalow's address. Then she merged onto the Pacific Coast Highway, sequined with taillights in the darkness, and drove north trying not to think the word *kill*.

After passing through two more towns without any sign of a tail, she pulled into a liquor store parking lot. She tried Jack and Bobby from the pay phone, got the usual response, and in the backseat began to go through the contents of the suitcase: a leather-bound book full of notations she could scarcely begin to comprehend, the carefully organized and coded communications, the sheer quantity of cash, assorted personal documents. A sense of mounting panic came over her as the vastness of what they'd planned—were still probably planning—emerged. But the sight of her own false passport and birth certificate—using the names Sophie Mortenson, and Mrs. Ivan

Lancer, and an old photograph from her brunette days—gave her a brief breath of calm. What could Alexei's possession of these documents mean except that he had not given up on her, that his sense of paternal obligation was real, that despite everything he wanted to give her another life? And then, realizing that even in death he was able to tug at her loyalty, melt her to his purposes, she had to shove open the car door and be sick on the already dirty asphalt.

It was while using Alexei's newspaper to clean the vomit off the edge of her car that she noticed the small item about the attorney general's trip to San Francisco that weekend. After that, she didn't think much. She wiped her mouth with the back of her hand, started up the engine, and drove steadily, never more than five miles over the speed limit, to the Lawfords', making a wild left turn across two lanes that elicited horn blasts from the oncoming cars.

She knew the man who opened her door—he'd worked parties there before—but even so he didn't immediately recognize her, dressed down as she was. "Miss Monroe—are you all right?"

"Yes," she said. *Yes*, even though every time she closed her eyes she saw her father's mangled leg, his blank face. The body torn open and the spirit gone, the whole human mechanism revealed as so many fragile, unreliable parts. When the security man reached for the keys, she pushed down the lock and closed the door. "Leave it where it is, I won't be long. Are Mr. and Mrs. Lawford here?"

"He is." He glanced at the other attendants nervously—there were too many of them, she thought, for an ordinary night at the beach house. "Let me park your car, and have you announced."

"No. No! There isn't time. I won't be long."

"All right, but—"

He was still protesting when she hurried past the gate, through the interior courtyard and the rooms of the house, which was lightly populated in the post-dinner hour with a few hangers-on. She found Peter outside, waving a lit cigarette close to his ruddy face, legs crossed dandy-like, his cocktail balanced on his lap so he could use both hands to punctuate the story he was loudly telling a handful of guests overdressed for a casual dinner party. Behind them the surface of the pool glowed.

"Peter—"

"Marilyn!" He leapt to his feet at the sight of her, but was not so surprised as to spill his cocktail. "Jesus Christ, are you all right? You look like hell, baby. Where are your shoes?"

"Uh . . . in the car, I think."

"Is that blood on her foot?" a woman lounging on a nearby deck chair drunk-whispered to her companion. There were six or so like her, staring at Marilyn with salacious pity, an expression she was pretty well acquainted with by then.

"Fine, I'm fine. Is Pat here?"

"She's on her way to Hyannis. But now listen, Marilyn—"

"Bobby's in California, isn't that right? Is he coming here, too, Peter?"

"I don't know about that, baby. I think it's a little family trip to San Francisco, with the children. You know, ride the cable cars, that sort of thing, probably no time to come visit us out at the beach . . ."

"I've got to talk to him, Peter. Can you get him on the line for me? You could, couldn't you? It would be better to see him in person, but the phone would be a start, and—"

"Marilyn, you've got to stop this," Peter interrupted her, wrapping his arm around her shoulders and drawing her away from the gawking guests, out of the glare of the upstairs windows and toward the beach. "You're acting like a madwoman, you know that, don't you?"

"I'm not crazy, Peter, please, you've got to listen to me, this matters more than anything—"

"Didn't Pat have a chat with you up in Tahoe? She was supposed to. You have to pull yourself together, baby. I know you and Jack enjoyed each other, but that's over. It's gotta be. And whatever happened with Bobby—that's over, too. There are already too many stories, and you know how once there's a little scandal people love to fabricate on top of that. Of course you didn't help yourself—that stunt you pulled at the Garden was practically pornographic."

"Forget the Garden. That was a thousand years ago, okay? This isn't about me and Jack. It's for Jack's safety. We've got to do something before they kill him. Okay?"

The muscles of Peter's face pulled in strange directions—he seemed unsure whether to be amused or afraid. With some effort he removed her hands from his shirt collar—where they had, unbeknownst to her, assumed a furious grip—and began to lead her back toward the house. "You can't say that kind of thing," he told her with quiet intensity. "I'm going to send you home—someone is going to drive you—and tomorrow I'll come around to check on you, all right?"

"No!" she shrieked, breaking his hold and darting backward. He turned, saw that she was tense and ready to run away from him, around the pool, if necessary. "You're going to listen to me, Peter."

"My god, Marilyn, what does that doc have you taking? We knew you were a little free with that stuff, but this is—I mean, Christ, I've never seen you like this."

"Peter—" She would have said more, but the sound had by then become too loud to ignore, the whooshing of the blades violent against the sea air. She and Peter went quiet and drifted toward the glass wall that separated the Lawfords' property from the public beach, watching the helicopter's vertical descent, its lights illuminating the hilly sand below.

"Marilyn," Peter implored her, grabbing her arm. "You can't be here."

She freed herself and ran through the gate at the edge of the pool deck, across the sand, which was damp with evening dew. Peter was behind her, but he was too late. The big blades were still *thwacking* through the night, but underneath, through the darkness, she could make out a man jumping down onto the sand and striding in her direction. Hope made her heart light and fast, but she still smiled, even when his features became clear and she knew it was Bobby. As much as she longed for Jack, it was better that it was Bobby—she remembered his fierceness, and thought he would know what to do; and his kindness, that day in Palm Springs, and felt he'd be a good one for taking confession. Even at a distance his gaze was unrelenting.

"Bobby!" she called, throwing herself into his arms.

"Marilyn." He held her for a moment, and with his arm around her shoulders, they began to walk toward the house. "I'm glad to see you," he continued warmly. "I was hoping we could have a little talk this weekend."

She could see Peter's silhouette against the illuminated house, the guests behind him arrayed on the patio furniture, in poses alert to a brewing drama. "Listen, we don't have much time," she said, putting her face close to his, holding on to the lapel of his jacket. "Peter thinks I'm crazy, but I'm not. You don't think that, do you? That I'm crazy?"

"Of course not. You're just sensitive, and you've been hurt."

"No. Bobby, Bobby, I've done something terrible. I didn't know what I was doing—I should have—I—"

"It's all right." He was rubbing her back as they moved across the sand where the wrens had left their crisscrossing, birdbrained tracks. "It's all right. There's isn't anything I can't fix."

"Good." She squeezed her eyes shut and told herself Go. "Listen, Bobby, the thing is, I've been spying on Jack. For the Russians. I tried to stop, but they wouldn't let me. And then I tried to tell him, but I couldn't. And I've killed somebody—the man who asked me to spy—but—but—I think they're still going to murder him—the president, I mean—and I have all these papers, and I don't know what they mean except that . . ."

"Shhh . . ." She was trying to choke down sobs, which was making it difficult to get the words out, and her vision was blurry with tears, although the pressure of Bobby's arm around her was unchanged. He gave no sign of surprise, or alarm. They were almost to the gate by then, and he whispered in her ear, "Let's go talk about this somewhere private, all right? Somewhere safe. We'll get a room at the Roosevelt. We'll take your car. Do you have the keys to your car?"

"Yes."

"Give them to me."

She fumbled in the pocket of her slacks for the keys, handed them over.

"Good. Now pull yourself together, try not to make a scene in front of these people. I'm here, and I'll get you through it. Just keep your head down, and you can cry later if you want to."

"Okay."

The helicopter lifted off behind them, kicking up sand and whipping their hair, making it impossible to say anything more. Peter was at the gate holding it open so they could pass, and Marilyn shielded her eyes with her hand as they hurried across the patio, through the house, out the front entryway. It wasn't until they were on the drive, out by the highway, that he released her, unlocking the front passenger door and holding it open so that she could climb in. He shut her in, and turned to say a few words to the sentries in the plain black suits. She watched him in the side mirror—his handsome, worried, asymmetrical face, the intensity with which he was giving instructions, and felt sad for his children, riding the cable cars without their father that weekend. In the rearview, she checked her appearance, wiped away the smudged mascara under her eyes. She was trying to pinch some color into her pallid complexion when a man—not the man she was expecting—slipped into the driver's seat and started up the car.

He was holding down the locks, so she could only crank the window. "You said—"

The kindness was gone from Bobby's countenance as he approached the car. "Marilyn, this man is going to take you to your psychiatrist's house. The address is 920 Franklin, you got that?" he said to the driver, who grunted yes.

"But—"

"You're lucky I'm not dumping you in a sanitarium right now. What Jack said to you he may have meant, for all I know. But that's never going to happen. You hear me? God help me, if you try and contact me or my brother again, I'll have put you where no one can find you."

His back was already to her when the man behind the wheel peeled away from the house, a second car tailing them up the highway. "Take me back," she said, but anemically, so that she almost couldn't blame him for ignoring her. As they drove into the city she began to wonder where Alexei's people were, if they were watching from passing cars or if they were waiting at her home. If Bobby really had planned to talk to her, and if so, whether Jack knew that he'd threaten to have her sent away, do the same thing the Russians had done to her. She still had no will to protest, a few moments later, when the driver dragged her across the Greensons' yard. He rang the doorbell, and she tried to straighten up, smooth her hair, when she saw their teenage daughter had answered the door.

"Can I help you?" Becky asked. Her hair was up in curlers, and a floral nightgown covered most of her body.

"Is Dr. Greenson at home?"

"No." Becky's eyes, wide with alarm, went to Marilyn. "They're at the Hollywood Bowl. The Henry Mancini Orchestra. Do you want me to call him?"

"No." Marilyn managed to summon a little force as she told the driver, "You can leave me with her."

"But Mr. Kennedy said—"

"Give her the fucking car keys," Marilyn said. "The concert must be over by now, Dr. Greenson will be home soon. Anyway, you can tell your boss I'm in good hands and I won't bother him anymore."

He was reluctant, but did as he was told. Marilyn stood on the steps to the house next to Becky as he crossed the lawn and climbed into the idling car that had followed them from the Lawfords' beach house, and watched it disappear down the hill.

"Do you want me to call Father? I could, they'd find him. He'd come right away."

"No." Marilyn took the keys from her and began to stumble over the grass to the place where they'd left her car. "Have him call when he gets back, though, just to check on me, see if I'm still around . . ."

"Are you sure you're fit to drive?" Becky cried after her.

"Yeah." Marilyn swung around for a final glimpse and, smiling sadly, called out, "Hey, darling, you know what? You can really do the twist. Good night! And good-bye, good-bye, good-bye . . ."

Of course she wasn't fit to drive, but that didn't deter her. Not after the events of the day. In fact, there was something maudlin and appropriate about steering the car into the nighttime city in such a frantic state. To die alone, in the land of freeways, mere miles from her birthplace, her car flying off a bridge or crushed against a traffic signal. That would be so much cleaner and simpler than waiting around for Alexei's people to find her. She drove recklessly with the window down, the night air sharp on her face. She got lost, and that was how she came upon the station. The big yellow building, lit from below like the picture palaces of her adolescence, with its deco ornamentation and palm tree fringe. As she crossed the parking lot, slipping between the black-and-white patrol cars, she had the sense of being far removed from any human activity—she could hear no voices, only the rush of vehicles on an invisible street—as though she were about to pass into another realm.

Inside the halls were wide and neon-lit, and smelled of old coffee cooked down in the pot. Now she heard the squeak of shoes, low murmurings, a file cabinet slammed shut. The first person she actually spoke to sat in an office by himself, his elbows folded on the big oak desk, a newspaper spread before him. He was wearing a white lab coat over a blue collared shirt, and his face was still pudgy with youth—he might have been born the same year she was, or later, even. The door was open, and *Chief Medical Examiner* was painted on its mottled glass, and she hovered there waiting to catch his attention.

"What do they call you?" she asked, when his absorption in the article— about a string of murders in what the paper termed a house of ill-repute— proved total.

"I am Dr. Noguchi," he replied, his focus cast down on the spread news- paper. "Dr. Thomas Noguchi."

"You're the top guy, huh?" she murmured.

As he glanced up he pulled his large, wire-rim glasses from their perch on his nose and put them aside. "I am the deputy coroner," he started to say. He stood up awkwardly and cleared his throat. "Oh my. You're—"

"Yeah?"

"Not wearing any shoes," he said, eventually, as though actually pronounc- ing her name would be too much for him.

"I guess I must have lost 'em someplace."

"Are you all right? I really don't think you ought to be barefoot here."

She glanced at her feet, but didn't see any reason for this to bother any- one. "If you're not the top guy, how come you're in his office?"

"Coroner Curphey usually goes home about ten on Friday evenings, and spends the weekend with his family."

"Sounds kinda lonesome to me. You're here by yourself all weekend?"

"I suppose he'd come in if there was a big case—but ordinarily there isn't much I can't handle personally, on my own. I—I can't think why that would be of any interest to you. What are you doing here, anyway?"

"This isn't what you thought it would be like, huh? All alone on a Friday night with Marilyn Monroe . . ."

"I'm sure I've never imagined any scenario of the kind," the deputy coroner replied, too quickly so she knew it was a lie.

She exhaled a disbelieving murmur and arched her back into the door-frame, cast her eyes down the hall. "I guess I just wanted to see what it's gonna be like."

"What *what* will be like?"

"You know, the end."

"The end?"

"Yeah. I always sort of knew I was the kind of girl they'd find in some seedy motel room somewhere with, I don't know, an empty bottle of pills next to the bed and a sad, sweet little note, leaving her favorite mink to the prop master's niece, in handwriting that's like hers but isn't. And then she gets wheeled in someplace like this. And every cop on duty gets a nice, big eyeful of her gorgeous corpse."

The coroner blinked, swallowed. He was trying to meet her gaze, but his focus kept slipping lower, where her breasts stretched the thin weave of her sweater.

"You wanna see them?" Her voice got smoky, and her hair, even unkempt as it was, did its job and fell coquettishly over half her face.

He swallowed. "Them?"

She began lifting her sweater, revealing the pale flesh of her torso.

The coroner leaned forward across the desk, neglecting to close his mouth.

She took two slow, swaying belly-dancer steps into the room, drew the sweater another few inches, above her first ribs. "You do, huh?" she whispered. "You want to see it all?"

The coroner's head bobbled on his neck as he felt across the desk for his glasses.

Then her shoulders drew back, and her smile disappeared. She dropped the hem of her sweater and tilted her head back. "No," she said. "I don't think you're going to see them just yet. After all, you'll get plenty when I'm dead."

FORTY-ONE

Los Angeles, August 1962

WALLS had been in a state of agitation for so many weeks that he was only ever able to fall asleep for a few minutes at a time. "You look like shit," his mother had observed that morning (out of disappointment more than concern, it seemed to him), and he could not tell her the reason why. The reason for his paleness, his bagged eyes, was that his friend who worked in the lab at the Bureau had finally gotten back to him regarding the flask that Marilyn had left in her hotel room back in May.

"Must be some case," he'd said, and explained that the contents matched a substance known to the Bureau because a Soviet scientist who had defected the previous summer had used it in negotiating a new life for himself and his wife in Dublin, New Mexico. According to the defector, the formula was his own invention, had been tested on numerous human subjects, and was meant to cause heart failure when ingested, but go undetected by typical Western autopsy procedures. Walls had hung up and closed his eyes, waiting out moments of dire intestinal turmoil such as he had never known, and which did not fully abate until he determined that the president was still alive and well (at least as of the printing of the morning edition). The flask, moreover, was with the Bureau. But the fact that a method of assassination had been delivered to the object of his surveillance, without his knowledge but under his watch, and that she'd had ample time to use it, was as terrifying as any he could imagine. The fact that she had not yet committed the act was as gentle as a lullaby.

He knew he should call Toll immediately. He was in over his head, and needed the full resources of the Bureau behind him. But the failure of his independent undercover operation socked him with shame, and he decided that so long as he could determine that Kennedy was safely in Hyannis, and Marilyn was in California, he would allow himself twenty-four more hours to bring her in on his own.

Since that day in early summer when the police had chased him off Marilyn's lawn and he had subsequently lost his job with Alan Jacobs's firm ("We both know that broad is crazy," Alan had apologized), he had tried to justify his solitary tactics by monitoring the movements of the president and the movie star on his own. This task had, briefly, seemed within his power—Marilyn was giving so many interviews, sitting for photographers in such a noisy way, that her whereabouts were quite generally known around town. Otherwise she was spending a lot of time either with Joe DiMaggio or Frank Sinatra, in which case the gossip columnists left a trail for him to follow. The president meanwhile kept coming or going from Hyannis Port all June and July, so the news was full of pictures of him boarding *Air Force One*, or sailing with his handsome, happy children. But somewhere along the way Walls had become distrustful. He no longer believed the statements of reporters or government officials, and was becoming leery of the evidence collected with his own eyes and ears. The more the world seemed to reassure him that all was well—Marilyn was trim and smiling; the president was a devoted family man—the more he believed otherwise, that those pretty images were in fact pieces of an elaborate conspiracy, and the underground movements of the most conspicuous people in the U.S.A. might, at any moment, erupt into a tragedy only he could prevent.

He'd gotten in the habit of monitoring the Lawfords' Santa Monica place, which the press had taken to calling the Western White House on account of the president's frequent visits there, and which he knew to be the setting for many of Kennedy and Marilyn's assignations. After dark he would park his car in the public lot and stroll along the sand, even though he had no proof of their having been anywhere near each other in months. It had occurred to Walls that the affair might have ended for some humdrum reason—maybe Mrs. Kennedy had caught on after that wanton rendition of "Happy Birthday," or perhaps Kennedy's desire had flagged, which was a possibility Walls ought not to have been caught off guard by.

The ritual soothed him, however, made him feel that everything was under control, and Nan Pettycomb, with whom he remained on drinking terms, had told him that Marilyn was still an occasional guest. And then, around midnight on Friday evening, after he had more or less despaired of finding her before his self-imposed deadline, he saw a helicopter descend to the beach, and a man who might have been the president stride across the sand, where he embraced a woman whose pale hair obscured her face.

As soon as the helicopter departed he sprinted toward the house, but they had already gone inside. A handful of people in evening wear drank cocktails on the far side of the swimming pool, talking animatedly and oblivious to the man who had rushed to the edge of the property and continued lurking in the shadows. He distinctly heard the name Marilyn said by one of them, but over the next half hour she did not emerge, and he saw no sign of her in the upstairs windows or balconies. Growing anxious, he had driven up and down the highway watching the Lawfords' for some sign of her, and had then camped at the corner of Fifth Helena for a long stretch. But her house remained dark all the while. Morning was lightening the sky, and he felt melancholy, and confessed to himself that this was the end of his solitary road.

Toll had not been pleased by the predawn call, but as the hours accumulated, as he took in the evidence that Walls laid before him, as he pored over the transcripts and began to see the logic, his esteem for his subordinate seemed to grow even as he became increasingly alarmed by the gravity of the situation. He made a few telephone calls, assured himself that the president was in fact in Massachusetts and not at the Lawfords', and told Walls to try Marilyn at home. Walls was shocked when Marilyn answered her own phone, and he could think of nothing to do but hang up as soon as he recognized her voice. After that, Toll rubbed his eyes tiredly and told Walls to go home.

"We'll decide what to do tomorrow. You're exhausted, and I need you in fighting form so we play this right. Go get your beauty rest, okay?" Walls must have appeared reluctant, because his boss rose to walk him to his car, at which point he administered a fatherly pat on the shoulder. "Great work, kid. And don't worry. We're gonna nail this bitch."

But he couldn't rest. He could only imagine things he might have missed, scenarios he hadn't yet considered. And on Sunday morning, having lain wide-eyed in the darkness counting twenty-two, and twenty-three, and twenty-four hours since he'd convinced Toll of Marilyn's secret identity, he found himself fully dressed in a black suit of Italian wool that would be stifling once the sun climbed high, driving past the gated palaces of Beverly Hills as though without a fixed destination, but all the while moving toward her.

In this he was not alone.

When he arrived her cul-de-sac was already jammed with vehicles, and a helicopter raged overhead. Walls, possessed by the notion that Toll had staged a raid already and cut him out of it, parked with his wheels on the curb, a few blocks up Carmelina, and jogged heedlessly into the fray. But it was a different boss he encountered at her gate.

"Douglass." For a moment Walls thought Alan would act surprised, but he seemed unable to summon the energy. His face was ashen, and his shirt was buttoned wrong so that its hem, which he had not succeeded in tucking under his belt, hung unevenly. "How did you—?" And then he answered several unspoken questions in rapid succession. "Oh, never mind. What does it matter now. I'm glad you're here."

Walls would have asked him what was happening if he'd had a single wit about him. Instead they started walking over the brick patio toward the house, where a pair of police officers stood at the door. "Who are those people?" he managed eventually.

"Press, mostly. I don't know how they found out—they got here just as I did. Maybe they heard it over the police radio, or maybe the operator who took Ralph's call couldn't resist making an anonymous tip."

"What did you tell them?"

"Nothing, yet."

What is there to tell? he wanted to ask. But there wasn't any need, because the police officers were standing aside to make way for the gurney pushed by a man wearing a checked sport coat and dark glasses who might have been of Japanese descent. A step behind him was a man with deep-set eyes and close-cropped, graying hair, in a tweed jacket. Walls could imagine him speaking in the steady, sober voice he knew as Dr. Ralph Greenson. As the procession moved into the sunlight, toward the hearse parked just inside the gate, Greenson reached out protectively, resting his hand on the white cloth that covered the body. In his face, Walls had a glimpse of what real sorrow looks like. Leather straps crossed the cloth, fastening her in place, and Walls found that he had involuntarily put his palm over his mouth as they shoved the whole contraption into the back of the vehicle.

The coroner's van drove slowly through the mob and away. For a while he and Alan stood together in silence.

"How did—"

"We won't know for sure until the coroner's report comes back." Alan sighed, lifted his gaze to the sky. "I hope to god it was an accident, but it smells an awful lot like suicide."

Walls, too, looked at the sky. He felt tricked. Three years of his life had been devoted to following Marilyn, listening to her weird little voice telling tall tales, watching her wallow and wiggle and lie. He had thought about her more than he'd ever thought about anybody. He still wanted to punish her for what she had thought she'd get away with. This was entirely too sudden an end—but maybe death was always like that. He had apparently held the vague notion that in a moment like this one saw something—a cloud unfurling, branches bending, a flash downpour—while the spirit freed itself. But the setting did not accommodate. Besides the crowd of photographers jostling for position on the street, all appeared perfectly ordinary. "Was there a note?" he wondered out loud.

If Alan replied Walls didn't hear it. He'd spotted Toll striding toward them, his brimmed felt hat tipped over his face and his trench coat flapping around his legs. He was flanked by five similarly dressed men, their shoulders broad under their black suits. Walls knew these men—he had trained with them, not so long ago—and he briefly remembered what he'd thought it would mean to be an agent of the Bureau. A rigorous and exciting life; inclusion in an elite pack. But as he watched the cavalcade approach, he felt apart.

"Agent Walls, who is this?" Toll demanded.

"Alan Jacobs, Marilyn's flack."

"*Agent* Walls?" Alan's mouth trembled and his eyes grew large, as though he might cry. Instead he slapped Walls across the face.

"Get him out of here." Toll was waving his badge in Alan's general direction, and Walls, hoping it didn't show how much the slap hurt, reached for his former boss's elbow to lead him away. "Not him, you."

"Me, sir?"

Toll didn't meet his gaze, he just tipped the hat lower. "We have an investigation to see to, and someone pretty important needs to talk to you. Agent Amberson will escort you. Now, Mr. Jacobs, let's not get in each other's way, what do you say . . ."

There was more to their conversation, but Walls couldn't hear, as Amberson was more or less pushing him through the gate. Walls looked over his shoulder, and saw how Toll's head bent toward Alan's in discussion as they strolled up the patio and disappeared into the house. The reporters and photographers assembled in the cul-de-sac called out to the two agents in their black suits for information, but Walls could only take a final glance at a crime scene he, too, would have done anything to understand.

The limousine was idling somewhat beyond his own poorly parked vehicle. Amberson pointed it out, and then retreated in the direction of Marilyn's house, leaving Walls alone. One of the rear passenger doors was pushed open from inside, so he climbed into the backseat and found himself opposite the attorney general of the United States. He wore a tailored navy suit, but his hair flopped over his forehead.

"Hello, Douglass. I'm Robert Kennedy."

"I know who you are," Walls replied as the limo began to move.

"We're all pretty impressed with you."

"We?"

"SAC Toll and I."

"So you know? That she was a—"

"Yes, I know what she was. Toll did the right thing. He called his boss, and his boss called me, and by chance I was in the area and able to come down and express my gratitude to you personally. My gratitude, and that of my entire family."

"Sir, I should be back there."

"Yes. You're right, of course. And I want you to know I respect that—your tenacity in this case."

"Thank you," Walls replied with more diffidence than he had intended. He cleared his throat, deepened his voice. "But I've got to go back and search the property. I know more than anybody about their operation and what they planned. If the Russians disposed of her, they surely made it look like an accident, or suicide, but I could—"

"It's not going to be that kind of investigation."

"What? But she—"

"She's dead, poor girl. She got herself mixed up with some bad people. But I did always like her personally."

"'Poor girl'?" Walls hoped he didn't look as wretched and incredulous as he felt. Perhaps at birth, but the woman he knew was sly, manipulative, capable of unspeakable betrayals—anything but a poor girl.

"Listen, she's dead. That's what matters. She can't do any harm now."

"But what about the Gent? He's still out there—"

"There was a homicide Friday night in a rented bungalow in a beach community south of the airport. A man who fits your description of her handler. They must have known you were on to them, that it was a matter of time, maybe they even knew you went to Agent Toll—someone in KGB decided to terminate the operation. Obviously they made the decision to eliminate the entire cell."

"Well." Walls exhaled in frustration and glanced at the window. "With all due respect, I don't know if that's obvious, sir. I'd like to make damn sure."

The attorney general leaned in, forcing Walls to return his gaze. The muscles around his blue eyes constricted, and Walls couldn't help but wonder how someone so young-looking could come across so grave. They had moved through similar rooms, but life had handled them differently. "Agent Walls, I'm going to be straight with you, all right?"

"All right."

"The president of the United States was having an affair—we don't want that generally known, but it's nothing new, and our boys in the press rise above that sort of tawdry reporting. That he was having an affair with a Soviet spy is another matter entirely. I don't think I really need to explain to you how deeply we need to bury this. Right now four people know—Toll, the Director, you, and me. And we're the only people who are ever going to know."

"But what about the agents Toll has combing the place?"

"They were told enough that they won't guess at more. They know that she was a girl with some personal problems—everybody knows that—and that she had a thing with the president—which plenty of people already suspect. Toll told them she kept a diary of things she liked to talk about with Jack—on sensitive topics, about his opinions and policies and so forth—and that we have to clean her place out, make sure there isn't anything incriminating she's left behind. Anything that might pose a threat to national security."

"Mr. Attorney General, I think you're making a mistake," he said with as much deference as he could muster given the fire in his chest. "You want to keep it a secret, sure. But I think this thing is much bigger than any of us know. I think you need to investigate it aggressively."

"You are permitted your opinion," Kennedy replied evenly as he switched the cross of his legs. "But you're not going to share it with anyone. Do you understand? Your file on Marilyn is going to be destroyed, and that's the end of it."

Out the window sprinklers were churning rainbow droplets across bright green lawns. A boy on a bicycle was hurling newspapers over grand, gilt barriers, and Walls, watching them because he didn't want to face the conversation he was having, realized how early in the day it was to feel so beaten. "Where are we going?"

"The Santa Monica Airport." Kennedy lifted his wrist to check the time. "My wife and children are staying at a ranch up in Gilroy, and I've got to join them. Mass begins at nine thirty. After I'm dropped off, my driver will take you wherever you want to go."

"Why did you need to tell me? Why couldn't Toll have—"

"Because this is between you and me. And because you're never going back to the Los Angeles division. You'll get a healthy severance—and for a few months, you can do whatever you like."

"You mean you want to buy my silence? I'm really not cut out to swan around poolside, you know, or jet off to Europe, or . . ."

"Yes, I knew you'd say something of the kind. And I wouldn't insult you like that. So I'll tell you what we're going to do. When you're ready, come back to Washington. Think about where you see yourself, where you want to go. Perhaps you'd even someday like to run for office. In the meantime, imagine how you'll get there, wherever you're going, whatever it is you'd like to become. Any job in government you are remotely qualified for, it's yours. Think about it; get back to me. I'll take care of everything."

They had stopped at a traffic light, and Walls, whose jaw was too set in anger to talk anymore, opened the door and climbed to the sidewalk. He had no idea where he was or where he ought to go, which was fine by him.

"Agent Walls." He glanced over his shoulder and saw the attorney general perched at the edge of the limousine's rear seat. "Can I count on you?"

"Don't worry. I'll never speak of it." As his gaze drifted over the clean concrete, he added bitterly, "Nobody would believe me anyway."

V

1963

FORTY-TWO

Dallas, November 1963

THE diner on the corner of Maple and Winchester had big windows and two exits, a good view of the street. She'd been there once before—maybe two months ago, maybe four. As Mrs. Ivan Lancer she often went to diners. In her old life, breakfast had not been her bag, except occasionally in liquid form. The meal itself had seemed utilitarian, and the timing conflicted with the hours that were her best bet for sleep. But now she woke with first light, and had come to like the atmosphere in places that served chicken-fried steak and pecan pie with vanilla ice cream and flapjacks under brilliant lighting. Of course, as Mrs. Ivan Lancer she rarely used a name (Mary, if politeness required) and always paid cash, and made eye contact only long enough not to appear evasive. The waitress behind the counter was having a bad morning, and she waved Marilyn to a stool without a second glance.

"What'll you have, honey?" the waitress drawled while wiping down the Formica to Marilyn's left, her head tilted away as she surveyed coffee levels in the mugs of the customers lined up against the counter.

"Eggs over easy. Rye toast, no butter. Coffee, black."

"You got it, hon."

"Thanks."

She went to bars, too, although she no longer drank much. Only when it would draw attention not to, and on those occasions she found she had lost her taste for alcohol. But like diners they were good places to overhear things, encounter people when their guard was down, and it was in a bar that she located Hank Foley. The first time he chatted her up it was at a joint called Florence's Hotsy-Totsy, and he'd implied that he was an oil-and-gas man, but the working girls said that when he was drunk he sometimes boasted of CIA connections. They warned her to watch out for him, said he hit with a closed fist. For a while she demurred, rattling her wedding and engagement rings at him with a coy smile. Holding out did its neat trick. He became more persistent, almost desperate, tried to impress her by hinting at insider knowledge of government intrigue. Finally she let him rub against her one night while Sinatra was on the jukebox; the next week, she told him her husband was out of town. They'd walked into the parking lot, and his alcoholic breath stung her eyes right before he shoved her against his car.

In the morning, as they lay together in the motel bed (Hank also claimed to be married), he'd observed, "You know, if you dyed your hair, gained ten pounds, and stayed out of the sun, you'd look just like Marilyn Monroe." He wasn't the first person to say this to her, although it happened less frequently than she would have imagined.

"But I like the sun," she had replied cutely. "And I'd be all wrong blonde. Anyway, we all know what happened to her."

"Yeah, that was a damn shame." He had shaken his head and lit a cigarette. "Beautiful girl like that."

Her understanding of the events of August 5, 1962, was mainly patched together from this variety of interaction. She skirted discussions of the presumed suicide of Marilyn Monroe, but especially in the beginning it had been a big story, and she'd been unable to avoid it entirely. Later she guessed that people recognized her unconsciously, and were moved to express their true feelings about the deceased movie star. She herself only knew that she said good-bye to her house, and to Dr. Greenson, and swallowed the drugs he'd promised her. The ones that would make her sleep like the dead for twenty-four hours. When she'd come out of it, in a broom closet in the morgue, the coroner, Dr. Noguchi, had been chain-smoking, and appeared deeply relieved to feel her pulse growing stronger. "I've never heard of anybody your weight taking that stuff and coming out of it," he'd said. Then she'd given him what she had promised, on her back on the autopsy table. That was the deal they had struck, the night she killed Alexei, when she had wandered into his office barefoot and distraught. After he'd smuggled her out of the police station in the trunk of his car, she had reminded him that if he ever told anybody she was alive he would lose his job and his medical license, everyone would call him crazy, that he might be institutionalized, and that she personally would not rest until she had taught him the true meaning of pain. He assured her that he had an unidentified body—five-six, a hundred and sixteen, bottle blonde—already picked out to autopsy and cremate for the burial, and she flinched, and tried not to think what befell that poor honey. Then she removed the contents of Alexei's suitcase—transferred to a ladylike tote—from the bus station locker where she'd stored it, and disappeared.

"Thanks," he had said, with what she could only comprehend as sincere gratitude.

In her youth, trading sex in this way hadn't seemed to cost her much. She'd traded shrewdly, and that had made all the difference. Later, after she'd realized that Arthur wasn't going to become everything she hoped, she'd given it away vengefully, to almost anyone. But that was a long time ago. With the coroner, she had to set her teeth and tell herself that she was doing it for Jack, to keep Jack safe. Luckily she'd still been groggy and had managed to hold the retching for when she was alone. By the night she was first treated to Hank Foley's labored breathing and copious perspiration, she'd come to think of herself as a kind of Joan of Arc, beyond the needs or denigrations of the flesh. Her skin was brown, her hair was an unremarkable shade of bark, and she had more or less forgotten the lure of her own glory.

It was not until recently that she understood how Hank fit in. They had left the Hotsy-Totsy together, not trying to hide it, and he was already cockeyed. "Hey, gorgeous, mind if we take a detour? I need to do a quick check on one of my people."

This was maybe their fifth assignation, and she had steered clear of him for the previous two weeks. She figured if she gave him the runaround he'd become stupid, try to show her how important he was. "All right," she'd said indifferently, gazing into her compact. "But I've got to be home by midnight in case my husband calls from the road. He was suspicious last time; if it happens again he'll load his shotgun, come looking for you."

Hank emitted a low, macho chortle and said something like "If it came to that, *he's* the one I'd be worried about," and then, "Why don't you leave that joker? We can go to Reno for the divorce, and Vegas for the wedding."

As they drove he went on trying to impress her that way, and she had continued to blow smoke out the passenger window of his Ford Galaxie. She was glad that her face was averted when they pulled up at a tiny clapboard house on West Neely where she finally glimpsed the man she'd come to Dallas in search of. Oswald was in the living room. She saw him clearly through the window, and the wife had her back to Lee trying to stop the baby from crying.

"Who were they?" Marilyn asked, a few minutes after they drove on.

"He's a pain in my ass. She's his pain-in-the-ass Russian wife."

"You mean they're commies?" She couldn't risk doing the doe-eyes that had worked so well for her as Marilyn, but with Hank, a skeptical tone had the same tongue-loosening effect.

"Sort of. We sent him over around the time of the U-2 debacle. We sent a bunch like him—U.S. Marines posing as socialist sympathizers. Marines are catnip for the KGB; they go nuts when they get their hands on those boys. We figured they'd pick them up, some of them would succeed in infiltrating, and some of them they'd sniff out and send back, but either way we win. The ones they send back give us a picture of their operation, how they handle defectors. But they knew right away with this guy. Locked him in a mental hospital, made it look like he'd attempted suicide, interrogated him, sent him to the boonies, got him to knock up one of theirs. Waited for him to get sick of Russian winters. Easy as pie."

"So he's a traitor? And she's controlling him with her bedroom wiles, something tawdry like that."

"Lord no. She's just a kid, and he's a nutcase. Unstable. Can't believe the Marines ever took him in the first place. Fancies himself some kind of boy-genius double agent. She might have some training, but she's low level, if she's anything. We've been trying to use the situation with Marina—that's the wife—get him to infiltrate communist groups here, but so far he just keeps fucking up. Like I said, pain in my ass."

Oh, Hank, you goddamn idiot, she thought.

But it was the final piece she'd needed to make sense of the jumble of coded messages and notes she had discovered in Alexei's bungalow. Dallas had already been her destination, almost as soon as her death was publicized, because that was where Alexei had been headed. Or anyway where his final airplane ticket would have taken him. The month that followed had been agony for so many reasons, but mostly what she remembered was the confusion over who she ought to be looking for, and how frustrated she'd been trying to make sense of the numerical messages from Moscow. She'd never known humidity like that, and had smoked cigarettes out the motel window, and watched how the elms wept with summer rain. She had tried not to cry too much, and tanned by her motel swimming pool once the storms passed, and went to the movies at night to quiet her mind.

The theater near her third motel had been playing old war movies, and one night she watched a Nazi melodrama that involved a book cipher, and realized what those numbers were for. It had taken her some months to find an antiquarian shop (she'd had to drive all the way to New Orleans) that had the same edition of the complete Shakespeare that lay on Alexei's unmade bed the day she'd gone to his Hell's Kitchen apartment. She had always suspected that he chose Hal as their code name for Jack to stroke her literary pretensions, but now she saw that it fit into the larger system, too. Perhaps everything in this life has at least two reasons, she'd thought as she began running her fingers over the pages of Alexei's diary once again. The codes had her thumbing to *Lear* and *The Tempest*, until she understood that a mariner named Oswald had been of interest to Alexei for a long time, and that he had returned to the country in June of 1962.

Lonely, imaginative, delusions of historical destiny, Alexei had written in November 1958. That might have been an observation about her, but in November of 1958 they hadn't spoken in almost ten years.

Likes publicity about self, Alexei had jotted in November of 1959.

This, too, might have been about her, but in the fall of 1959 she had been in New York avoiding the press, and her contact with Alexei was minimal. Once she had decided it was in reference to another publicity hound, this phrase had led her to the library, and an article that ran in the *Dallas Morning News* on November 1, 1959, about a local Marine named Oswald defecting to the Soviet Union. According to Alexei's coded messages, his mariner returned to the new world in June 1962, which was about when Alexei had tried to strangle her—the night he had told her that her replacement was already on his way. This time the newspapers didn't care—there was no mention of a Marine named Oswald in June 1962—but she was beginning to understand the scheme by then. She had the code, so she knew that Oswald had notified Alexei that he was living at his mother's in Fort Worth, but suggested his handler put off traveling to Texas a few months, as he was being monitored by a man named Hank Foley.

But she had not known, until Hank Foley had driven her down Neely Street at eleven miles an hour, where to find him. Or why Alexei, in his communications with Moscow, had begun, in the spring of 1961, to reference Oswald's twin.

"Some double agent," Hank had muttered, and clapped a hand on her knee as he sped off. But once he said it she knew it was true, and not in the way he meant.

There was Oswald, and there was Oswald's twin. Oswald was a lonely and imaginative Marine whom Alexei had encountered in California, probably while he was on leave, sometime in late 1958. Oswald's twin was a highly trained Soviet agent who had been groomed his entire life for a single, elite mission. Oswald was a troubled romantic, who believed his intelligence ought to mean something. It would have been easy for Alexei to manipulate him, as it had been easy for Alexei to manipulate her, and with the courtly, erudite Russian's encouragement, Oswald had returned to the base in Japan where he was stationed, and made himself conspicuous to CIA recruiters, who in turn had sent him off to renounce his citizenship at the American embassy in Moscow, prompting the newspaper mentions of which he was apparently proud. Oswald's twin was a skilled sniper, a master of accents, a perfect mimic, and, she presumed, indifferent to fame. In the summer of 1962, the CIA had made it easy for their agent Oswald, along with his new Russian wife, to return to the United States. But they had gotten Oswald's twin instead.

Maybe, like the "father" she had seen through a false mirror in Payne Whitney, the face of Oswald's twin had been reconstructed. He had been given the face of a former Marine with intelligence connections and a family to go home to in Texas. Of course, Alexei knew every detail of that connection, his habits of speech and the way he thought, and would have passed the information on to Oswald's twin, so that he could better play the part. With a shudder, Marilyn realized that the slight, dark-haired man she had been trying to locate in Dallas was not American at all. Was that twitchy, resentful gaze his own, or was it an exquisitely honed impression? The real Lee Harvey Oswald was still in Russia, if he was anywhere, and whether his fate was a labor camp or a grand apartment and a new girl from the provinces every month, she would never know. Apparently Alexei had not cared what had happened to him, or had not needed to be told.

She might have shared her theory with Hank, but she knew nobody truly important would need to brag and strut the way he did. He had no real power, and would only get in her way. She had continued their affair long enough to collect some tidbits about what he had been up to, Oswald's movements over the summer and early fall, when he had made trips to New Orleans and Mexico City. Hank had sent him on the first trip to try and infiltrate Castro supporters, and the second to try and get into Cuba itself (with the ultimate goal of assassinating El Comandante, Hank implied, although she doubted it), but both missions had failed. Hank chalked this up to incompetence, but Marilyn was becoming ever more convinced that the man he was calling Oswald had been born in another world and had failed on purpose. He might even, in the Soviet embassy in Mexico City, have been able to communicate with Moscow without the usual subterfuge.

"He's on his own now," Hank said disgustedly, and indeed, Oswald had gone on to procure an actual job for the first time in many months, moving boxes at the Texas School Book Depository on Elm. Marilyn learned this from her own surveillance, not from Hank, whom she was relieved to have no further use for. She expressed anxiety over her husband's possible hiring of a private detective, and from then on avoided Florence's Hotsy-Totsy.

A month passed. She switched motels twice, to keep people from remembering her, and also to shake off her dread, and she seemed to have succeeded on both counts. She considered several methods of terminating Oswald, but she hesitated, knowing that he had been trained to kill, as she had not. And she wanted to know for sure that she had the right man, that she really was putting an end to the last of Alexei's schemes. The weather was moody, the week before Thanksgiving, when the harried waitress slipped her eggs and toast onto the counter and refilled her coffee mug, and she had almost forgotten the details of Hank Foley's enthusiastic lovemaking, and these both did much for her spirits. She broke the yolk with the tip of her toast, and put it into her mouth distractedly.

"He has some nerve, coming to god's country," said the man next to her.

"That commie traitor," added his companion.

"That treasonous bastard."

"That pinko Harvard boy."

"Give me Friday off, boss." The man next to her chuckled as he lifted a phantom rifle, peered through a phantom scope. "I'll do 'im myself." As he imitated the sound of a gun firing, he jerked at the phantom kickback, and Marilyn, sitting beside him, felt it, too.

"May I see that?" She leaned in with a broad smile and indicated the newspaper in front of the one called boss.

"Sure thing, little lady, so long as you ain't one of those girls with cotton-candy brains swooning every time Kennedy comes on the TV."

"I'll tell you straight, I voted for him back in '60, but I won't make that mistake next year."

This seemed to satisfy the man, and he shoved the newspaper in her direction and went on loudly expressing his displeasure with the president, to the delight of the other men with their elbows on the diner counter. She might have been offended had she listened. But this kind of talk was always going on somewhere in Dallas, and she had quickly become absorbed in the paper and could no longer hear. Her heart was cold, and her mind had begun to tick. So this was how it happened. Where in the city was the man calling himself Oswald, and had he read the newspaper? Or did he already know what had been printed there for anyone to see? President Kennedy was in Texas as of yesterday, and tomorrow morning he would take a short flight from Fort Worth and proceed slowly by motorcade through downtown Dallas, through the canyon of office buildings on Main Street, passing Oswald's workplace right about noon.

FORTY-THREE

Dallas, November 1963

SLEEPLESSNESS she now regarded as a gift; and after she learned that Jack was coming to town, she did not want to rest.

That afternoon she took an extra thousand out of the reserve of cash she had found in Alexei's suitcase ("my inheritance," as she darkly referred to it in her thoughts), and trailed Oswald home from work. He had no car of his own, but she was familiar with his figure by then, his quick, purposeful stride, and spotted him when he left the Book Depository building and climbed into another man's car. She followed them into the leafy suburbs—not to the rooming house that he'd moved into about a month ago, after Hank washed his hands of him, but to the home of a Russophile divorcée where his wife had been staying as of late. Marilyn had speculated that their living apart was to protect her from what he planned, keep her isolated and unaware of his preparations. As she sat in her Pontiac listening to the pre-dawn rain hitting the metal roof, she wondered that he was there to sleep with her tonight because he knew he could be captured tomorrow, and never have a woman again. Were they really in love, or merely coconspirators? But in the early morning, when he stepped through the front door, she saw that there was another reason. The wife kissed him good-bye, and handed him a large package.

The same man drove him back into the city. Marilyn followed at a good distance, but arrived in time to watch him walk into the seven-story building from its Houston Street entrance, just before eight o'clock, still clutching the package. She knew she should stay. Wait to see if he left work early, monitor his movements. But she had learned the route of the presidential motorcade published in the *Times Herald*, the same illustration Oswald had surely memorized by now. She knew the layout of the Book Depository—once he'd gotten the job there, she had gone to the library to study its plans, and so knew its layout, its stairwells and elevators. Of course he might use whatever was in that package at another location, but her intuition was that he had taken the job there with a larger purpose. He must have known that it had big windows, a perfect vantage of the prominent plaza below. By eight the streets were already closed off to traffic, and policemen patrolled the area the president would be passing through. If Oswald tried to put a rifle together out-of-doors, they would find him. No—she felt sure that he would remain in the place where his presence would attract no notice, the place where he was expected to be.

The minutes passed slowly. She had never, in all her years of desperation, actually doubted in tomorrow, but she did now. Sitting in the darkness last night, outside the house where Oswald slept, she had remembered an evening spent with Alexei—this was before she really knew Jack, and the situation had seemed too wild to take seriously—when they'd drunk old-fashioneds in a bar that played a prize fight on the radio. He had been fatherly, and she had been a sucker for it. "Spying is much like boxing," Alexei had observed, another of his epigrams. "You study your opponent's feints and hooks until you know him like you know yourself. Often, in the end, one feels strangely closer to their adversary than to their lover."

She did not believe herself to have intimate knowledge of Oswald. His eyes were opaque to her; they revealed no motivation. But she had observed him carefully enough that she sensed what he was going to do almost as he did it. And she knew he was good, much better than she was, that he was more likely to survive their coming confrontation. She comforted herself that what she did was out of love, and that his motivation must be weak by comparison. She still loved Jack, and that was why she couldn't resist pulling away from the depository, heading to the airport to catch a glimpse of him. Tomorrow she might be dead, and she felt her resolve would be stronger if she saw him one last time.

Dallas was the perfect setting. The animosity that part of the country held for the eastern president with the civil rights agenda and the peace rhetoric was such that the law might actually let Oswald escape if he succeeded. But he wouldn't succeed, she told herself. He was better than she was, but he didn't control the weather, his bad luck—it was raining, and when it rained the president's motorcade was covered with bulletproof glass, a fact she had learned by studying the details of every report on Jack's public appearances since she'd gone underground. She knew how they protected him, and had imagined what gaps Oswald might take advantage of. Whatever he had planned for today he wouldn't be able to see through. But she would be there, she would make sure he was her man; and she would take him out.

As she drove toward the airport she listened to the radio. The local station broadcast speeches being made at the presidential breakfast in Fort Worth, and she half listened to the reporter's commentary. It was all business talk, war talk, lauding the Texas contribution to the defense industry, flattering the locals' Texan pride, which she had become well acquainted with over the last year. *B-58*, he said, and *Vietnam*. She only half paid attention, allowed herself to drift into the confident tone of his voice. "Military procurement in this state totals nearly one and a quarter billion dollars, fifth highest in the Union . . .," he was saying in that rousing orator's voice. "There are more military personnel on active duty in this state than in any in the nation save one—" He broke off, and for a fleeting moment she heard a note of the urbane, ironical man she'd known, as he muttered, "*And it's not Massachusetts,*" under his breath, and laughed at his own joke like a little boy while the crowd broke into applause.

She squeezed her eyes and gripped the wheel. It was enough, most of the time, to know that she was making right what she had done wrong, that she was living to keep Jack safe now. But when she heard him laugh, and remembered what it was to lie between sheets with him, far away from the world's troubles, she felt a seam rip open in her chest, and it took all her concentration to keep the car straight. So much depended on it; she had sacrificed too much already to succumb to emotion now.

Anyway, she was not the only one who loved him. When she arrived, several hundred people had already gathered on the tarmac just to see their leader with their own eyes, and maybe to touch his hand. The whole scene was perfect, like something in the movies. The airport was called Love Field, and the gray clouds drifted off, making room for blue sky, as the white jet plane descended through the atmosphere. Golden light filtered over everyone and everything. Mrs. Kennedy appeared first, in pink, and was handed a large bouquet of roses, and the president came after her, his thick, neatly trimmed bronze hair one shade darker than his skin. The spectators cheered, and her heart cracked over the white flash of his smile. Oh, how she wanted him. She had to glance away and think what a drab story it would have been without the parts where they'd been alone together, talking idly over a drink in some forgotten place. He jogged quickly down the steps and disappeared into the waiting crowd.

The jubilation of the throng told her where Jack was, as did the slow progress of his wife's pink pillbox hat. Marilyn kept glancing away toward the motorcade vehicles lined up ahead. What she saw made her body cold. There were no more rain clouds, not as far as the eye could see, and a team of men in dark suits was removing the clear, bulletproof bubble from atop the shiny black Lincoln that Jack would ride in. She turned and walked fast toward her own car. Her limbs were rigid with urgency now, and she was angry at herself for having indulged in sentimentality on this of all mornings.

She checked the pistol in her glove compartment for the tenth time that day, made sure it was loaded. Once she started up the engine, steered her car in the direction of Lemmon Avenue, she permitted herself four choking sobs. It wasn't pretty crying, and she didn't hold back. She had to get it out and make herself hard inside, and ready.

A long time ago, when she still believed that writers could be her friends, she had sat drinking champagne with a young reporter who had told her, offhandedly at the beginning of the interview, that she wouldn't have to worry about him running late because he had a date at eight. She'd held his attention long past midnight, saying very confessional things that kept him scribbling and bright-eyed. "I guess I always knew I belonged to America, and to the world. Not because I'm especially beautiful, or because I have any real talent, but because I've never belonged to anybody in my life," she had told him, not knowing why, just that it sounded interesting and would make him stay. By the time she saw the quote in a magazine she had forgotten the whole episode, and for years she'd wondered what had possessed her to say that. But now, on a Friday afternoon in Texas, she finally understood what those words meant.

FORTY-FOUR

Dallas, November 1963

HE would not have noticed her except that the sun came out just when the jet landed, and it flashed in her mirrored pilot's sunglasses catching his attention. She looked like any other Dallas housewife, her hair mousy brown and held back with a headband, her boxy jacket and black slacks unremarkable. But he happened to be looking at her at the same moment that the first lady appeared in the door of the airplane, wearing a suit of pink, nubby wool with black trim. Every other woman in the crowd gasped and jockeyed for a better view of her outfit. This woman stood away from the others, and when she saw Mrs. Kennedy she averted her gaze.

Walls had not been immediately fond of Mrs. Kennedy, either. She could be socially peculiar, almost shy, and while he allowed that a certain kind of man should be expected to stray from his marriage to some degree, he had, during the years he shadowed Marilyn Monroe, developed a distaste for the willful blindness Mrs. Kennedy had shown in the face of her husband's transgressions. This distaste was heightened last fall, when he had been assigned to the president's Secret Service detail. "You could have any job you wanted," the attorney general chuckled, when Walls came to collect on the promised favor. "And the biggest post you could think of was getting in line to take a bullet for my brother. Well, I guess we've done our job making it all look pretty glamorous." But Walls didn't see the glamour—the mood in the White House, when he started protecting its occupants, was gloomier than he'd imagined from the pretty pictures that ran in *Life*. The president was reckless in those days, like a man who has had a premonition of the end, and

Walls saw that behavior mimicked by his fellow agents. They picked up their boss's scraps, escorted the party girls to bars when their shifts were done, and often drank straight through to the beginning of the next workday. Every one of those girls seemed to Walls a potential threat, and he couldn't understand how the other Secret Service men could be so nonchalant about them. He was mocked for his seriousness, of course—"I guess you think Linda here is a Soviet assassin?" they'd laugh, tightening their grip on Linda's waist.

But Walls's sympathy for Jackie had grown, like every other American, when her third child died, only days after he was born, back in August. So it was that much more perplexing that this woman blanched at the sight of the first lady.

He knew her. He knew her like he knew himself. Despite her changed hair, her thinner figure, he would have known her anywhere. Every inch of his skin prickled. He shuddered, shook his head, but the phantasm did not dissipate. She was alive—Marilyn was alive. He felt struck dumb. All this time, she had been out in the world, and he'd had no idea, and he was sick with the thought of what she could have done already, but hadn't. When she turned suddenly and walked away from the hubbub, he followed as though in a trance.

As he trailed her wide, cream-colored Pontiac—he guessed it must have been at least five years old; it was larger, more curvaceous than this year's models—he realized he wasn't even surprised. His blood boiled, but he wasn't surprised. She had always been so much smarter than she let on, and her plan, the one he was beginning to comprehend, was shrewd. She was clever to have chosen Dallas—the president himself had joked darkly with his agents that morning about heading into nut country, how they'd hang him in a second here if they could, which Walls supposed was his funny way of telling his Secret Service men he appreciated what they did. Walls knew full well there would be security lapses—that the indifference of the local police, who were partially responsible for security along the motorcade route, would make it easier for her to carry out her plan. Plus the entire itinerary had been published in the local news, over his strenuous objections. The president's aides had insisted that a big turnout was necessary to the success of the trip, and Walls had by then developed the reputation of a square. A man overzealous in his duties, and thus easy to ignore.

Sweat beaded on his forehead as he calculated the time she'd had to practice her aim. He thought how her intimate knowledge of the president would help her now, teach her to intuit his movements, stalk him in the way Walls was able to stalk her. On the radio they were reporting how the president had darted into the crowd back at Love Field to shake hands. Even at a distance this made Walls nervous. He was convinced that the greatest danger to Kennedy at that moment was the supposedly deceased movie star now got up like a suburban mother, piloting an old station wagon through the streets of Dallas, but he couldn't help agonizing over the dangers posed by the large grouping of people on the tarmac. It would only take one lunatic, a few seconds of negligence, for their leader to fall.

The radio was reporting on the motorcade, and when they described the president's car without the usual protective covering, he ground his foot into the gas pedal and nearly rear-ended the truck in front of him.

"Shit," he muttered, and grabbed for his radio. "This is Agent Walls," he said.

"Walls, where are you? The motorcade took off already." It was Agent Peal, who was also on the first lady's detail, part of the group who remained at Love Field to keep the airport safe for the presidential party's takeoff that afternoon.

"They've got to get the cover on the president's limousine, do you hear me?"

"Too late for that," Peal said mildly. "It's a gorgeous day, Walls. The president's not afraid."

"Peal, tell them to stop the motorcade. Get the cover on. I've seen a suspect—a potential assassin. We've got to take every precaution."

The radio crackled. "Like in New York?"

Walls cursed under his breath. It was true, he had embarrassed himself in New York, caused the other agents a great deal of trouble, but he could not dwell on that now. "Listen to me."

"Ship's sailed, Walls."

"Okay. Fuck. Fuck!" Walls wiped his forehead with his sleeve. "Peal, listen, I am going to need backup. I am currently following the suspect downtown. Suspect headed downtown in a white Pontiac."

"Description of suspect?"

"She's five-four, brunette, mid-thirties, mirrored sunglasses, black slacks. A hundred and twenty, maybe, hourglass figure."

A low whistle. "Hear you loud and clear, Agent Walls." Was Peal laughing? Walls couldn't comprehend that anyone would find anything the least bit funny at this moment. "You chase that suspect. Just make sure you're back here by two."

"This woman is not a joke!" he shouted hysterically into the radio. "You have no *idea* what she's capable of!"

"I'll be looking forward to hearing all about her talents later." Peal chuckled lewdly. "Over and out."

Walls hurled the radio at the floor, but apparently Peal hadn't bothered switching off his radio, so he heard how the other agents went on mocking him as he followed Marilyn's white Pontiac.

She headed downtown, and he followed close behind and parked half a block behind her on Record Street. They were a block from the plaza, and he could see the railway overpass up ahead. The radio was now reporting that the motorcade had departed the airport, and would be making its way into the city, so he turned the volume low, rolled down his window. The lead car would be stocked with his fellow agents, their eyes scanning the pathway, waiting for any sudden movement; behind them the presidential limousine, driven by another agent, flanked by policemen on motorcycles, which in turn was followed by another Secret Service vehicle, then the vice president's car, the press car, a car for agents of the Dallas Bureau. Despite the chill in the air, his collar was soaked through with perspiration.

The area was eerily quiet. A policeman stood on the corner, gazing down the block, in the direction from which the president's entourage would arrive. The radio reported people lining the entire route, although they must be hushed with anticipation. There were only waiting noises, a shuffle of feet, the snap of a camera, as they waited to capture their moment. He heard a cheer from a long way off—the president was coming. Then Marilyn stepped out of her car, tucked a pocketbook under her arm, and dashed into the big brick building that occupied the whole city block and looked down on the plaza on the other side. Walls closed his car door very quietly, and followed her through the back entrance.

On the second-floor landing, he found her high-heeled shoes, but she had disappeared into the darkness of the stairwell. He, too, shoved off his shoes and jogged up the stairs in his socks. His sense of panic grew as he climbed higher and found no sign of her. Had she gone into one of the lower floors? Had he miscalculated? He figured she'd want to be higher, where she could get a clear shot; but maybe she had a contact on a lower floor. Did she already have a sniper's rifle set up? Had she managed to secure an office in the building? He was out of breath from running, and furious with himself for having not arrested her when she was in her parked car and he had the chance.

But he wasn't wrong. He came around the corner and saw her, at the top of the stairs, her silhouette against the sunlight streaming in what must be a large, open room. She was peering around the corner, checking that it was empty. Of course—she had not needed an office; she knew everyone would be down below, watching the show. She stepped back, took a breath, and removed a handgun from her purse. She checked that it was loaded, and pushed the cylinder into place. She never got a chance to cock it. Walls was on her, grabbing her at the wrist and waist, and hauling her back down the stairs.

"You fucking bastard," she hissed, and he knew that she had thought about him over the past year, too.

They struggled against each other. She was stronger than he'd imagined, more angular and determined, all elbows and teeth, but he held her tight. They staggered together, one lumbering body, pushing each other back and forth, feet slipping on the stairs. Outside a cheer went up, and she let go of the gun suddenly. He flinched as it clattered down the stairs, so his eyes were closed when it went off. Two things occurred to him at once: that neither of them was bleeding, and that a six-shooter was a terrible choice for killing a man at long range. Another shot rang out, which he could have sworn was behind him. In his confusion he relaxed his hold. She escaped his grip and jogged down a few more steps toward the gun. He grabbed her by the hair, yanked her backward, lunged for the gun himself. But the third shot echoed in his skull, and his shock slowed him. She was on his back, a knee against his kidney, reaching beyond him, as he slid down another few stairs, and the last thing he saw was her manicured hand seizing the gun just out of his reach. The blow fell at the back of his neck; and all color left the world.

The next thing he knew was a slap. He was slapped twice, and he shook his head, and discovered that he was slumped in a stairwell, looking into the ashen face of a man in a white police helmet. He recognized the man, and in the next moment he remembered how—they had met that morning, at the Dallas Airport, to go over the details of security for the procession of the president's limousine.

"Agent Walls, did you see him?"

"Him?"

"The shooter."

"Where is she?" Walls blinked exaggeratedly, trying to get his eyes to focus, his consciousness to become steady.

"She?"

"Marilyn—she was right here . . ."

"Who?" The officer exhaled, filling his cheeks with air. That morning he had seemed so brash, but he was something else now. He stood and began jogging up the stairs, toward the sixth floor, the big, open room full of midday sunshine. "Get yourself together, Agent Walls," he called over his shoulder. "The president's been hit."

EPILOGUE

Arlington National Cemetery, November 1996

THE guilt never lessened; it only became the fact of his life, the shape of his face, the story he knew best. He had rehearsed all the scenarios, every possible outcome, until he could replay each by heart without the directives of conscious thought. These took the place of memory. He did not believe in god, but he did try to do penance. Every November twenty-second he went with a cone of yellow roses, although his conscience knew this wasn't real penance. He went because he wanted to stand amongst a mourning crowd. It was always an awful day, but it was also the only day of the year he did not feel alone.

The government of Kennedy's successor had labored to promote the notion that Lee Harvey Oswald acted alone, murdering the president with three rapid shots from the easternmost window of the sixth floor of the Book Depository building. It had been made clear to Walls that he should forget his struggle with the woman in the stairwell. And how could he argue, anyway, with the attorney general, a man who had lost his brother, his president, his boss, and his hero in a single moment? He castigated himself for having not thought to do as Ruby had done, stalk the jailhouse, wait for a transfer of the prisoner, and do unto Oswald as he had done to Kennedy. Of course, with the passing of time, Walls realized that if the assassin had lived at least some questions might have been answered. He had friends who had been in the room questioning him, during those first wretched twenty-four hours, and they later related, while trying to numb themselves with bourbon, that while he never dropped the façade of a radicalized malcontent, he exhibited signs of a man trained to resist interrogation, and probably torture. That he was, at the very least, more than he seemed.

It had been thirty-three years, not a particularly meaningful anniversary. The president's widow had passed, and the day was cold, even more than could be expected in late November. The ceremony was over, and only a few spectators lingered watching the flame lick the frigid atmosphere. On the slope above the memorial, lying on the patchy grass as though it were the height of summer and the ground beneath her a verdant pillow—there she was. Her arms were spread like an angel, her head tilted back as she gazed at the thin blue sky. The roses were still in his other hand when he grabbed her by the elbow and jerked her to her feet.

The buried fury of three decades burned in his chest, his features weighted down with anger, but she stared back at him with clear, neutral eyes. She had that radiance of people who no longer have anything to lose, and nothing to prove. In the era when he listened in on her telephone conversations she had been older than him, further along in life, more experienced, but time had worn away such distinctions. They were both old now. She was still beautiful, her skin healthy and her spine straight, although her hair had gone completely white. She wore it long, undone, the way the flower children had, although the rest of her style seemed unchanged from her heyday. Her skirt fell below the knee, and her cloth coat was belted at the waist. It took him a minute to realize that the coat was flat over her breasts—where her breasts should have been—and then he understood that the radiance was something else. She was incandescent. The aliveness of her whole being glowed beneath the skin, but it was the vibrancy of life fighting for the final time. She wouldn't be here in the spring.

"What are you going to do, arrest me?" she said, without irony or fear.

He didn't tell her that he no longer had the authority for that. Instead he took her to the bar off Connecticut Avenue, where a long time ago he had perused the file of William Vladimirovich Fitin. They sat at a corner table.

He opened his mouth—but what was there to say? His hands covered his face, no matter how he tried to make himself look at her. He knew her silhouette at the top of the stairs like he knew the joints of his own hand, and he wanted to tell her sorry, for not understanding her intentions that day, but this seemed wholly inadequate to the situation. If she had been Oswald's lookout, she would have been there earlier, wouldn't have needed to go to the airport. Her focus would have been down the stairs, waiting for Walls, ready to stop him. If she'd been trying to kill Kennedy, she would have had more than that handgun. In the year after the assassination he had replayed and replayed the whole episode, mostly in bars, her elbows in his side, her nails at his neck, until he reached the conclusion that those were not the moves of an assassin but the desperate flailing of a woman trying to protect her man.

He sighed, pushed his chin into the middle of his palm. "How did you . . . ?" was the most he could manage to say. "You." He shook his head. "*You*, of all people."

"You mean, what happened to me that I should have ended up like this?" She leaned her shoulder blades against the wall. A vein pulsed in her forehead, and her gaze drifted off into the middle distance. "I was a beautiful child," she observed. His face must have twitched as though in disapproval, because she quickly added, "That is not a brag, nor is it evidence of some sentimental attachment to the little girl I used to be."

He sat back and listened while she spoke a long time. They were wary of each other at first, her words clipped and defensive, but she also seemed relieved to be telling all at last. At some point he went for drinks—the place was no longer a dive, and nowadays served champagne, but she asked for whiskey with soda on the side, and he was relieved to have the excuse to order a strong drink himself. As she went on she became more honest about what had been, and more elegiac, too. She asked him questions, and he answered, and their stories got tangled together.

Night had fallen by the time they were done, and the bar stools were mostly occupied, although their own corner was still private enough. The evidence of several rounds of drinks cluttered the table, and they had filled two ashtrays, and his mouth was dry. He dropped his face into his hands again.

Seeing his fatigue, she seemed to want to comfort him with small talk. "And what have you done with yourself? Are you married, Douglass?"

"Yes—I was. Am, I suppose, technically. But Gloria is the dean of Columbia Law now, she doesn't need me. For a while she came back to D.C. on the weekends, but she hasn't made the trip in a long while. She has a friend in New York, I think. I wouldn't want to ruin that for her by asking. You?"

She smiled faintly and shook her head.

"How did you get by?"

"Oh . . . It's not so difficult, you know, to live underground in this country. Especially when you're not greedy. Especially when you've already renounced so much."

"Do you miss him?"

For the first time she had to glance away, and as she fingered one of the yellow petals on the roses that were wilting in the barroom atmosphere, he thought she might cry. But she didn't. She put her drink on its coaster, stared into it for a while, and changed the subject. "You know what I keep thinking?"

"What?"

"That if I'd wanted to save him, all I'd have had to do was call you up, get the file you'd been keeping on me, and give it to one of the boys I was friendly with in the press wrapped in a big bow. Reporters were more discreet then, it's true, but I don't think anybody could have resisted it if they had documentation like that, about the man in the White House and Marilyn Monroe. If that had gotten out he couldn't have been president anymore, and then they wouldn't have had any reason to kill him."

"But you can't mean that." Walls drained his drink. He was ready to go; he wanted to sleep for a long time, if indeed he was still capable of sleep. "Politics was everything to him. I mean, think how hard he worked to become president. He was supposed to change the world."

"Yeah, that's true." She must have divined his desire to retreat, because she reached out for his hand to stop him, lacing her fingers through his. The warmth of her palm against his was so unexpected that he forgot the instinct to run. She was stranger than he could have guessed, and the history that was between them two and nobody else was as ugly as he'd suspected. But who else could touch him now? What was the harm in staying a little longer? He closed his eyes, and listened to her say, "Anyway, the world *is* different. And wouldn't there have been other work to do if he had lived? The scandal would have passed eventually, and maybe we'd have been better for it. All of us, I mean. I can't help thinking how, you know—it's not always our flaws that destroy us. Sometimes it's our big, beautiful ideas."

With her skin against his skin he felt pleasantly at sea—a sweet, rocking loss of control—and he didn't even realize she had stood up until he smelled her perfumed neck and the whiskey on her breath.

"Douglass," she said, and he knew why his mother had called him that. For the first time he heard its poetry.

"Yes?"

"I'm going to the ladies' room to fix my lipstick."

"All right."

"We're friends, aren't we?"

"Yes."

"Good friends?"

"Yes."

"When I come back, let's get out of here, find someplace quiet."

He opened his eyes, so he saw the way she walked past the pool table to the back. He had no idea what "someplace quiet" meant, or what he expected, or even what he wanted, but while he waited for her return he had no questions, only a sense that the answer to life's riddle was simple, and that he had known it all along. Even after he realized too much time had passed, went in the direction she had disappeared, thrust open the bathroom window to see the empty alley behind the bar, and finally burst onto the sidewalk, he was not exactly perturbed.

He ran up and down the street like a fool, and the bums laughed at him.

"Marilyn!" he called into the darkness.

"Marilyn," the bums chorused. "Mar-i-*lyn!*" and then they laughed some more.

The image of her pale honey face was still vivid in his mind's eye, the way her lips quivered before she spoke, making you eager for what she might say. But he felt hollow in her absence and weary with the years to come, as though by slipping out on him she had escaped their story, and left him to take it to the grave alone.

ACKNOWLEDGMENTS

THIS book has some brilliant fingerprints on it. I am so grateful to my great friend and editor Sara Shandler, to Lanie Davis who brought the light bulb, to Josh Bank, Les Morgenstein, Jennifer Rudolph Walsh, Amanda Murray, Georgina Levitt, Katie McGee, Kathleen Schmidt, Kristin Marang, Julie Miller, Natalie Sousa, Liz Dresner, Heather David, Devorah Backman, Bob Levy, Polly Aurrit, Tom Colligan, and Maya Galbis. I am also indebted to Katie J.M. Baker and Claudia Ballard for early reads. And many, many thanks to Adrienne Miller and Maura Sheehy, who gave generously of ideas and support during the writing process.